PRAISE FOR VICTORIA HELEN STONE

Follow Her Down

"A must-read for romantic suspe   ers
nonstop tension and a mind-ber   to
overcome the traumatic past she's
        —Melinda Leigh,   .or

At the Quiet Edge

"The plot's many twists and turns will stun and surprise readers. Suspense fans will get their money's worth."

—*Publishers Weekly*

"Sharp and sophisticated, *At the Quiet Edge* commanded my attention from the captivating first chapter to the electrifying ending."

—Minka Kent, *Washington Post* bestselling author

"An utterly compelling blend of family drama and suspense, *At the Quiet Edge* pulled me in and didn't let go. I read this riveting, twisty book in one sitting. Not to be missed."

—A. J. Banner, #1 Amazon, *USA Today*, and *Publishers Weekly* bestselling author

"I raced through the pages of *At the Quiet Edge*. This propulsive story places you inside a world of secrets, and locks you inside. And like our heroine Lily and her son Everett, it's hard to know who to trust. This is taut, heart-pounding suspense."

—Kaira Rouda, *USA Today* and Amazon Charts bestselling author of *The Next Wife* and *Somebody's Home*

"As a single mom, I couldn't help but identify with the complex dynamics between mother and son as each protected the other in this gripping thriller. It is a thrilling game of cat and mouse that kept me guessing all the way up to the jaw-dropping conclusion."

—Lucinda Berry, bestselling author of *The Best of Friends* and *The Perfect Child*

Evelyn, After

"Hands down, the best book I've read this year. Brilliant, compelling, and haunting."

—Suzanne Brockmann, *New York Times* bestselling author

"Readers will cheer on Evelyn when the power dynamic with her lying, cheating husband shifts, even while they watch her flirting with disaster in her steamy affair with Noah. A solid choice for Liane Moriarty readers."

—*Library Journal*

"Stone (a nom de plume of romance writer Victoria Dahl) . . . ably switches to darker suspense in a compelling story exploring what lurks behind a seemingly perfect life."

—*Booklist*

"Stone pens a great story that will have readers wondering what will happen next to the characters involved in this mysterious tale . . . Fascinating tale told by a talented storyteller!"

—*RT Book Reviews*

"Victoria Helen Stone renders the obsessions and weaknesses of her characters with scorching insight. Her sterling prose creates a seamless atmosphere of anticipation and dread, while delivering devastating truths about the nature of sex, relationships, and lies, often with a humor that's rapier-sharp. *Evelyn, After* reads like *Gone Girl* with a bigger heart and a stronger moral core."

—Christopher Rice, *New York Times* bestselling author

Half Past

"A gripping, haunting exploration of the lengths to which we'll go to belong, *Half Past* will hold you in its thrall until the very last page. Stone's expert storytelling, vivid characterizations, and tantalizing dropping of clues left me utterly breathless, longing for more—and a newly minted Victoria Helen Stone fan!"

—Emily Carpenter, bestselling author of *Burying the Honeysuckle Girls* and *The Weight of Lies*

"A captivating, suspenseful tale of love and lies, mystery and self-discovery, *Half Past* kept me flipping the pages through the final, startling twist."

—A. J. Banner, #1 Amazon and *USA Today* bestselling author of *The Good Neighbor* and *The Twilight Wife*

"What would you do if you found out that your mother wasn't your biological mother? Would you go looking for the answer to how that happened if she couldn't provide an explanation? That's the intriguing question at the heart of *Half Past*, Stone's strong follow-up to *Evelyn, After*. [It's] both a mystery and an exploration of what family really means. Fans of Jodi Picoult will race through this."

—Catherine McKenzie, bestselling author of *Hidden* and *The Good Liar*

Jane Doe

"Stone does a masterful job of creating in Jane a complex character, making her both scary and more than a little appealing . . . This beautifully balanced thriller will keep readers tense, surprised, pleased, and surprised again as a master manipulator unfolds her plan of revenge."

—*Kirkus Reviews* (starred review)

"Revenge drives this fascinating thriller . . . Stone keeps the suspense high throughout. Readers will relish Jane's Machiavellian maneuvers to even the score with the unlikable Steven."

—*Publishers Weekly*

"Crafty, interesting, and vengeful."

—*Novelgossip*

"Crazy great book!"

—*Good Life Family Magazine*

"Stone skillfully, deviously, and gleefully leads the reader down a garden path to a knockout WHAM-O of an ending. *Jane Doe* will not disappoint."

—*New York Journal of Books*

"*Jane Doe* is a riveting, engrossing story about a man who screws over the wrong woman, with a picture-perfect ending that's the equivalent of a big red bow on a shiny new car. It's that good. Ladies, we finally have the revenge story we've always deserved."

—*Criminal Element*

"Jane, the self-described sociopath at the center of Victoria Helen Stone's novel, [is] filling a hole in storytelling that we've long been waiting for."

—Bitch Media

"We loved being propelled into the complicated mind of Jane, intrigued as she bobbed and weaved her way through life with the knowledge she's just a little bit different. You'll be debating whether to make Jane your new best friend or lock your door and hide from her in fear. Both incredibly insightful and tautly suspenseful, *Jane Doe* is a must-read!"
—Liz Fenton and Lisa Steinke, bestselling authors of *The Good Widow*

"With biting wit and a complete disregard for societal double standards, Victoria Helen Stone's antihero will slice a path through your expectations and leave you begging for more. Make room in the darkest corner of your heart for Jane Doe."
—Eliza Maxwell, bestselling author of *The Unremembered Girl*

"If revenge is a dish best served cold, Jane Doe is Julia Child. Though Jane's a heroine who claims to be a sociopath, Jane's heart and soul shine through in this addicting, suspenseful tale of love, loss, and justice."
—Wendy Webb, bestselling author of *The End of Temperance Dare*

"One word: wow. This novel is compelling from the first sentence. An emotional ride with a deliciously vengeful narrator, Jane's tale keeps readers on the edge without the security of knowing who the good guy really is. Honest, cutting, and at times even humorous, this is one powerhouse of a read!"
—Brandi Reeds, bestselling author of *Trespassing*

False Step

"[A] cleverly plotted thriller . . . Danger and savage emotions surface as [Veronica] discovers that she's not the only one whose life is built on secrets and lies. Stone keeps the reader guessing to the end."

—*Publishers Weekly*

"Intense and chilling, *False Step* wickedly rewards thriller fans with a compulsive read that'll leave readers wondering how well they know their loved ones. I was riveted!"

—Kerry Lonsdale, Amazon Charts and *Wall Street Journal* bestselling author

Problem Child

"Outstanding . . . Readers will find vicarious joy in Jane's petty vengeances and unabashed meanness to anyone who tries to take advantage of her. Stone turns some very dark material into an upbeat tale."

—*Publishers Weekly* (starred review)

"This installment is highly recommended for fans of edgier psychological fiction."

—*Library Journal*

The Last One Home

"Stone gradually reveals her multifaceted characters' secrets as the intricate, fast-paced plot builds to a surprising conclusion. Fans of dark, twisted tales of dysfunctional families will be satisfied."

—*Publishers Weekly*

"The story gives just enough detail each chapter to keep the reader intrigued about where it is going to go next . . . family secrets will never be looked at the same."

—*The Parkersburg News and Sentinel*

"A slow burner . . . *The Last One Home* takes its time to set the scene for the twists and revelations that will come in the last chapters of the book."

—*Mystery & Suspense Magazine*

"*The Last One Home* is elegant and chilling, an indelible novel of family secrets. I couldn't put it down until I learned the truth about these finely drawn characters—the ending left me absolutely shocked and amazed, and I can't stop thinking about it."

—Luanne Rice, *New York Times* bestselling author of *The Shadow Box*

"Gripping and relentless, *The Last One Home* stalks you like the serial killer within its pages: you know danger is right around the corner, but you don't know when it'll strike. And just when you think you have the story figured out, Victoria Helen Stone rips the rug right out from under your feet. Highly recommended!"

—Avery Bishop, author of *Girl Gone Mad*

"In *The Last One Home*, Victoria Helen Stone weaves another sure-handed story, this one about mothers, the fierce love they have for their children, and just how far they will go to protect their progeny. This is a suspense novel that's in part a love story, as well as a chilling mystery. But it's the kind of tale that sneaks up on you, revealing discoveries in the last scorching chapters that flip the whole narrative on its head. Full of shifting family loyalties and recollections of the past, and creepy, alone-in-the-countryside vibes, this book held me, start to finish, in its mesmerizing thrall."

—Emily Carpenter, author of *Reviving the Hawthorn Sisters*

FOLLOW
HER
DOWN

ALSO BY VICTORIA HELEN STONE

FOLLOW HER DOWN

A NOVEL

VICTORIA HELEN STONE

Text copyright © 2024 by Victoria Helen Stone
All rights reserved.

Published by Lake Union Publishing, Seattle

www.apub.com

Amazon, the Amazon logo, and Lake Union Publishing are trademarks of Amazon.com, Inc., or its affiliates.

ISBN-13: 9781662521683 (paperback)
ISBN-13: 9781662514609 (digital)

Cover design by Caroline Teagle Johnson
Cover image: © Rekha Garton / ArcAngel

Printed in the United States of America

AUTHOR'S NOTE

Stratum is a fictional company, and Willow Canyon, Cold Creek, and Creekside Cabins are fictional locations. The highway through Willow Canyon, though similar to existing highways that connect the Sacramento Valley to the Tahoe area, is also fictional. Please excuse any authorly sleight of hand or artistic license with placement of government offices and other infrastructure.

Content warning: this story deals with grief, trauma, sexual violence, and addiction.

CHAPTER 1

The distant scream tore through Elise Rockwood's body, making her guts clench even as her joints went soft. The pail slipped from her hand and dropped with a thunk before it tipped over on the drying grass of her yard.

That cry had sounded like fear, not pain, and for a moment she couldn't get her breath back. Something was very wrong, and she'd had too many wrong things in her life already. It wasn't fair. She refused to respond.

Her brief refusal vanished like smoke when a child's high-pitched babbling broke through the buzzing in her head. This was her property and her responsibility, even when everything inside her was begging to run away. Finally an adult at the ripe age of thirty-five, she couldn't choose to ignore trouble and hope someone else would take care of it.

Elise took a deep breath and tried to center herself the way her therapist had taught her.

"Hello?" a woman called out. "Ma'am?"

Right. That was her. Elise was the *ma'am* here.

She flattened her face into careful competence and turned to hurry across the wide expanse of grass toward the woman and little boy who'd checked in to their cabin on Monday. They stood together, neither of them clutching any body parts in pain. Both simply looked troubled, thank God.

"Are you okay?" Elise called. "Is anyone hurt?"

"No, we're fine," the woman—was it Julie?—said. "It's just . . ." She pointed toward a sloping bank that led to the waterway that gave Creekside Cabins its name. "That."

Nodding as if she understood, Elise headed past her, trying to hide her hesitation and the way she had to force herself to walk around the picnic table and toward the water. She moved slowly. No one was injured. This wasn't an emergency. There was only something horrifying in the water.

It probably wasn't the same kind of horror she'd pictured in her mind for so many years, turning it over and over, different seasons, different terrain, the water tugging, dragging, pulling apart. No, it wasn't that.

When she reached the bank, Elise stared into the flowing water of the stream. In spring it would be a flood of icy snowmelt three feet deep, but today the creek was shallow and calm, clear all the way to the bottom. The rocks still threw up swirls of white froth, but the bubbles did nothing to disguise the stiff legs of the carcass or the eye that had been pecked out by crows. A nightmare stared up at her with a hollowed-out socket, half of its open jaw submerged.

"Mommy?" the little boy cried from behind her. "Is it dead? Is it still dead?"

Wincing, Elise bit back a sigh as the mother murmured comforting words. Yep. The raccoon was dead, and it definitely wasn't going to recover from that.

Elise might not either. Her guts loosened now, making her queasy as relief tumbled and wrestled with the anticipation of what she'd need to do. This was one of the worst parts about being a responsible adult. She was the one who had to take care of *things*. All the things. Even the ones she'd rather call some grizzled old man to do.

"Okay, I'll be right back," she said as she passed the woman and child, hoping her voice wasn't trembling as badly as her knees. After a few minutes of digging around in the toolshed, she returned to the morbid scene, clutching a black garbage bag in one gloved hand and her oldest shovel in the other.

"Sorry about this," she said as she edged down the rocks toward the dead body. "Nature can be pretty . . . gross." The boy nodded doubtfully, his eyes bright with tears. She held his gaze to put off the gruesome task for a few more heartbeats, but then gave in and turned to the water.

The clear mountain stream was the focal point of Creekside Cabins, and she couldn't leave the carcass as a surprise for other guests. The only relief in getting closer to the raccoon was that the roar of the water drowned out the sad questions of the little boy.

Even now at the start of autumn, the creek was surprisingly loud, and she probably wouldn't have bought this resort if her own cabin had been on the banks. The stream was beautiful, but it muffled every other noise, and Elise liked to keep her ears open for anything she didn't expect. If you lived next to moving water like this, anyone could sneak up on you. The sound also reminded her of her sister in ways she didn't welcome.

The guests loved it, though. The three tiny homes that edged right up to the creek went for an extra hundred dollars a night during high season.

"Why don't you go ahead and relax by the firepit?" Elise called over her shoulder. "I'll get this taken care of; then I'll bring out a s'mores kit for you and your son to enjoy."

She didn't catch the mom's answer, but she definitely heard the boy shout "S'mores!" and hoped burning sugar would help glaze over his trauma.

After taking a moment to stare into the oak leaves rustling in the wind, she told herself to stop wasting time. The spicy scent of turning leaves only laid a transparent veil over the stench of rotting animal.

She shook out the trash bag, then jerked back with a curse when pain burned through her arm. Sucking air between her teeth, she studied the scratch below her elbow before belatedly spotting the broken branch right next to her. Two points of it had gouged the tender skin of her forearm, and blood was welling up in parallel lines.

"Ow, ow, ow," she complained as she pulled out the drawstring of the bag and carefully hooked it onto the jagged branch. After steeling her nerves and parting her lips to breathe through her mouth, she hefted the shovel.

The raccoon's fur parted as she pushed the shovel under it, the shiny flesh pink and winking. Something moved inside the abdomen. Or maybe her shaking had done that. Regardless, tears sprang to her eyes, and sickness clogged her throat.

Don't think about that. Don't think about that.

Clenching her eyes shut, she shoved the handle hard, then hefted the weight and swung it toward the bag. She had to look now, and she tried to aim her focus above the jutting front legs instead of the seething abdomen, but it didn't help. The black fingers curled just like human hands exposed to the elements for too long. Just like—

Do. Not. Think. About. That.

The bag fought her, of course, plastic folding in and clinging, and she had to jostle and twist and shake until the lump of rot finally slid in with squishing resistance. Tiny claws caught on the plastic with a terrible skittering sound as if the dead animal wanted out.

"Shit!" she shouted, unable to hold back even for the sake of the guests. She'd earned the right to curse over this.

The rest went quickly. Elise held the bag at arm's length, trying her best to suppress a grimace as she passed the boy and his mom. Once she'd dropped the corpse in the dumpster, she wiped the shovel on a patch of crabgrass far from her cabin. Finally, she ditched the contaminated tool behind the shed for the sun and rain to sanitize. Let nature take it. Maybe she'd clean it and put it back in the shed after a month or so. Maybe not. She had plenty of unsullied shovels.

After opening the door to her cabin with her elbow, she scrubbed her hands under hot water until they were beet red, then cleaned the blood and dirt from her wound with alcohol, biting back a few more curses at the bright flashes of pain.

When it was done, Elise slumped with relief to have the whole disgusting task behind her, but her shoulders didn't quite relax. She could feel in her bones that the worst of it was still ahead, because tonight her dead sister would tiptoe into the cabin during the deepest, darkest hours to haunt her sleep.

But that was a horror she'd been living with for a long time.

CHAPTER 2

After she grabbed a s'mores kit and delivered it to the mom along with a couple of skewers, Elise lingered a moment, hoping to replace the boy's memory of the raccoon with something good. She showed him a video of a huge moose that had wandered slowly around the cabins the month before, totally unconcerned with everyone filming from the safety of their porches.

The mom smiled gratefully and pulled her son close as he licked melted marshmallow off his fingers, his face bright with sugar and excitement as he watched the moose. This time it was the right kind of excitement, not the "faced with the permanence of death" kind.

A few minutes later, Elise hurried back to her cabin, downed a glass of water, and restocked the hand sanitizer near the front door. The adrenaline had faded, and she felt fine by the time she collapsed into her desk chair. No worries, no stress.

Until she checked the reservations for the next couple of days and saw a familiar name.

"Seriously?" she asked the computer screen. "Daniel Serrano?" This was her penance for telling herself it would be a slow week. She glanced around in exasperation as if there were someone else in the cabin she could roll her eyes at.

Her place was a real log cabin: two bedrooms, a living area, and an enclosed sunroom that served as reception for the rentals now. Outside, a semicircle of nine tiny homes fanned out in what had once been a grassy clearing near the water. There were plenty of rustic rentals around the area, but hers was the only place equipped with modern tiny houses more suited to folks who didn't enjoy roughing it. Considering she was only three and a half hours from Silicon Valley and forty minutes from Tahoe, there were plenty of those kinds of tourists. She stayed fully booked during summer and ski season, but the third week of September was much slower.

Only two people were checking in this week, and apparently one of them was Daniel Serrano. Not a rare name, but not common either, and it happened to belong to a boy who'd grown up in her hometown eight miles down the highway.

If it was *her* Daniel, her childhood crush and older brother's best friend, did he know she owned the resort? And did her brother know he was coming? If so, Kyle had probably forgotten to tell her, because Kyle forgot a lot of things when he was in an obsessive mood, and he'd definitely been in an obsessive mood lately.

She wanted to call and ask him about the reservation, but that felt like a violation of some kind of privacy law. She decided to try subtlety.

Hey bro! she texted. Got anything going on this week? She didn't bother waiting for a response. Kyle treated texts like emails. He'd get back to her at his convenience even if she sent increasingly worried messages as the hours passed.

She already felt silly even asking. Daniel didn't matter. He was likely long married and settled down, and she was just . . . not making those kinds of mistakes anymore. No crushes, no one-night stands, and certainly no relationships with tendrils that crept deep into her past. No relationships at all right now if she was being smart. And she was.

"Bring it on, Daniel," Elise murmured. She was an ice queen. She was mature and stable. She made good choices and didn't get bogged down in her family's past. Or even in their present. Life was good, and she planned to keep it that way.

But first she had to replace that toilet intake valve in cabin 7.

She finished gathering the supplies recommended in the YouTube video she'd watched, then went to retrieve the pail she'd dropped by her side door. When she neared the row of cabins, the faint stench of decay touched her nose.

Elise shook her head. It was her imagination. Cabin 7 wasn't anywhere near the creek or the dumpster. She was only catching the scent of her own fear.

Not for the first time, she wondered if this creek fed into the Mokelumne River. Unless it took a hard turn to the south somewhere past the highway, she knew it must. Only one narrow spine of these hills separated Willow Canyon from the river, but she'd very purposefully never traced the creek path on a map. She didn't want to know, not for certain. She didn't want to think that this water, so clear and clean and perfect, might eventually twist over the last remnants of her sister's corpse.

"Stop," she ordered herself as she unlocked the door. Then she whispered a question her therapist had taught her. "Do these thoughts help you?" No, they definitely did not help. They'd only bring on nightmares.

It took half an hour to pry off the slippery plastic fastener and wrestle the old valve out of the toilet, but she had the new one installed in five minutes and walked out of the cabin full of triumph. She'd bought this place with a maxed-out mortgage and a ton of determination, but she'd had to learn handyman and accounting skills along the way. Before this, she'd never even owned a home, much less a whole complex. She was making it work, though. She was even—dare she say?—flourishing.

It was decidedly odd to feel that way. From her first moments of puberty and all the hormones that came with it, she'd thrived on chaos and a tough-girl attitude. It had seemingly served her well. She'd survived out there on her own, hadn't she? And many others hadn't.

But she'd been in a constant state of fight or flight her whole life. She'd never stayed in the same apartment for more than two years, and even those quick bouts of geographical stability had been fraught with breakups and job loss and endless, shifting change. Oakland, LA, San

Francisco, Portland, Seattle—finding the same tornado of a life in every successive city.

She'd thought she loved that. But then she'd lost a friend to suicide. The second friend in as many years. At age thirty-two, Elise had felt herself spiraling into depression, and she'd taken a hard look at her shitty life: A dozen pill bottles, only some with her name on them, all mixed up with empty beer cans and sticky glasses on her bedside table. The constant acid reflux and creeping headaches. The men she couldn't remember. The men she could. The unwritten list of bars she no longer went to, either because she'd been banned for screaming arguments and occasional fistfights or because those bars were an ex's favorite hangout. The bank account she measured in cents by the end of a pay period. The roots she cut off each time she left everything behind and moved on to a new place.

She'd owned little besides a couch that smelled of mildew, a mattress on the floor, and a car that needed a new transmission. She'd worked plenty of jobs: grocery cashier, hotel maid, bartender, roadie, server. But she'd never had a career, and she'd never had a future.

Elise had looked at it all and realized that if she took the wrong pill or two with her whisky, they'd call her a suicide too. That had pissed her off for reasons she didn't want to look at closely. Reasons that cropped up on late nights when she was too alone and too sober and missing her beautiful sister.

So she'd worked on it. She'd slowly weaned herself off the personal pharmacy. She'd gone to a few AA meetings to bolster her efforts to cut back on drinking too. And she'd found a therapist who'd asked Elise to challenge her fears and dare to confront her childhood.

Elise had surprised herself by saying yes. Challenging her fears felt like a fight, and fighting was her natural state. The pandemic had shrunk her world anyway, so it hadn't been hard to walk away from that life, from her friendships based on partying, from all her bad choices. And this time she'd run with the assurance that she was doing something right. She was moving in with her brother to confront her childhood and face the mountains of her youth. Oh, she'd still cussed out the world on a daily basis. She'd cursed all the bad luck she'd accumulated. But she'd tried. Was still trying.

Only recently had she come to truly see the common denominator in all these troubles: herself.

Working on her real problems wasn't as much fun as brawling through chaos, but it was definitely more peaceful, and running a rental business satisfied her need for surprise and occasional havoc.

As she finished scrubbing toilet germs from her hands, she had to let a phone call go to voicemail. But it was funny. She didn't mind getting her hands dirty these days. She'd felt like a servant at her old hotel job and had resented every filthy towel and urine-flecked toilet seat. Now she felt pride that she kept her property in good repair.

Once she dried off, she returned her brother's call. "Hey!"

"Why'd you ask that?" he blurted.

"Ask what?"

"If I have anything going on?"

"Because I was checking in with my loving brother. You know, making conversation?" He sounded suspicious, which made her feel guilty about her attempt at fishing for information. "Why?"

"I don't know. Things feel really off lately, you know?"

"Is that unusual?" she asked. She left off *for you* and tried to keep the sarcasm out of her voice. Her brother wasn't exactly a usual kind of guy.

"I don't know. I'm fine. I mean, I'm good. Is anything going on with *you*?"

Despite his reassurance, he still sounded edgy, so she kept it light. "I just fixed a toilet. And I had to haul a dead raccoon out of the creek. A child was traumatized. So that was pretty exciting."

"Hm."

"Kyle." She tipped her head back, summoning patience. "Are you really doing all right? Everything okay over there? It feels like you want to talk about something."

"How are you?" he asked, ignoring her questions. "Are you feeling better? Did he ever contact you again?"

Elise froze. Her brother was bringing that up after two weeks? She just wanted to leave it all behind, and this wasn't the first time he'd mentioned that stupid email. "Oh my God, Kyle. I'm sorry I even told you about that."

"Why?"

"Kyle," Elise growled, and all her patience flew right out the window. "I only wanted some advice, that's all. It's over, and there's nothing more to talk about. I told him I didn't want to see him, and he dropped it."

"And you're okay?"

She squeezed her eyes shut so hard she saw stars. Was she okay? Yes. Maybe. Mostly she felt grateful Christian had waited so long to reach out. A year before, even six months, and she would have shattered into pieces just so he'd feel the shrapnel.

Kyle wasn't the most intuitive brother in the world, but he obviously saw past her assumed serenity. Still, it didn't hurt to keep pretending.

"I'm fine," she said with deliberate ease. "Please don't bring it up again. I had a moment of weakness, and I appreciate you for talking me through it. But I need to feel like I can talk without you turning it into . . ." She slashed her hand through the air. "Another problem."

He didn't respond, but he stopped shooting questions at her, and that was as good as it got with her big brother.

She took a deep breath and tried again. "Listen, do you know if Daniel Serrano is back in town?" Her morals had apparently flown off with her patience, but at least she got a direct response to the question.

"Yeah. He's coming back. I told him to hit you up for a friends-and-family rate if he needed a place to stay."

"Oh. He's moving here?"

"His dad still owned their old place all these years. Someone's renting it, but Daniel's going to move back in to fix the house up and flip it next summer. Should make a killing."

Well, that was pretty interesting. "I saw his name on the books. He must have made a reservation online."

"Shit, I'm supposed to meet him there tonight. Totally spaced it." When he stopped talking, the line rustled as he shifted around. "But I should make an appearance," he mumbled, his mouth clearly angled away from the phone.

"It'd be good for you to see Daniel," she said, but her brother had already hung up.

She could tell he was distracted again. It happened on and off and had ramped up in the past couple of weeks. It wasn't his work in IT security distracting him, and it certainly wasn't his nonexistent dating life. His hobby was the problem . . . if you could call a passion for conspiracy theories a hobby. It definitely took up his free time and sometimes managed to pull him out of a bout of depression, but she was never quite sure if that type of diversion was a net positive.

The deep dives had been fun back in the old days before Elise had realized how they'd started. He'd delve into UFOs or cryptids like Bigfoot, and she'd enjoyed the stories. She'd even gone camping with him a few times, though she'd mostly joined for the cooler of beer and less for the Sasquatch hunts. Today his obsessions involved far fewer campfires and way more hours on the computer.

It *would* be good for him to see Daniel. Hanging out with a childhood friend would distract him and get him offline.

Kyle had been in a good place during the months she lived with him, busy with working on long-form posts about various spyware schemes. But since then he sometimes went dark, spiraling into obsessions. He'd always had trouble letting go of a topic, but she'd very specifically asked Kyle not to talk about her ex once she'd made the decision not to see him.

Lord, could she even call Christian an ex? An ex-*what*? He was more like—

Nope. She didn't have the mental space for him today. It was getting close to two years since their official breakup, and if Christian had a desire to reinsert himself back into her life, that was between him and his conscience.

Elise tucked her phone away and forced her shoulders to lower and relax. She tried to soften her face and jaw to head off the tension wrapping around her skull. She summoned her therapist's voice to ask, *How can you help yourself right now?*

Right. Simple things. Small actions she could control.

She opened the window above her kitchen sink to let in the chattering of the wrens gathered in trees outside. A chipmunk chirped furiously at them from somewhere farther off. This was good. Peaceful. She hadn't realized how much she'd missed nature during all those years of city living.

Her life was predictable now, steady and quiet. She would see an old friend tonight. Maybe hang out with her brother by the fire. Before slipping into bed, she'd make the rounds of this place she improved every day with her own two hands.

And before she fell asleep, she'd meditate instead of warding off thoughts of her sister with pills. That was how she could help herself. Better living *without* chemistry.

Everything would be fine . . . even if she had to force the issue.

CHAPTER 3

"So how's your mom doing?"

Elise didn't have to tamp down any anxiety to that question like she had in the past. She'd gotten used to the query after moving back to the area three years earlier. Still, she let Kyle field the response as she studied Daniel Serrano in the light of the firepit.

He looked good with lines around his eyes, his black hair still tousled like a messy kid's, but shorter than in his youth and already shot through with a little gray. Yeah, he looked really good, but she was relieved that she had only a comfortingly pleasant response to him.

Back when she'd been partying too much, she'd gone on point like a hunting dog when exposed to attraction. Tunnel vision always teamed up with a voice in her head telling her she should have him, *could* have him. After all, she'd learned long before that life was short and men weren't difficult to convince.

Kyle finally rumbled, "She's the same," into the silence. "My mom," he clarified. "I mean, she's better, but . . ."

"Oh." Daniel's brow creased with confusion. "But I thought . . . I mean, after the confession, I assumed she would . . ."

Kyle shook his head, and Daniel looked from him to Elise, the frown deepening. "But she always said she couldn't leave the house because Robin might come home, right?"

"Yeah," Elise drawled. "Right."

"Now your mom knows what happened to her. That didn't help?"

Elise took a hard swig from the beer she'd been nursing and shook her head. "I guess after ten years of staying locked in the house, Mom didn't know how to leave anymore. She's on disability now. Has to pop a Valium just to get herself to a doctor's appointment. It's not great."

"It's better," Kyle insisted.

Elise shrugged. "It's not great."

"Wow," Daniel said, leaning back into the lawn chair with a sigh. "I'm sorry. I didn't know."

"It is what it is," Kyle said. "And to be fair, Robin still isn't home, since her body was never found."

Elise tipped her bottle toward him. "True. But at least Mom can order anything she needs online these days. Kyle had to do everything for her for years, so that's gotten better. She has more hobbies now. She does seem more content."

Kyle had been the one to do everything for their mom because Elise had fled their small town like a bat out of hell on her eighteenth birthday and she hadn't come back until she'd passed thirty. Not even for holidays. It wasn't like things suddenly became cheery and festive because of a date on a calendar.

No, surviving the disappearance of a sibling had a way of screwing up a childhood. And an adulthood, apparently. Really, the whole family's past, present, and future took quite a beating, and holidays were the worst times of all. When she hadn't celebrated with friends, Elise had willfully ignored festivities as much as she could.

Their mother was agoraphobic and paranoid, and learning the truth fifteen years ago about what had happened to her teenage daughter hadn't corrected a decade of living with horror, guilt, and uncertainty. For ten endless years, she'd been absolutely convinced that if she ever left the house—even for a few minutes—her little girl would finally show up at the doorstep, needing help, needing her mom, and her mother wouldn't be there to save her. Something as harmless as a quick trip to the grocery store would leave her convinced Robin had made it home . . . only to be tracked down and snatched right back off her doorstep by whoever was holding her captive.

Their mother's terror had been real and heartbreaking. Elise had never doubted that. She'd been obsessed with her missing daughter. Obsessed with re-creating the day leading to her disappearance during the hottest, longest days of summer, obsessed with tracking down any information about white women of the right age range in any of the fifty states or Canada or even Mexico. And the worst part was, no matter how much of Elise and Kyle's childhood she missed, how could they be allowed to resent that? A mother was *supposed* to be obsessed with finding her lost child.

Robin always needed Mom more than either of them did, because Elise and Kyle were fine and free and *alive*, utterly safe in their own home, and . . . anything might be happening to poor Robin. Anything.

She'd been eighteen years old when she'd disappeared after a campground party in the woods. Kyle had been thirteen, and Elise had been only ten.

That had been the end of Elise's normal childhood, but Kyle had been forced to grow up even faster, feeding Elise breakfast and getting her to school, making her dinner and getting her to bed, then prodding their mom to remember school breaks and special occasions so their whole lives wouldn't fall through the cracks.

Poor Kyle. He looked quite a bit older than Daniel. Older than his years. She watched him as he and Daniel talked about the upcoming Sacramento Kings season. Her brother looked younger when he wasn't frowning.

He'd been scrawny throughout high school, but strong. He'd ridden his bike up and down the hilly highway to buy everything they needed. Friends and neighbors had offered rides, of course, but they weren't allowed to ride with anyone, not ever. Any nearby adult, no matter how well known, could be the person who'd taken Robin. Any stranger could be a monster, any friend a ghoul. They'd trusted no one and depended on only themselves, three bent tent poles holding up a lopsided world.

Now Kyle was decidedly into dad-bod territory, though his arms were still pencil thin and his shoulders hunched. Elise had a sudden vision of him dead at an early age, and she looked away from her brother to his friend, determined to think good thoughts.

Daniel had thickened up a bit too, but mostly through the chest. And thighs. And he still looked like a guy who smiled a lot. That was probably the reason she'd crushed on him in her adolescence. A shiny spot of cheer in her gloom. She'd wanted to be near him even before she hit puberty.

And now? Well, she was suddenly glad she'd worn old jeans and a huge flannel shirt tonight as a shield to keep his charm from settling on her, because the horniness she'd managed to bury over the past year was definitely stirring. Damn it.

"How's the cabin?" Elise asked to distract herself. "Is it big enough for you?"

He turned that gorgeous smile on her, and she tried not to squirm. "It's cool! Very cute. I love the Sasquatch."

"All credit to my big bro for the inspiration, of course."

Daniel laughed, tipping back his head and drawing Elise's unwilling eyes to his throat. She looked quickly away, trying not to imagine how warm his skin must be. "Man, Kyle," he said, "we had some fun setting traps in the woods, didn't we? Imagine if we'd had access to cheap trail cameras back then."

"Yeah, we could've been the guys to catch one. They're still hiding, though."

Chuckling, Daniel sank back into his chair and spread his legs toward the fire as he turned his smile back on Elise. Jesus. Did that heat in her belly mean she was healing and ready? Or was her body jumping right back into leading her astray? How could she know?

"This place is fantastic," he said. "Wasn't there an old pony ride here when we were young?"

"Yes! There's a picture in the reception area," Elise said. "I think I caught the tail end of the pony rides when I was about six. The last owner brought in the tiny homes nine years ago, but he wanted out after the fires in 2021. It happened to come on the market when I was looking for a new path."

"Were you in hospitality before?"

Elise grimaced. "Not really. I worked for a hotel for a few months. Did customer service here and there. But when I saw the cabins, something just felt right about it." What had felt right was the compromise of staying in one place, building a life, and letting the scene change with every new wave of guests. A happy medium between drifting like a tumbleweed and settling down.

Christian had been the one who encouraged her to jump right in. "You're strong as hell, Elise. There are only nine cabins. You could handle twenty." He'd helped her put together a business plan and even pushed her on a loan agent he knew. She still wondered if he'd pulled strings to make it happen, because her credit was hardly stellar.

"Well, you've done a great job with it," Daniel continued. "I'm surprised the cabins are nine years old. Mine still looks brand new."

"Thanks." Her cheeks warmed with the compliment. "I watch a lot of home-improvement videos and try to stay on top of the little things." She watched accounting videos too, but they weren't as exciting. Thankfully her mom was a bookkeeper who helped out when she could.

"And hey." Daniel twisted to look over his shoulder. "I really love the sign."

Laughing, Elise tipped her head toward Kyle. "In my brother's honor, obviously."

The nine-foot-tall two-dimensional Bigfoot stood at the edge of the highway, holding a "Creekside Cabins" sign and pointing one long finger toward the office. She'd had him custom painted wearing a plaid hunter's cap with earflaps.

Tourists loved him. She didn't have to do much advertising with all the social media photos people posted of themselves with the big guy. She'd even put a three-foot-tall boulder next to him so kids could scramble up and pose with Bigfoot. Pretty smart considering she knew nothing about kids and even less about publicity. Her Bigfoot sign was the best money she'd ever spent.

He was an easy decorating crutch too. Each cabin was outfitted with Sasquatch prints she'd purchased on Etsy and dotted with little plastic figurines. Surprisingly, she lost only a few every year, and she cleared a nice profit selling stuffed Bigfoots at check-in. The kids loved them even if the parents probably cursed her for stacking dozens of plushies on the shelf behind her desk.

My God, she was such a normie now. But this new life fit just fine. It felt like the kind of life she might have had from the start if her world hadn't hit the fan so hard in fourth grade.

"Maybe Mom's right to still be on guard," Kyle said suddenly, his eyes fixed on the crackling sparks popping from the firepit near her side door, far from the larger area meant for guests.

Elise had been so lost in thought that it took her a moment to stiffen up at the sudden topic change. "She's not," she snapped at him, but Daniel was already asking, "What do you mean?" and his words tangled up with hers, drowning them out. It was a perfectly reasonable question, but she wanted to curse him for asking it.

Kyle leaned toward Daniel. "How do we know that Phoenix guy really did it?"

"Because he confessed," Daniel replied as if it was the obvious answer. And it was.

"He was just a regular kid. He—"

"Stop," Elise interrupted. "I don't want to argue about this tonight." It was the one conspiracy even their mom refused to tolerate these days, but that hadn't stopped Kyle from bringing it up over the years.

"We're not arguing," Kyle said in that awful calm tone he used when her voice rose. "We're talking."

"Yeah, but we're going to argue if you keep talking, so just *stop*."

Daniel watched with wide hazel eyes, his gaze flitting between the siblings.

Despite her warning, Kyle smirked, his face set in a familiar smug expression. "If there's no merit to my questions, why do you get so weird and defensive about them? Is it because you know it's possible?"

"No. It's because Robin is not a cryptid, Kyle. She's not an internet riddle for podcast fans to solve. She's *our sister*, and it was bad enough we knew nothing for ten years. I'm not going on a goddamn mystery adventure with you just because you need her death to be more meaningful than it was."

"I—"

"It was stupid violence and homegrown misogyny, the same dumb shit that kills women every hour of every day. Sorry if that's not exciting enough for you to accept."

The fire popped in the silence her words had carved into the purpling evening air. A moment ago it had been a bright dusk, a happy reunion with a friend, and now their ugly family wounds crouched with them in the circle of Adirondack chairs. The vibrant yellow paint faded to the color of a healing bruise as the fire fought to make a space in the gray. Elise's fist looked just as sickly against the shiny wood. It looked like how she felt inside every time they *discussed* Robin.

Daniel cleared his throat. Kyle reached to open the cooler he'd brought, his face placid and self-satisfied at having set her off. He seemed to believe upsetting people was the same as exposing the truth, as if her anger were a symptom instead of valid emotion.

"Amber will be here in a minute," she muttered, pushing up from her chair, trying not to look as stiff or awkward as she felt. "It's good to see you again, Daniel."

"You too," he said, flashing a tight smile.

"Let me know if you need anything."

A blast of headlights hit her cabin before she'd even made it up the steps, but she didn't pause to wait for Amber. She let the storm door slap shut behind her and headed for the sink to dump the last third of her beer. These days she had no trouble stopping at one. The real problem that wanted to tug her back down was the temptation to avoid her pain at any cost.

She'd chased relief for years with booze and weed, pills and sex, that feeling of being swallowed by a huge blanket that promised to enfold her completely. But she could now process being upset with Kyle without chemical or physical thrills. It wasn't even difficult anymore. In fact, dumping the beer had been nearly as instinctual as downing it would have been a few years ago.

Hot damn, she was getting good at life. Maybe they'd put her in the next high school reunion update.

She heard the friendly chirp of voices outside, and then the storm door clapped shut again. "Special delivery!" Amber called, hoisting up a plastic bag as she appeared in the kitchen.

"My hero," Elise responded without a hint of sarcasm. Amber worked as a hairstylist in Tahoe three days a week, and they had a very special relationship based on mutually beneficial mooching. Amber brought Elise her favorite restaurant food a couple times a month, and in return she got to hang out in a home free of children, teenagers, or husbands for as long as she wanted.

They'd always known each other, but they hadn't been childhood friends, exactly. Amber had been friends with Robin, both of them eight years older than Elise.

Back then, Elise had been nothing more than a pesky younger sister constantly pushing open the bedroom door to find out what the teenagers were up to, equally desperate for their attention and scandalized by their rule breaking. Cigarettes, loud music, the occasional boy smuggled in after school let out. They'd absolutely fascinated young Elise.

God, Robin had been a blazing star. In her family's life, sure, but she'd shone for everyone. Like many firstborn siblings, she'd been driven and focused, but not in that standard, overachieving way. Robin had been focused on *fun*. On going to every party, trying every new hairstyle, joining every club. An extrovert who'd burst free of a family of introverts.

Elise had often wondered if her older sister had inherited their father's personality. He was a rolling stone who'd eventually rolled right on down the highway, disappearing from their lives. For a time it had seemed possible that Robin had simply taken off for the big city . . . until it hadn't.

"Do you ever take your dishes *out* of the dishwasher?" Amber asked with a groan as she wrestled the bottom rack free of the hulking beast of an appliance.

"It's only me," Elise answered as she unpacked containers of smoked turkey, coleslaw, and barbecue sauce on the scarred wood of her kitchen table. "Why would I bother putting the dishes away when they're going to end up back in the dishwasher again?"

"Because we live in a civilized society?"

"Do we, though?"

Amber sighed. "Good point. I peeled mandarin oranges for everyone's lunches this morning. I was being nice, you know? Sending my darling children off with a smile! Aaron walked by before I could finish packing, stuffed an entire orange in his mouth, and ate it whole. Then I had to stop Andy from copying him, because his mouth isn't quite as big as his seventeen-year-old brother's. Like, sometimes I feel guilty for not putting inspirational notes in their packs like those moms on Instagram, but I can't even cover the basics like 'Please eat like a human and not a bear.' Am I doing something wrong?"

"Everything, probably."

"Yeah." She sighed. "Yeah, screw it. They're all alive, right?" As her words settled between them, Amber froze, blinking hard as if someone had taken a flash photo of her. Her eyes went wide as she realized what she'd said. "Oh. I didn't—"

"Hey, you saved little Andy's life this morning!" Elise jumped in to pave over Amber's faux pas. All any mother could do was try to keep them alive, and sometimes all the trying in the world didn't work. There was no point rehashing that.

"I did, didn't I?" She flashed Elise a grateful smile. "Time to celebrate with food and TV. Are you up for another *Ted Lasso*?"

"Absolutely."

Amber craned her neck to look out the window before turning to set plates and forks on the table. "Daniel Serrano is looking pretty cute," she said, her voice slyly casual. "Says he's back here for the winter."

"Yep."

"Hmm."

Elise hmmed back at her, keeping her eyes on her plate. "Hey, it's slow here. I've got a lot of cabins open right now if you want to book one."

"You do need a haircut." She opened the appointment app on her phone, then toggled over to her calendar. Elise had successfully distracted her.

"And you could use a break before ski season starts up," Elise pointed out.

"True." Amber popped a piece of corn bread into her mouth and tapped her chin. Their mooching relationship didn't stop with food from Tahoe. Amber cut Elise's hair for free whenever she wanted what she called "a spa vacation." The spa consisted of one of Elise's tiny homes with unlimited hours of reality TV for a night or two and a Jacuzzi on the back deck. At home, Amber had four kids, three dogs, and a husband who worked all hours for the Department of Transportation when he wasn't on call as a volunteer firefighter.

"Oh my God, I think I might be able to get away Friday. You have anything free?"

"Absolutely. I'll put you in your favorite cabin."

"Now you're my hero. Hey!" She grabbed Elise's wrist as if she planned to wrestle the corncob out of her grasp.

"Back off, this one's mine."

"No, what happened to your arm? There's blood on your shirt."

Cursing, Elise twisted her elbow sideways to get a better look. "Shoot." She tugged up the sleeve of her flannel.

"Ow!" Amber cried when she saw it.

"I must have opened it up in the shower. Just a scratch." She pressed a napkin to it and dropped the corn onto her plate. She'd forgotten all about the scratch, but now it burned with pain again. "I'll get some ointment."

"Nah, that napkin will fix it right up. Trust me. I'm a mom."

"Nevertheless." Elise retreated to the bathroom and searched through the medicine cabinet for antibiotic cream, but she found only a spray. She peeled off the napkin and sprayed her forearm, then taped a little gauze to the still-oozing scratch.

When she closed the cabinet, she winced and made a mental note to never buy this shade of LED lightbulb again. She looked blue and tired, her hair an ash brown instead of chestnut. She'd let it grow out a bit over the summer, but maybe it was time for something drastic. A short cut she could cover with a knit cap when she didn't want to fuss with it during the winter. And it wouldn't hurt anything to look cute for Daniel.

Still, she couldn't deny the thought that crouched in the dark of her brain like a devil, telling her she should look hot as hell in case Christian disobeyed her wishes and stopped by. Make him eat all his regrets right in front of her.

She pulled the sides of her hair back, piled the waves on her head. Yeah. Hot as hell.

She'd always had long hair, had always loved her dark waves and the wildness of it after sex or a bleary-eyed afternoon wake-up. She'd looked as crazy as she'd felt inside for all those years. A signal to others not to fuck with her, a warning that she was on the edge.

But she'd cut it all off during her grief spiral after Christian. It was still choppy and wild but had grown down to her shoulders, easy to tame with an elastic band.

But if she could just cover it up with a fuzzy hat . . . maybe she could go a bit crazier. "Am I too old for a faux-hawk?" she yelled.

"Hell no!" Amber shouted back. "That would look amazing on you. Let's do it!"

"Hm." She leaned close to the mirror, eyeing the wrinkles starting to form around her eyes. The creases in her forehead had always been there, tension she'd carried with her since elementary school, and she'd be damned if she'd hide those marks life had left on her. Why shouldn't her suffering be on display?

"It's now or never," she murmured to her own face. She was thirty-five, and middle age was barreling toward her with no way to stop it. Well, only one way, and she'd definitely take age spots and wrinkles over death.

"Yeah." She snapped off the light and headed back to her food. "Let's do a faux-hawk."

"Yes!" Amber pumped a fist. "You're not busy Friday? I could come over and cut your hair, then hide away in my cabin. Start the weekend off right."

"Perfect." Her nerves shivered with the old, familiar joy of chasing every impulse. Split-second decisions were her happy place.

She tucked the leftovers into the fridge while Amber rinsed dishes; then Elise headed to the fireplace to arrange kindling and get a fire started. The wood was cracking and popping within minutes.

Amber had just dropped onto the couch when she cursed. "Shit." She glared down at her phone. "I can't stay long after all."

"Oh no. Everything okay?"

"Yeah, but I might have to get up early. Looks like John needs to head out at sunrise, which means I'll have to drive Abby to swim practice in Tahoe at the ass crack of dawn."

"It's not going to snow, is it?" It wasn't unheard of in September, and plow drivers would get the word before anyone else, but the winds felt way too calm to signal a big front.

"No, somebody went missing. Um." She shot a look at Elise past her lashes. "It's a grown man, though. Probably got lost hiking. Hopefully he'll show up before John has to head out with the search."

"That's too bad. You only have time for one episode, then?"

"Just one," Amber said, settling deep into the couch as she tucked a fluffy blue blanket tight around her. "Maybe two."

Figuring it would be more like three, Elise winked and grabbed the remote. But when the show started, she wasn't watching the screen. Her gaze drifted to the black square of the window and the sliver of new moon that peeked through the highest leaves of the tree. It was too dark out there. Too cold. Too fucking lonely. Whoever the guy was, she hoped he wasn't terrified or in pain.

God, she was caught on multiple hooks today, all of them tugging her toward memories she didn't want to touch. Elise tugged back. Robin was long gone, and nothing could ever change that. But she did have one sibling left.

"Sorry, hold on a second." She hit pause and hurried into the kitchen to open the side door. "Kyle, if you want to—" But Kyle was gone. The chairs were empty, his car had vanished, and only a faint wisp of smoke snaked out of the firepit. A glance toward cabin 6 showed a rectangle of light glowing in the darkness. Daniel had settled in, and Kyle had gone home.

That was for the best, she told herself. Kyle wasn't the type to drop a subject once he'd started gnawing on it, and then they'd argue again and she'd feel worse.

Still, another hook dug into her flesh with a sharp sting and tugged hard. But that hook was as familiar as the slide of a favorite earring going in. Guilt. Her closest family member.

She'd meditate before bed and hope for the best. Maybe she wouldn't have any bad dreams about being kidnapped after all.

Hey, baby sis!

You'd better be staying out of my things, or there will be hell to pay when I get home.

Good news here! Starting tomorrow I'm going to be a head counselor for the first time!!!!! One of the senior counselors got sick and had to go home because of mono. You know what that is? THE KISSING DISEASE! Glad you still think boys are gross because THEY ARE. Except for Marco—he's cute and tall, and he made me a polished wood necklace with my initials on it. Isn't that the sweetest? That's a secret, so don't tell anyone. Someone at home still thinks we're dating, but I told him we aren't, and summer doesn't count anyway. I'm away at camp for two months! Why would I want a boyfriend?

You're smart to say you never want a husband, but you are NOT SMART to stay home from camp. There aren't that many spiders, I swear. Don't be a baby! Tell Mom you want to come for the last July session. It's only two weeks. I can hook you up with extra desserts and all the best activities because I'M A HEAD COUNSELOR. Haha.

Tell Kyle I say hi. He never writes back, so I refuse to write anymore. See you soon, especially if you come to camp with me!

XOXO
Robin

CHAPTER 4

"I'm heading out with a search, but my boy can handle a quick trail ride," the man on the phone said. He owned the mountain version of a dude ranch a little farther down the road.

Elise leaned out the door and aimed a thumbs-up at Julie and her son. The day had dawned sunny and warm, and the boy had found a reception-room brochure promising safe family fun on horseback.

"You've got a good mount for a seven-year-old?" Elise asked.

"Yep, no worries. Our oldest mare can't be spooked even if you try. I'll have Junior saddle her and pick a calm gelding for the mom. You said they'll head over about now?"

"Yep. Twenty minutes or so, okay?"

When he answered, Elise gave another thumbs-up and a grin to the boy, who let out a whoop and actually kicked up his heels.

"You're good to go!" Elise called to the mom. "Plug the address into your phone, and you shouldn't have any problem finding it. It's a paved road all the way up to the ranch gate."

The woman thanked her with a smile that was decidedly less enthusiastic than her son's, prompting Elise to laugh. Usually it was an overexcited parent trying to pump some enthusiasm into kids who were glued to their screens.

"You'll be great," she reassured her. "They're saddling up two gentle horses for you. You'll need sunscreen at this altitude even in fall, so take some with. And be sure to show me pictures when you get back!"

"Oh, we will!" the boy shouted.

Elise felt a brief pang of bittersweet joy. She didn't want kids. She couldn't even imagine it. But she enjoyed these glimpses of families lighting up with excitement. She took special pleasure in the way small children glowed when she opened the door to a tiny home and showed them some of the secrets inside. Not all of them. She knew they'd want to discover their own. The little shades that pulled down over the bunks. The mini sink that fit into the tight corner of the bathroom. Some of the kids would later ask breathlessly if she knew about one thing or another, and in that moment she felt like a fairy godmother.

She'd never had that feeling before this. Contributing positivity to the lives of strangers felt . . . nice.

Retreating back to the kitchen to pour a third cup of coffee, Elise rubbed her tired eyes and considered sneaking in a nap while Julie and her son were gone. Daniel had taken off early that morning, and nobody was scheduled to check in. And she was definitely dragging.

Her hopes for a dreamless night had been in vain. She'd been visited by all her old childhood demons, and to chase them off she'd finally gotten out of bed at 4:00 a.m. to read some of her favorite letters from Robin. She'd sent dozens over her summers away, all of them decorated with doodles and swirls and stickers. A few still smelled of perfume, and one stank of berry-scented ink. Between Elise, their mom, and Robin's huge group of friends, she must have written for an hour every night.

But even those cheerful letters hadn't worked for Elise, and she'd had another familiar dream during her last hour of sleep, of someone behind a wall, banging and breathing hard. Sometimes she thought it was Robin, but usually she knew it was the monster who'd stolen her. Still, Elise's demons passed quickly these days. Hopefully she'd sleep like a rock tonight if she could power through.

Her nap decision was made for her when she heard the rumble of a vehicle stopping at her driveway and glanced out to spy the familiar brown of the UPS truck. The new microwave for cabin 8 had finally arrived, and she needed to get that installed above the two-burner stove.

Elise headed out to the road, strutting with premature pride. Another new project to master, another notch in the measure of her new competence, and this had to be more fun than working on a toilet.

Within minutes she had her earbuds in, blasting Wet Leg as she unpacked the microwave and read the installation instructions. She was on a stepladder, eyeing the old screws she'd need to remove from the cabinetry, when a shadow flickered somewhere in the cabin.

Whipping around, she tugged at an earbud, pulling it free to swing against her chest. There was no one there, no stranger looming in the open crack of the doorway. But last night's dreams were fresh in her mind, screaming of danger. That old constant terror that the boogeyman who'd taken Robin would come back for Elise. They'd started right away after the disappearance, and they'd returned with a vengeance when Elise had been thirteen and finally hitting puberty.

You look exactly *like your sister.*

Jeez, you scared me. I thought you were Robin!

Does it feel weird looking just like her? I mean . . . it's weird, right?

Yes, it had been weird. It had been horrible. The comments and looks from people in town. The terrible, surprised grief she'd catch in the eyes of her mother when she wasn't quick enough to look away.

But worst of all had been the fear that whoever had taken Robin would want Elise too. That he was waiting and watching. Aside from Elise's darker hair, she and her sister could have been twins, separated by eight years and one tragedy. It was why Elise had never bleached her hair, never even gotten highlights. She'd already felt hunted, and out in public she imagined a flashing arrow above her head. Lightening her hair might turn her into a target.

Or into a ghost.

A shadow passed the doorway, blacking out the yellow slash of sun again.

Elise's fist tightened around the screwdriver. She took one quiet step toward the door, then flinched when a new song cut through a silence she hadn't realized had fallen. Elise tugged the other earbud free and pushed it into the pocket of her jeans.

Grass crackled beneath a foot somewhere close by.

"Hello?" she called gruffly, hoping it was only Daniel returned from running errands. She wasn't normally this jumpy. These stupid nightmares and dead animals and her brother's ridiculous paranoia . . .

Another footstep. Another brief flash of dark. "Ma'am?"

She relaxed at the hard voice, not knowing why. It just didn't seem like a killer would use that tone. He'd be oily or sly or high pitched. None of which made sense, anyway. Robin's killer was dead. He'd seen to that himself.

Elise pulled open the door and took a defiant step out to find a surprise waiting for her. Not a killer, but a cop. The sight of a sheriff's deputy facing toward the highway jolted through her like a shot of electricity. More rage. More memories. They'd barely bothered to look for Robin and had spent ten years making excuses.

"Can I help you?" she asked, fully aware that the police had never helped *her.*

The deputy's blue eyes flashed with irritation when he turned to find her standing only a few feet from his shoulder. "Elise Rockwood?"

"Yes," she said, her voice icy. But that ice melted when an image of her guest and the little boy on horseback flashed before her. Then she thought of her brother, and everything else fell away. "What's wrong?"

Another deputy walked around from the side of cabin 7, head cocked and face suspicious.

"We have a few questions for you, ma'am," the blue-eyed man said. A few questions? So it wasn't an accident or a health scare.

That was a relief, but her wariness returned, and she squinted at the guy's name badge. Harrison. "Questions about what?" When he ignored her, she stepped farther out onto the small wooden deck of the cabin. "Is my brother all right? Did something happen?"

"Ma'am, when was the last time you saw Christian Valic?"

The world stopped spinning and set her soul tumbling. She pressed her toes hard to the wood planks to keep her body from weaving, but her eyelashes fluttered before she could get control of herself. The cop was watching far too closely, but she couldn't seem to regain her equilibrium.

Why would this man ask her about Christian? Why would *anyone*? Only one person knew about him, and her brother wouldn't spill her secrets. "I . . . I'm sorry. Christian?"

Her feigned ignorance didn't work. She could see by the hard light in those pale eyes that he'd noticed her shock. His mouth twisted at the side, giving away self-satisfaction and drawing her attention to a nick in his cheek where he'd seemingly cut himself shaving. "Christian Valic," he said flatly.

"I . . ." She shut her mouth and swallowed hard. "What is this about, Deputy Harrison?" The second man had taken up position a foot behind Harrison's shoulder, hand on his gun belt. He wasn't threatening her but clearly didn't trust her. When his eyes touched her hand, she glanced down to see the screwdriver clutched tightly in her numb fingers. Ah.

Elise reached slowly out to set it on the wooden rocking chair to her side. It rolled off and clunked onto the deck. What the hell was going on?

"Ms. Rockwood, Christian Valic's vehicle was discovered at a trailhead yesterday evening after he failed to return home as expected. We recovered his phone on the trail last night."

Her gut turned. Was he dead or injured? Christian was athletic and health conscious for a man in his forties, not exactly someone she'd worry about going for a trail run, especially around here, where he ran nearly every day. But he could have fallen. Could have had a medical issue. Still . . .

"That's terrible," she managed, "but I'm still not sure why you're here. Unless it's Switchback?" She tipped her head up toward the hill that rose on the other side of the highway and the trail that snaked through the trees.

The small parking lot lurked a quarter mile down the road, but during the winter she could see scraps of the trail from her land. Snowshoers trudging up, fat-tired bikers barreling down. There was a steep drop-off on the other side of the peak. Had Christian—?

"No, ma'am." She jerked her gaze from the treetops to the cops. "We're here because we suspect foul play."

"Foul play?" Elise shook her head, not needing to feign confusion this time. "I don't understand. You said he was on a trail. He was running . . ."

"We assumed that, yes."

"But?"

"But new evidence indicates otherwise."

She had no idea what that could mean, and his stubborn expression didn't promise an explanation. Fractured thoughts began to pepper her with dark images, and the hair on her arms rose.

Foul play. What did that mean? Assault, kidnapping, murder? "I still don't understand what this could possibly have to do with me," she said, her voice going reedy at the edges.

"You do know Christian Valic?"

There was no reason to deny it. Probably hundreds of people knew Christian around here. "Yes."

"So you acknowledge that you have a relationship with Mr. Valic?"

"No!" she yelped as panic lapped at her brain. "What?"

"You have a relationship with Christian Valic." A statement, not a question. This man already thought he knew a lot about her.

"I don't!"

"All right, Ms. Rockwood. Let me rephrase that. Did you have a sexual relationship with Mr. Valic in the recent past?"

Her mind thrashed against the sea of fear threatening to drown it, tossing out excuses like hands reaching for rope. It wasn't recent. It felt like ancient history. And it hadn't just been sex. But maybe it hadn't really been a relationship, either. *Say no, say no, the answer is* no.

Instead she offered the most illogical excuse of all. "Christian Valic is married."

"I'm aware. Mrs. Valic is the one who called us to report him missing. She's extremely upset."

"Yes. Of course."

"You didn't answer my question, ma'am."

Deputy Harrison looked to be in his midforties. He'd likely been doing this job a long time, dealing with both small-town crimes and the complexity of many thousands of visitors coming through every year. He looked seasoned and wary. Better not to lie, and there was no reason to. She hadn't done anything illegal. The best thing would be to tell the truth so they could move on to finding him.

Christian. My God, he was *missing*.

"We had a friendship," she said past clumsy lips that wanted to hold her secrets back. "It's over. It's been over for a very long time. I haven't even seen him in passing. We don't . . . we don't run in the same circles." Her hand rose of its own volition to gesture at the cabin behind her.

Christian was rich. Silicon Valley rich. And she was a woman running a cabin-rental business that was mortgaged to the gills. She cleaned toilets and washed linens. Christian probably hadn't touched a washing machine since his twenties.

"When was the last time you spoke to him?"

"I don't know. A year ago? More than that."

"I guess I'll need to rephrase again," Harrison said dryly. "When did you last have contact with him?"

Her face heated. The nape of her neck prickled. How could they know about that? Had they already gotten into his account and searched emails? It was the only explanation for why they were here, why they were asking any questions at all. "I . . . We . . ." She cleared her throat.

The deputy's face tightened, and his eyes nearly disappeared into a narrow squint.

"Yes, we exchanged emails recently. About two weeks ago. It was no big deal. And I certainly haven't seen him."

"I take it things ended badly." Another statement pretending to be a question.

She stood a little straighter and uncrossed the arms she'd folded protectively over her chest. "Regardless, I haven't seen him. However it ended, it *ended*. If something happened to him, I can't help with that. It has nothing to do with me. I don't know anything."

"So you didn't threaten him?"

"What? No!" That word leapt high and loud, flying off into the sky, but the grunt he offered in response conveyed deep fathoms of doubt. His skepticism didn't scare her, though. The idea that she had ever threatened Christian was absurd. She'd never even threatened to tell his wife about the affair. She had too much pride to stoop to setting fire to his marriage.

That thought smacked hard into her gut. "Deputy," she said, starting to reach a hand toward him before realizing he might consider that a threat. "I promise this has nothing to do with me or our previous friendship. *Please* don't say anything to his wife. She doesn't deserve that. Christian will come home soon, and she doesn't need to be thinking terrible thoughts about him in the meantime."

When the only response was silence, she tried again. "It's over. It's been over for a long time. He was separated when we first . . ." She waved a vague hand. "But he worked through all that." Bitterness flooded her tongue at those words. *All that.* As if Elise had been a terrible plague. But she forced herself to continue with the truth no matter how hard it was to get out. "Please don't blow up his life. They have a good marriage. He's happy with her."

Tears pricked her eyes. She'd never said those words before, never even thought them. But it was the truth, despite what he'd done with Elise. It was one of the reasons she hadn't pushed him harder. He'd *wanted* Elise, wanted the base thrill of her wildness, but he'd loved his life. "Neither of them deserves to have their lives destroyed just because he twisted a knee or . . . whatever you think happened."

He stared at her, eyes piercing, brow crimped down. She met his gaze and refused to look away. She'd done something wrong, yes, but she hadn't done *this*.

"We discovered his phone on a bench only fifty feet from the trailhead."

"Okay. Maybe it fell out of his pocket?"

"Maybe. His health app tracked his steps. He walked to the bench, sent a text, and then the phone didn't move for seven hours until we found it."

She nodded, worried but unconvinced. He could have set down his phone and forgotten it, and that would offer the simplest explanation of his disappearance. During a run, he'd fallen or broken an ankle, and then he didn't have a phone to call for help.

But Harrison still stared, waiting for her to say something. She looked to the other deputy, another white guy, younger and plumper, then back to Harrison. Just finding the phone didn't seem like enough to indicate foul play. "You—"

"Where'd you get that scratch on your arm, Ms. Rockwood?"

"Scratch?" She looked down at her right forearm, and there it was. The angry twin gouges from the branch she'd scraped yesterday. She'd taken off the bandage to let it scab over, but now she put her fingers over the wound to cover it. When she realized how that must look, she lowered her hand. "I was doing some maintenance down by the creek yesterday. I scraped it on the point of a broken branch. That's all."

A click snapped from his phone, and she glanced up to see it pointed right at her arm. He'd taken a picture of her injury. Heat flashed up her chest to her neck and face, and she knew she must be bright red, her skin sending signals of nonexistent guilt. And the damn wound was exactly a day old and looked it. Not healed over but not oozing blood.

"Do you have any other injuries you'd like to reveal?"

"No!"

"This is a good opportunity to come clean. Maybe something went wrong but you didn't mean anything."

"There's nothing to come clean about!" she said, her voice practically a yelp.

"All right, then," he drawled, sly hostility in his tone. "I'm sure we'll have more questions later. You're not planning any trips, are you? Gonna be in town for the next few days?"

She nodded, fear making her throat click dryly when she swallowed. The other deputy made to leave, but she held up a hand before Harrison could turn away. "You said Christian sent a text. What did it say?"

The deputy smirked and nodded as if she'd posed exactly the right question. "Let me know if you hear anything, Ms. Rockwood. We'll be in touch."

CHAPTER 5

She couldn't let this derail her. Christian wasn't part of her life anymore, so it didn't matter if her knotted heart sang with pain at every beat. He was fine. And if he wasn't fine, he wasn't hers to grieve. Christian didn't love her, she didn't love him, and he'd excised her brutally from his world, trimming her existence from even his thoughts.

He'd needed to do that, he'd said. Needed to concentrate on his wife and the life they'd built together for over twenty years. Needed to make up for his most shameful secret: Elise.

And how could she argue with that? She was the other woman, a homewrecker, an interloper, so how could she demand anything? She hadn't even wanted him like that, not as a *husband*.

It might not have hurt with such sharp pain if she hadn't known he was fully capable of cutting her from his mind with surgical precision. He had that kind of willpower. It was part of the secret of his success. And my God, she'd hated him for that. Despised knowing that while she thought of him endlessly for months after their break, he'd locked her into a sturdy box and shoved her into the attic of his brain.

She'd never had that ability, which was the secret of her failure to launch. Her mind had always been a roil of restless darkness, latching on to any shiny thing to distract from what she couldn't escape.

You're just a late bloomer, he'd murmured into the bare skin of her shoulder when she'd lamented that she'd only started building a foundation in her thirties. She'd been nothing like him, the id to his ego. They'd snapped together like magnets. And now he might be *gone*?

No. He was fine.

Standing inside cabin 8, the door now shut and locked behind her, Elise scrubbed a hand hard over her forehead, trying to free something. A comforting thought or a helpful insight. But no amount of pressure worked.

The microwave. She'd install the microwave and move on with her day. That was her job. And whatever the cops thought, this had nothing to do with her. If he'd sent a text, it was to someone else, and that digital trail would lead the police to bother that person instead of her.

She mounted the stepladder, raised the screwdriver, and promptly burst into tears. "Please let him be okay," she sobbed. "Please."

Christian had been her best friend once. He'd been her lover and her crutch and her delight. And despite the bad things they'd done, he wasn't a bad person.

She'd tried so hard to get her shit together when she'd moved back to California. She'd worked full time, gotten up early, flossed every day, and started indulging the dream of Creekside Cabins as soon as she'd seen the "For Sale" sign.

She'd taken up jogging, stopped smoking, and found a therapist she truly trusted. But she hadn't wanted to give up on the belief that she was cool and edgy. That she'd suffered more than most and had the kick-ass scars to prove it.

She wasn't *like* other people, wasn't like other girls, and she'd still wanted to yell *fuck off* at everyone who asked too much of her.

Christian had been one way of doing that. She hadn't realized it at the time, of course. He'd just been hot and funny and forbidden. A slightly older married guy who looked at her like she was a bad decision he wanted to make.

They'd been friends at first, striking up a conversation at a local watering hole as they both nursed beers. From then on she'd flirted mercilessly with him every time he set foot in the bar. She'd gone frequently, just for a beer or two, to get out of her brother's place and maybe to prove she could still drink socially without spiraling. When Christian had started dropping by more often, she knew it was because of her.

She'd felt *bad*, and she'd loved the thrill of that after too many months of being good. It wasn't like she was going to sleep with him, right? He'd been nothing but respectful.

It had been months before they'd started texting and meeting occasionally for lunch. Then he'd said his wife was leaving, that they both wanted a separation.

Shit. What a disaster it had all been.

But it had been definitively over, and now *this*? The rot of it was seeping through all that healed tissue, threatening to spread pain. His wife hadn't deserved the initial betrayal, and she certainly didn't deserve this awful, metastasized ruin of what they'd done.

Elise pressed her hands to her face and wiped the wetness from her cheeks. She could bear this worry. It was penance, really, for wanting what wasn't hers. She'd always wanted what wasn't hers, because that meant she didn't have to fear losing it. Not that it always worked out. Not that she hadn't fallen hard anyway.

"He's fine," she said aloud to herself. Christian would turn up in the next hour or two, injured and embarrassed, and his wife would clutch him and kiss him and never know the truth. He could get back to that new, grounded life he'd written to her about, and Elise could keep working on hers.

The beep of a car honking out on the highway snapped her out of her emotional spiral. "He's fine," she repeated, and her heart calmed a bit. She removed the last of the old microwave fastenings and wrestled the packaging off the new parts.

An hour later, she wiped down the glass door and nodded at her latest accomplishment. Another new skill, another step in the right direction. But she still braced herself for bad news when she put her hand to the doorknob.

When she emerged from the cocoon of her temporary hiding place with lowered brows, ready for another blow, all that greeted her was the sight of the steep hill across the highway. She knew he wasn't up on Switchback, but she stared at it, hair rising on her arms even as the sun pressed heat into her face.

"Hey," a man's voice called, and she was so caught up in her staring she didn't even startle. She only said, "Hey," as she turned her body in his direction, her face following slowly, reluctant to let go of the view.

Daniel stood on the deck of his cabin, a hand raised in greeting, and she forced a smile she didn't feel. She wasn't in the mood for smiling, but he was a customer, after all, not just a cute guy.

He stepped off his porch and met her on the grass. "Where do you buy your supplies around here?" he asked, tipping his head toward the box she carried. "Got any good tips?"

"I needed an especially small microwave, so I ordered online. Whatever you do, don't buy in Tahoe. But you already know that."

"Yeah, I figured I'd head down to the valley for any big purchases."

"I do a lot of my own repairs, but let me know if you're looking for help with plumbing or electrical while you're working on the house. I'll give you my best contacts. And Jamie Springer is a great roofer."

"Oh, I remember her brother. Played soccer with him."

"Unfortunately, I think he's in prison now."

Daniel winced. "Yikes. Sorry to hear it, but . . . that sounds right, actually. He was kind of an asshole."

Chuckling, she shifted the box and stepped toward her cabin. "I'd better get back to it."

"Hey, I'm sorry about last night." Daniel gestured toward the box in an offer to take it, but when she shook her head, he stuffed his hands in the pockets of his jeans and followed her. "I didn't mean to bring up a sticky subject."

Last night felt a hundred miles away now. "No big deal, really. Not in our family."

"Kyle seems good, though." He didn't notice the doubtful look Elise shot his way. "Man, I wish I had the sort of skills to get into tech, but programming is a foreign language to me."

"You and me both. What were you doing before this?"

"I was a park ranger for about eight years."

"Whoa! Sounds like a dream job."

"Well, the location was unbeatable, the tourists were okay, but the pay made it feel more like a hobby."

She winced. "Yeah, I've heard it's not exactly lucrative."

"I'm glad I did it, though. These days I'm working on informational projects for the state parks. Mostly online, a little travel."

"Sounds perfect for spending time working on your dad's house. I was sorry to hear he died, by the way." He nodded and made no comment. "How's your sister doing?" she pressed.

"Great! She's an RN in San Jose. In high demand and doing real well. She has a wife and kids, white picket fence. The whole package."

"That's good to hear."

"And I get unlimited free medical advice, so that's a big plus. Hey, listen . . ." He followed her to the recycling bin, where she set the box down to break up later. "Would you want to grab dinner tonight?"

Her body stuttered with shock or excitement or both. It seemed her flannel shirt camouflage hadn't worked as a force field. He'd probably glimpsed the stir of horniness in her eyes. "Oh, I . . ."

"Haven't been to Harry's in a long time."

Harry's was a seasonal drive-in where teenagers gathered in droves during the summer, the same as they had twenty years earlier. She knew for a fact that Harry's summer season closed in ten days. There was still time to go and relive their adolescence, flirt over greasy fries and burgers. Her pulse sped at the thought of teasing him, bumping his knee with hers, leaning over a bit to show off her cleavage as she'd done with Christian.

Christian. The butterflies in her stomach rioted, threatening to spew out. "I'm sorry. I can't get away."

"Oh, sure." She didn't miss his quick glance at the empty parking area near her cabin.

"The other guests will be back in a couple of hours, and I try to stay close in case I'm needed."

"Of course. Got it. Another time."

The butterflies solidified to a stone. She hated the disappointment on his face, not least because it echoed her own. She'd always liked him. She still did. "You should go to Harry's!" she said too brightly. "It'll be closed soon."

His easy smile barely betrayed any tension, but it was there. He might not ask again. "Maybe I will."

She couldn't go with him. Not with this new worry about Christian. But it would be over soon, right?

He was starting to turn, and she felt a little panicked at pushing him away. How could someone who'd been broken for so long know if a decision was right or wrong? Would she have agreed to a date before this police visit? Maybe. Maybe she was stable enough to risk it. Maybe she wouldn't ruin their friendship with her old chaos. And surely this issue of Christian being "missing" would be resolved within a few hours.

She stared at Daniel's back as he stepped away. "Next week?" she blurted out.

He jerked to a stop and swung back to raise his eyebrows at her. "Next week?"

Elise nodded, and when his smile bloomed back to life, something inside her bloomed too.

"All right," he drawled. "I'll check in again in a few days." He gave a small wave even though he was only standing five feet from her, then spun to head back to his cabin.

She watched Daniel walk away, her heart fluttering. It felt like she'd done the right thing for once. She wanted something, but she'd put it off and tamped down her impulsive nature for a week . . . because where the hell was Christian?

Elise tugged her phone from her pocket and began typing. Did John have to go out on search this morning? she texted Amber.

Three dots appeared immediately. Yes! And he's still out. Now I have to do all the pickups too! Ugh.

Wow, no word on the guy? Which trail is it? Big Hollow?

Midmountain.

Elise winced. She'd hiked Midmountain with Christian once. Well, they'd done more than hike, actually. She knew it was one of his favorite trail runs, close to his house and peppered with stunning views, especially this time of year.

She thought of him pushing her against a huge spruce, the bark digging into her back, his mouth playing gently against hers. God, she still missed that. The chemistry, the easy fit of their bodies together.

She missed him, and sometimes she feared she always would. Feared she'd whisper his name on her deathbed decades from now, like some tragic character in a novel. Now that worry had vanished, replaced with sharp rocks and high cliffs and the fervent wish that Christian's marriage would play out into old age.

I know we haven't spoken in a while, but I'd love to grab a coffee and talk.

When she'd opened that unexpected email from him, her heart had nearly pounded its way out of her chest. Why would he reach out after so long? After she'd finally exorcised him from her possessed heart?

Been doing a lot of work, a lot of therapy, and there are some things I need to say face-to-face, if possible. In case you saw me . . . I pulled into the cabins

the other day but realized it wasn't fair to surprise
you that way. OK if I drop by again?

His request had filled her with terror. Not of him, but of herself.
Terror at the way her entire soul blossomed at the idea of seeing him
again. She'd already been thinking of what to wear, how to look her hottest while maintaining an illusion of not having tried at all. An old tank
top, maybe, with an unbuttoned flannel shirt "accidentally" sliding off
her shoulder. Tight jeans. Her hair pulled back but beginning to loosen
from its tie, tendrils framing her face as she opened the side door to let
him in the way she'd done so many times.

He'd loved her cabin. She suspected part of that had been the fun
of slumming it, but he'd also been proud of her. He'd given her a lot
of advice about the purchase, the loan, how to research property and
forecast potential income and costs.

The very first time they'd slept together had been after she'd finally
signed the papers and made the place hers. They'd had drinks to celebrate, and he'd told her about the separation. Then they'd had each
other.

His wife had been a phantom. Someone Elise had never met, a face
she avoided looking at on his social media. Savannah Valic had been less
than real, and so his marriage had been easy for her to ignore.

Elise pressed her fingers to her closed eyes until she saw stars.
Midmountain Trail. The spectacular views were provided courtesy
of a rocky ridge and steep drop-offs. He could have slipped. Could
be caught in a crevice or on a narrow ledge. Had they checked every
pocket, every cliff? She hadn't noticed helicopters today, but the trail
was nine miles toward Tahoe, so any emergency vehicles would have
come in from that direction.

Or had he been meeting someone new there? A new lover they'd
assumed must be Elise? Or was it another woman from his past he'd
reached out to after therapy?

Jesus. The pain stabbed through her like a knife to the gut. Stupid to feel that way after two years, but he told her he'd never done that before. And at the end, he'd told her he'd never do it again. But he could have been a serial cheater, a serial liar. She couldn't put her trust in warm eyes and hot kisses.

Before she'd even thought about it, Elise snatched her keys from the hook by the side door and headed for her car. She peeled out onto the highway and drove east, Bigfoot shrinking smaller in her rearview mirror.

Leaning forward, she gripped the steering wheel hard, weaving through the curves as the road wound through the narrow pass into national forest land. The creek flashed into view, peeking through trees when it curled close to the road, turning into narrow, foaming torrents when it dropped down in two- or three-foot falls. She shivered and turned on the seat heater even though it was a perfect sixty-five degrees outside and the sun blazed through the windshield.

The shivering had only just subsided when she neared the trailhead parking lot and saw dozens of vehicles parked along the road. Her trembling immediately returned.

The lot was so packed that she couldn't have turned in if she wanted to. But she couldn't join the search for him, couldn't ask any questions. She shouldn't even be seen there, but she still slowed to a crawl, her eyes searching desperately for any sign of good news.

A group of men stood in the parking lot, dressed in brush pants and camouflage hats, and they all looked grim. The three horse trailers she spotted showed empty windows like dead eyes looking at her. The horses and riders were still up on the trail, which meant Christian hadn't been found. Not yet.

Movement drew her eye back to the road, and when she spotted a law enforcement vehicle approaching, Elise hit the gas too hard and lurched back into motion. Sweat prickled her brow, and she chewed at her bottom lip as she drove toward Tahoe and tried to summon the courage to turn around and dare to pass the search area again. It took her three miles, but she finally did it, pulling a sloppy three-point turn in the driveway of a campground.

She was halfway back to the trailhead when lights strobed behind her, and she startled so hard her hands jerked away from the steering wheel. A low whine leaked from her throat as she wrapped her fingers back around the wheel and eyed the cop car coming up fast in the mirror. She flicked her signal as her heart hit only every other beat, stuttering until she began to see stars from the lack of oxygen. But when she eased over to the shoulder, the car flew past her with a whoosh that shook her vehicle on its springs.

"Oh," she said, frozen in place for nearly a full minute before she eased back onto the road. "Never mind, then."

Just before she reached the trailhead, she watched a sheriff's truck peel out of the parking area and flick on its own lights. Nothing to do with Christian's search, only an accident up ahead, maybe. Two miles closer to her cabins, she reached the intersection of a county road that cut to the north and realized she could just make out the fading red and blue splotches of light through the little canyon. Her shoulders slumped with relief.

By the time she got home, her stomach was growling. She occasionally forgot to eat when she was stressed, but never for long. Her stomach didn't believe in making a bad situation worse. But she only had a short time to freshen cabin 3 before the guests returned, so she rushed to grab towels and hurried inside to make the beds.

It was 2:00 p.m. before she managed to toss bread into the toaster and started mixing up tuna and mayo and relish, but before she could finish, Julie and her boy pulled into the lot, their faces still animated from their adventure. Elise smiled and headed outside for some good news to lighten her stress.

"How was it?" she called as their car doors flew open.

"Amazing!" the boy yelled. "Junior said I was a natural!"

"Was it scary?"

"No, it was great!" He nearly screamed the last word, prompting his mom to wince as she smiled.

"It was a little scary," she said. "It felt very high up."

"The trail?"

"No, the horse. He's never going to forget this. Thank you so much for setting it up. He's over the moon."

"I'm just happy he had so much fun."

"He had a blast." The mom glanced up and chuckled. "Hey, Jesse James," she called. "The police are here. You'd better vamoose!"

The boy took off toward the cabin, his laughter trailing behind him as all the blood left Elise's head. The police were indeed here.

She thought she'd left them behind two hours before, but a now-familiar sheriff's truck crunched over the gravel of Elise's driveway.

"Thanks again!" the mom called over her shoulder. Elise could only manage a wave in response.

Why the hell were they back?

Maybe it was good news. Maybe they were here to let her off the hook and reveal that Christian had been found.

Harrison's eyes locked with hers and bored right into her as he drove the last twenty feet.

"Ms. Rockwood," he drawled as he and his partner stepped out and slammed their doors hard. He slipped on his western-style hat as if he wanted to make himself even taller before he approached.

"What's going on? Is Christian all right?" Her sentence rose at the end as hope took it higher.

"Ma'am. We'd like you to join us at the station."

"Me? Why?"

"Because we need to discuss your whereabouts yesterday afternoon."

Hope flew away and left her behind, feet pressed to the unyielding ground. No one was bringing her good news.

CHAPTER 6

"Yesterday?" she echoed, stunned by the deputy's words.

"Yeah. Where were you between the hours of . . . oh, let's say 9:00 a.m. and 8:00 p.m.?"

"But . . . why?"

"Because I believe you were with Christian Valic just before his death, and I'd like to ask a few questions about that."

The stench of that dead raccoon snuck back to her on a wave of sudden heat, either her imagination or from a breeze sneaking over the dumpster thirty feet away. "No," she whispered.

Christian was dead. Somehow he was dead, and she'd had a chance to see him one last time and said no. Because she'd still been angry, still been hurt, and mostly because she'd still been in love.

Love. Or whatever malformed semblance of love she'd managed to conjure in a heart impossibly twisted by scar tissue. Now it was too late. It would always be too late.

"Ms. Rockwood."

"We broke up almost two years ago," she insisted, the sentence rising too high and loud at the end. A confession to her last sin. "I haven't even run into him in a year! But he wanted to meet. Wanted to talk. He emailed me, and I . . . ."

"You what?"

"I said no. I refused."

"This was yesterday?"

"No. No, it was almost two weeks ago." She had to explain. It was too awful otherwise. "I was scared."

His eyes narrowed. "Scared of what?"

"No, not like that." She swiped a hand through the air, chopping off his stupid suspicions. "I couldn't face him. H-he . . ." Her jaw shook, teeth chattering. "What happened? Are you sure he's dead? Maybe he's lost. Maybe you'll still find him."

"His body was recovered from the Mokelumne River two hours ago."

The Mokelumne? That fucking river. The same river that had hidden her sister's body from her for so long. Now it had taken Christian from her too?

Elise pressed her hand to her chest, rubbed her fingers hard against her breastbone. Christian had been floating in that water. His body had probably caught in branches like the limbs of that raccoon, his fingers curled into stiff hooks, fingers that had once laced warm and needing through hers.

She remembered the awful pink wet of the animal's skin splitting. She—

"So where were you yesterday between nine and eight?"

Elise blinked at the ground. "I was here. I'm always here."

"I don't suppose anyone can confirm that?"

She glanced up, irritated that this man was bothering her when Christian was *dead*. "Yes. My guests. I had to help with an animal carcass they found in the stream."

"What time was that?"

"I don't know. Around lunchtime. Twelve thirty, maybe."

"What about before that? And after?"

"This is ridiculous. I was here all day. I replaced batteries in smoke detectors. I fixed a toilet. I had a beer with my brother and his friend. I had dinner with another friend. I never left the property. And I told Christian I *wouldn't see him*. There are emails."

"Right. But then you changed your mind."

"I have no idea what you're talking about."

"We've seen the texts, Ms. Rockwood. About meeting at Midmountain Trail."

Betrayal tugged her heart to her throat. "From *my* number? I don't think so. You're questioning the wrong woman. That was somebody else. He was probably seeing someone new!"

He crossed his arms and stared at her, waiting for something she was never going to offer. His head tilted as if he were studying a puzzle. "Somebody else, huh? So that's what you were angry about?"

Elise rolled her eyes. "I wasn't angry. I was over it. I'm happy Christian is working on himself—" She gave her head a hard shake, biting back a little hiccup of shock. "*Was* working on himself. But I didn't owe him help with that. I couldn't jeopardize my own peace of mind to help with his. I just . . . I couldn't. I've had to concentrate on getting my own shit together."

"I see. How about you come on down to the station and you can explain all that."

This time she couldn't swallow her fear. It refused to budge. She stepped back, arms rising up from her sides as if they meant to protect her from attack from any angle. "What? No. I was here all day. This is ridiculous."

"Then let's clear it up."

"There's nothing to clear up! You can speak to my guests!"

"You know what? I think I will. I don't suppose those guests who saw you are still here?"

"They are! Cabin 3. I can get her right now if you want."

He held up a hand and offered that smarmy smirk again. "We'll speak with her, ma'am. Please wait in your office."

The deputies turned and left her there, gaping at their backs, jaw dropped and eyes blinking. This was madness. Her life had been utterly normal yesterday, and now . . . Good God.

Elise pressed a hand to her mouth to hold back the sob welling in her chest, but it never rose. It stayed lodged there, caught in her lungs, a fist against her heart, ruthless knuckles pressing hard. *Christian.* His sparkling eyes, the slightly crooked nose, the tortured worry in his brow, and that genius, nimble mind. All of it just . . . gone.

Bitter sweat from her hand touched her lips and filled her mouth with a taste like grief. She had no idea how much time passed before she realized Deputy Harrison had stopped in front of cabin 3 and turned to glare at her from a distance. He tipped his head toward her front steps, and Elise obeyed because she had no reason not to. She didn't want this stranger to see her, anyway, didn't want his hostility dirtying up her pain.

She hurried, stumbling where the grass dropped half an inch to the gravel, weaving a bit as her head spun in the bright sunlight. She made it up her stairs and lurched through the entryway, the darkness swallowing her whole when she shut the door behind her.

The shadows helped relieve the stars circling in her brain, but then the stars sparked in her eyes and she had to lower herself slowly to the wood floor, hands searching out the surface to keep her body from tipping over.

She sat down, and . . . that was all she did. She didn't cry. Didn't think. The dark wrapped around her, and she sat with it, drawing slow breaths until her eyes adjusted and the rectangles of light around the window blinds finally revealed her cabin. The dark log walls made it feel like a cave sometimes, but she wanted a cave today. Wanted to stay inside for months until this storm passed.

She knew she should be thinking, puzzling out what the hell was going on and why Deputy Harrison had accused her of being involved. She should be calling someone or at least googling what to do when the police asked hostile questions. But she did none of that. She just curled in on herself and stared past the office doorway into her living room.

The thump of footsteps on the front stairs startled her, and she twitched out of her stupor. His knock was a hail of bullets as she scrambled to her feet to reach for the knob. Deputy Harrison stood there, his partner lurking at the bottom of the steps like a witch's familiar.

Elise wanted to ask what her guest had said, but that would seem panicky and suspicious. She knew what the woman must have told him because it was the truth. Elise had been around all day.

"Could you come on in with us to answer a few questions?"

No. That was the wrong door to open, especially when she had no idea what was really happening. "I—I can't leave right now. This is my business and I'm the only one here."

Harrison shifted, hooking a thumb over his tactical belt, his face scrunching up with a displeased scowl. He glanced over his shoulder at his partner. "All right," he finally drawled. "What time would you be able to come in?"

"A guest is checking in tonight. I don't know when they'll arrive. Check-in is anytime between three and seven."

"Ma'am, a man is dead. Surely there's someone you can call to cover for you."

There were people she could call, but she had no intention of making this easier. Whatever she said in a room with them would be recorded. All her sins would become part of the record. Everyone would know.

"It's the slow season," she said numbly. "My summer help is gone. It's just me, and I can't leave. I've told you everything. I can't help you."

He looked over his shoulder again, and he and his partner shared a glance that didn't bode well for her. Harrison finally turned and retreated down the steps, but only so he could pull the radio at his shoulder closer to his mouth and convey a message. "We've got a problem here."

Elise. *She* was the problem. She'd always been a problem. Her shoulders rose, neck going painfully tight as a terrible feeling swallowed up her body and screamed that she'd made a mistake. She should have gone with them instead of escalating.

But they were already telling themselves a story, adding spice to the truth that she'd been a homewrecker willing to take risks and hurt others while shucking off the rules of society. Surely a woman like that must be unstable and potentially dangerous, like old sticks of sweating dynamite.

A cabin door slapped shut, and when she looked up, Daniel was standing on his deck, frowning directly at her and the deputies. She met his gaze and held it, and he must have seen her fear, because he jogged down the three steps and headed toward Elise's place. For no good reason, she felt relieved.

He didn't quite make it, though. The deputies heard his footsteps and moved to meet him halfway. This time they didn't order Elise to go inside, and she heard Daniel's side of the conversation and snippets of Harrison's words.

"I got here around four," Daniel said. "Elise checked me in."

Harrison's voice was low, but she heard the words ". . . she leave?"

Daniel shook his head, eyes meeting hers again. She gave him a shallow nod. "She gave me a tour, we talked about the cabin. I was moving my stuff in for a few minutes, and she was at her place. I didn't see her drive off at any point. Her brother came by before six. We talked for a bit; then we had beers over at Elise's place around the fire."

"With her?"

"Yep. About forty-five minutes later, a woman came by with dinner. Amber. After Kyle left, I went back to my cabin."

"And the rest of the night?"

Daniel shrugged. "I came outside to smoke around seven thirty, eight. Amber's truck was still there. That's all I know, man."

"Came outside to smoke what?"

Daniel shot him an exasperated look and didn't answer.

"Are you in a romantic relationship with Elise Rockwood?"

"What the shit?" Daniel asked, his words half laughter. "I'm renting a cabin. Before this week I hadn't seen her in about twenty years."

Elise's fear eased back toward frustration. Had Harrison time traveled from the fifties? A middle-aged cop angry about devil's weed and harlots? He pulled his radio up again, hooded eyes sliding back to Elise as he stepped away from Daniel. His partner still hadn't said a word and was starting to creep her out.

She could feel Daniel's eyes on her, but she kept her attention on the real danger and watched as Harrison scowled. He wrapped up a crackly conversation on his radio before striding toward Elise. "Make time to come in tomorrow morning, or I'll take you in. Understand?"

Nodding, she kept her gaze locked tight on him as the deputies returned to their big Chevy Tahoe and got in. She walked down the stairs and watched very carefully until they pulled away and took off down the highway.

"What the hell was that about?" Daniel asked, joining her to watch the truck disappear.

Elise slumped and let the big log that supported the porch roof hold her up as well. "I have no idea. A man went missing yesterday. They . . ." Her throat thickened. "They found his body in the river today. For some reason they think I know what happened."

His hazel eyes went wide. "Do you?"

"No. He's an old friend I haven't seen in a long time."

"I'm sorry. Are you okay?"

When he reached to put a careful hand on her shoulder, tears finally wet Elise's eyes, the first offer of kindness too much to bear. "Maybe. I'm not sure."

"Shit, Elise. I'm really sorry."

She knew he'd hug her if she leaned into him. God, she needed a hug so badly right now, and the weight of his palm promised comfort. But Daniel was already too involved. She couldn't let her guard down and accidentally reveal too much of the story. Her pride wouldn't let her.

She ordered her body not to sway closer, yet it did. The world went blessedly blank when he wrapped his arms around her and she was covered for a moment. Shielded. She hadn't felt that sheer relief since the last time Christian had held her, offering respite from a world that had always been cruel.

Then he'd emailed with his own cruelty three days later, a tortured, selfish cry for understanding in "an impossible situation."

Remembering it, Elise pulled away and tucked her pain back into her body to deal with later.

"Thanks," she croaked.

"Hey," he started, but she backed away until her heel hit wood. She'd wanted Daniel, wanted his kindness and connection, but now the darkest depths were lapping at her life again, threatening to turn into a tsunami.

"I . . . I need to make a couple of phone calls. I appreciate you letting the cops know I really was here all night."

His brows rose a bit, and she knew what he must be thinking. That he had no idea if she'd been here *all* night. But she let the statement stand because it was the truth.

"Let me know if you need anything," he said. When she didn't respond, she caught the quick frown, a wince at her withdrawal. But then he nodded and turned to walk toward his cabin.

He paused after only a few feet and spun back. "Did I know the guy?"

Elise shook her head. "Tech guy. He moved here from Silicon Valley a while ago."

"Yeah, I definitely don't know anyone like that."

With a nod, she retreated into her home, tugging her phone from her pocket. Time to find out what the hell had happened to the only man she'd ever loved.

CHAPTER 7

I heard the search team found the body, she typed, brow furrowed over the cold distance in those words. But Amber didn't know anything about Christian, and that was the way Elise meant to keep it.

Her friendship with Amber had been fairly superficial until Christian had ended things. After a few weeks of grieving, Elise had started leaning more heavily on Amber for distraction and companionship. She'd dropped hints to her friend about a heartache that had left her reeling, but she'd certainly never revealed who the man was.

Dots appeared in the text box, ratcheting her tension even higher as she waited for the terrible details. *A fisherman found him. The body was in the river about four miles downstream from Midmountain.*

She breathed a sigh of relief at the vague picture and offered more false distance in her response. *Oh no. Did he fall?*

Guilt scraped over her for pumping Amber for information, but desperate times called for desperate measures. Hopefully her friend would never find out, or at least be forgiving if she did. But Elise knew Amber wouldn't forgive the sordid truth. She'd been married for a long time to a handsome man, and she could rage for an hour about young hussies trying to get her husband's attention. With zero sympathy for cheaters, she'd toss Elise aside like trash if she discovered the affair.

John says the cops have no idea, Amber wrote. Head injury, but that could be a million things. Midmountain doesn't quite reach the river, but it's only a half-mile sidetrack to that overlook.

Elise pressed harder. There were a ton of cop cars around the trailhead earlier.

Yeah, he's a rich guy so they're playing CYA until the autopsy just in case. Probably just clumsy. Those city guys think nature is a playground.

Elise slumped. There'd been a head injury, but as Amber said, that could easily have been from a fall. What could they really know? Except Harrison had asked her about those texts. Elise knew she hadn't sent them, but who had?

She pulled up that damned email from Christian. It had landed in her inbox like a detonation, setting off a mild panic attack and a major crying jag.

Hey there, Elise. Long time no see.

I know we haven't spoken in a while, but I'd love to grab a coffee and talk. Could I come by? Or we could meet for a drink? Been doing a lot of work, a lot of therapy, and there are some things I need to say face-to-face, if possible . . .

I have things to apologize for, things to explain. I can't make everything right, but I can be more honest with myself and with you starting today.

For a dizzying, frightening moment she'd thought Christian had wanted back in. The pleasure had been almost as hot and shocking as the fear. But that hadn't been it at all. He'd only been working on himself.

After some intense therapy, I'm doing well. Things
are good with Savannah and with the rest of the
world. With one crucial exception. You. And until I
resolve that and get some closure, I can't fully grow
as a person.

He hadn't wanted to get back together; he'd only wanted to assuage
his guilt. How fucking infuriating was that?

But with all the therapy and those good intentions . . . what
if he'd confessed to his wife? People did that sometimes, taking the
pain off their heart and putting it right on someone else's. What if
Savannah had been the one who'd texted him to meet her and she'd
gotten violent?

Elise couldn't quite imagine that. She'd tried to avoid knowing much about the woman, but she knew Savannah was a gentle
vegan who fostered animals and went on yoga retreats. According
to Christian, she was subject to debilitating bouts of depression, not
violent rages.

The most likely possibility was still that another woman had been
texting him, another lover, another betrayal. Of course it was.

Her heart told her that didn't feel right, that casual sex hadn't
been his thing. They'd been friends for months before he'd ever made
a move. He simply wasn't a serial cheater. Then again, her heart was
idiotic.

She needed to talk to someone, and her brother was the only one
who knew the truth. He'd been the one she'd finally sobbed to when
she'd realized the affair was truly over. And he'd been the one she'd called
when Christian's last email had knocked the wind out of her. She'd
needed someone to hold her up and help her stay strong.

Can you talk? she texted him. Maybe come by later?

He actually responded right away. A little swamped with work but
I can call.

Yes please!

It came as no surprise when she had to wait a few minutes, pacing back and forth, then downing a glass of water to try to wet her parched mouth. Somehow she was just as dry after the water as she'd been before.

God, what must her guests think? A very good chance now existed that if that woman left a review, she'd mention something about the cops investigating the owner. *Cute place, but I wouldn't want to be there alone.* Elise would have to talk to her this evening. Tell her the police were simply canvassing the area and speaking to anyone who'd known the man.

When her phone finally rang, she stabbed her finger hard at the button.

"What's up?"

"Christian is dead," she said without any preamble.

"What? Your Christian?"

"Yeah. He went missing on a trail yesterday. They found his body in the Mokelumne River today."

"Ho-ly shit." She heard him swallow, and his chair squealed with movement. "They . . . Are you . . . ? Wow. I'm sorry, Sis."

"Thanks." He was the only one who could truly understand, but she didn't feel comforted. It didn't help at all. She pressed the heel of her hand between her eyes. "The police came here asking questions."

"The police? That's really weird. Why are they questioning you?"

"I don't know. They think I was involved."

"Involved?" He snorted. "Involved in what?"

She sighed. "I don't know. He went missing on a trail, he might have just fallen, but for some reason the cops are suspicious. They knew about us. About the affair."

"Jesus." Kyle blew out a long breath. His chair creaked again, and she wished she were there in his crowded home office, just to be with someone. "How did they know?"

"No idea. Those last emails are the only thing I could think of. Christian wasn't explicit about what he needed to atone for, but the context was pretty clear. The police said I was obviously angry and that I asked to meet him."

"But you didn't, right?"

"No! You know I didn't."

"You told me you wouldn't, but we all have weak moments, Sis."

"I didn't. I told him it wasn't a good idea and I didn't want to see him." She suddenly remembered the rest of her email and had an epiphany. "Um. I also unfortunately made a joke they might think was a threat."

"What does that mean?"

"It was an inside joke. I said, 'We can talk when you're dead.'"

"Oh shit. Are you kidding? Why would you say that?"

"It didn't mean anything! We used to say we'd obviously been a couple in a past life, and it evolved into jokes about death."

"Why would—?"

"I was playing it cool!" she cried. "You told me to be lighthearted, remember? Pretend as if he hadn't devastated me by sending a fucking email. Like, he's moved on with his life and everything is wonderful, and I get angry about one stupid email? I wanted him to think I didn't care!"

Kyle responded with a long silence that made her start to curl in on herself with horror. "Hey, I get it," he finally said. "Nothing to be done now, anyway. No worries."

She huffed out a humorless laugh. "A lot of worries, actually."

"Okay, maybe a few. How did the cops leave it?"

"They want me to come in for an interview."

Kyle cursed, and his chair squealed like a wounded animal. "Good God. Why?"

"I have no idea. I told them I was here working all day."

"And we were together in the evening."

She nodded. "I told them that too, but this asshole deputy demanded I come in. I said I couldn't get away from the cabins today, but they made me agree to come in tomorrow."

"No. That's a bad idea."

"No shit! But this guy threatened to come back and take me in himself, and I can't have guests see the owner of their quaint little motel hauled away in handcuffs as a murder suspect!" Her words rang in the silence of the cabin, and she realized she'd been shouting. A glance out the front window showed no one around, thank God. Her cheeks were icy with tears.

"What the hell is happening, Kyle?" she whispered, swiping at her wet cheek in irritation. "Why do they think someone killed him?" She panted into the phone, waiting for him to tell her anything that made sense.

"Listen," Kyle said. "There's been some talk online—"

"No," she snapped. That wasn't the kind of answer she was looking for. "Don't start that. He probably fell off the trail and they're being ridiculous. It wasn't a Sasquatch or the government or a hit man. It was just an accident, and now Christian is dead, and they think I did it!"

"All right, calm down," he muttered, obviously irritated by her dismissal.

"'Calm down,'" she repeated. "Seems like the perfect time to freak out, actually."

Kyle sighed again, but he dropped whatever conspiracy he'd been about to push. "True. You're not really going to go in, are you?"

"I don't have a choice. If law enforcement keeps hanging around or, God forbid, they actually haul me in, it's bad for business. They can look at my phone or whatever they need to do, because I didn't see him or text him."

"If you do that, you need to get a lawyer."

"No. They'll only focus harder on me if I act guilty. I don't have anything to hide. I didn't set foot off my property yesterday. Plenty of people saw me here. And—oh my God. Hold on a second."

She minimized the call screen and opened Instagram. "Yes! I just remembered I posted a picture on Instagram before lunch. So I was here before lunch, here after lunch, here to check Daniel into his room, and here to see you and have dinner with Amber. I'll show them everything, and then they can concentrate on some real answers."

"I don't know, Sis," he said, his voice tight.

"Kyle, I don't *have* an attorney. I'd have to spend hours figuring that out, then fork over money I can't spare. The summer season was good, but it wasn't *that* good. I'm barely breaking even."

She couldn't deny that her shoulders ached with anxiety at the idea of talking to the police, but she didn't want to involve anyone else in this. She wanted to lay all her cards on the table so they wouldn't need to divulge any of this to the rest of the world.

Her brother growled, obviously displeased with the idea. He didn't trust cops. Then again, he didn't trust corporations or government or people in general, so his feelings weren't much of a guide.

"You have an appointment?" he asked.

"I'll go sometime in the morning. I have a guest checking out early tomorrow. I need to go reassure her that Creekside Cabins isn't a hotbed of criminal activity. If her imagination runs wild, she could leave a hell of a review."

"Maybe you'd get some lookie-loos," he said. "Or ghost hunters."

Elise snorted. "Well, if things get worse, I might change my mind. But hopefully this will be over tomorrow." Then she'd have plenty of space to think about Christian and deal with her grief in private.

That was the moment it occurred to her that there would be a funeral . . . and that she couldn't go. "I'll be in touch," she muttered, getting off the phone quickly before she lost it.

There were too many parallels with her sister here. A loss she couldn't grieve properly. No funeral to help her process. And part of her heart drifting dead in that same cold river. How could that be? What were the chances?

At least she hadn't fought with him the way she'd fought with Robin before she'd died. It was bad enough she'd refused to see him, but if she'd sent that first response she'd typed out . . . A fierce, ugly relief opened up inside her that she hadn't told Christian she hated him.

She'd been swallowed by rage when she'd finished his email, furious that she'd read the first two paragraphs thinking he wanted to confess his love, wanted her to take him back. She hadn't even wanted him back, but she'd wanted his *hope*. The same kind of hope she'd once had for him. Unfulfilled and denied and too late and not enough.

Or maybe that hadn't been it at all. If he'd simply shown up, would she have opened her arms and legs and forgiven him everything?

No, that couldn't be true. Not if she wanted to hold on to any shred of dignity.

Whatever the reason, Christian's signoff, "see you soon," had turned her vision red. The arrogance of it. The absolute confidence that of course she would see him, of course she was yearning for him . . . it had sent her over the edge.

Her fury had poured out of her, complete with a dozen f-bombs and countless hot tears. She'd called him a piece of shit, told him she hated him and had never loved him, not for a second. She'd told him to go straight to hell and rot there, perpetually thinking about how fucking mean he'd been to her and to his wife, to his whole family. And how goddamn *typical*, another selfish man who had *everything* and always wanted more.

What if she'd actually hit send? She would have borne the burden of it not just emotionally but legally, because if the cops thought her little joke had been threatening, they would have had a field day with her actual rage.

Instead of hitting send, she'd walked away from her computer and called the only person who knew about the affair. Kyle had talked her down. He could be surprisingly smart about relationships for a man who had never had a long-term partner and only a few short-term ones. He loved to read and take in information, and that covered science-based stories about human emotions and even the occasional advice column.

If you really feel all that stuff, he'd said, *that means you're still in this relationship with him, still in love with him. That kind of intensity only gives him power, Lise. Did he sound that emotional about you?*

No, he certainly had not. All he'd been looking for from her was closure. And fucking growth. Gross.

After she'd spent half an hour on the phone with Kyle, rehashing exactly how she'd fallen for Christian and how he'd turned his back on her, Elise's anger had receded and left behind sadness. She'd reopened her laptop with a heavy heart, but in the end, she hadn't wanted him to know about that either. She and Kyle had agreed that she would be reserved and give Christian nothing, not even a little morsel to discuss with his therapist, no nutrient for his growth.

Hell, she'd even thrown in some lighthearted humor to show how much she truly didn't care. That hubris had been a mistake, but it could have been much, much worse.

Okay, she needed to get her shit together and go speak to her guest. Being red-eyed and upset certainly wouldn't help rehabilitate this situation.

Elise blew her nose, then wet a washcloth with ice-cold water and pressed it to her eyes. Once she looked normal, she pasted a serene look on her face and headed out to putter around near cabin 3. Her ploy worked. The boy flew out of the cabin with a phone in his hand to show her pictures of his trail ride along with a very long video. The mom followed soon after, mouth quirked in an awkward grimace and hand outstretched as if to restrain her son.

Pretending not to notice, Elise bent closer to look at more pictures he'd taken, most of them half-blurry photos of the back of his horse's head and the gray whiskers exploding from its ears. The mom walked over, peering warily at Elise.

"Is, um, everything okay?" she asked, tipping her head toward the parking area.

Elise flattened her mouth and shook her head as she straightened. "A friend of mine was involved in an accident," she said in a low voice.

"It's pretty upsetting. No one knows what happened, so the police are asking everyone if he was around yesterday. If they saw him, was he behaving erratically?"

The woman's face opened up with sympathy. "Oh no. Is he okay?"

After glancing down at the boy, who was still staring at his pictures, Elise shook her head.

"That's awful. I'm so sorry."

"We'd just exchanged some emails, and they seemed to think he might have come here, but I haven't seen him in over a year. And now . . ." She shook her head again. She wanted to let a little of her actual grief show, but she couldn't seem to call it up. It was hiding itself. She hoped it would hide forever.

"Yeah, they did ask if I'd seen a man here anytime in the past couple of days. Which of course, I had. But when they showed me his picture, I didn't recognize him. I told them you were here all day too."

"Thanks. I just hope they figure out what happened. He was up on a trail, and . . . Who knows." She rubbed a hand across her dry eyes. She'd feel guilty about her acting if she had anything to cover up, but she was only trying to bolster the truth. "But I'm sorry if the police disturbed your vacation."

"Not at all. We've had an amazing time here. The cabin is perfect, and Jake loves the little bunks. It's been a great trip."

"Are you still checking out tomorrow? Do you know what time?"

"Early. By eight, I think. We've got a five-hour drive ahead of us."

"No worries. I'll be in the office when you're ready."

She avoided looking at Daniel's cabin on her way back, but her caution didn't pay off. She heard his door open after she passed, and her whole back went tight with painful awareness.

"Hey!" he called. "How are you doing?"

She slowed with a reluctance she hoped wasn't insulting, but she couldn't lean on him like that again. For so many reasons.

"I talked to Kyle a few minutes ago," he said as she turned to offer a wan smile. "He asked me to look out for you."

Elise raised an eyebrow. Men. "I'm fine."

"Well, just a warning, then. He said he was going to stop by tonight and hang out, but I think he wants to make sure you're okay. Big brother and all."

Kyle wasn't exactly a typical big brother, but she figured it was a nice gesture. "Thanks for the heads-up."

"I thought maybe I'd pick up some pizza for me and Kyle. You want in?"

She meant to say no, but she figured she owed him a little gratitude for letting the cops know they were being ridiculous. It'd be safe to spend time with him if Kyle was around, and her therapist always told her to ask for help when she needed it.

Well, there was a first time for everything, and if she couldn't drown her sorrows in wine and pills, pizza was a good second choice. "Sure, but bring it over to my cabin. I have an adult-sized table and chairs we can use."

He chuckled and glanced toward the open door of his place and the mini table that folded out from the wall. "Perfect. Let me know if you need anything in the meantime. Or if you want to talk."

"No, I'm just . . . still processing."

A bit of tension appeared between his brows, but he kept his voice light. "I get it."

God, Daniel was honestly nice. An attractive, decent man who seemed interested in her and wasn't married. He had a job, he loved his family, and he sipped his beer instead of downing it. He seemed . . . normal.

If she hadn't gotten this terrible news, she might have tried entering into a healthy relationship with open eyes and honesty. Make an attempt to get all the excitement she needed out of every-day moments and positive interactions. Could she do that? Settle down and live a normal life, let go of her white-knuckled grip on her heart?

Well, she wasn't going to find out now. As of today, her disastrous relationship history had crash-landed with a married man pulling her into an investigation over his sudden death. It was quite a capstone to the endless march of fucked-up but very exciting men she'd left in her wake. She always chose guys who were emotionally unavailable so that she never had to worry she'd depend on them for anything.

Daniel, on the other hand? He seemed solid as a boulder. And a boulder was way too much weight for her to hold right now. He'd slip from her hands and roll down a cliff to his doom. Or he'd crush her. Either way, it was a no. Which, of course, made her all that much more tempted.

His arm flexed when he reached to shove black waves of hair off his forehead, and Elise looked away. She hadn't seen her therapist in two months. She really should set up a phone call, at least.

"Pepperoni okay?" he asked.

Nodding, Elise stepped away to make her escape. "Perfect."

Her phone dinged with a text message, but before she could tug it from her pocket, an ancient Toyota hatchback zipped up the driveway. She watched with near admiration as the rickety red vehicle bounced over a pothole. Well, it was mostly red. The hood was a bright and shiny yellow, clearly cannibalized from another old Toyota. Duct tape held one of the side mirrors in place, though it listed toward the ground.

An old white man with a ponytail of dyed-black hair nodded gruffly when he got out, then walked past her and into reception without a word. Tonight's guest had arrived, and he'd come wearing a bolo tie and high-top Converse.

Though it was a few minutes before arrival time, she checked him in without any protest, trying to keep up a friendly chatter. He answered only in grunts and paid in cash for one night, nodding when she told him checkout was eleven.

Dying of curiosity about this character, she hoped she'd see him by the firepit tonight and get the chance to eavesdrop on his life as a needed distraction. Maybe she could offer a beer and see if he'd open up a little, because he was exactly the kind of guest she loved to watch roll through. She craned her neck to watch him disappear into cabin 8 as she tugged her phone from her pocket to read the text she'd missed.

The smile faded from her lips, and she tossed her phone on the desk with a horrified gasp.

Everything had just gotten exponentially worse.

CHAPTER 8

Who is this? How do you know my husband?

"No, no, no," Elise muttered, grinding her fist against her forehead, hoping enough pressure would change her reality or wipe her from this version of it. Sadly, she continued to exist and so did the phone and the message. There was only a number, no name suggested by her smartphone, but there could be only one person writing to Elise about a husband.

She stared until the message shook into a blur; then she took the only action she could think to. She ignored the text.

Savannah Valic obviously had no idea who this number belonged to. Maybe it was a burner phone. Or a spoofed number used for anonymity. Elise would ignore it, and the woman would go away. If she didn't, Elise would block her. Her stomach burned with acid, but she was determined to stare a few moments longer and then tuck her phone away like nothing was happening.

Is this Elise?

The message appeared even before the notification buzzed, and Elise jerked so violently that the phone slipped from her sweating hand and tumbled across the entryway rug.

"No!" she said again, more firmly this time. This wasn't happening. She wouldn't allow this to happen. It was bad for her, but it would be much worse for Savannah. "Fuck," she said, then repeated it more loudly, drawing the word out into a moan.

Christian might have lied about how his separation had played out, but that didn't absolve Elise. She knew he'd been lying, and she'd slapped his promises over her guilt like a bandage and washed her hands of it. After all those months of flirting, she'd wanted the lie.

It was true that Savannah had left him, apparently had rented a cottage on a desolate stretch of coastline in Northern California to think about her future and "reconsider" their marriage. But it was also clearly true that when she'd returned after two weeks, she hadn't come back to live as a roommate with her husband.

Of course, Christian had sworn that they were only trying to work out the details of the separation and prepare their college-age son for the divorce, but Elise had known he was lying. She'd argued with him about it on occasion when she'd been looking for a fight. But she hadn't kicked him out of her bed. In fact, he'd been the one to finally leave, and that had been almost ten months later.

For all that time, Christian had been the perfect boyfriend, frankly, with or without a wife. Elise had been free to concentrate on her new business, unburdened by a twenty-four-hour obligation to care for a man's endless domestic needs. She could barely handle her own.

He'd come by three or four times a week. Sometimes just for sex. Sometimes for a hike or even to help with work around the cabins. He'd spent the night fairly regularly too, reinforcing that his marriage was no longer a real commitment. But Elise had suspected those were the nights his wife had gone to the city with friends or off to visit family.

He hadn't promised her anything, though, and she'd never asked. In fact, she'd told him, *Let's do this forever. Exactly like this.* Separate lives with shared nights. The perfect relationship for a stray cat like her.

The ugly truth was that she'd offered that wish as permission. *I don't care if you're lying; this all works for me.*

He'd laughed in response and whispered, *God, I love you,* delighted that she demanded so little. Elise wasn't like other girls. She never had been. She wanted hard sex and easy love, and my God, didn't that make her hot as hell? What a goddamn treat. A manic, bitter dream girl.

But that was what hurt so deeply. That she'd asked for nothing from him, and it had still been too much to offer a woman like Elise. She wasn't even worth the easiest path.

When he'd left, trailing soft regrets and apologies, she'd hated him for weeks and months. When that had faded, she'd hated herself. No one would give her more respect than she demanded. She was the one who set the bar on the ground in her relationships. She wanted to risk nothing, and that was exactly what men put on the line for her.

When that realization had sunk in, Elise had finally gotten serious about therapy, and a whole year had passed since she'd sent him a late-night email or checked his social media. And finally, yesterday he'd taken their secret to his grave. Or so she'd thought. But apparently he'd somehow revealed it to everyone now, including his wife.

Shit.

The phone rang, pumping adrenaline into her veins so ruthlessly she had to press a hand to her chest to soothe the pain. The phone's vibration against the hardwood floor was muffled by the rug, and she had the strange thought that it sounded buried beneath the floorboard, her own trembling telltale heart. Elise could acknowledge it or she could go mad. For the moment, she chose madness and stared until it went quiet.

But then what? Savannah clearly knew her name. It wouldn't be difficult to track down an Elise in this collection of tiny towns strung along the highway like cheap charms on a bracelet. If she didn't respond, the woman would likely show up here, and God only knew what kind of breakdown a furious widow might have in front of any guests.

Cursing again, Elise left the phone on the floor and paced into her living room, then back.

Okay. She could acknowledge the text and find out what Savannah knew. Elise could downplay it. Make it better. She was living the straight-and-narrow life now, but she'd bulldozed her way through the world before this, cheating and lying her way out of endless complications.

She snatched up her phone and opened her texts. Who is this? she asked.

Three dots immediately appeared. It's Savannah Valic. Is this Elise? Are you ER?

Yep, she sure was. She imagined that Christian must have had her contact info under her initials. And someone had found that damned email with her name on it. Hopefully he'd covered other more incriminating tracks. Faced with exposure, Elise held her breath and dove in. Yes, it is. I'm very, very sorry about your loss.

No dots this time. Just silence. Was she weeping? Had she thrown the phone across the room? While Elise was in the midst of weaving a hundred different tales, a response arrived with a gut punch. Were you sleeping with my husband?

All the breath left her body, and she merely floated. She'd never truly imagined this moment even in the thick of it. She hadn't thought of Savannah at all if she could help it. And now? How the hell to respond to a woman whose husband had once told Elise he wanted her forever? That he loved her? That she made him feel like an unhinged sex addict?

She decided to go with some surgical precision in her choice of lies. No. Christian and I were friends. I haven't seen him in more than a year. Why would you ask that? All true as long as she didn't think about what she'd omitted in the spaces between sentences.

The police asked if I knew you. Said he'd been communicating with you and was supposed to meet you that day on the trail.

That's not true, she answered, carving out the one falsehood she could easily call out. We had no plans to meet and I was working all day. No idea why they think that but they've already confirmed with witnesses.

The phone screamed, and Elise yelped. Shit, Savannah was calling again. And she knew Elise was holding the damn phone right in her hand. "Aaaah," she screeched, horrified, torn . . . and then she answered with a strangled croak.

"Hello?"

"I saw the email," Savannah said on a rush. "I didn't . . . They showed it to me, and I read as much as I could in that second, and I want to know if you had an affair with my husband. You did, right? What else could he have meant? He said . . . he said he hadn't been honest with you. He said he needed to apologize!" Her voice was hoarse and pleading. Defeated. She sounded like a woman who'd been screaming for days.

Tears pricked Elise's eyes. How the hell could she possibly respond? What could she do? "Listen," she said, then offered nothing but silence.

"Just tell me the truth!" Savannah sobbed. "I need to know, or I'll never get past this. He's dead, and I just . . . I want the truth about him!"

No. Not the truth. Not for this woman in this kind of pain. But Elise had to offer something. Savannah wasn't an idiot, and Christian's words hadn't exactly been circumspect. "It was a long time ago," Elise managed. "You were separated. For a few weeks, I think? We went out on some dates. That was it."

When she heard a high-pitched sigh in response, she swallowed hard and made herself do the right thing. "Christian loved you. But he was confused and hurt about the separation. That was all."

"R-really?"

"Yes. We'd been acquaintances for a while." Those dry words radiated pain through her body. Acquaintances. My God. "I was a shoulder to cry on while you were gone."

"Did you . . . did you have sex?"

Elise knew damn well there was too much emotion in their email exchange to explain it away as a couple of dates. The full text would make its way to her eventually along with anything else Christian hadn't erased. That kind of sloppiness was unlike him. But maybe their interaction had felt less dangerous with the relationship as dead as a fossil.

"We did," she finally whispered. "I'm sorry."

"Oh."

"But you were separated." The lies were getting easier.

"Was it an . . . an *emotional affair*?" She said the phrase like she'd read articles about it. Like she'd heard it discussed in a workshop.

Elise grimaced. "I don't really know what that is," she said. "But he broke off contact a long time ago. He was committed to your marriage. Please don't doubt that."

"Oh, thank God," she cried. "Thank God. I thought . . . But we were separated. That's true. It was a terrible time. I was so withdrawn. I was struggling. I'm the one who left, so I can't . . . That makes sense, doesn't it? That he'd slip a little?"

Elise's throat clogged up. Her whole chest turned to cement. "I'm so sorry. I'm at work, and I have to go. Okay?"

"All ri—"

Elise hit the button before a sob burst from her and pulled her grief out on a wail. Christian was gone, and he'd loved his wife and wanted a life with her. Elise had been an accident, like catching a sleeve on fire. Like a slip and fall. And now he was dead.

She powered down her phone, tossed it on the counter, and went to curl underneath her comforter the same way she'd hidden when she was a scared little girl who'd done something wrong. At least she didn't have to worry about loose-lipped cops anymore. They'd already screwed up everything.

CHAPTER 9

She must have dozed off, because the next thing Elise knew, her brother's favorite music was invading her dreams. He played it incessantly in whatever vehicle he owned, an album by Richard and Linda Thompson, who'd broken up years before he'd even been born. First it had been a cassette tape in their mother's old car, but he'd eventually upgraded to a CD, ignoring Elise's vigorous complaints over the years. She'd called him all kinds of names over that fucking music, and he'd never even dignified her with a response.

She hadn't learned until her twenties that it had been their father's favorite album. She'd never really known the man, but Kyle had been seven when their dad walked out and never returned. Her heart broke now for her big brother, who couldn't release his death grip on this sad and final tie to a father who'd abandoned him.

When the haunting music abruptly stopped, she opened her eyes and realized she'd left her bedroom window cracked, and Kyle had parked in a space near it. Whatever she'd been dreaming of had been replaced by his intrusion. Thank God.

She jumped from her bed to race to the bathroom and brush her hair. Her swollen eyes were a lost cause at this point, but in her experience there was a fair chance neither Kyle nor Daniel would notice. She heard them talking before her front door opened and someone tapped on the interior door frame.

"Hey, Sis. Daniel brought pizza."

The scent of pepperoni hit her, and her stomach growled. "There's beer in the fridge!" she called. "Or Coke!" The beer was a trophy for her. Proof that she was fine. Proof that she didn't need AA or some other crutch to win this fight. She was still strong and scrappy and could kick the world's ass as needed.

She touched her pocket, looking for her phone, then realized she'd tossed it on the counter earlier. The memory of Savannah's phone call tried to crawl back into her head with slimy fingers, and she shoved it away and rushed to join the men. Hopefully company would keep that at bay.

They were already deep in conversation about old-school Nintendo games when she walked in. Elise grabbed a piece of pizza and let their voices wash over and drown everything else out. Nobody said anything about her red eyes.

"You still going to see the cops?" Kyle asked, jerking her back into the real world.

"I am." When Daniel frowned in question, she shook her head. "They want a formal interview, and I want this over with. It's absurd."

"I think it's more than that," her brother grumbled.

"Since I'm not involved, I don't see how it could be."

"Well, I told you I've been seeing things online, Sis."

Daniel grabbed another piece of pizza. "About this guy's accident?"

"If it was an accident," Kyle said. "Christian Valic was involved in some shady shit."

Elise clenched her jaw, ready to explode at Kyle, but that would raise questions for Daniel. Like why she cared so much about this dead man she hadn't seen in a year. She bit off a huge piece of pizza and chewed hard, telling herself it didn't matter what he thought of her.

"Drugs?" Daniel asked as he shot her a cautious look. She ignored it.

Kyle shook his head. "More like shady business. His company got involved in some deep crap. Data tracking. Selling info to the highest bidder. Typical privacy evisceration disguised as capitalism. Aside from that . . . he was around here back in the day."

Daniel raised a finger and hurried to swallow a bite. "Back in what day?"

Now it was her brother shooting her a quick look. She glared daggers, trying to head off whatever theory he was about to spout, but he didn't stop. "Back when Robin disappeared," he said.

Elise choked, then shot to her feet, coughing.

"Hey," Daniel said, holding up his hands to slow things down.

"This is bullshit, Kyle," Elise bit out. "Absolute bullshit. Another rabbit hole about Robin? You're starting this again?"

"But it's true," he insisted. "He came to Willow Canyon."

"Who cares? You were around then too! So was Daniel! So was everyone in the damn town."

It wasn't as if Kyle was breaking any news. Christian's whole reason for settling in the area after he'd retired early had been his amazing memories of coming here every summer as a kid, first with his parents, later with college friends. The only revelation tonight was that Kyle had decided to incorporate Christian into his obsession with Robin.

He'd come by his tendencies honestly. In those first years, any clue, no matter how flimsy, might send their mom on a days' long mission of frantic phone calls. Later, it had been emails sent via slow dial-up on a clunky donated computer. Kyle had started helping her with online sleuthing, however primitive it had been back then. Then he'd never stopped.

He'd had a new theory every year before Phoenix had confessed, and he still circled back around to poke at them on occasion. But this was too much. She backed away and held her arms tightly across her chest. "How could you do this right now?"

"I'm sorry, but I can't ignore what's right in front of my face. He and one of his partners sold their stake in Stratum after a falling-out that none of them are willing to discuss. And they were all here that summer, Elise. They rented a cabin for a month."

"Are you kidding me?" she yelled.

"It's true."

"I don't care if it's true! You can't do this to me. It's fucking mean. He just died."

"But *how* did he die?"

"Get out," she growled, then repeated it in a scream. "Get out!"

Furious grief crashed over her, her vision actually going dark at the edges as if she might black out. One second Kyle was there at the table. She heard the dull screech of chair legs across the floor, and then he was gone, the front door closing quietly behind him.

Elise panted, fists clenched over her breastbone, ready to brawl.

"Hey," Daniel murmured, and his hand touched her shoulder. She hadn't even realized he was still in the cabin, but his warmth seeped through her shirt just as it had the last time she was upset. Then his soft voice enveloped her. "Let's sit down, okay?"

The fury was already fading, leaving her knees weak and shaky. She let him guide her over to her own couch as if she were helpless. Maybe she was. Her knees collapsed, and she landed safely on the worn cushions.

"I have no idea what that was about, but I'm sorry," Daniel offered.

"He . . . He won't accept that her death was meaningless. It was a jealous boy who lost it and killed her. Just more stupid, senseless violence, and that's not enough for him. He wants it to mean something, when all it means is that men kill women all the time."

"Yeah, he obviously struggles with it. He told me earlier that we can't be sure Phoenix did it. You know, I knew him."

"Phoenix? I was too young. I don't think I ever knew him."

"He played soccer, and even though I was still in the junior league, I'd see him at tournaments and practice. He seemed like everyone else, but I heard he drank a lot sometimes."

She nodded. Phoenix's suicide note had blamed alcohol, claiming he remembered only bits and pieces of that night, just enough that it had tortured him for a decade. He wasn't quite sure what he'd done to her or why, but he'd loved her. And when he'd realized she was dead, he'd thrown her body in the river.

But Elise knew why. Phoenix Whit had killed Robin because she'd broken off their one month of dating and brazenly dated several other guys afterward. Her sin had been daring to think she didn't belong to any man.

Elise dropped her head back and stared at the vaulted wood of the ceiling. She spied a cobweb up there. Then she spied several more. "I understood it when he and Mom would put their heads together and brainstorm more ways to look for Robin. But once Phoenix confessed, Mom let it go. A couple of years ago, she finally told Kyle she couldn't discuss it anymore."

She shook her head with a growl. "He just gets lost every once in a while. He gets sucked into his conspiracy communities, because he needs something bigger to explain his suffering. They all do. That's what they're looking for. An explanation for their absent fathers, their addictions, their divorces and layoffs and military service, and all the everyday heartache of trying to survive in this world. I think the idea that we're dealt so much pain for no reason at all is too heartbreaking to endure."

"But you manage to do it."

"Barely." She cracked a smile. "We all have our vices. I've been working on myself for a few years. Kyle is just a little behind the curve. He'll catch up. He'll be okay."

"He took on a lot." He gestured toward nothing. "Back then."

She tipped her head toward Daniel, surprised a teenager had noticed that about his friend. The teen boys she'd hung out with hadn't noticed much at all unless it had to do with sex or weed. "He did. I try to cut him slack, but God, it feels impossible sometimes."

"I can see that."

When he stared at her a bit too long, Elise relaxed into it so much that she panicked and sat up, slapping her hands on her thighs. "I'm exhausted. I think I'd better wrap things up."

When she pushed to her feet, he followed her. "All right. You know where I am if you want to talk, Elise."

"Thanks—" She was only turning toward him to say goodbye, but she saw the exact moment he thought she wanted another hug. She'd exposed a weakness, and now he was wrapping her up again, tucking her into his shoulder. She knew she needed to push him away, but her arms refused. Instead, they folded into her body and accepted the embrace.

It felt so good. Not exciting, just a balm on all the places that hurt. She let her head fall, let her face find its way into the crook of his neck. Sorrow and fear surged inside her, like her heart had been lanced. Then she breathed in the scent of his skin and realized how much she wanted this. Daniel with his strong hands and soft soul. She'd always wanted this.

So she pushed away, stumbling a bit in her haste to stop her emotions. All of them. She couldn't do this, not now, not with Daniel. He was so sweet to her, and she couldn't ruin that with the truth that she'd always been awful and nothing about that had really changed.

His mouth was an O of surprise, his brows rising with worry.

"I'm sorry," she rasped. "I'm just . . . all screwed up right now."

His nod contradicted the absolute confusion on his face, but he soon schooled his features into a calm mask. "Anyone would be," he assured her.

But that was the problem. She wasn't like other girls, and not in that cool way she'd always pretended. Her childhood had broken something inside her, and she couldn't offer a man like Daniel anything good.

Oh, she could pretend for a while, get him close enough to really hurt him when she slashed him to bits and spiraled back to who she'd always been. She could only love a man who promised nothing. No gain, no pain. With therapy she could now see that fatal flaw, but she definitely hadn't managed to fix it.

"I could stay," he said softly, gesturing toward the couch as if to assure her he didn't mean to crawl into her bed. But she knew what the answer would be if she asked.

"I'll be okay," she said, managing a distant smile. "I just need sleep."

"Sure. Of course." He cleared his throat. "I'll leave the rest of the pizza for you. Comfort food."

"Thanks." She had a feeling there'd be a lot of stress eating in her future.

In fact the stress eating started as soon as Daniel walked out. She locked the doors, turned off the lights, and took a bottle of beer and another piece of pizza to bed with her.

She couldn't allow Kyle's obsessions any space in her brain, and she couldn't allow Daniel to even brush up against her heart. Once the beer began to work its magic, she loaded up an episode of *Broad City* and pretended the rest of the world didn't exist. Just until tomorrow. Tomorrow it would all come rushing back whether she could handle it or not.

CHAPTER 10

"Ms. Rockwood, I'm Lieutenant Lopez. I believe you already know Deputy Harrison."

Elise stopped cold in the doorway, causing the front-desk officer to bump into her shoulder. She'd been expecting to find Harrison and his spooky familiar waiting for her in the interview room, but this new guy was a shock. He was taller and younger than the deputy, with a narrow face and sharp jaw. She felt a twinge of glee that his superior rank must hurt Harrison's pride.

That twinge, however, was vastly overshadowed by a rush of anxiety. Lopez was an unknown quantity, and Elise had to fight the instinct to spin right around and walk back out. She wasn't under arrest. She could leave if she wanted to.

But she'd come to clear things up, and leaving would make everything worse, so she stepped inside and took the chair Lieutenant Lopez indicated. The cheap molded plastic, even grayer than the gray walls, was ice against her thighs. She tried her best not to tremble.

"Thank you for volunteering to come in, Ms. Rockwood," he said, voice gentle and brown eyes exuding friendly warmth. This guy must get a lot of confessions, pretending to be people's buddies. He was good at it. Instead of a sheriff's uniform, he wore a blue dress shirt and nondescript silver tie. "Obviously we'd like to clear up any questions about what happened, so why don't you tell me about the last time you saw Christian Valic."

Easy. "I last saw him over a year ago, so I'm not sure how much that could help."

"A year ago?"

"More like thirteen months, I think. It was a brief encounter. We happened to run into each other." That was before she'd finally given up drinking at bars. He'd had the nerve to show up at the place where they'd met. She'd told him he was rich and could hang out in Tahoe if he wanted a drink.

"Things were too hostile after that?" he pressed. "You two had a bad breakup?"

She took her time answering. Christian's fortune had been made on data mining and tracking. He didn't use the cloud, and he'd instructed her on how to switch to a secure email provider that would autodelete messages after a set time so they'd leave no trace during his so-called divorce. Another red flag. But she knew that meant the police couldn't have any emails from that time period, so they couldn't read the vitriol she'd flung his way during the weeks after their breakup.

She'd always been the one who did the leaving, or at least the one who blew things up. She'd been thrown into a dark spiral by Christian's sudden, quiet departure from her life.

"Things weren't hostile," she said carefully. "They were a little fraught, but we were adults about it. I'm not really a long-term relationship person, and he clearly wanted to make his marriage work."

Fraught, yes. Fraught, like her driving past his gated mountain home, checking his very occasional social media posts, stalking his digital talks and interviews. She'd clicked through the same dozen pictures of him online over and over.

Even months later, she'd emailed him, trying to strike a friendly tone as she seethed inside. But that was it. He'd responded with careful politeness, pretending happiness to hear she was doing well, then ignoring her when she snapped and responded with anger.

"Did you know Mr. Valic was married?"

"Yes."

"He didn't try to trick you? Or maybe he made a few promises he didn't keep?"

Well, that was a loaded question. He'd tricked her the way men had been tricking women for centuries: absolute obsession at the start. Christian had fallen hard. He'd showered her with lust and love. Morality and logic had peeked their twin heads up only after the initial blast of that fire had burned out. So yeah, he'd tricked her.

"No," she said coolly. "Not at all."

Lieutenant Lopez slid a printed piece of paper to her. It glowed against the cheap walnut veneer of the table. Elise recognized the email even before Lopez pointed at it. "He says here that he lied to you."

"He did, in a way. I won't pretend I didn't call him a liar at the time. But whatever he wanted to have with me, I could see he was tortured by the idea of divorce. He loved his wife."

"Don't they all?" Lopez said wryly, clearly hoping to draw her into a shared viewpoint.

Elise ignored him. "Savannah was his touchstone, and her family had become his family, but they'd been together since college. They'd lost their sense of connection. That was what he told me, anyway." Elise shrugged. "He struggled with a lot of guilt, so I wasn't exactly surprised when he went back. He was worried about his relationship with his son too."

When she fell silent, he waited for her to say more. Elise sighed. "I'm a grown woman, Lieutenant. I took what he told me with a grain of salt. When a separated couple is still living together . . ." She cocked her head, raising her eyebrows. "I'm not stupid."

"Is he the one who broke things off?"

"Yes."

"You must have been angry."

Angry? She'd been furious. Because he'd loved her with very few demands, and that had given her the space to open up and love him back. Truly. For the first time in her life, she'd felt like there were two adults in a relationship, not teenagers pushing and pulling and scream-ing about devotion.

But she'd been wrong, of course. They'd just been two teenagers sneaking around and enjoying the thrill of it. Jesus, she'd been so blind. Mostly to her own faults, but also to his.

"I was hurt," she answered carefully. "But as I said, I've never been a long-term kind of girl. I don't even want to live with a partner, much less get married and settle down. I moved on, Lieutenant. Which is why I haven't seen him in over a year, not even when he requested it."

"So you didn't contact him this week about getting together?"

Elise unlocked her phone and slid it across the table. Lopez caught it. "Look through whatever you want. I emailed him back, and that was it. I didn't text or message him, and I was at Creekside Cabins all day. I took pictures, posted to Instagram, excavated a dead raccoon from the creek after a little boy found it, checked in a new guest, and spent the evening with friends and family. I even found an email I sent around three in response to a query. Take your time looking."

He took her up on the offer and spent a few silent minutes clicking around on her phone.

"Are you even sure about what happened?" she pressed. "That it wasn't just an accident?"

His eyes flickered up and then back down, and she felt sure that was a sign of doubt. How could they possibly know if he fell or was attacked?

He scrolled through a few more pages without answering. "Would you mind if we kept your phone for a day or two, ma'am?"

"Yes, of course I'd mind. Deputy Harrison already spoke to my guests, which I hope won't come back to bite me on reviews. He *knows* I was on my property. When do you think I had time to sneak away and drive to the trailhead so I could . . . do what?"

He raised an eyebrow in question at that.

"If I'd wanted payback, I could have told his wife at any time. An easy choice, since that wouldn't be difficult *or* illegal. But I didn't want to hurt him or his wife. Now you've clued her in for no reason at all, which was just cruel."

That caught his attention. He leaned forward. "What do you mean? How do you know that? Did she contact you?"

Elise stared at him without answering. Considering what she'd done to the woman, she felt strangely protective of Savannah now. "She's trying to mourn her husband." She shifted her eyes to Harrison. "There was no reason to do that to her."

"Ms. Rockwood," the lieutenant said, "would you mind showing me your arm? I hear you have quite a scratch."

When Harrison's straight mouth pulled up into an ugly smile, real fear flooded Elise's veins for the first time, and the last of her snide comments dried in her mouth. She suddenly saw that this wasn't a meeting; it was a trap, and the jaws were about to snap shut.

CHAPTER 11

Heat rose to her skin until her cheeks burned, and when she realized the flush screamed guilt instead of anxiety, Elise's skin only went hotter.

She could tell them a hundred times how she'd scratched herself, but how could she prove that? Even the boy and his mother had been too far away to see it happen.

Aware of Lopez's gaze on her face, she tried to keep her expression neutral, but what would that mean to him? Not smiling looked too much like a frown, half a smile looked like maniacal glee. She tugged up her sleeve to draw his eye there.

"I caught it on a broken branch while I was trying to get the raccoon out of the creek. The boy was very upset, and I was moving too quickly."

He touched her wrist, leaning closer to the parallel wounds. The distance between the marks brought to mind desperate fingers clawing for purchase. "Pretty deep scratches."

"Not really. They're already scabbed over."

He grunted and sat back, eyes returning to her face. She told herself to look straight at him, but then she tugged down her sleeve, and her gaze jumped from her arm to his face and back to her arm again, refusing to land on him. Did she look guilty? Probably, because she felt guilty as hell.

What if they asked her to take a lie detector test and she failed because of her own worries? Her fear puffed up into anger at the thought.

"I assume you've heard that Mr. Valic's body was found in the Mokelumne River," Lopez said, looking back down at a folder. "I've been reading up on you, Ms. Rockwood. You have a connection to that river, don't you?"

"You mean my sister's murder? The one this office barely investigated and didn't solve? Yeah, I do have a connection to that river, and I can promise you I don't go anywhere near it unless I have to."

"It's quite a coincidence, though."

She slumped back, crossing her arms, then immediately uncrossing them. "Is it? How many people have died near that river since my sister disappeared twenty-five years ago? Are you going to connect me to all of them?"

"All right, Ms. Rockwood," Lopez continued, "what if I told you we've seen texts you sent to Christian Valic the evening before his death?"

The fear broke through again at that vague accusation finally made real. Why the hell did they think she'd texted Christian? Had someone set her up? Was it Savannah? "If you have texts, they didn't come from me. Did they say my name? Come from my number?"

"Not precisely."

"Can I see them?"

Lopez glanced over at Harrison, who frowned, his whole reddish-tan face going into the movement. "Yeah, I don't think—"

Whatever Lopez had been about to say was cut off by the crack of knuckles against the metal door behind her. She spun around to see the door open only slightly, and then Lopez was up and heading for it. "Excuse me a moment."

The door whooshed open, then whined as it closed until the final clang alerted her that this was not a normal, cheaply decorated conference room, though it was easy to pretend. There was even a plant in the corner, but it was obviously plastic, and the whole thing looked lightweight enough not to be used as a weapon. But the door? The door was jailhouse sturdy. She could get up and try to leave right now, but she wasn't entirely sure the thing was unlocked, despite her "voluntary" status.

She glanced around for cameras so she wouldn't have to look at Deputy Harrison's ugly sneer or prickly buzz cut. If she looked too long at him, she'd blurt out a recommendation that everyone should use sunscreen when living at high altitude.

There was no two-way mirror like she'd seen in the movies. She imagined they were no longer needed since she'd spotted three cameras facing her at different heights. There were probably more behind her too. If anyone was watching, the cameras were likely high-def enough to catch the bead of sweat forming at her hairline. She scratched it away, surprised she could be so icy and sweaty at the same time.

Minutes passed while she stared at the dusty plant and ignored the dyspeptic gurgle of Harrison's stomach. Judging by his big biceps, she guessed he probably worked out a lot and needed frequent protein breaks. He looked like the worst kind of cop, and she could easily imagine he'd show up on the news someday, accused of something.

The door clanked open behind her. "Deputy," she heard Lopez say.

Anxiety crawled over her skin when Harrison got up and left her alone in the room. What the hell was happening? Had they searched her cabin while she was out and decided her old death-metal CDs were another sign of guilt? Were they combing her toolshed for possible weapons? What if they'd found blood on that rusty shovel and decided it was Christian's?

She turned her chair to the side so she could watch the door. Nothing moved past the one narrow rectangle of reinforced glass. All she could see was an off-white wall and another closed door.

She should have prepped more for this. Scrubbed her hard drive or dumped it in the river. She didn't have any of those ancient emails from Christian, but she'd saved some snippets in a hidden document, keeping them as relics. Just a few poetic phrases or intense paragraphs Christian had written to her during their time together. And the whole text of his brief breakup.

On her worst nights, she'd pored over his words for hints of what he'd really meant when he'd written them. But once she'd gotten past those first few months of mourning, she should have deleted them all. She hadn't even opened them since last year, not until his death.

Stupid, stupid. Then again, Christian had obviously gotten lax and ceased cleaning up his own digital trail. If he'd been more circumspect, she wouldn't be here right now.

A blue-sleeved arm came into view in the glass, and the door opened one more time.

"Sorry about the interruption, Ms. Rockwood." Lieutenant Lopez propped the door open instead of returning to the table. "I'm afraid we've got something else to attend to, so I need to cut the interview short. I'll be in touch if we have more questions for you."

"Oh? Oh!" She sat there stunned for a moment before she realized he was holding the door open, and she should get the hell out of there. "Thank you," she said as if it had been a business meeting. He offered a distracted smile, his eyes still looking down the hall.

"I appreciate you coming in." He handed her his card as she brushed past. "Front door is straight down that way. I'll be in touch."

After thanking him again, she hustled past lots of people with guns and too much power over her life. She burst out the front doors into a damp and dreary day, and the flat gray clouds were the most beautiful things she'd ever seen. Though she hadn't really thought she'd be arrested, it had been a possibility, and that fear had opened a spiraling sinkhole of anxiety in the back of her mind.

She'd been arrested once in her misspent twenties, after a drunken bar argument had turned into a fistfight, and that had been bad enough even when she had very little to lose. She was happy she had a bigger, better life now, but it truly upped the stakes when dealing with law enforcement.

Amazingly, Lopez hadn't asked her not to leave town. Did that mean they'd figured out their mistake? Maybe it was all over.

How strange to feel happy that Christian's death might have been an accident. How awful. But awful she was. She almost smiled as she speed-walked to her car; then she let out a stream of whispered curse words as soon as she was shut inside.

God, what a relief. She got out her phone to text Kyle that they'd let her go without much fuss. As soon as she started typing, she remembered she wasn't talking to him and put her phone away.

"Dickwad," she muttered, feeling guilty even as she said it. He was all she had, really. Her mother couldn't come bail her out if she needed it. How could you lean on a person who could barely hold herself up in a breeze? Mom had enough on her plate. She'd always had enough on her plate.

Elise hadn't seen her in a month, and she knew she needed to go by, but she hated even walking into that house. Grief had soaked into the walls along with the smoke from her mom's menthol Virginia Slims.

Determined to soothe herself, Elise drove to the tiny coffee shack at the edge of town, then hit the highway back toward home, switching hands between the steering wheel, a ham-and-cheese croissant, and a large caramel latte. Her new happy place was *not* eating jail food at any point in the foreseeable future.

She was thankful she'd finished the croissant when she left behind a long stretch of dense forest and saw a sign for the Midmountain Trailhead. Her mouth went immediately dry, and her throat burned with acid. The parking area was back to normal, with two cars parked and a golden retriever bouncing down the trail toward the lot.

The world moved on, and she'd need to move on too. But she meant what she'd said in that interrogation room. She hadn't wanted Christian or his wife hurt, and now they both were. Badly.

Although she made a note to herself to reserve time with her therapist ASAP, when she got home she found two new reservations had been made online, both of them for Sunday night. Two couples traveling together, maybe, or a family who wanted to spread out. She processed the reservations and then took a quick walk around the grounds to ensure the property looked nice and neat.

Sometimes when she stopped to restack the woodpile for the firepit or retrieve a hummingbird feeder for refilling, Elise felt like an impostor. Like she was in disguise and hiding out from problems she'd left behind in half a dozen cities over her life. One day, she thought, someone would spot her and realize she was a fake.

But sometimes, like today, she felt firmly attached to the soil beneath her feet. Like she'd finally landed in the right place and all the parts of herself she'd shed through the toughest years were slowly making their way back to her. Bits of her heart, her childhood, her truth floated on the breeze like dandelion fluff. She never felt them land, but she became more solid over every month that passed.

What if Robin had never disappeared? If Robin had been the wild and wandering sister, could Elise have been the quiet one, content with what she had? Would she have stayed in Willow Canyon like Amber had, settled down and satisfied with a larger world glimpsed through a sister's frequent letters?

She couldn't picture it. Marriage, motherhood, cooking after a busy day at work. The part of her that could imagine that life hadn't flown back to her yet, and she felt sure it never would. But just having this place was enough. Here on her property, she could be the sun and let the world revolve around her.

She was okay. Even after this awful loss, she was going to be okay. Today, that felt like triumph, and between that and the caramel latte, Elise had enough energy to push through and prep Amber's cabin.

The decision to cut her hair short had been an impulse, but today she felt a deep urge to chop it off. Death was the ultimate breakup. Christian was gone, and she needed to mark the change. The hair would be a weight lifted somehow. She had no idea how it worked, but the same gesture had been happening for millennia, so there must be power in it.

By three forty-five the small hot tub on the deck of cabin 1 was steaming in the cool air, the key was under the mat, and Elise was freshly showered and ready. At four o'clock on the dot, she walked outside to see Amber striding across the grass from her cabin, a wineglass in hand and her styling kit in the other.

She grinned and held up the glass when she spotted Elise. "You have no idea how much I need this! Don't stop by after six, 'cause I'll be outside naked."

"I figured. Daniel is staying a few cabins over, so try to keep it relatively contained."

Amber shrugged. "A married woman has to have some fun, doesn't she? Looking isn't touching!"

"True. And you do still have a hot bod."

"Aw, thanks, sweetie. That's a nice lie. So are we still going real short, or did you already chicken out?"

"Cut it off," Elise commanded.

Amber held her wineglass high. "Let's goooooo!"

Forty-five minutes later, Elise blinked back tears as she surveyed the results. Her sides and the nape of her neck had been shorn close and faded up into long waves that cascaded over her forehead. She wasn't the same woman she'd been a few days ago. It seemed right that she should look as different as she felt. Like she'd donned armor.

"Hey, are you okay?" Amber asked.

"Yes, I love it." She looked tough again. A girl who could handle anything thrown at her by life. Or death.

"You don't normally get this emotional over a cut. Is it too much?"

"No, I just . . . I'm arguing with Kyle, that's all. I'm stressed out."

"Aw, poor baby. Do you want to come hang in the hot tub with me? Would that help?"

Elise managed a hoarse laugh. "I wouldn't dream of imposing." When she rubbed a hand over the shortest buzz of her hair, goose bumps chased along her arms at the feeling of prickly fur. "No, I'm good. This feels great."

"Your neck looks amazing. Like a goddamn swan!"

"Thank you. You're dismissed. Go enjoy your skinny dipping."

As soon as Amber was gone, Elise went to the bathroom to stare at herself in the ugly light. Her face was tired and hollowed out with sadness, but her hair said she was a punk bitch who could persevere. And she could.

In the old days, she would have immediately piled on eyeliner and lipstick and headed out to show off her new look, stir up a little fun, and get blasted or high or both. Tonight she just switched off the light and went to peek in on any front-desk duties.

The ponytailed man who'd checked in yesterday had already left, dropping no clues about his life before disappearing. Disappointing, but at least he'd been no trouble, and she could add him to the cast of strange characters who kept her staid life interesting.

When she opened her reservations, a new request for Sunday night took her by surprise. Odd. Sunday wasn't usually a hotbed of activity even during busier seasons.

She assigned the guest to a premium cabin, then opened a new window to stare at the three reservations. It could still be a large group on a road trip together, but a new suspicion made her nerves crawl.

Elise googled Christian's name and saw that an obituary had been published. She quickly scanned the text, unwilling to dwell on who he'd left behind. But when she found what she was looking for, her heart sank. A "service of remembrance" was planned for Monday morning at Christian's home, less than ten miles from Creekside Cabins.

If asked, Elise would have guessed he'd have a funeral in Palo Alto, where he'd lived and worked for so long. But he'd loved his estate here in the mountains. Five gated, wooded acres in the Timbers, an enclave of exclusive homes in easy driving distance of the ski slopes of Tahoe.

He'd loved hiking the game trails that crisscrossed the road near his estate, and he'd often texted Elise pictures of moose and turkeys and even a black bear. He'd left his Silicon Valley life behind completely, and he'd been content with his new world.

When her phone rang, she answered it in distraction, registering her brother's name only after she'd already hit the button. "Hello?"

"Did you hear?" Kyle asked, his voice low and secret.

She shook her head, confused why he'd ask about the funeral. "About Monday?"

"About Jeremy Quinn."

Jeremy Quinn? The name sounded vaguely familiar, but frowning harder didn't bring any details to mind. Then she realized what this must mean. "Did he kill Christian?"

"Hell, maybe. But he's dead now."

"What do you mean? Who is he?"

"Jeremy Quinn was one of Christian's partners at Stratum. I told you there was something going on." His voice rose. "These people are being picked off!"

"Wait, wait," Elise said in a rush. "What are you talking about?" She remembered the name now. Christian had mentioned him once. He was one of the two college friends he'd founded his company with.

"Jeremy Quinn was shot to death today. Early this morning. He was having breakfast on his own fucking patio in Los Altos, and someone shot him through the head."

Elise sat down hard in her office chair. The air had gone heavy around her. "That can't be. What are you saying?"

"There aren't any official details yet; I'm only telling you what I've seen on the boards. This is connected to Christian's death, Elise. It has to be."

She could barely process his words. "That was just an accident," she whispered, trying to convince herself. "Christian fell."

"Apparently not. Something fucking weird is going on. Did you talk to the police this morning?"

"Yeah."

"What time were you there? Did they ask you about Quinn?"

"No. They didn't say anything about that. I was there until about nine forty-five. Then they let me go. I can't . . ." She trailed off, her mind drifting from whatever she'd been about to say. Had Christian really been murdered? She'd convinced herself that Deputy Harrison had too much time on his hands and an overactive imagination.

"Don't go anywhere, Sis. I'm coming over. I'm worried you could be in danger."

CHAPTER 12

Elise thought of the cops and their suspicions. Then she thought of Savannah Valic and her ugly doubts. She couldn't deal with more darkness piled on today. She couldn't deal with Kyle.

"I'm fine by myself, Kyle. This has nothing to do with me. And honestly, I want to be alone."

"I'm not sure you should be," he insisted, unfazed by her rejection. "Listen . . . I have my suspicions, but did Christian ever tell you what happened between them? Him and his partners?"

Her knee bounced with anxious energy. She wanted to get off the phone, to organize her thoughts without Kyle adding more to them. "No, he never talked about that."

"I'm not surprised. It seems like bad blood of some kind. Christian and this Quinn guy both left Stratum in the same year."

She bit back a groan. "So what?"

"So now *they're both dead.* Something super shady is going on. You don't think you're in danger?"

"Why would *I* be in danger?"

"You know why."

No, she didn't. She had no idea what Kyle was talking about, because she never had any idea what he was talking about.

She remembered the door of the interview room opening, the sudden shift in the lieutenant's attention, the way Elise hadn't mattered to them anymore. They'd been notified about Jeremy Quinn's shooting.

That had to be it. But that meant none of this had anything to do with her. She'd never even met the man.

"These two deaths can't be a coincidence," Kyle said, interrupting her thoughts. "I'm just glad you weren't involved with Christian anymore. What if you'd been with him on the trail?"

She squeezed her eyes shut at the thought. It was already a mess of lies and secrets. "Do they know who did it yet?"

"Not that I've heard. There's been nothing about the third partner. Billy Jackson. I bet it was him."

"Jesus." Elise muttered a few more curses under her breath. "Why would he kill them?"

"Are you asking me?" Her brother paused, waiting several heartbeats before he continued. "Because I think I know why, Sis, but I don't want to piss you off more."

"Oh God. Please don't bring up Robin again. This is so stupid."

"Elise, I know Christian was a boyfriend to you and that's how you see him, but these men were dangerous. I started looking into it when you told me you were sleeping with the guy."

"You *what?*" she snapped.

"Seriously, do you know what kind of information Stratum collected? From everywhere in the world? They had secrets about people, and they knew how to use them. His business was about power."

Why did she feel shocked that he'd spent time researching her married lover? She should have known he would, but she'd told him about the relationship in a fit of desperation. "Okay," she sighed. "Fine. I get that part. Big, bad corporate power. But he left the company years ago, way before I even met him."

He echoed her sigh, though his exhale sounded more like a curse. "I don't like anything about this, Elise. It feels all wrong. I'm coming over. Give me thirty minutes to wrap up here."

She wanted to be alone, but it wasn't even 6:00 p.m. yet. What was she going to do all evening? Pace around and spin anxious fantasies about what had happened to Christian while getting more and more freaked out?

"Okay," she conceded. "Sure. I'll see you soon."

Good God, she needed a drink, but these days she made a point to only have a beer when she *didn't* need one. Because one beer wouldn't be enough for this situation. Not even close. Instead, she mixed ginger seltzer and some orange juice and downed it, pretending it was a cocktail. Funny enough, she felt calmer even as she paced outside to spend some of her nervous energy on making the evening rounds, in case anyone needed her.

Nobody needed her. The grounds looked tidy and secure. She heard a faint splash of water when she drew near cabin 1, and that made her smile, at least, imagining Amber living it up in the hot tub.

After she'd untangled a strip of orange plastic that had blown in from the road and caught on an evergreen, Elise cut across the lawn toward her cabin. When a car pulled to a fast stop out on the highway, she winced, her whole body tightening with dread at what could be coming next. More cops? Christian's wife? *Reporters?*

The car had stopped past some trees, but she could make out the chatter of several people talking, then multiple car doors slamming. Holy shit, it was a SWAT team.

The distant scrape of feet against asphalt floated to her, and she braced herself, ready to run. But running from a SWAT team would be a terrible idea. She should just drop to her knees and hold up her hands.

Before she could decide, a family of five walked into view on the highway's shoulder and gathered around Bigfoot. She stared in silence as they snapped a dozen pictures, laughing together, the teenage daughter flashing a peace sign. They finally dispersed and disappeared. Car doors slammed.

It was Bigfoot they'd wanted. Not her.

Staring at the giant Sasquatch made her think of Kyle and her family and Robin. Instead of sorrow, an unsettled fear opened in her belly, so she retreated to her cabin to grab the big hatbox hidden on a shelf in her closet.

The sky-blue box was filled with letters from Robin. Elise dug out a green envelope covered with glittery star stickers and opened it. There it was, the one and only time Robin had mentioned Phoenix, the boy who'd destroyed everything.

> *Hey, baby sister!!!*
>
> *You didn't write back last week. Don't be a slacker. Even Phoenix has written four times since I got here, and we only went on three dates. He's sweet but too serious for me. He never wanted to do anything, just hang out alone. Girl, I need to LIVE. Bad enough being stuck in that dinky town as it is. But I'm desperate for letters, so it's all good. I get more than anyone, not that I would ever gloat. Heh.*
>
> *It's hot as hell in this cabin tonight, but I don't even care because it's my last week and I'm determined to enjoy every moment until I get home. And then . . . I can't WAIT for college in September. You'll come visit me in Santa Cruz, right? We can have sleepovers at my dorm whenever you want! We just have to get Mom to drive you down. Then I can drive you back and do my laundry.*
>
> *I'm still mad you didn't come for July session, but we'll have a blast when I get home. One more week, Elisey!*
>
> *Miss you!*
>
> *XOXO*
>
> *Robin*

CHAPTER 13

Elise had never even noticed the boy's name, not until he'd confessed to killing Robin. Her sister had dated so many boys and had so many friends that the police hadn't known where to start.

They claimed to have interviewed hundreds of people in the area, but if that were true, Elise imagined the "interviews" had consisted of a simple query: "Do you know anything about Robin Rockwood's location? Did you see her that night? Next witness, please."

But even that questioning hadn't started until it was too late. The night of her disappearance, Robin had been at a late-night party in the woods where she'd been drinking, clearly a girl running wild. At eighteen, she'd no longer been considered a vulnerable child, just an irresponsible and messy young woman.

Four days had passed before their mother's increasingly loud insistence had stirred up the interest of the sheriff, but his inquiries had been halfhearted at best. He hadn't cared about some drunk runaway who slept around. Girls like her were prone to go missing.

A week after, when none of Robin's best friends had heard from her and no money had been withdrawn from her bank account, their mother had written to the local paper with a plea for help.

The letter had worked. Nearly sixty people had been gathered around that bonfire the night Robin went missing, and most had been eager to help. When half of them had come forward with stories about talking to her or seeing her or who she'd been dating, the search had only grown more jumbled.

Robin was gone. Just gone. And no one would ever find her. Her leg bones were sticks caught between boulders. Her skull a goblin in an underwater cave. Crows had taken her hair for their nests and tucked her earrings away as treasure. Coyotes had probably chewed her knuckles as snacks.

She was yet another lesson in what happened to young women who drank and dated and danced. Women who were careless or at least not care*ful*. Robin had been a lit sparkler, blazing too brightly, spreading trails and sparks everywhere. Any one of those embers could have caught and grown into a fire that consumed her.

Or maybe she'd only blown away to parts beyond, a bottle rocket of a girl with the same inclinations as their father. Maybe, like him, she'd moved on to a better life and left Elise and Kyle behind.

Elise had half believed some of those theories, because they gave her hope. Hadn't Robin complained endlessly about small-town life and how she couldn't wait to get out? That had been the reason she'd chosen UC Santa Cruz. The social life and endless activities had drawn her, a girl who hated going to school and sitting in classes.

The first day of college orientation had been another terrible milestone. Another day Robin hadn't reappeared.

That was when the story had shifted in Elise's ten-year-old mind. The idea of attending a big university could have become too much for her sister. Hadn't she laughingly threatened to run away to Hawaii dozens of times? Maybe she'd just . . . left.

But she'd known deep in her soul that wasn't true. Robin wouldn't do that to their mom or her siblings. She would have sent letter after letter about her adventures. Elise knew that, but she'd still hoped . . . until her teen years when she'd turned furious.

Their mother, on the other hand, had been sure from the start that Robin had been kidnapped. Not killed, though. She'd said she would have felt that in her bones, if her firstborn had died. She'd believed with every speck of her soul that Robin was alive out there and needing her mother.

She'd bent over notebooks and files and their worn computer keyboard, calling out progress or new leads as she worked. It was a terrible way to live. It wasn't living at all, really. And her mom had been dead wrong. If mother's intuition was a real thing, it could apparently be papered over with desperate hope.

That hope had turned to something else, and that something else had infected Kyle as he'd helped, eventually taking over the online research for their mom. In fact, Kyle hadn't moved out until age twenty-four. After Phoenix confessed, Mom had lost her taste for theories, so Kyle had finally been free. Or maybe he'd gotten tired of their mother explaining that Robin wasn't truly missing anymore and there was nothing else to follow up on.

Elise glanced through a couple more letters, some of them just elaborately folded notes kids used to trade when cell phones had been too expensive for the average teen. Back then, no one had bothered with them in this area. Service was still spotty even today. Cell phones couldn't be relied upon.

As she closed the hatbox, she heard the crunch of wheels on gravel and tensed, but then her brother's music leaked past her cabin walls. Kyle. He might be eccentric, but he would always be there for her. She only called her mom with good news, because whatever was going on in Elise's life, her mom's suffering was worse.

She tucked the hatbox back into her closet, touching her hand to it for a moment as a goodbye before going to meet her brother.

The white file carton Kyle carried preceded him into the cabin. "Oh boy," Elise muttered, realizing he was going to offer *that* kind of help. It was a measure of how lonely she felt in that moment that she didn't turn him away. "Can we please talk about the tech stuff and *not* about Robin?"

"Sure. But I printed out all of it."

"Just try not to piss me off. I can't take more today."

He made a huffing noise that sounded like assent as he set the box on her coffee table, and she dropped the argument, proud of herself for letting it go. Maybe she'd finally left her long adolescence behind.

"You look weird," he said, ruining any pretense that they had a mature relationship.

"Wow, thanks. I got a haircut."

He shrugged and flipped off the top of the box, letting it fall to the floor while he dug through a four-inch pile of jumbled papers inside. For a guy in tech, he sure loved paper. "So," he started, "all three men dropped out of Stanford after their junior year to start Stratum. And boy, it paid off."

As soon as Elise sat down, he shoved a printout into her hands. It was a picture of Christian with two other white men, their arms around each other's shoulders, all of them dressed in expensive jeans and blazers. They looked incredibly, impossibly young.

She stared at a Christian she'd never known, full of arrogance and ambition, too young to hold so much power. The color photo was perfectly lit and focused, a PR shot for budding entrepreneurs.

Kyle pointed at the shorter guy with blond hair. "That's Jeremy Quinn."

She jumped a little as if she'd heard the gunshot. "Are they sure he didn't do it himself? Maybe he argued with Christian, and it got out of control, and then he felt awful after the accident . . ."

"From what I've seen online, the police aren't considering that. Probably didn't find a gun at the scene."

"Right. That would make sense."

"Okay, so . . ." He handed her a few more papers. "This is an article about Stratum. How much do you know about data mining?"

She glanced past her lowered brows. "Seriously? How much do you think I know?"

Kyle sighed. "All right. Read the article. I can't really explain it for a layperson."

"Layperson," she muttered, but she scanned the pages as quickly as she could.

Kyle started talking again before she could finish. "Stratum didn't just passively mine data for clients; they were one of the firms that marketed some of the first third-party cookies to extract information for other companies. They developed their tracking software before it was completely ubiquitous; then they bought up a couple of other start-ups in the industry. They knew the ins and outs of every side of it."

She nodded. So far it was easy enough to digest.

"Stratum got off the ground at exactly the right time. On websites first, and then smartphones hit the market, and everything really took off, because now they didn't just have data about your online shopping habits and your internet searches; now they had data about your location, where you worked, where you lived, whether you commuted by car or train, your dating habits. Hell, your smartphone knows how long you sit on the toilet every morning."

"Stay classy, Bro."

"Listen, it knows your porn preferences too, down to how much time you spend with each subgenre, so imagine that."

"I'd really rather not."

"Don't worry. I'm old school."

Elise kicked his leg. "I have no idea what that means, and I definitely want to keep it that way."

He grunted. "Hey, I had to hear about your dirty little affair."

She rolled her eyes and scanned the last of the article. "But it's all put in one big pot, right? They accumulate data on millions of people and identify trends and habits."

"I mean, sure, that's *part* of what they do. But how randomized is it when they know the address where each data point sleeps at night?"

A ring of familiarity let her know that Kyle had explained this to her before, but she'd never truly thought about it.

She didn't use the most invasive features of her phone and turned off location services on photos and social media. That seemed sufficient obstruction for a bit player in the game of life. If anyone was spying, they'd find her a pretty boring mark. Even during the affair, she and Christian had mostly met for hikes or for dinner at her place. They'd never gone to seedy motels or fancy resorts. She'd never even been to his house.

Well, not inside it. She'd certainly driven by. Maybe she'd even hiked around it once or twice at a low point.

She sat up straight, thinking of the million times she'd checked his Facebook and Instagram feeds. Had he known that? Her data-broker ex-lover? Had he spied on her, seen her movements, watching the little dot that hovered near his property?

At first she'd been stalking him, hoping for glimpses of his life, maybe even a chance to run into him. But later, when she'd finally metamorphosed from love to terrified avoidance, she'd timed her trips to the local health food store in the late evening, just before they closed. She'd only stopped by favorite restaurants when she was sure he was busy with some online conference or on vacation. She'd been a newly recovering addict, desperate to avoid the taste or temptation of Christian Valic.

"Wow," Kyle said. "You must have some creepy porn. You look horrified."

"Shut up, Kyle," she muttered, curling back into the couch.

"Do you remember that big push for a comprehensive data privacy law about eight years ago?"

"Kyle," she said wearily. She sighed and rubbed her temple. "No, I don't remember anything about data privacy laws."

He grumbled something about ignorance and bliss that she ignored. "Well, news flash." He waved his hands. "Right now we have a patchwork of laws, and altogether they add up to jack shit. A real breakthrough bill was gaining momentum before two of our California representatives changed course and killed it. Guess who went to visit them in DC right before the bill died?"

"Christian?"

"And his two partners, yes. They all flew out together to try to stop it. Do you think they just made a solid argument that it was a good idea to keep invading Americans' privacy?"

"Maybe?"

"Sure. Or maybe they confronted those politicians with detailed information on their most immoral and illegal habits."

She stared at him. "That's it? That's your conspiracy theory? That *maybe* Stratum used private information to influence a couple of politicians because you imagine it could be true?"

"These representatives had already signed on to the bill. What do you think would change their minds?"

"Money and lobbying."

"Don't be naive. This is Stratum's whole business. They traffic in *information*, Elise. They can control anyone with the right data. Your phone is *you*. Do you get that? It's a digitized version of your entire life, and companies like Stratum can spy on anyone in the world. They know who wants an abortion, who's getting online therapy for a drug problem, which married man is looking up the age of consent in his state."

"Kyle—"

"They know which billionaires own which shell companies and who's sending money to white supremacists while publicly funding progressive charities. Even doctors and hospitals sell your data these days. This isn't a conspiracy, Sis. It's not chemtrails or the Denver airport or a flat Earth. Those idiots out there claiming Bill Gates is tracking us with a vaccine are posting about it *from their smartphones*! They're willingly carrying their trackers around. Data mining isn't a conspiracy. It's good old-fashioned capitalism. Money is power, and information is worth more money than anything."

Now this was familiar territory. Kyle didn't consider himself a conspiracy theorist. Those people were beneath him. He was a conspiracy *realist*. She'd heard his complaints a hundred times before. *Why would billionaires use a public website for sex trafficking when they could procure anyone with untraceable cash? Why would a cabal develop a whole new disease when the flu shot is distributed everywhere and reformulated annually? If there's a deep state controlling elections, why can't they get their president elected every time to start with?*

Those low-hanging conspiracies, he claimed, were food for the masses, meant to distract from the real scandal: the control of money and power played out right in our faces every single day.

"What does any of this have to do with Christian's death?" she asked with an exhausted sigh.

Kyle looked energized instead of tired. "These three lifelong friends clearly had a major falling-out soon after that trip to DC. Christian sold the bulk of his Stratum shares to his partners six months later for nearly two hundred million dollars. And Quinn sold out four months after that, leaving Jackson with majority control of the whole company. You're sure Christian never gave you a reason the entire partnership blew up in the space of four months?"

She scoured her brain for memories, but their relationship hadn't really touched on a company he'd left before she met him. "He said he loved the work but hated the job. I'm not sure what that meant. But I know he didn't associate much with his old friends. He said they were all very different people than they'd been as kids."

"Right. So it was personal."

"I have no idea. He hated the constant grind, the pressure, and he just wanted out. He never went any deeper than that. He seemed happy to be a nature nerd here in the mountains, free from those obligations."

"And now the two partners who left the company are dead, and the last man standing is alive and well."

Elise curled tighter and chewed on her thumbnail. "Maybe someone wanted payback for whatever they were wielding over them. Or maybe someone wanted to silence them."

"Then wouldn't they go after the guy who still holds the power?"

She shrugged. "He's probably got way better security than a couple of tech retirees. The company value has gone up a lot the last few years, from what I've seen."

She'd asked Christian about it once after her phone fed her a story about Stratum's stock prices. It had obviously assumed her online interest in Christian Valic must extend to the company he'd founded. He'd laughed and said he didn't care how much money he'd left on the table. He now had the life he wanted. He had peace.

God. Her phone really did know everything.

"But what if a vengeful data victim isn't the killer?" Kyle asked. "What if it's Jackson?"

Elise poked him with her foot. "Kyle, that's crazy."

"Not as crazy as the two of them being murdered in the same week, though, right?"

Shit, he had a point. He handed her another article. This one featured a more recent picture of Billy Jackson by himself, posed in slacks and a gray cashmere sweater in an office, nothing but blue sky and perfect white clouds beyond him. A man at the top of the world.

"Why?" Elise asked. "Why would he do something like this? How does that make sense?"

"Because they know things he doesn't want known. This is a man with a visceral understanding of how much power anyone can wield with something as common as a drugstore thumb drive."

"And he'd risk everything he has for that? Years after they left the company?"

Kyle shrugged. "Obviously he wouldn't do it himself. He'd hire a hit man. A good one. Not much risk to him at all."

He started digging around again and pulled out another paper. "I checked his whereabouts. He was at a public event the day Christian went missing, and he was in Iceland today. Absolute deniability. All he has to do is act scared that he's next, hide out for a while, throw away a million on extra security. Hell, he could come out of this looking like a brave survivor instead of a suspect."

Elise stared at the picture of Jackson, the arrogant crook of his mouth, the intensity of his dark eyes. His hair was expertly styled with a cut that probably cost hundreds. Christian's style had been northwestern woods. Flannel shirts and messy waves of brown hair that always needed a trim. A beard sometimes, other times just scruff. She couldn't imagine the Christian she knew in an office like that, though she knew that version had once existed.

She glanced into Kyle's box and saw the mound of paper it still held. "What does any of this matter to you? It's up to the police. These crimes were about Silicon Valley, not Willow Canyon."

"I'm not so sure about that."

His face went tight with a familiar look. Kyle had their mother's wide mouth, and it now echoed one of her more common expressions: bitter certainty.

Elise shook her head, an easy denial of what she saw coming. "I can tell by your face that you're about to piss me off, so stop right there."

"Again, I have no idea why you're so opposed to hearing facts, even if you don't like them."

"Again, I said drop it."

He blew air out in a long, frustrated stream. "All I'll say is this: Christian purchased his land here a month after that trip to DC. And I think his decision to build a home here in Willow Canyon is the wedge that broke the whole friendship apart."

"That doesn't make . . . No. I'm not going to engage on this. You've managed to convince me that Christian's death probably has something to do with what went on at Stratum. That makes obvious sense considering Jeremy Quinn's death. But he died in Los Altos, not here. I really can't go through this shit with you again, Kyle."

He shrugged. "Fine. We'll see. But I want you to be careful. Seriously, Sis. You're mixed up in something you don't understand."

Elise bristled at the patronizing speech, but he wasn't wrong, because she sure as hell had no idea what was going on.

He packed up the box and tucked it under his arm. "Don't go anywhere with people you don't know. And be on the lookout for strangers where they shouldn't be."

"Now you sound like Mom."

He rolled his eyes. "I'm serious, Elise."

"I run a motel, Kyle. Strangers hanging around is kind of crucial to my business."

"Stop being a brat. You know exactly what I mean. Watch out for people who don't fit in."

She did know. But she didn't dare tell him that she'd already booked several cabins for the memorial, and they were likely going to be a different clientele than she normally hosted. Less hiking gear and more expensive suits. Though the real tech billionaire set would probably rent a ski chalet or one of the expensive estates near Christian's home, even if it was only for a night or two.

"You should go see Mom," Kyle said as he hefted the box, hitting Elise with another jab she wasn't expecting.

"Sure. I will."

"She actually managed a little garden this year. Stop by and get some carrots so I don't have to take them all. In the meantime, I'll do more research and keep you in the loop."

Elise surprised herself by saying something she'd never said before. "Yeah, let me know if you find anything else."

The world was full of wonder these days. Or maybe it was just fear.

CHAPTER 14

"Hi, Mom!" she called out. She was trying for brightness but sounded frantic instead.

"Elise?" her mother asked uncertainly from the kitchen, as if she still hoped it might be someone else.

"It's me. I brought some rolls from Lupe's."

She emerged from the back, wiping her hands on a towel. "Oh my God, what kind did they have?"

"I got you three orange glaze and six cheddar."

"Perfect. I'll freeze the cheddar for lunches."

Her mom hurried over, a bit of a limp in her step from a bad hip. When her eyes rose from the bag, she came to an abrupt stop. "You chopped off your hair!"

"I did!" She rubbed her hand over the fuzz at the back, still thrilled at the feel of it. "Love it? Hate it?"

"Well, you certainly look hip."

Elise laughed at the sidestep but decided to accept "hip" as a compliment. Her mom trimmed her own hair, despite Amber's frequent offers for a free cut. It was always in a braid, the ends of it still light brown, the rest gone gray.

"It suits you," she said, stepping forward to give Elise a quick hug and a peck on the cheek before she took the white bakery bag. "You want coffee and a roll?"

"Just coffee, thanks. I ate my roll on the way here. Couldn't resist. My whole car smells like warm bread."

Her family home was fifteen minutes from Creekside Cabins, but the true transition was that one second between opening her car door and stepping outside. The smells and sounds immediately thrust her right back to childhood. The pine-scented crunch of needles under her feet from the huge, unruly ponderosa that dropped detritus all over the steep driveway. The distant cawing of crows no matter the season. The quiet pall from the house itself.

She was home, for better or worse. Mostly worse. Her stomach had tightened before she'd even gotten up the cracked cement steps, which was why she'd eaten her roll in the car. Dead bugs littered the front steps of the house as they always did, proof that the porch light was still left on 24–7, just in case. A beacon. Or a plea for help.

Inside was a time machine, nothing changed or updated since the disappearance, aside from one beige couch replacement. A gigantically fat tabby trotted over to rub against her leg. "Remind me of his name again?"

"Pierre."

"Of course. What a sweetie." She gave him a chin scritch and smiled at his engine-like purr.

"He's scared to go outside," her mom whispered as if to save him from shame.

"Good! He probably saw some horrifying shit before you rescued him." Her mother loved taking in strays, but they'd gone by in fairly quick succession. These hills were full of predators. Maybe Pierre would survive locked in here for a while.

The cats seemed to satisfy whatever caregiving instinct Mom needed to indulge. She wasn't the type to make suggestions about marriage or grandchildren. Elise suspected she didn't want more family to worry about.

Though there had been a year or two during Elise's teen years when she'd mentioned the idea often. *Robin could have kids now. Have you thought about that, Elise? I could be a grandmother right now.* No, Elise hadn't thought about it. Instead she'd thought, *You could be a mother too, if you tried.*

Ugly thoughts from an ugly child. She'd never known how to process her twin devils of anger and shame, and it felt strange to think other people had an angel on one shoulder to counter all that pain.

Stuffing those memories down, she followed her mom into the kitchen, the old linoleum crackling under her feet. "You look great," Elise said.

Her mother had been frail and stick thin for years, but the decades of staying inside had finally caught up with her. She'd gained a lot of weight, but she'd been healthy until her last checkup, when her doctor had diagnosed her with dangerously high blood pressure. She hadn't quit smoking, but she'd dropped a few pounds.

"How are you feeling?" Elise pressed.

"Fair," she answered with a shrug. She was on meds, and she'd taken up gardening instead of walking, because the garden was only a few steps away from the back door.

"Kyle says you have carrots growing."

"Oh, don't let me forget to give you carrots and beans before you go! I've got too many."

Elise retrieved two mugs from the dark oak cabinet and put them close to the coffeemaker as her mom waved off her help. When Elise sat at the table, she found a half-finished puzzle taking up most of the space.

She stared at her mom's familiar back, the shoulders hunched now, though she was only sixty-six. How could anyone stay straight after hauling the load she'd carried?

"How's work?" Elise asked. In their previous life her mom had been an office manager. Now she did bookkeeping from home for a few local businesses. With the meager disability payments the state allowed for her agoraphobia, she made just enough to stay in the house.

"Slow this time of year, but that's good. I'm not taking new clients, and the old ones are dying off, literally and figuratively. I'll wind down for a few years to put off taking social security."

"Sounds like a plan. The work is probably good for you, anyway."

Shrugging, she brought the coffee over. "Keeps me busy. So what brings you by?" The slight edge in the question was obvious, the implication that there must be a reason, because her daughter certainly never dropped in to hang out.

"Nothing really. Just here to steal carrots."

That shocked a laugh from her, and Elise smiled. Her mother had healed a bit sometime during all those years Elise had been gone. Maybe learning the truth had finally let her move on in the grieving process. None of them had been able to grieve before Phoenix's confession; they'd been too busy waiting for the next blow.

"Do you still have all Robin's letters?" she asked. A stupid question, but she knew it wouldn't be unwelcome. Her mom still loved to talk anything Robin.

"Of course."

"She only mentioned Phoenix once in the letters I have."

"Yeah." She glanced through the steam of her coffee and stared out at the backyard. "It's frustrating. I found two times she used his name in my letters, but that was it. Only two. There were other boys she mentioned for weeks."

"He feels so insignificant," Elise said quietly.

"He does." Her mom sipped from her mug and nodded. "He *was* insignificant. He was nothing."

"I don't know how much he talks about it with you, but Kyle still doesn't accept the story."

Her mom sighed so hard her body deflated. She cupped her hands around the mug as if she'd taken a sudden chill. "I know. It's hard to accept. But it's more than some people ever get. If that man hadn't left a suicide note . . . Well, we still wouldn't know anything." She took another sip of her coffee, then a big gulp. Elise realized she was trying not to cry.

She'd been meaning to ask if her mom thought Kyle could be getting worse, hoping to grab on to any hope his theories couldn't be real. But Elise couldn't put this on her mother. She had to figure it out herself.

"I still wish we could have her back," her mom admitted. "But it is good to know *something*."

Elise reached out and patted her hand. She never knew how to handle other people's tears. She'd spent too many years trying to hide her own to have any kind of healthy relationship with emotions. She'd had no safe harbor to express them, so she simply . . . hadn't. They hid in her flesh now. In her bones and tissue, burrowed deep like parasites.

"At least we know she was somewhere peaceful," Elise said. "He didn't toss her in a garbage dump somewhere." She winced, realizing how dark her words were, but her mom nodded.

"That's true. The river is beautiful." Her mom sat up straighter, her face brightening. "Honey, do you want to visit her room? It's been a while."

"No. No, thanks."

It was a shrine, of course, and Mom always seemed to think she'd take comfort in it the way she did, but the sight wound Elise into a ball of tension and ugly, secret resentment. It was why she'd moved in with Kyle instead.

The bedroom had been Elise's room once too, much to Robin's chagrin. In a three-bedroom house, the girls had to share, no matter the age difference.

A week after Robin's disappearance, her mother had burst into the bedroom at six in the morning, overwhelmed with anxiety and shaking Elise awake. "The police will need all these things. I left them another message. They're going to need to comb through the entire bedroom and see what's here. Come on, baby, I'll help you pack some stuff. You can sleep in my bed tonight."

Elise had slept in her mom's bed that night, which had been easy since her mom rarely slept in those first months. When she did, she lay on the couch that had been pulled within inches of the front door so her head rested only a foot from the knob. Elise had slept in her mom's bed the next night too. Then for the week. Then for months and years.

Her mom never had gone back to sleeping in her room, and eventually it had become Elise's domain, the dresser space shared with her mom's clothes. The tiny bathroom countertop grew crowded between their toiletries and Elise's growing collection of lip glosses and a shoplifted mascara or two. Finally, at age thirteen, she'd cleaned out the bathroom drawers and thrown away all the unused crap in there. Her mom hadn't even noticed.

"That was good," Elise said, finishing the last of her coffee quickly. "Thanks." She noticed a couple of puzzle pieces on the floor, likely courtesy of Pierre, and used that as an excuse to push back from the table to retrieve them. "I'd better be heading out. No reservations today, but someone could show up looking for a room. I just wanted to check in and bring you the rolls."

"Oh, let me dig up a few carrots!"

"Sure. I'll help if you tell me what to do."

She followed her mother outside to a pair of raised beds. Pierre trailed them only as far as the doorway, settling in on the metal threshold to sit in the sun and watch from a safe distance. A smart cat and a perfect companion for Mom.

After slipping on the gloves she was handed, Elise followed her mother's lead and loosened up some soil before digging in deep and working a carrot free. It popped up easily, and she marveled at how beautiful the color looked against the black dirt. She felt less enthusiastic about the green beans her mom was snapping off, but she'd take them home and . . . steam them? The carrots she'd dip in ranch.

She had six carrots exhumed after only a few minutes of work and felt remarkably accomplished considering she hadn't grown them.

"Get out of here!" her mom suddenly screamed. Elise tried to jump up and fell on her ass.

"What?" she yelled in a panic.

"Darn rabbits. I've been thinking about making rabbit stew all summer."

Elise twisted around to see a cottontail at the edge of the yard in the shadow of a pine tree. It watched them from between two gray rocks, whiskers twitching as it nibbled a weed. "Do you even know how to make rabbit stew?"

"No, but I'll learn."

"Liar. You like animals too much."

"Humph." She tossed a pebble across the yard, and the rabbit turned and took off through a break in the brush. Elise recognized it as a break she and Kyle had created during old adventures.

The hike up the hill had felt like a dangerous trek, the woods a vast wilderness, but she'd been safe with Kyle. At the end had been a castle. A fortress.

She stood and wandered toward the nearly invisible gap in the serviceberry bushes. "Is our place still there?" she asked.

"I'm not sure. Haven't been back there in years."

Elise edged some of the leaves apart.

"I'm going to wash these off for you," her mom said, rising with a grunt and dusting off her gloves.

"Okay, I'll be right back." She pushed past the bushes and found the trail. She could see tracks of deer that likely wandered in at night to snack on the garden, Bambi and Thumper teaming up.

Shielding her face from a few thin branches, she pressed on, rising steadily away from her mom's property and up the incline toward the clearing where she and Kyle had built their grounded version of a tree house.

When their dad had left, he'd cleaned out his shitty homemade toolshed, taking everything valuable, and the small outbuilding had rotted in the backyard until Kyle had eventually pulled it apart. Together, they'd carted the pieces up the trail, their hands torn up with splinters and scrapes.

Rebuilding it in the woods had been a half-assed effort, but that had all changed after Robin's disappearance. After that, they'd both thrown themselves into the project with manic determination. They'd needed an escape from the doom and darkness of their home. Mom had resisted at first, terrified to let them roam the woods, but she'd eventually lost her focus, and they'd gained some freedom.

Elise was surprised when she reached the clearing. It had felt miles away from everything back then, yet the walk couldn't have been more than five minutes, even uphill.

She laughed a strange, high guffaw at the sight of their fairytale land, their refuge. As magical and fortlike as this place had seemed to her, it was nothing but a collection of stained plywood sheets topped with off-kilter metal roofing. Mildew climbed up the sides to the height of past seasons of snowfall, and weeds crowded in from everywhere.

She drew closer, remembering whole days spent in the shade of that flimsy roof during the summer, reading books and trading a second-hand Game Boy back and forth.

Bending close, she tried to peer through the cracked-open door, but it was too dark to see much. A log they'd used as a chair. A small chest where they'd stored books and where Elise had later hidden liquor. The shed was nothing more than a palace for spiders now, and she imagined there were black widows lurking beneath the years of leaf cover that had blown in.

Still, she was glad she'd come. This was one of the few good memories from her childhood that didn't involve Robin, and it felt safe to think about. She could take it out later and reminisce without that awful bitterness that coated everything else.

Kyle had been such a good brother. She needed to cut him more slack and stop getting so impatient with his thoughts. They might be a bit out there, but he was smart as hell. He always had been.

When she stepped back, her heel kicked something solid, and she looked down to see an empty beer bottle. It wasn't from her youth; the label was too modern. Another bottle lay nearby.

The shack was on US forestland, so she wasn't surprised that others might come by and lounge on one of the pieces of tree trunk they'd collected. People hunted wild turkey back here and even did some bow hunting for deer. A couple of faint game trails snaked in different directions, but the firepit had been taken over by poison oak. Surely no one had been here in a long time.

Still, she felt glad her mom was passionate about locking every door behind her when she came inside. Just in case.

Elise picked up the two bottles she'd spotted and tucked them under an arm to walk out of the past and into the present. She'd done her good deed for the day, picking up some trash. It was time to retreat and leave the fantasy behind. Luckily, she had years of practice to fall back on, and she barely noticed the heavy weight of reality pressing down as she trudged back toward the sun.

CHAPTER 15

Watch out for people who don't fit in. Elise's pulse quickened as a man in a beige cashmere sweater closed the door behind him and blinked, his eyes trying to adjust to the shadowed reception room.

"Can I help you?" she asked when his gaze finally focused on her behind the desk.

"I'm checking in," he answered, sounding confused to be there. Perhaps he hadn't expected the Bigfoot sign.

"We're happy to have you! Can I get the name on the reservation?"

He gave his name and glanced around with a curiosity that edged close to suspicion. Or was he gathering intel? His black hair appeared freshly trimmed, and the thick scruff on his face was edged to accentuate his sharp jawline and expose the perfect brown skin of his cheekbones. Was he a dandy or just disguised as one?

"All right, you're in cabin 2, one of our premium Creekside Cabins. And it looks like you're only staying for one night?" As she took his credit card, Elise dared to ask her most pressing question as if it were a normal thing to address. "Are you here for the memorial?"

He finally turned his gaze back to her, face opening up a bit. "Yeah, I am. Are there others here?"

The confirmation ratcheted her tension up another notch. "You're the first, but I believe there are several reservations."

"Oh good." He smiled, looking relieved. Because he wouldn't be staying in the backwoods alone or because he'd have backup? Kyle was really starting to get to her.

"I'll walk you over and show you how the heater works. It's getting down to forty-eight tonight. Just the one key?" She directed him out first, but her neck prickled when he fell behind her on the walk over.

This job had never felt dangerous before. She was isolated at the edge of town, with nothing to her east and only a surveying office to the west, but the highway was right there. Regardless, she felt very alone today despite the sunshine and the faint roar of cars passing.

Hyperaware of her own safety, she opened the door to cabin 2 and handed the man a retro metal key before waving him in ahead of her. She kept her feet planted outside.

"It's cozy, but you should have everything you need. There's a list of nearby restaurants and essentials on the fridge, along with the Wi-Fi password."

"Thanks." He was barely paying attention and already had his phone out to check for messages. Elise explained how to turn the heater on or set the fan for fresh air and excused herself.

Another vehicle was pulling up as she walked back, but it was only Daniel. He honked and got out with a big smile. "Hey, Elise! Great hair!"

She touched the shorn nape and felt an honest-to-God blush heat her face, remembering the way she'd pressed into him for comfort. Then she blushed harder remembering how she'd practically pushed him away. She couldn't even manage flirting without being hurtful.

She tried to offer a natural smile. "Thank you. It felt like a good time for a change. Haven't seen you around much. Been busy?"

"I'm helping the tenant load up a storage unit. He should be out in a day or two, so I'll be moving in soon."

"I owe you a room refresh tomorrow. Need more towels or anything else today?"

He waved away the offer. "How have you been?"

"Okay. I think I cleared things up with the cops."

"You're off the most-wanted list?" She ignored the urge to get closer when he winked, to use him as a distraction. It wouldn't be fair to use him in any case, but it felt even more wrong while she was mourning Christian. But Jesus, she'd been mourning that man for a long time.

"We'll see," she said, keeping things serious. "Someone was shot in the San Jose area, and they think it might be connected, so I'm hopefully off their radar now."

He'd been reaching into his truck for a toolbox, but he swung around, eyes widening. "Are you kidding? So Kyle was right about that company?"

She felt her stomach unknot a bit that someone else had confirmed the logic. Kyle wasn't spiraling. He was actually on to something.

"Must be a lot to take in," Daniel said. "Kyle said you were close to the guy who died."

Elise crossed her arms and stepped back a little, worried her brother had said more than that. "Sure, I guess. But not recently."

"Speak of the devil."

For a split second she thought Christian was there, and she was swinging around to follow Daniel's line of sight when she remembered his death. How many times would that happen? When would reality sink in and stop moving aside for hope?

It was Kyle driving toward them to park next to Daniel's truck. She actually felt relieved to see him after two days of searching in vain for more information about either death online. Whatever the police knew, they weren't sharing much with the press. As resistant as she'd been before, she craved Kyle's intel now.

Jeremy Quinn had been shot from a distance while having breakfast on his back deck in the foothills of Los Altos around eight in the morning. His wife was out of the house at the time. His housekeeper was there but heard nothing, and she didn't discover his body until eight forty-five. The police claimed to have no suspects in the shooting, and the articles made only glancing mention of Christian's death in connection.

Stratum corporate PR issued one paragraph expressing sorrow and shock over both men's deaths and extending sympathy to the families as well as to "the entire Stratum family who knew and loved these men, who weren't only founders but were inspirations to our entire global team."

Ugh. Christian would have hated that. He'd walked away from those people. They weren't family to him.

"Hey, Daniel." Kyle nodded at his friend before turning to Elise, that same file box in his hands. "Sis, can we talk?"

"Yeah, what's going on? The police aren't saying anything."

"They're fucking scrambling, that's what's going on. Shit is going to hit the fan."

"What shit?" Daniel asked.

Kyle stood a little straighter. Instead of answering Daniel, he met Elise's gaze straight on as if daring her to doubt him. "I think there's evidence these guys killed Robin."

It didn't quite hit for a moment, this violation. She'd been so eager to hear more about the Stratum connection that she was still waiting for it. But Daniel responded with the shock that was rolling toward her on a slow-moving train.

"Seriously?" he exclaimed. "The police are saying that? That's just . . . insane."

"Oh, they're not *saying* it," Kyle responded smugly. "Frankly, I doubt they have any idea yet. But it'll all come out eventually. I've been tracking down the proof."

"Wow. Okay."

But it wasn't okay, and Elise was drawing herself up as if she meant to scream or punch or explode. She pulled a breath in slowly through her nose, jaw clenched too tight to let it pass her lips.

Daniel looked from Kyle to her before putting a hand on her brother's shoulder. "Hey, man, maybe we should take it down a notch and discuss what you found."

"They were right here that summer," Kyle said, ignoring Daniel's hint to back off. "I don't mean I *think* they were here; I mean I have proof. It's an article from some business magazine that went under in 2006. I'd seen snippets, but a contact finally found it in an archive. In the interview, Christian talked about the summer they spent brainstorming Stratum and building it from the ground up. He actually said they were in Willow Canyon, so no one can dispute that."

Kyle put the box down and began digging through it while Elise glared at the top of his head, trying to burn a hole in it with her rage. "You can't do this," she said, her voice rising. "You can't just tell me Christian murdered our sister and *pretend that's fine*. It's not fine to say that. It's *not fine!*"

He didn't look up from his search. "I know you were in love with the guy, but facts are facts."

"Kyle!" Her head whipped to Daniel, and she caught the way his eyes went round with shock. "What the hell," she whispered.

Daniel studied her expression for a moment before stepping back with a quick nod. "I'm going to let you two talk, all right?" His tone was already more distant, already pulling away from her.

She nodded, her head loose on her neck, chin bobbing over and over as Daniel spun and hurried toward his cabin. He'd left his toolbox in the truck bed.

"Here!" Kyle stood with whatever printout he considered a prize. "Listen to this quote. 'That summer was when Stratum was truly born. We rented a cabin up in Willow Canyon. It was August, perfect mountain weather, and it was the exact environment we needed. We brainstormed twenty-four hours a day. Well, we left a couple of hours a day for fun. But that month was an intense bonding experience. We were like brothers when we left that place. We had each other's backs.' That was *Christian*. He said that."

"*So what?*"

"So what? Did you hear what I just read?"

She could only stare at him, jaw aching with tension.

"They had an 'intense bonding experience'? They 'had each other's backs'? What the hell is he talking about? They rented a fucking cabin for a month. Something happened that summer, Elise. *Robin* happened."

Elise, normally the loud-mouthed one in the family, could barely speak. "His memorial is tomorrow," she muttered past lips that felt disconnected from her nervous system. "Tomorrow. And I can't even go. Why are you doing this?"

"I'm not trying to be cruel. I'm telling you what I found. And what I found is that they were here that summer. Then Phoenix confessed to her murder out of the blue ten years later. Why do you think that is?"

"Because he killed her," she whispered. She wanted to be somewhere else right now. Anywhere else. She'd been ready to listen to him. Ready to believe. And now this madness?

Kyle had been the rock in her life, but suddenly he was a landslide.

"No," he insisted. "Phoenix Whit was set up. He died and left that supposed suicide note in November of 2009. They took Stratum public two months later. They needed that episode tied up and *gone* so nothing could come back and haunt their stock prices."

Her heart ached with a pain like tearing fabric, the muscle fibers stretched too thin to hold. "This is ridiculous, Kyle. You're finally losing it. You're not okay."

"I'm fine. Come inside. I'll show you everything I have."

A car pulled up, the grinding of the gravel so loud it sounded like her skull being scraped from the inside. The absence of engine sound told her the Mercedes was an electric model, a gleaming black car that cost over a hundred grand. Yet another danger had pulled into her life.

A wisp of a blond woman hopped out of the passenger seat. Elise stared at her.

"Oh my God," she cooed, "it's so *kitschy*, I love it. Did you see the Bigfoot? So cute! We have to take a picture, Ty! Come on!"

Elise watched as the driver emerged and studied him for any hint of threat. He was flat-faced with cool resignation, but he took out his phone and followed behind the woman as she raced toward the sign.

"Shen Lu is going to die when she sees this!" she yelled. "I told you this would be fun." She didn't sound like a woman in town for a funeral, but she'd probably barely known Christian and was here to make an appearance.

Elise, still numb, her head still strange and loose, stared after them without looking back to Kyle. "I need to check them in," she said dully.

"I'll meet you inside." Kyle hefted up his box and disappeared through the door.

At least she didn't have to worry that these two guests were a team of assassins. Killers probably wouldn't document their movement with pictures. But who knew? Elise was living in a bad novel, wasn't she? And she desperately wanted to burn all the pages.

Instead of screaming at the top of her lungs, she walked very slowly inside, sat at her desk, and folded her hands to wait, hoping it was too dark for the guests to see the crazed wildness spinning in her eyes.

As soon as she had them checked in, she was going to walk into the living room, find a weapon, and murder her only remaining sibling. Hopefully their mother would forgive her.

CHAPTER 16

A ream of paper had exploded in her cabin. Though Elise had calmed a bit while walking back from cabin 1, she still flashed to thinking about an easy murder-scene cleanup when she saw the paper Kyle had spread over every flat surface. Half an hour in front of the fireplace, and the blood spatter evidence would be gone.

But she probably wouldn't murder him. *Probably.*

"Clean it up," she snapped. "We're not talking about this."

"Just listen to me, Elise." When she shook her head, Kyle threw his hands in the air. "Listen! Please! We need to look through Robin's old letters. You still have some, right?"

She stopped shaking her head and frowned. "Her letters? Of course I have them."

"Good. I have too many other details to track down. You can't possibly object to looking for names, can you? How could that hurt anything?"

She counted to five. Then she counted to ten, remembering how her brother had helped her so many times over the past decades. She could get him through this. Calm him down. "Whose names?" she asked.

"Jeremy. Billy." He paused as if even he hesitated to say the third name. "Christian. We need to see if she mentioned any of them. If she was dating one of them or if she talked about a big party she was looking forward to. Something at a cabin, maybe."

Elise's eyes filled with tears. She didn't know if she wanted to hug him or shake him. "Kyle, I was only ten. She wouldn't have told me about some kegger with college guys." But Robin had mentioned boys in her letters all the time, hadn't she? She shook her head. "She wrote to me from camp. She didn't write when she was home."

"Who did she write to, then? She was posting letters every single day. You shared a room with her. You must have seen the envelopes. Or maybe you heard her talking on the phone. She certainly did that a lot."

"I . . ." She squeezed her eyes shut, summoning more patience. "I'll look through my letters, all right? But even in your ridiculous theory, she wouldn't have met them until she came back from camp. So what's the point? Kyle, you need to step back from this."

He stood straight and pointed at her. "You should ask Amber. She might remember something. And she has her own letters."

"Amber doesn't know anything about Christian. I'm not bringing this crap up with her."

"She doesn't need to know why. Just tell her your crazy brother wants to know."

Elise winced at him calling himself crazy. But with the power of that word being spoken, she knew she didn't believe it. Yes, Kyle was easily hyperfocused and desperate for answers and as screwed up from their childhood as she was. But no matter how intense he got about his theories, he always followed them through and walked away when he was wrong. He needed to stare this in the face, and then he'd see that he wasn't being rational.

"What do *you* remember?" she asked. "You were thirteen. You'd know more than I would."

He shifted papers around, his eyes scanning them. "I was a late bloomer. All I cared about was Pokémon and riding my bike. I sure as hell didn't know anything about parties, and mostly I was looking to get time away from a house full of girls. No offense."

Rubbing her tight neck, Elise dropped onto the couch, her anger shrinking back into sadness. "This has nothing to do with Christian, Kyle. You're imagining that."

"Just *listen*." He snatched up a couple of pale-pink papers from the sea of white. "If there was a party around here, Robin was going to it, right? She even wrote to Mom about it that summer." He snapped the paper straight. "'I'm eighteen now, and I don't need a curfew anymore.'"

"Where'd you get that?"

"Mom has a lot of letters. I need to go back and read them more thoroughly. Just listen. 'I'll be at college in September. You have to give me more freedom. It doesn't matter if I'm out at 2:00 a.m., I'm with *friends*.' Friends is underlined three times."

"Well, she was sure wrong about that, wasn't she?" Elise said.

"Yeah, but I guess Mom finally agreed."

Elise nodded. "I remember Robin staying out all night a couple of times after camp."

Kyle joined her on the couch, still clutching the pink papers. Elise took them from his hands and pressed the wrinkles out on her thigh.

"She was out a lot that week," Kyle said. "I spent the night at Daniel's the night before she disappeared, so I don't think I'd seen her for days. Maybe in passing. We hadn't talked, I know that."

She wanted to wrap her arms around him and squeeze these terrible thoughts from his head. Instead she leaned her head on his shoulder, picturing him as that awkward thirteen-year-old boy who'd taken such good care of his little sister during the worst days of their lives. "A lot of her friends were leaving for college at the end of August. She was enjoying her last moments with them. You shouldn't feel bad that you barely saw her."

He shrugged, the worn flannel of his shirt rubbing against her cheek. "I guess. But I kind of ignored her that year."

She blinked her burning eyes, trying to fight off the tears. It didn't work. "We fought a lot, you know," she admitted. "She didn't want to share a room with a ten-year-old, and I didn't want her to treat me like the little kid I was. I'd go through her things. Try on her clothes. She constantly called me a brat and a pain in the ass. I—" Her voice hitched as her breath caught on the sharp and jagged grief. "I told her I couldn't wait for her to go away. Half the time that wasn't even true. But half the time, I was sick of her."

"Shit." Kyle shifted, raising his arm up to awkwardly work it around her shoulders. "You were just a kid. Sisters fight."

"I know. But for a while I thought maybe she did go away. I thought she was tired of me and us and this place, and she decided to get the hell out."

"I did too. Mom never did, but I thought she'd run away. I thought she was boy crazy and she'd taken off with some loser but she'd turn up right before school to pack up her stuff."

Sighing, Elise let the tears fall down her face and soak into his shirt. "God. She was so excited about college. She would have made the most of it. I went to the campus to see a friend once. Robin would have been in fucking heaven there. It's only a few minutes to Santa Cruz and the beach. And there were people *everywhere*."

"Sounds awful," Kyle said dryly, and Elise laughed and wiped her eyes.

She felt calm now. Too exhausted to fight him anymore. "Christian didn't have anything to do with this," she said. "It's a story you made up."

"Maybe. But two people have been murdered. I didn't make that part up. There has to be a screwed-up reason for two friends getting killed, Lise. You get that, don't you? You're looking for a reasonable explanation for someone behaving unreasonably, but you're never going to find a comfortable answer."

She wanted to protest and deny. Wanted to shove his shoulder and tell him he was wrong, wrong, wrong. But he was right about that one thing. Something awful was happening, and it was obviously a dark and secret story of some kind. But it wasn't *this*. It couldn't be.

"I'm just glad that other guy was killed while you were with the police," he murmured. "At least they'll stop looking at you now and search for real answers."

She nodded and finally gave in. Just a little. "I'll ask Amber. But that's it. You have to leave me alone after that. I have enough emotional trauma right now, don't you think?"

"Eh, you're pretty tough," he said as he squeezed her in a tight hug.

But she wasn't. She really wasn't. Not anymore.

CHAPTER 17

Did he love you?

Elise stared at the message in confusion, then rubbed her eyes and checked the time on her phone: 5:50 a.m.

"Oh damn," she croaked when she saw who it was from. It was the day of Christian's service, and Savannah had woken up thinking about her dead husband's affair. Or maybe she'd never gone to sleep.

Regardless, this was exactly why Elise had cursed Deputy Harrison. She was embarrassed for herself, yes, and maybe selfishness was her true motivator, but whatever Savannah was feeling was a thousand times worse.

This time her heart didn't hurt at all as she told the lie. If it *was* a lie.

No, he didn't love me. It was nothing like that. We were friends, then we saw each other a few times. That's all.

At this point, Elise wanted it to be true. Yes, he'd told her he loved her over and over. But men said a lot of things they didn't mean when they wanted sex. Married men most of all.

When he'd broken it off, she'd called him a liar a hundred times. She'd known deep in her bones that he'd manipulated and lied and used her to get what he wanted.

Many months later when parts of her heart had healed, she'd let some of that go. He'd had feelings for her. She knew that. He claimed he'd never cheated before, and she had believed him. They'd made a mistake. Both of them had.

But now? Now she hoped their affair had meant nothing, because that made it easier for everyone, including her. What the hell was love, anyway? How could anyone separate the strands of it from lust and novelty and obligation and guilt? Was it love if it only lasted a couple of months? Was it love if it lasted for five decades with breaks and betrayals along the way? How could she, of all people, ever know?

But she did know one thing, and she needed to say it. He called you his touchstone, she typed, her eyes too dry to make any tears. He said you were his family.

A new message appeared. I miss him so much.

Oh God. This was too much. Elise closed her eyes and let her head fall back, praying the phone wouldn't chime again. "I miss him too," she breathed, barely daring to make a sound even in her own bed. But she'd missed him for a long time. It was an old ache, not a fresh agony, not really.

The phone dinged. She squeezed her eyes until she saw stars. She couldn't do this. She couldn't. But she'd taken something from Savannah, and she owed her something back.

Elise opened her eyes and lifted the phone. Thank you, it said. She groaned and pulled the covers over her head to escape back to sleep.

Her escape attempt failed, so twenty minutes later she forced herself out into the chilly room and jumped in as hot a shower as she could stand. Considering all the designer-clad folks who'd passed gingerly through check-in the day before, she eyed her closet as she styled her hair into a subdued wave. Her wardrobe was a mishmash of ancient work clothes along with leggings and some nice sweaters she'd bought on clearance. The whole thing was supplemented by a lot of T-shirts she'd collected over the decades from local bands and obscure tours.

She resented her sudden self-consciousness and wanted to put on her oldest ripped jeans and her Grass Widow T-shirt in protest, but that felt disrespectful today, so she decided to wear all black. Once she'd tugged on a pair of nice leggings and boots and topped them with a black cable-knit sweater, she even put on a little makeup and her smallest gold stud earrings. These people were here to mourn, and if she couldn't go with them, the least she could do was put up an appearance.

She set two coffeepots to brewing and had a brief vision of Savannah doing the same thing for her guests. There must be friends and relatives staying in that huge house, people there to support and protect her. Her son and her parents, at least. His parents too. God, his poor parents.

The remembrance ceremony started at nine thirty, and the details had encouraged people to "find peace in the beauty of his favorite place and share memories of Christian" until a formal eulogy at ten. A reception would follow in the garden. It sounded beautiful, honestly, and she wished she could go. Wished she could stand in his favorite place and share memories with . . . complete strangers.

She didn't know anyone in Christian's life. No one who'd known him before Elise or after. She'd been separate. A way station. And she had her own path of travel today, however reluctant she was to make the journey.

She didn't believe Kyle's claims, not for a second, but they'd bruised her. She'd agreed to ask about Amber's stash of letters, and it wasn't just to talk Kyle down from this bad trip. She wanted to look and find proof that he was wrong. She needed to show him that Christian wasn't bad, that their relationship hadn't all been wrong and ruined. That it had been something good for a month or a week or one fucking hour.

She'd find proof, and then she'd help Kyle find a therapist. Or maybe a doctor. Even if he'd been able to control his obsessions in the past, he could be losing his grip on them, and he might need more help than she could give. Elise had always been the crazy one in the family, and she refused to pass on the crown to her strong and steady brother.

After forcing herself to choke down a piece of toast so the coffee wouldn't sour her stomach, Elise unlocked the front door and swept the pine needles off the steps. A squirrel barked at her from above, threatening or warning the others, she couldn't know until an acorn or two rained down.

At seven, the reception door finally opened, and Elise straightened, pasting on a placid smile. It softened to a real one despite her tiredness when she saw it was Daniel.

"I was dropping something off at my truck and smelled the coffee from outside. You mind sharing?"

She gestured at the pots, trying to ignore how cute he looked in gray sweats and a faded old park ranger T-shirt. "Help yourself. You're a guest. I'll even grab you all the toilet paper and shampoo you want while you're here."

"Tempting. Hey, you look all dressed up." He gestured with an empty coffee mug, then winced. "Shit. You're going to the funeral, aren't you? Listen, I—"

"No," she snapped. "No, I'm not."

"Oh. Okay." He looked away from her to fill his coffee cup, the silence drawing out between them.

She felt guilty for cutting him off like that, but she wasn't going to talk to him about Christian, and she didn't want to talk about missing the service.

Daniel tried again, clearing his throat. "So Kyle came by my cabin last night."

"Oh?" Kyle could have said anything, and none of it was good. But as she waited for Daniel to ask about her affair with Christian, he posed a different question.

"Do you think he's doing okay?"

God. How the hell was she supposed to answer that? She raised her eyebrows in question.

"He has a lot of thoughts about these deaths," Daniel said. "It sounds like . . . I don't know. He's a little obsessed, maybe?" He looked uncomfortable, head ducked and mouth tense.

She tried to swallow the knot in her throat. She wasn't sure if Kyle was all right, but she didn't want to betray his privacy either. Not unless it got worse.

"I think he's okay," she said. "He gets overly focused sometimes, but you know that. This was kind of his hobby even back in the old days, wasn't it? Researching stuff?"

His shoulders relaxed. "That's true. He used to pull me along with him sometimes."

"Bigfoot," she said.

"Bigfoot," he agreed. "I couldn't tell you how many hours we spent looking for tracks. Yeah." He nodded. "I just wanted to be sure. His theories are kind of wild."

"That's one way to put it." She only had to prove Kyle wrong, and she could point him on a less damaging path.

Daniel sipped his coffee and studied her for a moment. "You don't honestly think there's anything to it, do you?"

Her face went hot, worried he'd press for more about Christian. "About the stuff with Robin? Definitely not. Kyle just needs to work through it. I told him I'd check out one thing for him and that's all; then hopefully he'll drop it. He starts posting on message boards and—" She waved a stiff hand. "He and his community get each other pumped up."

"Just be careful," he warned. "Don't let him pull you in."

She bristled a little, as she always did when someone told her what to do.

"This guy Christian," he started. "Kyle said—"

When the door opened behind him, Elise nearly groaned with relief. Whatever he'd been about to ask about Christian, the conversation was over now.

The first man who'd checked in the day before stood uncertainly in the doorway, a buttery brown leather satchel in his hand. He looked at Daniel and hesitated as if he didn't want to get close to Daniel's old sneakers and worn sweatpants. Daniel took the hint and excused himself.

"Text me if you want to talk later," he said as the guest stepped back to let him out. "You've got my number."

But no way was Elise taking him up on that. She didn't know why it hurt so much for Daniel to know something ugly about her. Maybe because he'd been something clean and pure in her life. Something she'd never had the chance to fuck up. Not yet, anyway.

By nine o'clock all the funeral guests had checked out and Elise was alone. Even Daniel's pickup was gone.

She stood in the window, staring out at the highway at the cars moving east, disappearing into the trees. How many of them were going to Christian's home? Had they truly known him? Did they even care about saying goodbye, or had they come for appearances' sake?

"Screw it." She grabbed her keys.

A few minutes later she was behind a silver BMW, waiting in a long line of cars turning left into the Timbers. She was among them now, the people from his life, maybe even the people who'd wanted him dead. Goose bumps rose on her arms as she turned onto the smooth black road that immediately began twisting and turning up the mountain.

It was real all of a sudden. Christian's death and Quinn's too. Quinn had been shot, and if the cops were right that someone had texted Christian to come to that trail and then smashed in his head . . . then a killer was out there.

Or maybe the killer was right here.

The cars ahead of her slowed to a stop. She glanced in her mirror at the huge black bumper of a truck. The trees pressed up to the road, branches cutting off the early sun. She had no idea if she was near Christian's property.

When the car in front of her inched forward, Elise stayed at a stop, letting space open up so she wasn't boxed in. Just in case. In case of what, she had no idea.

Jesus, her brother had her on edge. Still, when the other cars disappeared around a curve, she followed, determined to participate in this pilgrimage. Surely she deserved it more than anyone popping in for an hour or two.

Once she'd cleared the curve, she spotted Christian's driveway, the gate open. Two big, shiny cars pulled out, and two more vehicles pulled in. Dozens of cars lined the long driveway, and the entry to the house directly across from his was full as well. The owners must have volunteered the space.

Past that, cars were parked on the right shoulder of the road as far as she could see. A valet jogged down the road toward the gates, another one hot on his heels. She couldn't be trapped by them, she shouldn't even be there, so when the truck in front of her pulled in, Elise hit the gas and sped past the whole circus.

She drove a quarter mile, then doubled back to a driveway that clearly hadn't been used in weeks. Half of these houses were only occupied on select weekends during ski season. The waste boggled her mind.

She pulled her car tight against some brush and slid on her largest pair of sunglasses before getting out, then walked downhill toward Christian's funeral, telling herself no one could recognize her. No one knew her, not even Savannah.

Once she was past the gates and on the driveway, she could see white chairs set up close to the house. The huge house loomed above them, all steep-pitched rooflines and huge timber beams. The perfect bright-green lawn screamed of continued irrigation even into autumn.

When a car pulled up behind her, Elise startled and darted to the side, squeezing between two parked SUVs, putting them between her and the other mourners.

They milled around in pairs and clusters on the lawn, beautiful people in dark clothes, aside from one woman who wore a very short lavender dress and a huge black hat with a veil, as if she were playing the part of a gleeful young widow at an old man's graveside.

Elise picked her way along the rocky edge of the driveway, craning her neck to view the scene. She admired that Savannah had decided to go with this setting, even with all the wealth and power in attendance.

The bright high-altitude sun cut through the spruce trees, painting the grass with stripes of vivid green amid the shadows. The sky was searingly blue, and half a dozen different birdcalls danced on the breeze.

Her eyes welled at how beautiful it was, a perfect send-off for Christian.

Past the rows of chairs stood a lectern and microphone, and past that was a line of tables draped with flowers. A hundred arrangements, maybe more, surrounded by tall stands of more flowers. She imagined there wasn't a cheap carnation in sight, and every mourner looked beautiful in their solemnity.

She almost laughed at the contrast with the last funeral she'd gone to. She hadn't snuck into that one, but she'd skulked around all the same, jonesing for a drink to enhance the Valium she'd already taken. Her dead landlord, Brenda, had been the motherly type to her tenants, and dozens of mourners had attended.

There had been no beautiful people there wearing beautiful suits. Half the attendees had worn T-shirts and jeans, a few in shorts and flip-flops. The service had taken place in a dingy strip-mall church with plastic lawn chairs as seating, and some of the sprays of flowers had been clearly enhanced with unnatural colors of dye. But the tears had been genuine, the grief real. Here there wasn't a turquoise flower in even the smallest arrangements, and the eyes of the guests stayed dry.

When a group of people moved away from the flowers, Elise's stomach clenched into a fist; then that fist twisted everything inside her. An urn sat at the end of one table, the space around it surrounded by small photo frames. That vase of polished metal hid what was left of Christian. The greasy dust inside was all of him. A handful of nothing.

Two women in conservative gray suits passed in front of the urn, blocking her view. They fussed over a board, setting it on an easel, and when they stepped back, Elise swallowed a high-pitched moan of dismay.

A huge posterboard picture now sat only a foot from his remains. Christian stood in a sunbeam in a forest, his arms and smile wide and open. Beneath a blue beanie, his face glowed with joy and a pink flush of cold.

He'd just finished a ten-mile trail run. Out of frame, a simple picnic awaited him, bologna sandwiches and sliced strawberries and a thermos filled with whisky-spiked coffee. Elise knew that because she'd taken this picture. She'd made the sandwiches and sliced the berries, and she'd lounged, laughing, on his lap as he ate.

She pressed a closed hand to the pain in her chest, tried to grind it away with her knuckles, but it wouldn't go.

Impossible that Savannah had chosen this picture. Unless she'd known. Unless she'd done it on purpose to taunt or defy or—

No, that couldn't be. Elise and Christian had been on a one-night camping trip, and no doubt he'd claimed to be going with a friend. There were no pictures of Elise on his phone, certainly none of them together. But he'd looked so happy and handsome in that moment that Elise had grabbed his phone from the blanket and snapped this shot for the pure joy of it. For his joy of *her*. She'd wanted him to remember it.

"No," she whispered as the fist opened inside her and clawed her to shreds.

She stepped out into the drive and stared, willing a gust of wind to sweep down the hill and fly the photograph away. She wanted to run across the lawn and snatch the picture from the stand, tuck it under her arm, and get it the hell out of this place. It shouldn't be here, not with Savannah, not with their son. Another telltale heart, thumping with accusation.

That bitch in the purple dress moved into view and stood next to the board to make a peace sign and snap a selfie.

"Fucking hell," Elise ground out.

A faint squeal hit her ear, then a rumble. Elise watched the woman check her phone; then she posed again with a sad gaze angled toward the picture.

"Ma'am?"

Elise swung her head around, startling at the shiny white grille right next to her. Her eyes rose to the windshield and the wide-shouldered man behind the wheel as he stuck his hand out the open window and waved. "Sorry," she murmured as she stepped back to press herself against a car and let him pass.

A face turned to watch her from the backseat, but she couldn't make out more than a pale oval past the tinted windows. A man, she thought.

When the pearl-white SUV stopped under the timber portico, a guy in a black suit jumped from the passenger seat to open the back door, his head swiveling back and forth, scanning the people around him. The driver waved off the valet who approached as the other back door opened and a second man wearing a slim black suit got out, buttoning his jacket as his gaze swept the lawn.

The figure she'd seen in the backseat finally emerged, and she recognized the guy's styled hair and round face immediately. It was Billy Jackson, the last surviving partner.

As Kyle had predicted, the two men who now stood at his side appeared to be bodyguards, with eyes that never stopped scanning the surroundings. Jackson glanced to the driveway, and Elise quickly worked her way back between the parked cars to hide herself. But he'd stared right at her, hadn't he? He'd studied her face as he passed.

Damn it.

Elise twisted around to flee to the road and her waiting car. She couldn't stay here. A man Kyle suspected of murder had just seen her and possibly recognized her.

Wow, you look exactly *like your sister.*

No, that was stupid. She didn't believe any part of that, though she wasn't quite so convinced he was innocent in Christian's and Jeremy Quinn's deaths.

She'd made it past two cars, glancing nervously over her shoulder, when something caught her eye and snagged her to a stop. She stepped back and peered through the cars toward the lawn.

A man in a suit was slightly turned away from her, speaking to a woman in a gray dress, but he looked familiar. The shape of his shoulders, the wave of his hair, even the way he moved a hand as he spoke. Frowning, she squinted, trying to place him.

When he pointed toward the flowers and turned a bit, Elise gasped so loudly she slapped a hand over her mouth to smother it. It was Daniel. *Her* Daniel. But what the hell was he doing here? He didn't know Christian. He *couldn't*. He'd only just moved back to town.

When Daniel turned toward her, she panicked and let her instincts take over, ducking down as she hurried along the uneven edge of the drive. He was far away, and she wore sunglasses, but she didn't want to take any chances. She found her feet moving faster, her heart beating harder. Sweat bloomed under arms, prickling.

The gate seemed a mile away, but finally she reached it and rushed past a straggling valet. Panting, she jogged up the narrow shoulder of the road, feeling safer only when she had her car door closed and locked behind her.

Her ragged breathing cut through the silence; her hands shook against the wheel. Why the hell was Daniel there? That didn't make any sense.

"Okay," she whispered to herself, "calm down. You're not living in a movie, and this isn't a conspiracy." She blew out a long breath and tried to calm her pulse. "Right," she said. "Right."

This wasn't a conspiracy. She would ask Daniel, and he'd give an explanation, and then she'd feel stupid for letting her brother drag her down.

The road was quiet when she pulled out, but when she passed Christian's driveway, the white SUV Jackson had arrived in sat there, crouched like a pale predator . . . and then it pulled out and followed her down the mountain.

"It's not a conspiracy," she reminded herself. But she sped up and flew past the curves too quickly, hoping to get away. By the time she reached the highway and took the hard right turn toward home, she'd lost him. In fact, she'd probably never been in his sights. He'd likely pulled over and parked in a driveway the same as she had.

Still, when she neared Creekside Cabins, she watched the rearview mirror and didn't turn on her signal. She slowed, hesitated, and then drove straight. It was time to get more answers, and she wouldn't find them in her cabin.

CHAPTER 18

Amber's box of letters was far bigger than Elise's. "Jeez, Amber, did she write to you every day?"

"Only when we weren't at each other's houses."

Elise sifted through the huge pile of envelopes and origami notes. "Incredible. Did the police ever read these?"

"They asked me to turn over anything from that month. There were only five notes because we were together all the time after she got back from camp. She slept at my place three nights in a row, I think."

"I remember her being gone a lot."

Amber grabbed the broom she'd dropped when she'd disappeared to retrieve the box. "We were both upset we weren't going to the same school. But I hoped to keep my grades up and transfer to Santa Cruz after my first year." She snorted. "Then I didn't even go, of course." Her sweeping picked up speed. "I knew she hadn't run off. You think she wouldn't have written to *me*? It was ridiculous."

Amber had apparently decided against college once Robin went missing. "I'm sorry about school. I don't think I knew about that."

She shrugged. "I wasn't really excited about college, and my parents couldn't afford it anyway. I was only going because a lot of my friends were. I'd rather be doing hair and setting my own hours than working in an office for some asshole."

Elise opened a letter and scanned it, her neck prickling at the sight of the first new words from Robin she'd seen in years. The letter appeared to be two pages of advice from her sister about Amber's boyfriend at the time, accented with an insane number of exclamation points. "There's a lot of personal stuff in here. Do you want to screen these?"

"Oh, I think we're both old enough to deal with the realities of a teen girl's chaotic love life. Spoiler alert, I wasn't pregnant, my period was just late, probably because I weighed all of a hundred pounds back then. Also, Tommy Fellows was a terrible kisser. Felt like he was trying to suck my soul into his throat." She shuddered. "I'm so glad I haven't had to date in two decades."

"I don't recommend it."

Amber winced. "Sorry."

"Listen, no one is making movies about how heartwarming the dating scene is. Then again, no one makes movies about how awesome marriage is either."

"Touché."

Elise held up the letter. "I promise I'll be careful with these. But if you want me to read them here, I will."

"Go ahead and take them, just bring them back when you're done. What are you looking for, anyway?"

It was Elise's turn to shrug. "Kyle has a bug up his butt again. You know how he is when he gets fixated on something. He's got some new theory that's going to drive me bonkers. Speaking of, do you remember going to any parties with college boys that summer?"

Amber dumped the dustpan contents into the trash. "Are you kidding? All we wanted to do was go to college parties that summer. We went to Tahoe a lot too. You remember how it was. All the camp and cabin parties around here were pretty mixed as far as ages. Otherwise it would have been the same fifteen people over and over."

That was true. There'd been plenty of skeevy guys in their twenties hanging around when Elise was a teenager. Older guys too, as long as they had weed. Her mom had been so overprotective and paranoid that Elise had rebelled by taking too many chances. She'd been rebelling against her own fears too. Then there'd been the vague, unexamined thought that if she also went missing, maybe she could find Robin. Jesus, she'd been young and dumb.

She lifted a stack of letters and rifled through them, looking at the date stamps. "Do you remember anyone named Jeremy Quinn or Billy Jackson? They were college guys." She hesitated. "Or maybe a Christian?"

"I couldn't say. It feels like a lifetime ago. There was a Christian who went to our school, though. Christian Price?"

"Yeah. I remember his brother. But Robin wasn't dating anyone special, right? I feel like she would have told me."

"No way. She was ready to tear through that Santa Cruz campus. These mountain boys weren't tying her down."

Elise laughed. "Of course."

"But Phoenix was always looking for her at parties. When I heard his name, when he killed himself . . . I didn't feel shocked. It was almost like 'Oh, of course.' You know? I felt surprised I'd never considered him before, but he was just a skinny guy we'd known since junior high."

Nodding, Elise closed up the box, trying to block the memory of her sister and Amber curling their hair in the bedroom, music blasting from a cheap boom box while Elise tried to stay quiet so the older girls would forget she was there.

"Hey," Amber said, snapping her from her thoughts. "Are you doing okay? You seem a little down lately."

When Amber put an arm over her shoulders, grief welled up in a rush. It snuck up on Elise so quickly it almost escaped her control before she realized it was getting loose. She inhaled sharply, a shocked hiccup that wanted to transform into a sob.

"Aw," her friend crooned, pulling her into a hug. "What's going on, sweetie?"

Elise shook her head. "I'm just tired, I think." Her voice was thick and hoarse, but she managed to swallow the tears.

"Don't let Kyle drag you down with this. We already know what happened to Robin. And hey, in the good-news column, I checked on your mom this morning, and she seems really good." Amber eased back and searched Elise's face for tears, then nodded at her dry cheeks. "I also scored fresh green beans, so the kids will be super stoked."

Laughing, Elise stepped back and busied herself with putting the letters away and picking up her purse. "Mine are still in the fridge."

"Don't make me mother you too. They're delicious. Eat your green veggies, Elise."

"Fine!" She grabbed the box. "I'll get these back to you quickly."

"Oh, you know who'd have more letters? Valeria. If she kept anything, I mean. She moved to LA that summer because she wanted to be an actress, remember?"

"Valeria! I forgot all about her."

"She was closer to Robin than to me, so we lost touch, but I think she's on Facebook. I know Robin wrote to her that summer. Neither of them could afford long-distance charges, that's for sure."

"Thanks, sweetie," Elise said. "That's a great tip. I'll try to track her down." She gave Amber a quick peck on the cheek before things could get emotional again, then hauled the box out to her car. Once out of sight of Amber's house, she pulled over on the shoulder to search for Valeria Vasquez on Facebook.

When she found her, Elise immediately recognized the woman in the picture. She might have a few wrinkles now, but Valeria still looked like a pixie with a pointy chin and big brown eyes surrounded by dark curls. She'd been a sweet girl who was quieter than Robin's other friends.

After sending her a quick message, Elise looked up and realized she'd parked just before her mom's street. So close, but the gulf between them felt unnavigable, and she had no idea why. She didn't resent her mother's pain. She didn't begrudge her the terrible grief.

Still, Elise hadn't quite understood when she was young and selfish, a child who needed her mom, her *real* mom, not this aching beast made of heartbreak and worry. She'd matured into some kind of understanding later, realizing that time might heal most wounds, but not *that* one. Time had no place in it. It didn't matter if it had been one year or five years or nine years. Each day could still be the *one day* out of all those endless months that Robin might return.

Recently Elise's therapist had helped her reach an even more painful truth. For her mother, Robin hadn't gone missing once. She'd gone missing every single day Robin didn't come home. Each morning, her mom opened her eyes and her daughter wasn't there again, and then again every night. Thousands and thousands of times she was snatched away until the truth finally came out.

So no, Elise didn't begrudge her mom all those years of pain. But she didn't know how to recover from it either. How to build something new. No one had ever taught her that, least of all her mother. And *certainly* not her father, who'd walked out before Elise had known him.

He hadn't even reached out after Robin's disappearance. Some newspaper reporter had tracked him down once, and he'd seemed resentful the police had questioned him about his own child. *My ex-wife didn't want me in their lives, so I stayed out of it. If I'd been there, this wouldn't have happened, but I wasn't even allowed to see them.*

That hadn't been true. The problem had been child support and his refusal to pay it. He'd made his own choices, and he must have been content with them, because he hadn't come back once, not even to join the search.

Elise had fantasized about it at the time. She'd thought her dad might return. That he might roll into town and demand answers and plead regret. He'd help find Robin, of course, because that was the kind of thing dads did, and then he'd be back in their lives, attentive and so damn sorry.

She squeezed her eyes shut at the raw memory. God, she'd been so full of need back then. That was the bloody core she'd eventually clawed out of her heart, that pitiful, whining *need*. Anger had filled the void, but it had never obscured the sheer desperation. Afterward, she hadn't needed anyone, damn it, but she had needed *something*.

Whatever that something was, she hadn't found it. She touched the box of letters.

Amberrrrrrr!

I'm so glad I'm not doing August session at camp. I can't wait to see you! And we'll both be home until mid-September, so don't start crying yet, girl. Anyway, you're going to come visit me ALL THE TIME. (Do I have to come to Fresno too? Fine. But only once.)

I'm kind of freaked out that everyone at college will be smarter than me. I'm pretty sure I barely got in. Don't let me flunk out, okay? Because you know I'll be just the dumbass to go to the beach during midterms. If either of us starts failing, let's promise to have a study weekend. For real.

What are you going to do about Rodney? You're not going to try to do long distance, are you? That is not the life for a freshman hottie like you. Fresno is a hell of a lot bigger than Cold Creek.

Uh, do NOT let him see this letter, though. He already thinks I'm a bad influence. Hell yeah I am!!!

I'll see you in ONE WEEK!!! We will be the queens of summer!!! I love youuuuuu!

XOXOXOXOXO

Robin

CHAPTER 19

"There's nothing here, Kyle. I read everything she wrote to Amber that summer. No Jeremy, no Billy, and definitely no Christian. And she didn't complain about any creepy encounters with college guys. There is a Chris mentioned twice, but that could be anyone."

Kyle went straight to the fridge and grabbed a beer. Either he was trying to grow a beard or he hadn't shaved in a week. He looked tired, which only added to the knot of worry in her stomach.

"I need to show you something," he said, his voice low and dark.

Her heart fell. He wasn't even listening to her.

She was too tired to deal with a possible mental-health crisis. The night before, she'd stayed up way too late reading letters, bringing her sister's ghost into the cabin as she'd followed Robin through her adolescence.

Elise had been too young to remember what her big sister had been like at twelve or thirteen. She'd always known her as the outgoing, confident older teen, filled with all the energy and bravado of that age. But she'd been much less sure of herself in junior high, worrying about whether she was pretty or her clothes were cute enough to pass muster with the other kids.

She'd gossiped like a fiend back then too. Well . . . she'd gossiped right up until the end, but her earlier letters were tinged by an anxious need to tear down the girls she didn't like. That nastiness had faded as her confidence had grown, and watching her sister blossom on the page had warmed Elise's heart.

Something she'd held tight inside her had loosened in the small hours of the morning. Maybe it was the grief for Robin she'd never had the chance to process. Perhaps when she got past this weird episode with Kyle, she could really sit with the loss for a while. Her therapist would undoubtedly say she'd never truly grieved and it was past time.

She discovered her sister had lost her virginity at fifteen to a nineteen-year-old. They'd worked at summer camp together, and Elise cringed at the idea of an adult counselor sleeping with a junior counselor while they were surrounded by camp kids. Robin had called him "soooo sexy and experienced." The boy—or man—had moved on to a new junior counselor within a week, of course, deflowering his way through the teenage girls. Disgusting.

Robin had written a letter to Amber dotted with actual tear splotches and thickly underlined curse words about that asshole, but she seemed to have recovered two weeks later when she'd fallen hard for a boy her age and had a much better time messing around with him.

But aside from all the fascinating details of watching her sister grow up, there hadn't been much on the page. Through the dozens of boys she'd crushed on or ignored or loved or slept with over the years, none had been named Jeremy or Billy or even Chris. A total bust.

Now she was grieving both Robin and Christian, and Kyle ignored it all to type away on his keyboard. "Are you ready for this?" he asked.

"Sure," she said, wanting to get it over with.

"I asked people to post pictures of Christian from his early years here in the Willow Canyon area."

Elise blinked her scratchy eyes. "I'm sorry, you did what? Which people? And *where*?"

"On Christian's memorial Facebook page."

"His wife created a memorial page?" That didn't sound right.

Kyle's nose wrinkled. "I get the impression it was his mom."

That made a bit more sense. His family was from a small town in Nebraska and was probably active on Facebook. His younger brother lived in Florida with three kids, and grandparents needed a way to stay in contact. They hadn't discussed their families much.

Though they had talked about Robin once or twice. He'd been caring and kind about Elise's loss, shocked that she'd gone through that. But he'd never mentioned being in Willow Canyon when it happened. She shoved the thought away, refusing to let Kyle unbalance her.

"Are you even on Facebook?" she muttered.

"No. I created a dummy account."

"Kyle . . ." She dropped onto the couch with a dramatic groan.

"None of that matters. The point is I pretended to be someone who'd known him here in town and remembered hanging with him that summer. I said he loved talking about his summers here when he was a little kid. Asked if anyone had pictures from that year in August because I didn't have any."

"Are you serious? You just asked outright?"

"Yes, I did. His mom posted a picture of him as a teenager at a cabin." He turned his laptop toward her, and there was sweet-faced Christian, his hair flopped over his forehead and nearly covering one eye. He was skinny as a rail with a huge grin that showed off a mouthful of braces as he held up a very small trout for the camera.

"Congratulations," she said, her voice edging toward hostility. "Nice picture." Why the hell was he forcing her into a tragic slideshow of Christian's life? It was just mean.

Kyle opened another photo showing Jeremy Quinn standing on a tree stump in front of a cabin. Not an adolescent but a young man. "Here we go," her brother said.

"Kyle, we already know they had a cabin around here. It's starting to worry me that you're so focused on this."

He ignored her and clicked away. "This morning someone posted *these.*"

She squinted at the small squares until he enlarged one of them, but she still had to lean close to see any detail. The outdoor scene was dim and crowded with people. Her gaze roamed, searching for the brightness of Robin's smile or the narrow face of a young Christian, but she found neither. She couldn't imagine what had captured Kyle's interest. Maybe David Koresh was in the background. Or Bigfoot.

"Do you recognize the place?" he asked.

She shrugged. It was trees and people, campfire smoke hovering above their heads, a small building with a restroom sign on the edge of the crowd. "No idea. Moon Lake, maybe?"

"I think so." He opened another. Two boys held beers toward the camera, their mouths open with laughter, each of them making bunny ears behind the other's head.

"That one is Tommy Fellows." She pointed to the muscular boy on the right. "I hear he's a terrible kisser."

"Behind them," Kyle snapped.

Sighing, she refocused on the dozen people caught by the flash of the camera. A bunch of kids in T-shirts and tank tops, beers and cigarettes in hand. Then she spotted a familiar face, and her breath caught in her throat.

"That's Phoenix Whit," she rasped, stunned to see a picture of him from that summer, that August, maybe even the week he'd murdered their sister. He looked normal and relaxed, not at all like a man about to ruin so many lives, including his own.

"Yep, that's Phoenix. And look who he's talking to."

At first she was focused on the girl next to him, who clearly wasn't Robin. She was a short Asian girl Elise didn't know. Then she leaned in to look at the boy at her side, his face turned toward Phoenix. Dark hair, round face, a jutting brow that shielded his eyes. "Is that *Billy Jackson*?"

"Yep. Billy Jackson knew Phoenix."

She hesitated, still focused on resisting Kyle's ideas. "Well, lots of people knew Phoenix."

He enlarged the next picture without responding. And there she was. Their sister.

For a moment, she was all Elise could see. Robin, who looked just like her. Robin, who smiled and waved at the camera, her arm around another girl's waist, their heads leaning close.

God, she looked so alive. So fucking alive. Eyebrows flying high and one foot pointing in a playful pose.

"They knew each other," Kyle growled. "They *all* knew each other."

Elise's exhaustion vanished with a pop. She reached out to touch her sister, her finger hovering over the laptop screen for a long moment before it sank in that there was nothing to touch. The image looked like Robin, but it was only electronic signals and cold plastic and the horrible, sinking realization that maybe Kyle wasn't crazy after all.

CHAPTER 20

Elise pulled her gaze away from her sister's smile and scanned the five other people in the photo. At the very edge of the scene, his back to Robin and face turning toward the camera, was a boy she'd never mistake for anyone else.

It was Christian. *Her* Christian.

She stared dumbly, feeling nothing. Because even if Kyle was right about this, it meant *nothing*. They'd been in the same area at the same time. They'd met at least once, or maybe only been near each other. It was the same reason the police had been forced to interview a hundred different young people. Summer in the mountains was for late nights and socializing after the kids got off their seasonal minimum-wage jobs.

"Did he ever tell you he knew her?" Kyle asked, and she was surprised at the sympathy in his voice, the careful cadence.

She shook her head. "No. But they were only at the same party. That doesn't mean he even talked to her, Kyle."

"Okay, did he tell you he was *right here* when it happened? That he heard about her disappearance? That he helped in the search or followed the story or *anything*?"

She shoved the laptop toward him and curled up on her corner of the couch. She didn't want to do this. She'd always hated talking about Robin. There was a reason she'd spent her life being tough and untouchable and drowning every awful feeling in booze and pills. So she'd told Christian very little. "I only mentioned her a couple of times."

"So you did talk about Robin. And he withheld pertinent information."

"He didn't withhold anything." He hadn't, had he? "I said I had a big sister who died when I was ten." What else? She'd said Robin went missing, that they'd never seen her again. But what had Christian said in return?

Her old friend, rage, rose up to drive off the pain. "This is so ridiculous!" Her voice echoed off the timber walls and up into the shadows of the vaulted ceiling. "What are you even saying?"

Kyle dug a notebook and pen out of his box and began writing. Elise glared at the logo of a big chain hotel on the pen as it scratched. "In 1999," he muttered, "the three founders of Stratum rented a cabin here for the month of August. They mingled with the locals at parties, and I doubt they were living like monks, right? They were twentysomethings high on the possibility of making millions."

He underlined August 1999. "That same month Robin disappears, and for some reason, Christian never talks to you about that. Nothing about what it was like dealing with massive police canvassing and even a few roadblocks. What it was like to know a girl who went missing. Your *sister*."

"Jesus, Kyle, maybe it meant nothing to him because he didn't actually know her!"

He drew a line on the paper and moved on to 2009. "In 2009, two months before Stratum is set to go public, the case is finally solved. What a coincidence. Phoenix, a local friend of theirs, suddenly writes a brief note claiming responsibility for Robin's disappearance before conveniently turning up dead. The Stratum public offering goes off without a hitch. No one ever asks any questions about August of 1999."

When pain flashed through her arms, Elise realized she was digging her nails into her skin as she clutched her body tight. She loosened her grip, but her hearing went dull with the rush of her pulse. "It is a coincidence. You're the one drawing a line there."

He drew another line. "In 2016, after the Stratum boys kill that data privacy bill, Christian purchases land here and begins building a house. He's drawn to this place, obviously. Why is that?"

"Because it's beautiful."

"Sure. Then right after his land purchase, there's a falling-out between the partners. A fight big enough that he sold all his shares to the other partners and got out. Why? Did he spook them by returning here? Was his guilt overwhelming his greed? What was it?"

"Oh my God, Kyle, he wanted to retire early. People do it all the time. He wanted time with nature and freedom, and he wanted to do it in a place he loved. It wasn't about August of 1999. He'd come here with his family years before that."

Kyle ignored her and kept talking. "Then four months later, the relationship further fractures. Jeremy Quinn sells out too. I can only assume something about Christian's departure was the last straw for him also."

"You're assuming a lot," Elise insisted.

"Okay. Let's move on. In . . . was it 2021? Christian meets you."

She felt dizzy, as if the couch were spinning so slowly only her lizard brain could sense it. "Yes. I moved back in March, and we met a few months later."

"And how did that happen, Sis? I'm going to guess he approached you. Is that correct?"

She ducked her chin and rested her forehead on her clenched fists. "It wasn't like that. We were both sitting at the bar. We just *saw* each other."

But that wasn't quite true. She'd looked up to find Christian staring at her. She'd raised her eyebrows in question, and he'd smiled and looked away. But *somebody* had to look first. There was a fifty-fifty chance it would be him.

"And then what happened?" Kyle pressed.

"Nothing! Nothing happened! He didn't blanch like I was a ghost or demand to know who I was. You're being ridiculous."

"How is it ridiculous? Because the rest of the timeline is that after he quit and moved here, the partners cut their ties. You said yourself that he didn't associate with his old friends, these men who were like *brothers* to him. Then a couple of weeks ago, he reaches out to tell you he wants to be honest with you, and all of a sudden he's murdered?"

"It's ridiculous that you're implying someone I loved killed my sister! Because then what? He pursued me because I looked like her? That's *sick*! Don't you get that?"

"So he did pursue you."

"Fuck!" she yelled, jumping to her feet, her tense muscles exploding into action. "No, he didn't pursue me. We knew each other for months before anything happened. We just *liked* each other. We talked at the bar. We had lunch. He gave me business advice. We were friends!"

But that hadn't been all. Not really. Hadn't he seemed fascinated by her? Hadn't he watched her like she was a rare treat? A bewitching puzzle? She'd assumed he'd loved her rebelliousness, her mysterious darkness, but what if he'd been pulled in by a darkness that wasn't mysterious at all?

"Why are you so pissed off?" Kyle asked.

Elise barked out a rough laugh. "Can you think like a normal human being for once in your life, Kyle? Christian and I had a relationship. It was real. We had love or as close as I'll ever get to that. Now you're trying to make me believe his interest in me was really a sick obsession with my dead sister. That he didn't want *me*—" She punched her knuckles against her breastbone, reveling in the sharp burst of pain. "He just wanted to get closer to a girl he'd murdered. Do you get why your absurd fantasy might hurt?"

Kyle's voice got much quieter. "They knew each other, Elise. And he never told you that."

She chopped a hand through the air, cutting him off. "You've chased a million different ideas over the years, Kyle. This is just another one. I can't trust you. No one can trust you!"

"No one can trust me? *Me?*" He finally lost his infuriating cool, but watching his face redden with anger wasn't satisfying. Not at all. "I've been here the whole goddamn time, Elise, looking out for you and Mom. So don't try to pretend you can't count on me when I'm trying to help you again!"

The air in her cabin was too thick, too hot. She paced back and forth, mouth open to pant, but she couldn't get enough oxygen no matter how deeply she breathed. She'd been telling herself this whole time that Kyle was stitching the entire scenario together out of paranoia and obsession, but those photographs were real. He hadn't made them up.

"Elise—"

She rushed for the door and stumbled into the reception area before she burst outside and grabbed for the porch railing to support her body. Bent over, she sucked in cool air and watched motes dance before her eyes. She couldn't tell if they were gnats or a lack of oxygen.

A gentle hand touched her back. "You okay?" her brother murmured.

"No," she wheezed.

"I'll get you a glass of water."

She didn't want his water. She didn't want anything from him. But she was too weak to protest, so she hugged the railing and pressed her side against the big timber at her hip.

This wasn't real. It couldn't be. Chemistry had pulled her and Christian together, an electric current that flowed between them whenever they were near. It hadn't been some sick lie. It had been *real*.

Her mind spun in nauseating, uneven circles. She had seen the sincerity on Christian's face. The love. Or had that intensity only been obsession?

When Kyle pressed the water into her hand, she knocked it away. "I need a real drink."

"Wait. You mean a beer?"

She nodded. He stood still for a moment, but when she ignored him he retreated back inside to do her bidding. She heard the pop of a cap, and when he delivered the bottle, she grabbed it and downed the whole thing in one long pull.

Kyle cleared his throat. He knew she didn't drink like this anymore, but desperate times called for desperate measures.

Her head felt lighter within seconds. So did her body, the familiar delicious ache oozing into her joints. Unwise or not, the beer sure as hell felt good. The pounding of her heart slowed. Alcohol might be a crutch, but she'd been about to tumble and fall.

"I'm sorry, Lise. I've been turning this over for a while. Since that first time you told me about him."

"Why?"

"I don't know. I felt protective or something, so I looked him up. Some married asshole had broken my sister's heart, and I wanted to see who he was. At the time, I noticed that he and his cronies had come here way back when. I kept it in the back of my head. I wondered if he knew who you were. Who Robin was."

"Maybe he knew something," she conceded. "*Maybe.* It's not like I can ask him now. But Christian didn't hurt her. He wasn't like that, Kyle. Despite what happened between us, he was a good guy. The three of them lived together that August, but if one of them killed Robin, it doesn't mean all of them were involved."

"True," he admitted.

"And I'm not buying that any of them were. Do you really think Jackson had something to do with the other two being killed? Because the only evidence right now is your guesswork."

"It seems pretty damn likely," Kyle insisted.

"Or maybe they crossed the wrong person, and someone is seeking revenge on all three. That still seems like a good possibility." He nodded, and she looked away, out at the hills that eventually led to Christian's home, his favorite trails. And to the place he'd died. "He saw me yesterday."

"Who did?"

"Jackson. I . . . I went to the memorial."

Kyle drew back, truly shocked for the first time since he'd started this mess. "You didn't."

"Well, I didn't *go* to the memorial. I just stopped by before things started. I felt like I had more of a right to say goodbye than a few hundred of his work colleagues."

Kyle clutched his hair dramatically. "Well, that was fucking stupid! You saw Jackson there?"

She cleared her throat. "He was driving by, and . . . he kind of looked right at me." She didn't mention Daniel. She didn't want to ruin their friendship before she had a chance to talk to him herself.

Instead of responding, her brother turned and stormed back into the house. When she followed, she found him standing at the fridge, downing his own beer as if she'd sent him over the edge.

"It's not a big deal. He can't know who I am. It's not like I still look exactly like Robin. I'm practically middle-aged, and I was wearing sunglasses."

"Elise, of course he knows who you are. He killed Christian for making contact with you."

"Oh my God, just stop. That's so fucking stupid. We had a lot closer contact than that two years ago."

"Use your brain! Christian set up a private email back then, right? You told me that should have been your first hint he wasn't actually getting divorced. But that last message you showed me came through his work. CVC is his consulting firm, isn't it?"

"Yeah, but . . . CVC is just him. He only used it to set up appearances and educational stuff."

"That doesn't matter! It's not anonymous. Even with encryption, anyone who's spying can see who it came from and who it went to. And I know your damn Yahoo account isn't exactly holding up your end of any encryption. They saw it, Elise. Either Jackson or someone on his team saw enough to know that Christian was doing something he shouldn't do."

"But his email didn't say anything about Robin."

"No, but he spoke about the truth."

"Who would jump to conclusions and kill him for that?"

Kyle began pacing, his thumbnail caught between his teeth as he thought. His energy infected her, and fear began winding through her for no good reason. "Jackson could have called him," her brother said to the floor, his mind far away. "He might have asked what the hell he was doing. Or . . ."

He stopped, eyes going wide as he looked up at her. "He could have used your voice?"

"What are you talking about?"

"AI voice cloning. It's a thing now, and Jackson would sure as hell have access to it. A few recordings of you speaking, and he could have AI ask Christian anything."

Now he sounded like he was talking about a futuristic space novel, and not even a good one. "If that's even possible, who would have recordings of my voice?"

Kyle shook his head, exasperated. "Your Instagram videos, Elise. Don't be stupid. You post promo stuff for the cabins all the time."

Elise stepped back, shocked out of her denial. She had posted a few tours of the property last year. But this was still way out of the realm of possibility. "Even if that could all be true—and I don't concede the point—why would Jackson murder Quinn too?"

"That's easy," her brother said, as if they were trying to solve some stupid online mystery. "Quinn got spooked when he heard about Christian's 'accident.'" He made exaggerated air quotes. "He could have looked into it or even accused Jackson of being involved. This guy is not a warm and friendly CEO, Elise. He's cutthroat, and his tendrils reach into a lot of powerful lives."

There was absolutely no way she could continue this conversation sober, so she grabbed another beer and popped the cap. Kyle threw her a questioning glance, but when she raised her eyebrows and stuck out her chin, he held up a hand in quick surrender. Today was not a day for restraint. She needed this beer.

She carried it to the living room and paced back and forth, wishing she had something stronger.

Did she even believe any of this bullshit? No. There was no way. But two men were dead. Something had caused that. Some*one*. And there was a decent possibility it was the man who'd stared directly at her just the day before.

A sudden, dark suspicion about the other man she'd seen there roared into life. Kyle had been setting up traps, creating fake identities and playing around with Christian's memory online. Her previous caution flew out the window. "Oh my God, you sent Daniel to Christian's memorial service, didn't you?"

Kyle drew his chin in, his forehead crumpling in a frown. "What?"

"I saw him there. Don't try to deny it."

"I have no idea what you're talking about." His eyes went wide. "Wait a minute. Are you serious? *Daniel* was there?"

For a moment she doubted her own eyes. Were all these chaotic thoughts causing her to lose it? But she was sure it had been Daniel. She'd known him since she was a toddler. "Yes. He was wearing a suit and mingling with the other guests."

Kyle stared at the fireplace for a long moment, his eyes unfocused. "Daniel?" he whispered before jumping up to rush to the front window.

"You didn't send him?"

He lifted one of the blinds and peered out at the cabins. "Did he see you?" he barked.

"I don't think so. He wasn't looking in my direction, and I left as soon as I spotted him."

"Jesus. I'm going to have to think about this, Elise. This could be real bad."

If Kyle hadn't sent him . . . But no. Now she was spiraling. This was absurd. "It's Daniel, though. He can't be mixed up in this. Are you sure he wasn't following up on something you—"

"I'm going to need to do some serious checking up on him. Because if it was anyone but Daniel Serrano, I'd say he showed up out of the blue just before Christian's murder, and isn't that convenient?"

"Oh, come on, Kyle. Daniel isn't a hit man."

"I can't picture that either, but maybe he's only here for recon. He might not even know who he's working for or why."

Elise set her empty bottle on the table with a crack. "I don't believe that. I might believe some of what you've said, but Daniel is just Daniel. I'll ask him what he was doing there."

"No, you won't. Not until I check him out."

She ignored him and deliberately changed the subject. "When I talked to Amber, she reminded me about Valeria. Do you remember her?"

To her surprise, Kyle stopped his pacing and blushed. "Wow. Valeria. That's a blast from the past. I had a big crush on her. She used to ruffle my hair whenever she said hi to me. I guess that's all it takes for puppy love."

Thank God she'd distracted him. "She's still in LA, but I messaged her on Facebook to see if she has any letters." She opened Facebook on her phone to check. "No response, but I'll try to find her on Instagram too."

"Good. I'll keep monitoring the memorial page. Jackson is probably already trying to track down my fake account to see who's asking questions. I'll have to be careful. And you need to be careful too." He glanced toward the window again. "Maybe you should stay with Mom."

"I'm not staying with Mom."

"Stay with me, then. You're not safe. With Daniel—"

"I've been here with him the whole time. And he's checking out tomorrow, moving into the house. I'm not worried about him." And she wasn't. The man obviously had a reason for being at the memorial. All she had to do was ask him about it. Right?

Kyle dragged a hand over his scruff. "I could clean out the spare room again. It's pretty packed with—"

Elise cut him off. "I'm *fine*, Kyle."

She had no idea if she was, but she desperately needed to be alone. If she had to spend hours listening to her brother's ideas, she'd never be able to separate his thoughts from her own. And if she was going to get drunk, she didn't want to do it in front of him. He'd worry.

But really, there was no reason to worry. She knew how to restrain herself these days. She simply didn't want to do it anymore.

CHAPTER 21

Elise woke with a start, pushing up on her elbows in confusion. The light was wrong, too warm and sliding over her at a strange angle. When she realized she couldn't see anything past the glare and the gunk in her eyes, she rubbed her face. Where the hell was she?

Her head ached and her stomach roiled. She had to wipe her eyes one more time before she could make anything out. A glance toward a blessedly dark corner of the room finally gave her vision the chance to adjust. There was her cold fireplace. It seemed she'd slept on her couch.

"Shit." She swung her legs down and sat all the way up, wincing at the way her heartbeat invaded her skull and thumped like a cheap drum. Then she spotted the rough wood of the coffee table and the bottles spread across it. A couple of beers and one damning blue bottle of gin. She had a very vague memory of calling in a delivery order.

Elise had to bite off her groan of regret because acid started climbing her throat, and she feared she might vomit. Instead of fighting it, she welcomed the opportunity to purge this crap from her body and ran straight to the bathroom.

Hangovers were the only thing that had saved her from sinking all the way into destruction years before. She had friends—even tiny, birdlike women—who could drink to a blackout state every night and pop right up with no effects the next day. That was an easy prescription for blacking out every night, slowly and steadily killing your most vital organs. But Elise had always been forced to deal with misery and illness after a big night out, which had curbed her worst tendencies. Thank God for small mercies. The smallest, really.

As soon as she'd washed out her mouth and brushed her teeth, she stormed back into the living room to throw away the bottles. She poured the rest of the gin into the sink and tossed that bottle too. Then she forced herself to drink a huge glass of water, eat a small piece of toast, and swallow some ibuprofen.

She'd slipped up and lost control, but she'd been in a bad way. No point beating herself up over it; she'd simply get back on track.

When Elise finally checked the time on her phone, she cursed. It was nearly noon. No wonder she'd been so damn disoriented. Cringing with guilt, she unlocked the front door and propped it open to dissipate the smell of beer.

A glance outside showed that all the parking spaces were empty. She liked to think that if she'd had cabins full of guests, she wouldn't have been irresponsible enough to stay up until 2:00 a.m. getting blind drunk, but she couldn't honestly say. She'd spiraled hard, rereading Amber's box of letters, then browsing through those few snippets of emails she'd saved from Christian.

That thought sparked something in the back of her very muddled mind, and Elise found herself back on the couch, looking through her laptop again. The document where she'd pasted bits of their relationship was already open and waiting for her. Halfway into the six pages, she found the paragraph that had caught her eye.

You make everything else go away, Elise. My past, my shitty actions, the things that haunt me at night. Whatever I did before doesn't matter anymore, because with you . . . those things are rectified.

Rectified. Was that a strange choice of word? Did it mean something much bigger than she'd thought? What if there was a small, sick chance Christian had thought loving her might cleanse him of whatever damage he'd done to her sister?

Her stomach clenched, threatening more rebellion, so Elise closed her laptop with a snap.

How the hell was she supposed to get answers from the dead? She'd be better off visiting one of those psychics who hung out a shingle during peak tourist season, as if they'd be living in a crumbling cabin with rusted-out cars in the yard if they had insight into the beyond.

At least Daniel seemed to have left for the day already. She moved to the kitchen window and verified that his truck was gone, then realized she had the perfect excuse to spy on him. She owed him a housekeeping service.

Pressing her lips tight together against another surge of stomach acid, she looked past the reception desk to her housekeeping kit, then back to Daniel's cabin. It wouldn't be wrong to go in. She'd already told him she'd refresh his room.

Screw it. She grabbed her cleaning kit and a stack of towels and walked quickly across the grass to his door. Once there, she knocked with a shaking hand, then peered through the window when there was no answer.

A pair of sunglasses sat on the small dining table, so he obviously hadn't packed up yet. "Housekeeping!" she called into the empty cabin. When she drew the key from her pocket, her face burned, but she kept repeating to herself that she had every right to go inside.

He'd left a paperback on the loveseat. When she clocked it as a spy thriller, she tried not to take that as a sign. A pair of Vans were tucked under the table, but other than that, the compact living area was clean. Even the kitchen only revealed one dirty plate and a coffee mug in the sink. A bag of potato chips and a couple of apples took up most of the counter space.

She moved guiltily past the kitchen area to the bedroom and bathroom. Clutching the towels to her chest, she turned on the bedroom light and looked around.

Daniel had pulled up the comforter, and his clothes were hung neatly in the closet. She edged closer to the open closet door, ducking her head to look for a sniper rifle or other hit man gear stored under the clothing, but she only saw a pair of dress shoes.

Dress shoes. Right. There, on the farthest left side of the space hung a navy-blue suit. She hadn't been mistaken about who she'd seen.

Elise hurried to the bathroom to stack the clean towels on the shelf next to the shower, then went back to the bedroom to open the drawers tucked under the bed. They were empty aside from some socks and underwear that she gingerly moved aside to check for contraband. When she didn't find any, she grabbed the used towels from the bathroom and darted back out to the kitchen.

She checked the kitchen drawers too, then turned in a slow circle to see if she'd missed any hiding spots. She wasn't surprised to discover nothing else; because Daniel wasn't a spy, he was a friend.

"Damn it, Kyle," she muttered, cursing her brother for infecting her with his paranoia. But was it paranoia if he had a right to be worried? Two men had been killed, so *something* dark was going on. But Daniel Serrano?

He'd been nothing but nice to her from childhood on, nothing but supportive of Kyle. She'd talk to Daniel tonight and strike this off her list of anxieties.

Elise hauled the towels outside and said a quick prayer of thanks that he wasn't waiting at the door. Another small mercy. Her therapist had taught her to practice gratitude, and she was damn thankful she hadn't been caught.

But she'd practiced gratitude too quickly, because when she looked toward the parking lot, Daniel was walking around his truck, and he stutter-stepped at the sight of her lurking in front of his open door.

"Oh shit," she whispered, trying to fight the rush of blood that went straight to her face. Either he was in the wrong for being an undercover operative or she was in the wrong for snooping through his things. Either possibility was a vise around the back of her neck.

After hesitating a moment, Daniel raised his hand and grabbed an empty duffel bag out of his truck before heading across the lawn.

I was replacing towels, she told herself. *A totally legit service.* She hadn't replaced the sheets or taken out the garbage, though. Did that make her look more suspicious?

"Hi!" she brayed, her voice trembling and loud.

"Hey there!"

She stepped down to the grass and bounced the dirty towels high. "Just, uh, bringing fresh towels to your room!"

He frowned. Oh God, he *frowned*. "Right," he said dryly. That one skeptical word clutched her heart in its grasp.

Her pulse pounded in her ears as he stalked toward her, his mouth twisted with displeasure. When he finally reached her, Elise scrambled back a step.

"Damn," he said. "I tried to catch you earlier, but the office was closed. I'm checking out tomorrow. So I'm sorry you wasted your time."

Her chest loosened. "Oh?"

"With the towels," he said at her gape-mouthed stare.

"Oh. Of course! No worries. I should have been by yesterday, but . . ." But what? She couldn't tell him she'd gone to the memorial. "I got busy. You were out of here pretty early yesterday. What were you up to?"

"Me?" He shrugged. "Just working on the house. You know. Early bird and all that."

Early bird? Elise stared at him in absolute shock. She'd seen him there, and now she'd seen the suit and dress shoes. Instead of answering her question, he'd only created ten more. Because why the hell would Daniel Serrano lie to her about that memorial service? Now she was too spooked to ask. She'd wait to see what Kyle had to say, because it seemed he might be right again.

"Sure," she said weakly. "Right. Well." She lifted the towels again. "I'd better get going."

"I'm going to pack up a few things and take them over to the house. But I haven't unloaded my furniture yet, so I'll sleep here tonight."

Nodding, she hurried away. Maybe he really hadn't unloaded yet or maybe he had one last job to do before he moved on. Like murdering her.

Her neck burned, but she refused to look back and see if he was watching. This was ridiculous. First, because she was being violently paranoid about a man she'd known forever. Second, because if he was going to murder her, being the only guest around during her death would invite way too much suspicion. He'd wait until after he moved out for sure.

Strangely, that thought didn't make her feel better as she hurried toward the side door and the old mudroom outfitted with an extra-large washer and dryer for the cabins. She dropped his towels in the washer and started it, then regretted her quick action when the machine fired up and the noise blocked out everything else. She needed all her senses right now.

After she washed her hands, she paused, frozen. She should do something. Call her brother, maybe, or start making escape plans? Instead she stared into the garbage at the bottle of gin she'd emptied into the sink that morning. It glinted in the afternoon light like a jewel.

She only had to get through one more night with Daniel there, sleeping a few dozen yards away. Once he checked out, she could think about shutting down the cabins for a bit. She could get in her car and drive away until Kyle put this puzzle together. Then her life would get back to normal and *she'd* get back to normal, toeing the line and pulling her weight in the world. But tonight, she just couldn't.

Screw it. Elise grabbed her purse and keys, and after a quick check that Daniel wasn't coming, she locked the front door behind her and hurried toward the parking lot. She made a wide half circle around Daniel's vehicle, but when she rounded the back, she stopped with such horrified quickness that her feet skidded on the gravel, and she had to throw her arms wide to stop from falling. Not the impression she wanted to make on the woman standing there next to a gray Lexus.

"You're Elise?" Savannah Valic asked, her voice a soft tiptoe across the space between them.

"No," Elise answered.

The woman's delicate face fell into a frown. "You're not?"

For one ridiculous moment, she thought about lying. She hadn't started with that intention. She'd only been denying Savannah's appearance at her home. But perhaps she could carry on with it, pretend she'd dropped by the cabins to deliver something. Point Savannah toward the office and peel out while the woman was still waiting for her knock to be answered.

She could stay with her mother or her brother, tell Daniel to drop the key in the after-hours slot when he was ready to leave. Elise could stay gone for weeks until this woman forgot about her.

She nodded. She had a plan. Distract and retreat. But instead of following through, she opened her mouth and accidentally spoke the truth. "I wasn't expecting to meet you."

Had anything ever been truer than that?

CHAPTER 22

As she led Savannah into her home, Elise's skin buzzed with frantic self-consciousness. "There's coffee," she said, gesturing toward the big pots with a jerk. "Or I could make you herbal tea." That seemed like the kind of thing a woman into yoga and veganism might like. She'd have to remember not to offer cream.

And why was she thinking about such meaningless things as she opened the door to her living area and gestured her ex-lover's widow toward the table?

"Tea would be good."

Thank God. Now Elise had something to do besides sit down with Savannah and look straight into her face. She filled the electric kettle and clicked it on, then looked through her cabinet for her nicest herbal tea. She didn't think Celestial Seasonings would be Savannah's go-to brand.

A chair scraped behind her, and Elise wondered if she'd left crumbs or sticky spots on the table. But what did that matter? Her entire home was a reassurance to this woman that Elise wasn't a peer. Her husband had been slumming it and would never have traded his real life for this mess.

Or maybe Elise looked like the ultimate gold digger, reaching for a taste of the finery that belonged to Savannah and her son. "Sugar?" she asked without turning around.

"Do you have honey?"

"Sure." She opened another cabinet and tried to hide the bear-shaped bottle of supermarket-brand honey as she squeezed a little into a mug.

The lever of the kettle popped up too quickly, and Elise's stalling was finished. She filled the mug and dropped a tea bag in, then grabbed a small plate and spoon from the dishwasher before delivering the whole thing to the table.

Savannah was small and delicate, her wrists tiny, the skin beneath her green eyes bruised. They looked about the same age, despite that she knew Savannah was almost ten years older. She likely had the best estheticians money could buy, and she clearly hadn't started out with forehead wrinkles before her twenties. Her honey-blond hair fell in full waves around her shoulders. In a word, she was beautiful, and Elise felt cheap and clunky next to her.

Desperate to put off whatever this conversation might hold, she made another mug of tea and added white sugar out of sight of Savannah, before she returned to the table to sit across from her.

"This is good," Savannah said, nodding toward the mug as she set it down. Elise felt thankful she'd had the sense to grab one of the hand-made ceramic mugs and not the unicorn mug emblazoned with *I poop rainbows.* She imagined Savannah's cabinets were all glass fronted to show off her gorgeous stoneware, not a Corelle plate or ancient plastic tumbler in sight.

"H-how are you doing?" Elise stammered, because she couldn't think of anything else to say.

"I'm okay, I guess. Or not. It's hard to tell, I'm so tired."

Nodding, she tried to grab on to another thought. "And your son? How is he?"

"Poor baby. I don't really know. He's trying to be supportive, but I can't see what's going on inside him, you know? I'm trying to give him some time. I think he's in shock."

"I'm sure."

"Do you have kids?" Savannah asked.

Elise shook her head, feeling like the complete opposite of this woman. Maybe she could call Kyle and tell him the mystery was solved and it had nothing to do with Robin. Christian had obviously been pulled into this affair by the opposites-attract phenomenon. Not *his* opposite, but his wife's. Elise was poor, prickly, hulking, and vulgar, and Savannah clearly was *not*.

"I'm not sure why I'm here," Savannah said softly, and Elise definitely had no answer for that, so she sipped her tea. It turned sour in her stomach before even a few seconds had passed.

Christian had loved this woman, not in lust or infatuation the way he'd loved Elise, but deeply. She tried not to feel jealous and failed miserably. But she deserved this discomfort. She'd already lost Christian and grieved for him. What must Savannah be going through after living a real life with him and loving him until the end?

"I keep thinking what a good grandfather he would have been." Savannah chuckled and tipped her head up. "Isn't that odd? I know Liam won't have kids for a long time, but I can't stop picturing Christian with more gray in his hair, taking little kids for hikes. He was a good dad, but he was so busy when Liam was young." She fiddled with the spoon. "God, he would've loved having another shot at that. Camping, fishing, skiing. He would have been so amazing."

Elise swallowed. She'd never imagined anything like that for Christian, another reminder that they'd only known each other in a bubble. "I'm sorry," she murmured. "It must be worse with all this uncertainty."

"About you?"

Her face went hot, her mouth dry. "No, I meant the investigation. The other murder."

"Oh right. They won't tell me anything. You know, they really thought you were involved at first."

Elise nodded, thankful that she'd used the past tense.

"That was part of the reason I freaked out so much. I thought he'd ended it recently with you. That he'd broken your heart and maybe . . ."

She laughed. "I don't know. I guess I should have been afraid you'd kill me too, but I had to question you. I had to *know*. And I'm relieved to find out it was a long time ago. That it meant *nothing*."

Ah. Savannah wasn't all fluff and down, and Elise felt the knife slide deep. She couldn't defend herself, not in good conscience. She could only sit and take it as images of Christian flashed through her mind. His eyes crinkling with a smile. The surprising boyishness of his sleeping face. The way he'd held her safe enough to let her guard down and love him back.

Savannah watched her closely, either checking for falsehood or enjoying the blow, but Elise was good at drawing her softest parts into a shell. She nodded and took another sip of tea, willing it to stay down.

"What did he want to tell you?" Savannah asked.

From behind her armor, Elise suddenly realized she should feel fear. What if this ambush had nothing to do with emotions and everything to do with murder? Savannah could have killed her husband. Or perhaps she'd been threatened by Jackson and ordered to fish for information from Elise.

"I'm not sure what he wanted to tell me," Elise finally answered. "We didn't speak."

"Really? He seemed intent. He didn't even call?"

"No."

Savannah slumped a little, curling around her tea as she raised it to her lips. She looked vulnerable again, which allowed Elise to feel braver.

"Why did he want to move here?" she asked.

Savannah blinked slowly as if confused by the question. She gave the barest of headshakes and didn't answer.

"You two could have lived anywhere when he left Stratum. Why here? I've always wondered," she added hastily.

"Oh. He wanted to get back to nature, and it was close enough for me to go to the city to see friends. He said this area reminded him of who he'd been before everything changed."

The hair on Elise's arms rose, pulling her skin tight. "Changed how?"

"With Stratum, I suppose. He said this was where his old life ended, and he wanted to get back to that."

His old life ended. Because of the company or because of a trauma? Elise had talked to Christian about it when they'd first met, and he'd said something similar, but she hadn't been looking for clues. She hadn't known she should. "He said he came here a lot when he was young," she prompted.

"Yeah. His parents had a cousin with a cabin."

"Was that the cabin where he stayed with his college friends too? Do you know where it is?"

Now the woman really looked confused. "I don't know. He took me there once to reminisce, but I wasn't paying attention."

Despite that it would help nothing, Elise felt disappointed. Had she thought she'd be able to feel something if she found the cabin and stood in front of the door? The ghost of her sister? Or even the ghost of Christian?

"I wanted to take a picture with your Bigfoot once," Savannah said, cutting off Elise's questioning. "Christian wouldn't pull over. We actually got into an argument about it because I didn't understand why he was being so rude. But I guess now we know. He didn't want me showing my face here."

Savannah meant that he'd been afraid Elise would see them and run out to start trouble. She thought it more likely he'd wanted to spare Elise the humiliation of watching as he took cute pictures with his cute wife in front of that stupid, shabby sign. But Savannah wouldn't want to hear that. She needed Elise to mean nothing.

"We weren't in contact, if you're wondering," Elise offered, though she wasn't sure if it was out of sympathy or caution. "He did reach out with that email the police showed you, but that was the extent of it. I hadn't seen him in a long time. We didn't talk. He never tried to keep in touch afterward."

"So why did he want to see you?"

"All I know is what he wrote. He said he was in therapy and working on himself. But I didn't want to see him."

"Because you still had feelings?" Savannah pressed.

Elise allowed herself to grimace. "It felt like I'd moved on, and no offense, I wasn't interested in being part of his growth or journey or whatever it was. I'm not . . ." She gestured toward her living room, the sagging couch and scuffed floors. "I have my hands full running this place every day. That's what I have energy for." She left off the second part. That it must be nice to have time and money to spend on yoga and daily therapy and healing retreats, but some people had to deal with their problems on the move from the moment they were born.

Savannah nodded. "He changed a lot in the last couple of years. He really tried to put in the time, you know? I did too. Things were better than they'd ever been. We were going to take a big trip to Iceland. Mineral waters and the northern lights. Now . . . Jesus. Now I guess I need to start canceling things."

Elise couldn't listen to how beautiful their relationship had been. The future they'd anticipated together. If Savannah was innocent, Elise owed her something, but did she owe her an exposed wound and a handful of salt?

Holding her breath, she let the pain settle. Savannah would be pelted with reminders every single day. A flight to be canceled. An email about the dental appointment scheduled months in advance. One of his socks showing up in her laundry.

Elise had tossed all her own reminders of Christian in the trash the week after he broke things off. Her pain had nothing on Savannah's. It wasn't even close. "I'm sorry," she said again, and she meant it, but she had bigger problems now. "Who do they think did it?"

Savannah gave that bitter chuckle again. "I've been so obsessed with you I've barely paid attention to the investigation, which is really stupid, isn't it? Shouldn't I care more about that?"

When Elise held her tongue, Savannah looked up with a sharp gaze, and that was the first time she looked like a true danger. Was the delicate vulnerability all an act? Was it a tool she used to get through life? Elise felt a distant admiration at the thought.

But then the moment passed, and she turned back into the grieving widow. "They haven't told me much lately. I might be a suspect myself. But they definitely asked a lot of questions about Stratum."

"About . . . Jackson?"

That sharp look again. "Yes. Why do you ask?"

Elise shrugged, trying to buy a few seconds to think. "It just . . . seems like the obvious direction, right?"

"Yeah. There was bad blood there."

Elise tried to hide the jolt that went through her at those words. "I didn't realize. Why was there bad blood?"

"A million things over the years. Billy could be ruthless, and Christian didn't believe in following every killer instinct. He hated that going public meant pushing exponential growth over everything else. He wanted to invest in the employees, in building something solid."

Elise didn't process much after *killer instinct*.

"He was a good man," Savannah said, though it sounded so much like a question that Elise had to nod in response. Yes. Despite everything, he had been a good man. Probably.

She didn't speak. What the hell could she tell this woman about her husband that she didn't already know? They'd been partners. Elise had been a pothole in the road they'd traveled.

Could she have been more if she'd only asked for it? She didn't think so. Her great appeal had been her loose ties, fluttering in the wind like something that needed to be caught. Once you caught them, then what? A tie was a tie, and the knots with Savannah were more secure.

"I should go," the woman said, setting down her spoon with a clank. "I don't know why I came. The police were already mad when they found out I'd talked to you. Maybe they think we teamed up."

She laughed again, but the amusement crumpled, crushing her laugh into a sob.

"Oh," Elise said, getting up from her chair, but Savannah waved her off and squeezed her eyes shut. One deep breath and she was calm again. "I won't cry in front of you," she whispered.

Elise dropped back into the chair. She'd want the same thing too. To seem strong and together and absolutely not falling apart. "I'm sorry," she said one more time.

Savannah pushed herself carefully up like a woman afraid her legs wouldn't hold her. But they did. "I'd like to ask you not to tell anyone. I don't want people looking at me that way."

Elise nodded. "Of course." She didn't want anyone looking at her that way either.

"Who already knows?" Savannah pressed. The gesture she flicked toward Elise spoke of distaste. "About you and Christian?"

Elise piled yet another lie onto all the others. "No one." Kyle might work in tech, but his path would never cross Savannah's in a million years.

"Good." It was her last word, and she walked away and disappeared into the reception area. When Elise got up to escort her out, Savannah was already gone, the front door left open. A few moments later, her car started, and she backed out quickly before swinging around and racing down the drive, gravel pinging and dust churning up behind her like she wanted to leave a physical reminder of her pain, if only until the wind took it.

Elise stared, her heart a slow, heavy thump in her chest. She'd never hated his wife because the woman had been no more than an idea, but today she was real. Now she couldn't hate Savannah *because* she was real.

Elise was the one who'd been a fantasy. A phantom removed from the real world of deadlines and dirty bathrooms and tax planning and illness and in-laws and problems at school. She'd always been removed from that world because she'd set herself to the side, nothing more than a flashy sign on the side of the road where people could stop to amuse themselves for a moment.

Caught up in her regret, she picked her purse back up and headed for the door, knowing she'd need to numb herself again.

The anticipation of an ice-cold gin and tonic filled her mind so completely that it wasn't until she had one foot out the door that an awful thought hit Elise. She'd made a terrible mistake.

The memory of what she'd said to Savannah seized her with such fear that she scrambled back inside to slam the door and lock it tight. She'd promised Savannah that no one else knew about the affair with Christian . . . which meant Elise had set herself up as the last threat that needed eliminating.

CHAPTER 23

Chewing her thumbnail, she faced the darkness of her blank laptop screen and focused on nothing. She'd been treating Savannah with an empathy born of sticky guilt, but despite her frail wrists and bruised eyes, Savannah wasn't helpless.

Christian had sold his shares of Stratum for something like $150 million. With smart investing, he might have been worth half a billion when he died. And now it was all his widow's. She had power Elise couldn't imagine.

Maybe it was all an act, and she hadn't loved Christian at the end. Maybe his decisions and his power had been twin barbs beneath her skin, digging and tearing until she craved a clean break.

Her husband had sold his shares and moved his family from Silicon Valley and all its luxuries to a gilded wilderness. Instead of living among her peers, she'd been shut up on an estate surrounded by half-empty mansions and villages dotted with trailer homes. Instead of having the best schools down the street, their son had been in a mediocre private school a forty-minute drive away. Perhaps she'd come back from the separation determined not to make it work but to take everything he had.

After all, instead of grieving their separation, Christian had jumped right into an affair with a foul-mouthed local with all the morals of a stray cat.

Could Savannah have found out about that email? Or could Jackson have intercepted it and told Savannah all about the secrets of August 1999? Her mind twisted and turned, looking for connections.

Elise could imagine the conversation, the laying out of ugly facts. The real reason for her husband's obsession with Willow Canyon. The secret he'd been hiding. The sick affair with the sister. The danger and filth he might drag Savannah and her son into. What if Jackson had offered her freedom from all that with no repercussions?

Because Savannah was free now, wasn't she? More than that, she was also incredibly rich. She could return to the bosoms of her peers, and she'd barely be a blip on the detectives' radar. After all, her husband might be dead, but so was another man, and Savannah certainly wasn't a sniper.

And what had she meant when she said Jackson had a killer instinct? Was he just another ruthless CEO, or was he a step beyond that?

Then again, how much of a step was it when corporations routinely cut safety measures and sick pay to increase earnings by exponential amounts? When they moved factories to countries where workers were locked in dormitories as forced labor? Maybe a couple of dead men seemed like nothing to a man who hung out with mining moguls and factory barons who had blood on their hands every quarter.

Her heart beat harder at her growing belief that Kyle could be right. Maybe Elise had been looking at all this from the perspective of a bug looking up at a beast. How could she understand how a man worth a billion dollars might think? How could she comprehend the casual evils of power?

Elise put the heels of her hands to her eyes and pressed until she saw phantom fireworks and her eyeballs ached. God, she'd been so worried about Kyle, and now she was losing it, following thoughts down twisted tunnels until she couldn't see anything in the dark.

"Oh God," she moaned, telling herself that the simplest explanation was most likely. Except . . . the simplest explanation was that the spouse was always the main suspect, and that didn't make her feel any better, because she hadn't made one mistake with Savannah; she'd made several.

First, she'd expressed too much interest in Christian's past. Second, she'd asked about Jackson, clueing Savannah in that she knew enough about the man to be suspicious. Then she'd topped it all off by telling Savannah that nobody else knew about any of it.

She woke her phone to text Kyle about Savannah's visit, but her eye caught on the pop-up notification on Facebook.

Valeria. When Elise opened the app, she found two messages waiting. Both were from Valeria, and her pulse fluttered in her ears, muffling the rest of her hearing.

> *Elise! It's been so long! You're all grown up now!* 😄 *I love the rental place you're running. So fun. I'll have to come by and see you next time we're back. We try to make it up every few years. As for the letters, I was couch surfing that summer and didn't manage to hold on to much, but I know I kept Robin's last letters when I heard she'd gone missing. I can't tell if that feels like yesterday or a lifetime ago. I'll check and see what I can find. Good to hear from you.*

The second message had arrived an hour later and was frustratingly short.

> *I found them! Give me your email address. I'll scan everything and send them over right away.*

Right away? That had been hours ago. Elise grimaced and quickly typed in her email address, along with a friendly response she tried hard to make coherent.

Impatience coursed through her as soon as she hit send. She paced for five minutes, skin crawling with discomfort, before she grabbed her keys and dared to set foot outside again.

She couldn't go on like this without a drink, not with her memories and emotions all breaking apart into pieces that cut and scraped against her soul. She'd lost too much already, hadn't she?

She'd accepted what had happened to Robin, and she'd moved on and made a small life for herself. Just this. Just a job and a home and a friend or two, and the knowledge that if she couldn't trust anyone else, she could at least trust herself.

Now what the hell did she have?

She slammed her car door, but while she was putting on her seat belt, something roared behind her. She twisted and spotted the grille of a truck and then a flash of white as it skidded to a stop next to her.

Dumbstruck, she sat there as the truck's door opened. This was it. It was her turn.

She caught only a glimpse of a face before the man moved around her, and it took two heartbeats to register that it was Daniel. Relief churned through her like a storm.

It took two more heartbeats to remember Daniel was a threat too, and that was one beat too long. He was at her door, mouth a tight downturn of tension, brow pulled into a hard V.

"We need to talk," he said past the glass, and oh God, word had gotten back to whoever was pulling these strings, because why else would Daniel be this upset with her?

When she shook her head and started her car, he drew back in shock and raised a hand. "Elise! I didn't know!"

Didn't know what? That he was working for a murderer? That she was next on the list? She wanted to pull away, but what if he was trying to help? Couldn't she use a little fucking help?

But she couldn't get out. No one else was here. And she damn sure wasn't letting him into her car. Never let danger into your car. Never let anyone move you to a second location. Never—

"Elise?"

When she threw her car into reverse and hit the gas, Daniel scrambled back. She steered in jerky corrections, barreling back twenty feet before skidding into a three-point turn. She drove almost all the way to the highway, until her world was filled with passing cars instead of birdsong. That was where she stopped, leaving her engine running as she opened her door and stepped out, phone in hand.

Daniel was still frozen next to her cabin, his mouth an O of shock.

"You didn't know what?" she shouted.

He looked from side to side, then back to her, his shoulders rising toward his ears as he shoved his hands into the pockets of his jeans. "What the hell, Elise?"

"If you want to talk," she called, "let's do it out here." When she jerked her head toward the road, he took a tentative step forward before pausing as if to consider his options. After a few long moments, he started toward her. He'd been serious before. Now he looked twisted into knots, as if she'd thrown a wrench into his plans. Good.

"What is this all about, Daniel?" she demanded when he drew within fifteen feet.

"I don't know. I just heard it myself. Someone texted, and . . ."

"And what?" She braced herself for a terrible truth. That the monsters were at her door. That Daniel had helped lead them there.

He glanced back at his truck like he was still confused about how she'd gotten away. "He didn't say anything to me. I've never even heard of that podcast. If I'd known, I would have talked him out of it."

She shifted back, frowning so hard the muscles of her forehead trembled. "What are you talking about? What podcast?"

Daniel frowned just as hard. "The podcast Kyle was on."

"I have no idea what you're saying."

"He was a guest on some conspiracy show. He told everyone that these murders have something to do with Robin. You didn't know?"

She checked her phone as if the screen would offer an answer. There were no messages, but who would text her about something like that?

Amber was too busy to spend her mornings trolling the internet, and anyone else . . . Well, she didn't have anyone else, did she? Her world wasn't too small; it was too big, far flung and spread out among hundreds of friends and lovers she'd found easily and discarded in a flash. They didn't know where she was from, didn't know about her sister, and certainly wouldn't associate her with these murders.

"I don't understand," she said, her words chewed up by a passing truck.

"Hold on. I'll send the link."

He'd either added the Creekside number to his contacts or he had her number for some other reason, because the text dinged right away. She looked dumbly down at the name of some podcast she'd never heard of.

"What did he say?"

"He said these murders are obviously related, and he thinks they have to do with the disappearance of Robin twenty-five years ago. He said both men were here that month, and he has pictures of them all together. He thinks they raped and killed her."

Panic blasted through her, and the sweat that had bloomed everywhere on her body when Daniel had appeared now turned to slick ice on her skin. "What did he say about me?" she demanded.

Daniel shook his head. "Nothing. But he's coming back on next week, so I can't promise he won't mention you then."

He hadn't ruined her yet, but he would. "Jesus, Kyle," she spat, but Daniel distracted her by stepping closer.

"Stop," she said, raising a hand.

He stopped. "What's wrong? Why are you acting like this?"

"There's a lot of weird shit happening, and I don't know who's involved."

His head dropped, bending his neck in a weary curve. "Kyle really got into your head, huh?"

"No! Don't blame this on him. It's *you.*"

That jerked his head back up. *"Me?"*

"Yes, you. Have any deep, dark secrets you want to reveal?"

He had his dumbfounded look down pat, and her anger returned full force with his stupid wide-eyed shrug.

"You lied to me," she said, nearly spitting the words. "I saw you at Christian's memorial! So you had some reason to be there, and you also had a reason to lie to me about it later. How can you explain that, Daniel?"

"Oh." He slumped a little. "That."

"Yes, *that*."

"I'm truly sorry. But I *can* explain."

She rolled her eyes, because she'd heard that before. Men always had an explanation, but it was her choice if she was going to keep accepting the bullshit.

"I did lie," Daniel admitted, his lovely hazel eyes pretending regret, "but only because you really tensed up when I asked if you were going to the funeral. Your face went pale. I thought you were trying to avoid talking about it or thinking about it. That's all."

"That's *all*? That's your explanation? How about you explain what the hell you were doing at the funeral of a man you say you didn't know."

His head bobbed quickly, trying to calm her down with his agreement. "My cousin Clara is an event planner in South Tahoe. This is her slow season, so she needed help with organizing and setting up. The chairs and lectern. Outdoor carpet. And then tables for dining in the backyard. She doesn't have a lot of staff on hand until ski season gets going and the J-1 workers return."

"Clara?" Elise whispered, her head swimming.

"She's a few years older than me. I'm not sure you ever knew her."

Convenient, maybe, but he looked so sincere, his hands open at his sides, turned up in a plea, his eyes unflinching when he met her gaze. And he looked so damn sad. What the hell was she supposed to do with that?

"Did you think I was involved in this?" he asked.

She rubbed her forehead, pushing hard to free up her brain. "I don't know what to think. Nothing makes any sense." Her temples began to throb.

"Elise, come on. When Kyle let slip that you were in love with the guy . . ."

"Don't!" she warned. "That's nobody's business!" When he reached toward her, Elise stepped back, and he snapped his hand away as if she'd screamed.

"Shit, I thought . . ." He dragged a clawed hand through his hair, glancing up at the sky for guidance. "You and I . . . Can we go inside and talk?"

Alarm flared through her at the suggestion. "No, we can't."

"Okay, sure." He moved back a step, putting more distance between them. "I'm sorry I lied about the funeral. I just wanted to avoid a difficult topic. But I think this stuff with Kyle is . . ." He gestured toward her phone. "Please listen to the podcast. This isn't healthy, Elise. Be careful."

Her mind spun. Of course this wasn't healthy. A sister being murdered wasn't healthy either, but it was still real and all-encompassing, so he had a lot of nerve implying she was overreacting.

But what the hell was Kyle thinking, making this Stratum theory public? If it wasn't true, he'd look insane. And if it was true . . . Shit, it looked more and more like it was, and Elise couldn't let her guard down, not even with Daniel. "You're leaving, right? You can drop your key in the box when you've cleared out. I'll email the final receipt tonight."

He looked hurt by the distance in her words, but Elise couldn't help that. She'd hurt plenty of people for less important reasons. She wasn't taking any chances with two dead men in her rearview mirror.

"I've got to get going," she said as she edged back into the open doorway of her car. "I'll listen to the podcast."

"Stay safe, okay?"

Elise didn't know how to answer that, so she closed her door, locked it, and drove away without bothering to try.

CHAPTER 24

She mixed her third gin and tonic, trying to numb a stomach that kept knotting and turning as she listened to Kyle's interview. She was swimming through his words, shocked not by what he said—he'd explained it to her already—but from the way the entire theory was laid out so logically, each fact leading ruthlessly to the next.

Kyle made it sound like the truth must be inevitable. And that meant terrible things for Elise: that she'd loved a murderer, or something close to one. That she'd been a kind of perverted avatar for her sister's corpse.

But that couldn't be, because how could she survive it?

She gulped as much of her third drink as she could, and then she called her brother. He didn't answer, but she wasn't in the mood to give up and called him right back. He finally picked up the second time she hit redial.

"Are you in danger?" he asked.

"No."

"Then I'm busy with work."

"Don't you dare hang up. Don't you dare! How could you tell everyone?"

"Oh," Kyle said, his irritation softening. "You heard the podcast?"

"What do you think you're doing?" she cried, her gesture wide enough to slosh a splash of cocktail over her hand. She put her knuckles to her mouth before lowering the level in the glass by taking another big drink. "You have the nerve to complain about me showing my face at a funeral when you drew a giant target on both of us with that interview?"

"I'm getting the truth out there. People have been treating Jackson like he's under threat. Now they're taking another look at him and his past."

"They're going to come after you now!"

"Better than them coming after you. Are you drunk?"

"No!" she answered, her tone exposing her lie. Anyway, she wasn't drunk. She'd only had two. And a half.

"I thought you weren't doing that anymore," he said, his voice an infuriating whine in her ear.

"Yeah, well, I just found out my last boyfriend probably wanted to get to my dead sister through my naked body, so I've declared a holiday from sobriety, Kyle."

"Does that mean you believe me?"

Elise groaned and slipped lower on the couch, cradling her drink against her chest as if it were an emotional support cocktail. She'd never had a dog or a cat or even a hamster. Pets always left. They only lived a few years. She couldn't handle love when it was shadowed with the anticipation of deep grief.

Or maybe she just couldn't handle love, period.

"You do believe me," Kyle said, and she felt like she finally had his full attention, no screen to pull his eye from her, no thoughts spinning through his ears.

"I don't know," she whispered. "I don't know. I don't know. I'm . . ." Her throat swelled up with an awful ache, squeezing her voice to a rasp. "I'm just so sad, Kyle."

"I'm sorry, Lise. I really am."

She coughed or laughed, she wasn't sure which, but she managed to dislodge the sorrow. "It's better than being scared. I escaped that after the first drink, so mission accomplished."

"You don't have to be scared anymore. That's why I did the podcast. Now they understand I know everything, and the public will too. So there's no point in coming after you, Baby Sis. That would only prove the whole case."

She pressed the side of the icy glass to her hot face. He was right. She didn't have to think about slipping up with Savannah anymore. "But now I have to worry about you," she countered.

"Nah. I'll be fine. We're both safer with everything out in the public."

Elise stared at the dark crack where one of the blinds didn't quite reach the windowsill. She'd left the lights dim, but she wondered if she should do more to block any line of sight. "I don't want anyone to know, Kyle. About me and Christian." Tears spilled down her cheeks and dripped into the glass. "Please. No one needs to know that. I thought he loved me. And now I feel so fucking ashamed. I feel disgusting. I thought we were . . ."

What had she thought? That she was the one woman sleeping with an honest and honorable married man? That he'd meant his whispered words and the promises he made with his body? So many promises. It had all felt so *real*. But apparently her barometer for reality was broken just like the rest of her.

"There's no way to stop this," Kyle said. "The truth is going to come out one way or another."

"Don't say that."

"Jackson has to pay for what he's done. Do you want him to get away with it just to protect your reputation?"

This time it was a real laugh, because how stupid did that sound? She'd burned her reputation to the ground the first moment she'd had a chance, because a woman's reputation was only a leash meant to make her heel. But she still had pride, and that couldn't survive this.

Her heart, though . . . that was a lost cause. It had only been a tiny sprout peeking up from dry dirt, and it had been summarily ground back into dust.

Good riddance.

But her pride? Yeah, she'd never be able to trust her own instincts again. Never be able to even trust her body to pleasure. Who was she without that? It felt like the same seismic shift that had broken her when she'd become a girl without a big sister.

"Poor Robin," she murmured. "What do you think really happened?"

"I'm still not sure. You never got anything from Valeria?"

She'd forgotten about that in her eagerness to drown her sorrows in good gin. "I don't know. I'll check my email after this."

"Okay, let me know anything you find. Want me to come spend the night?"

No, she wanted to be alone. She wanted to drink and rage and put on loud music. She hadn't been lying when she'd said she wasn't afraid now. She was too pissed and in pain to fear anything, like the punk bitch she'd always been. "I'm good. Concentrate on watching out for yourself. You're in this now."

"Oh, believe me, I know. I have a couple of trusted contacts who are holding files for me on the off chance something happens. But I made that clear in the interview."

Right. That sounded familiar, though her ears had been a bit muddled by rage as she'd listened. She hung up, and the podcast picked up where it had silenced itself for the phone call as she listened for the second time.

The host seemed extremely eager to buy into Kyle's story, taking every opportunity to rail against information as a commodity and, of course, the wealth and power imbalances in this country. She let them talk as she checked her email, but stopped the playback as soon as she spotted that a treasure trove of eight image files awaited her.

After snatching her computer from the table, Elise started downloading the files and waited impatiently for her internet connection to complete the task. It took long enough that she had plenty of time to finish her drink. She thought about getting herself some water, but the files were finally there, and she set her glass down and clicked on the first one.

Robin's familiar loops of handwriting filled her screen, and Elise said, "Hey, Big Sister," without meaning to. "I mean, I know you're not here," she mumbled. "I'm not stupid."

She didn't believe in spirits, though she'd wanted to for a long time. If Robin's soul had been anywhere around, she'd have given them a sign, surely? "I guess you were too busy at that big college party in the sky, huh? I bet those angels are hot."

Okay, maybe she was drunk. Really drunk. The realization surged through her on a wave of pleasure. It felt great to be back, baby.

"Concentrate," she ordered herself.

Hey, Superstar! How's Hollywood? I'm so excited you got an actual audition!!! All my fingers are crossed right now! Yes, even while I'm writing this! HAHA I know you're going to kill it. You're so talented, and you know it. That's the key. You present yourself like a girl with the whole world ahead of her. And you're beautiful too. Double trouble.

Elise rubbed her dry eyes and scanned ahead. She'd pore over every word later. Memorize them. Dream of them. But for now she needed answers, and it was clear from the next paragraph that Robin had sent this letter right after she got home from camp, but there was nothing helpful. She glanced over the rest of it and moved on to the next image. When that one was a bust, she got up to pour another drink. She needed to keep this buzz at the right level: kick ass and confident.

Minutes later she opened the seventh image and found it was the backside of the letter she'd started in image six. A glance at the bottom of the page showed that it must continue into the last file too.

. . . have to let me know when you find a permanent place. If it's soon enough, I could drive down to see you

before school starts. Otherwise I might not see you until Christmas! And you can always come visit me, of course.

I hope my roommate is cool, or she's going to hate that I've already invited everyone to visit. Oops. I wish Katy had decided to room with me, but she's in honors housing, the snob! As if I'd ever get her into trouble. Haha.

Speaking of trouble, I met a cute guy from Stanford this weekend. I know, I know. Rich kids. But he's nice. I'm hoping he'll be at the bonfire Wednesday. If not, I'll make out with someone else. More on all of that later!

Breath ragged and hands unsteady, Elise raced through the rest of the note, then opened the last image file, but Robin didn't mention the Stanford boy again. "More later," she muttered to herself as she looked one more time. But Robin must have meant she'd write again after the bonfire.

Elise scanned back and checked the date. Robin had written it only two days before her disappearance.

After lurching to her feet, she paced clumsily around, one hand rubbing the prickly nape of her neck. A cute Stanford guy. How many fucking Stanford guys had been hanging around with locals that August? Five? Ten?

Or had it been only those three?

CHAPTER 25

A phone was ringing somewhere. Her phone, if the ringtone was any indication.

Elise swept a hand over the comforter, first on top of it, then beneath. Nothing. But the phone stopped ringing, so she pulled her arm back into warmth.

She'd just returned to sleep when a text dinged, bringing her back to consciousness. Groaning, she crooked her arm over her eyes and tugged the covers higher. A cold front had clearly moved in overnight, because it was way too chilly to get out of bed.

She wasn't hungover, at least. She had a vague memory of making mac and cheese very late in the evening, so it seemed the carbs had absorbed the last of the alcohol and saved her from herself.

When Elise finally dared to open her eyes, she spotted her phone on the far end of the mattress. It lay dangerously close to the edge, but she didn't have to brave the cold to get to it. After sneaking her arm back out from beneath the covers, she eased herself over to retrieve it.

"Oh jeez," she groaned when she saw the stack of alerts on the lock screen. Texts from her mom, a missed call from Amber, and a missed call and text from Kyle.

That was when it hit her. Valeria's letter and the mention of the cute guy from Stanford.

Christian. It had to be him.

But no, she was being biased. She thought Christian the obvious owner of that description, but Quinn had been boyishly cute too, and even Jackson had been okay in a 1990s bully kind of a way. Robin could have been talking about any one of them.

She touched the alert from her mom and frowned at the message. Do NOT come over. I won't even answer the door if you do. She'd sent it at one thirty in the morning.

"What?" Elise muttered, scrolling back farther. The previous message didn't reveal much more. You can pick up the letters tomorrow. NO DRIVING.

"Oh shit." The text poked a tiny hole in the dam of her memories, and suddenly her mind was working. First in a slow leak, then in a rush.

She'd called her mom late last night, and she remembered the effort she'd put into enunciating very carefully when she'd asked her about . . . what? Whatever they'd spoken about, her mother had lost her temper when Elise had said she was coming over. *You're clearly drunk, Elise. Go to bed. We'll talk tomorrow.* Elise had stubbornly insisted she needed the letters right then.

The letters. She sat up straight, no longer feeling the cold. For some reason, her pickled brain had worked through a puzzle the night before, and she'd had a late-night realization that there might be more of Robin's things she and Kyle had never seen.

She'd called her mom and asked if the police had ever returned the evidence they'd taken from the girls' shared bedroom, evidence they'd collected almost two weeks after the disappearance.

There wasn't much, her mom had said, her voice creaking with sleep. *I wanted them to take everything, but they only took a few notes and a T-shirt from her dirty clothes. Said they needed to get her scent for bloodhounds or something. But I don't believe they ever tried that, despite what they told me. I don't believe they did much of anything.*

And they kept all of her stuff?

Yes, but they finally dropped the last of it off a year or so after Phoenix confessed and did their job for them. I just tucked everything back into her dresser.

It was late morning now, almost ten. Elise jumped out of bed to get dressed. She was brushing her teeth when she paged through the texts she'd sent Kyle the night before, all of them belligerent demands.

Do NOT tell that podcaster about me, Kyle.

I don't give you permission, you asshole.

It's nobody's business but mine.

Are you trying to ruin my fucking life?

He hadn't responded to any of them, probably because she'd sent them about the same time she'd called her mom. His text from this morning only said, You up?

She wiped her mouth and was about to return Kyle's call with an apology, but something stopped her just before she hit the button. Anything she told him now would wind up on that podcast. He'd said as much, hadn't he? He wanted the whole truth to come out, not bits and pieces.

That was what she'd been thinking at one in the morning. That everyone would know about her and Christian, a relationship so private she hadn't even told any friends. Now, if she told him about Valeria's letter, about the cute Stanford guy, he'd spill that too, plus whatever else she found at her mom's house. She needed to think carefully before she gave him more information.

Right now, she'd grab the letters in that dresser, get some food and coffee, and then make a decision about what to tell Kyle.

Once she brushed her wild hair into submission, Elise looked less like a woman who'd gone on a bender and more like a tired thirty-five-year-old dealing with the normal stress of adulthood. Still, she tugged a gray knit cap over her hair and hoped the pillow creases across her cheek would fade before she got to her mom's. Then again, her mother already knew she'd been blitzed the night before, so what did it matter?

The shame she felt came as a surprise. She'd never bothered trying to hide her drinking before. She'd worn it like a badge. But now she felt embarrassed to knock on her own mother's door. If the evidence wasn't waiting there, she would have avoided her mom for weeks, but she had no choice. Time to face the music.

Unfortunately, quite a bit more music awaited her than she'd anticipated. When Elise opened her front door, Amber was standing there, hand raised to knock.

"Oh hey!" Elise chirped, grateful she'd already cleaned up as she faked a good mood. The cold air sent a shiver through her.

"Hi." Amber didn't sound chirpy at all. She sounded downright tense as her breath puffed white in front of her. "Are you okay?"

"Sure, why?"

"Uh, because you called me in the middle of the night."

Her stomach sank, doing a double flip on the way. "Oh" was all she managed to say as her mind followed the tumble of her gut. Had she confessed everything? Babbled about Christian?

"My phone was muted, but you left a message." Amber's face had drawn into a tight frown, and Elise's heart sank. If she'd told Amber the truth last night, she'd have to face it later. But not now. "I . . . I'm so sorry. I'm not sure what I said, but please don't jump to any conclusions."

"You didn't say much, just that you wanted to talk. So here I am. You seemed pretty upset."

"Okay. Yeah, I'm sorry." Relieved, she immediately latched on to a lie to keep her anxiety at bay. "I had a bit of celebration last night. Daniel checked out, and he was the last reservation on the books for a while. I think I'm going to take a break. Clear my head."

"It didn't sound like much of a celebration, except that you were obviously drunk. What's going on?"

"Nothing, really. It's been a stressful season."

Amber glanced past Elise, clearly expecting to be invited in. Elise had never kept her standing in the doorway before.

"I'm on my way to my mom's," she said, edging past Amber to close the door behind her.

"Elise, I'm worried about you."

"No, don't worry! Everything's fine!"

Amber put her hands on her hips and leaned closer. "Everything is not fine. You're acting weird, and you're lying to me."

Elise felt her face flush and couldn't do anything to stop it. "I told you I've been stressed."

"Stressed enough to start getting drunk again, apparently. I thought you were done with that." She raised her eyebrows in clear question, but Elise ignored it. "And you mentioned Robin again last night. What the hell is going on, Elise? Is this about that stupid podcast Kyle did?"

She winced. "You know about that?"

"I haven't listened to it yet, but John heard something about it. I assume that's why you asked me for those letters. And last night you said something about that Christian guy too."

She'd been starting to turn away, to ease toward the porch stairs and her waiting car. But that question stopped her cold. "I . . . What did I say about him?"

Amber must have seen something like the truth in Elise's face, because she narrowed her eyes. "You also asked about that name at my house. You asked if I remembered anyone named Christian from that summer, *and* that's the name of the man who died on the trail last week. That's not a coincidence. Tell me what the hell is going on."

"Nothing!"

That final false note seemed to pierce something in Amber's mind because she suddenly drew back, her chin tucking in as her eyes went wide. "Jesus, Elise. Did you have something to do with that?" Elise shook her head, but Amber kept talking. "You were fishing for information when John was still out on the search. Oh my God!"

"No, no, no," Elise promised. "It wasn't like that. I wasn't involved. The police already cleared me."

"*Cleared* you?" Amber's shout echoed out to the hills. "Cleared you of *what*?"

Everything was spiraling out of control. She couldn't lose the only real friend she had.

"Just listen, please. I knew him, okay? Christian Valic. I knew him, and Kyle thinks he started up a friendship with me because of Robin. At first I thought he was crazy, but now I think it might be true."

Amber was shaking her head, so Elise rushed on to cut off whatever denial she had brewing. "Just *listen*, Amber. There are pictures from that summer! Pictures of Robin at a party with Christian and that other man who was shot. Do you remember any of that? I'll have Kyle send you the photos. You might recognize them. Something is going on here, and I don't know what it is."

Amber's eyes were even wider now. "What the hell are you talking about? Phoenix Whit killed Robin. We all know it was him because he admitted it. There's no mystery here."

"He's in those pictures too! They *all* knew each other. Wait, I'll see if Kyle left copies." But when she reached for the door, Amber grabbed her wrist.

"I don't want to look at any pictures, Elise. This is not okay. *You're* not okay."

"You said you came here to talk, and I'm talking to you!"

Amber let go and threw her hands wide in exasperation. "I came to talk about the fact that you called me, drunk and crying, at almost two in the morning! I didn't come to review Kyle's latest conspiracy theory with you! Have you considered that if you were sober, you wouldn't be getting sucked into this?"

"That's not what this is about!" Now Elise was shouting, and she didn't care. If Amber wasn't going to listen, she wasn't going to keep trying to explain, so she stomped down the stairs to get on with her plans. "Christian knew Robin and he never told me. Doesn't that seem a little suspicious?"

"I didn't even know the guy," Amber said from behind her as Elise stormed toward her car. "And you couldn't have been very good friends if you never told me about—" Her footsteps went silent, but Elise kept walking.

"Oh my God," Amber said almost too softly to hear.

Elise was feet from her car. She'd scoot around to the driver's side and get in, and then—

"Were you *screwing* this guy?"

Her heart dropped out of her body and rolled away. It was the one thing Amber couldn't abide. Cheating. It hadn't bothered Elise too much when they'd discussed it, because her cheating days had already been over. But she'd tried calmly explaining that the "other woman" trope was tired nonsense. The onus was on the person in the partnership, the person who'd made promises and commitments. And life was complicated. Love was complex. People grew and changed.

Amber had rejected all of it, complaining bitterly about nasty bitches who bragged about their rich married boyfriends while getting their hair cut and colored. So Elise lied to her one more time. "No. I wasn't."

But when she got into her car and Amber didn't try to stop her, she knew her friend didn't believe her, so Elise drove off and left her behind. If their friendship was over, Elise wasn't going to beg and grovel just to get dropped like a stone anyway. She needed a friend who'd help her through this. Help her process the bone-deep horror that she'd let a man who'd killed her sister into her body. That she'd loved those defiled hands.

"No," she said aloud when tears began to press at her eyes. "No crying." She couldn't show up at her mom's house looking like a hot mess. She'd stay calm and keep it together.

Amber hadn't seen all the evidence. She couldn't understand it. Someday, when all of this was over, Elise would apologize and try to explain. If Amber couldn't accept that, then she wasn't a real friend, and Elise would have to move on and make new ones. She met people every damn day during the busy season. No fucking worries.

She felt nearly calm by the time she reached her old house, but as always, as soon as she got out, her muscles started going tight. Today old memories were egged on by her own embarrassment, and she was weighed down by dread by the time she knocked. The icy wind snatched at her like ghosts tugging at her clothes.

Her timid tapping must have been too quiet, because no one responded. She knocked again before opening the door a few inches. "Mom?" The house was so still it seemed to be holding its breath, and when she slipped inside, it felt almost stuffy from the sun beating in through the big front windows.

Frowning, Elise listened for a hint about her mom's whereabouts. She had to be home because she never left.

"Hello?" she called out, taking a few steps in. "Mom!" she called again, and this time a bit of fear invaded her voice. She'd discussed that evidence on the phone last night. What if someone had been listening? What if the letters held valuable information, and she'd clued them in to exactly where they were?

Elise turned left and moved quickly down the short hallway, going first to her mother's bedroom. Both the bedroom and bathroom were dark, so she immediately moved back toward Robin's room. *Her* room. It looked neat as ever, nothing disturbed.

She took a step inside, intending to open each of the nine drawers of the long white dresser to see if she found an evidence package, but something thumped in a different part of the house. She froze, straining her ears to listen. Terrible pictures began to slide through her mind. Her mom on the floor. Her mom locked behind a closet door. A man waiting around the corner with a gun.

She squeezed her eyes shut for a brief moment, trying to gather some courage when her body wanted to stay as still as possible. Her mother might need her, so she had to be brave.

Tiptoeing, Elise forced herself to move down the hallway, carefully avoiding the spot across from the bathroom that always squeaked, just as she had when she'd snuck around during her teen years.

The corner leading to the kitchen came too quickly, but she couldn't pause or she'd freeze, so she crept steadily forward and tipped her head out to look.

Her mom wasn't in the kitchen, either at the table or by the fridge or collapsed on the linoleum. No one was in the kitchen except Pierre, who blinked lazily at her from the heat register next to the back door. The thump could have been him jumping to the floor.

She turned toward the living room. Maybe—

There was a crack of a door opening, a whoosh of wind, and she realized someone was coming in the back. A cry sprang from her mouth as a figure swathed head to toe in black appeared, face hidden behind a ski mask.

Elise drew in a breath to scream just as the person's eyes focused on her.

"Oh Jesus!" the figure cried, pressing a gloved hand to their chest. "Elise!"

"Mom?" she yelled.

"Are you trying to give me a heart attack?" her mother snapped as she tugged the ski mask off, revealing her familiar face and gray hair.

"Me? You're dressed like a home invader! Why the hell are you wearing a ski mask?"

"It's cold out there. I had to cover the garden last night. Looks like everything survived the frost." She shot Elise a narrow look. "Despite what you think, I do set foot outside the house on occasion."

Elise winced, recognizing a vague echo, a memory in those words. She'd said something like that to her mom the night before. She'd been furious, demanding that her mom drive the letters over if she was so worried about Elise getting in the car.

"Sorry," Elise murmured. "I had a few too many last night. I'm sorry I called so late."

"Well," her mom huffed, "at least you didn't get in the car like a damn idiot. The stuff is in the top left drawer. Feel free to grab it on your way out. I have things to do."

Elise had been dismissed, and she deserved it. "Sorry," she said again. If there was anything else to say, the words failed her, so she retreated back to the bedroom. They weren't big talkers in this family, and the avoidance hadn't fallen far from the tree.

Robin's twin bed was on the side of the room next to the window, with Elise's bed wedged in by the closet. The headboards were identical curves of shiny white lacquer, separated by a matching side table. The long dresser took up most of the opposite wall.

Her mom had bought them the furniture when Elise was seven years old, and she'd felt like a princess at the time. She could now recognize it as a cheap set that had probably only cost a few hundred dollars, but she'd been convinced the redecoration was somehow the start of a glamorous new life for her and her sister.

Robin had commandeered the dresser drawers on her side as well as the three smaller drawers in the middle. She'd also taken up two and a half walls with pictures of her friends and her crushes and posters of the bands she'd loved. Her taste had ranged from Eminem to Alanis Morissette to TLC. Even the middle-aged Aerosmith had a spot on her wall.

Ancient tubes of makeup still sat on the left side of the dresser, and Robin's name badge from camp hung on the mirror above it along with some plastic beads and a green glowstick on a string.

Elise's side of the bedroom was mostly blank. Anything that had meant much to her had been moved to the master bedroom when she'd been shifted there, but she'd left a snapshot of herself posed with Robin tucked into the frame on her side of the mirror. She hadn't wanted her sister to come home and discover that Elise had taken her picture down.

In the photo, Robin was wearing a long red sweater. An oversized green scrunchie held her blond hair back in a high ponytail. She'd wrapped her arms around Elise from behind, and they posed in front of the Christmas tree, Elise wearing her red-and-white candy cane pajamas. Their last Christmas together.

They looked so happy. Despite that Robin had seemed so grown up to her little sister, she was practically a baby in the picture, her cheeks still smooth and plump with youth. Seventeen and just beginning. Seventeen and never started.

Elise looked away, reaching for the top left drawer, but she had to ignore the lurch of her heart when she saw a faded pink outline on the dresser's surface. She'd spilled nail polish, and Robin had yelled at her for ruining the dresser, but when Elise had started bawling, Robin had relented and given her a hug.

This was exactly why Elise never came into this room. It wasn't a shrine; it was a trap, and if she wasn't careful, she'd sink too deep and be stuck forever.

She yanked open the drawer, and there it was, a clear plastic bag with a few notes inside. It sat on top of a crumpled paper bag. She retrieved the smaller package and eased open the paper to see blue fabric inside. A T-shirt. Elise pressed the bag closed and shut the drawer with a clap, afraid some ghostly scent of her sister might touch her if she didn't get out of there.

"I'll bring these back," she promised as she rushed through the living room. "Thank you." But when she stepped outside and drew a deep breath, she had the strangest feeling she might never be back at all. More avoidance, probably, but the hair on her arms rose just the same. Elise told herself it was only the cold.

CHAPTER 26

Barely two minutes of driving later, she passed Daniel's house. It sat off the road, mostly hidden by a gnarled oak tree and huge pines. She could see his driveway if she looked. She didn't look.

She knew tourists saw an idyllic hamlet when they passed through. Even most of the residents saw Cold Creek as paradise. All Elise saw were shadows, which was why her new place was miles down the road.

Still, that therapist must have been right about facing things, because Elise had made real progress since coming back. But yes, she was backsliding a little. Before she could get nervous and change her mind, she ordered her phone to call her current therapist, then felt nothing but shivering relief when there was no answer. "Hi, it's Elise Rockwood," she said when prompted to leave a message. "Let me know if you have any available appointments in the next week or two." Done. She'd made the effort and acted responsibly. Kudos to her.

When she got past the shallow curve of the ravine that defined the town boundary, she glanced down at the bag on the passenger seat. There were three folded pieces of notepaper and one envelope ripped carelessly open to reveal blue paper inside. That was all they'd taken? All they'd cared to read? How cruel.

Elise glanced back up to a windshield filled with the red glow of brake lights, and she had to slam on her brakes so hard the antilock system kicked in and thumped beneath her foot like a struggling animal. Panicking, she aimed the car toward the shoulder, then panicked again when she saw it was only a foot wide. Before she could slide down the incline that led to the creek, her wheels finally caught the blacktop and held.

Silence swooped down and covered her until she could hear water past the windows, splashing against the edges of tumbled boulders that had slipped into the creek.

The rearview mirror showed another car approaching, and Elise cringed, but that driver slowed to an easy stop behind her. A long line of vehicles waited ahead, but within a few seconds the brake lights began to flicker off and the line inched forward.

When they'd finally moved a good forty feet, she spotted the problem. Two sheriff's trucks and an ambulance blocked the lane. It wasn't until she finally reached the scene and was waved around that she spotted a white pickup in the creek.

With all the emergency vehicles, she couldn't see much, only the side of the pickup framed by two paramedics balanced on the steep incline. A fire engine pulled up just before an officer directed her back over to the correct lane and the highway opened up.

Frowning, she concentrated on the road, ignoring a pull at the back of her mind. The highway stretched from the Sacramento Valley all the way to the Tahoe area, so anyone could have been driving. Even if it was a local, pickups were a common vehicle around these parts.

It wasn't until she pulled up to Creekside Cabins ten minutes later that she remembered the white Ford Ranger that had parked in her lot for nearly a week. "Daniel," she whispered, turning her head back and forth as if she'd spot him. The crash had been only a few minutes from his house.

Feeling equal parts ridiculous and anxious, she swung her car around and returned to the highway. When she hit the traffic jam, she parked at the start of a chained-off fire road. Just as she got out, the ambulance began wailing. It passed her, heading for Tahoe, no doubt, and she turned to watch it go before sprinting across the road.

Tense from the traffic as people accelerated past, she hurried up the highway. The firefighters were already packing up their truck and didn't pay her any mind. Elise could see the pickup now, and she spotted a Ford logo. Shit.

"Ma'am." A sheriff's deputy stopped her with a raised hand.

"Was that Daniel Serrano?" she asked as she ignored the cop and kept walking, craning her neck for any recognizable belongings.

"Ma'am, please head on back to wherever you came from. We're trying to clear this scene."

"Just tell me if it's Daniel," she insisted, but she could see from his hostile glare that she wasn't getting that information. "I saw the accident," she said, tossing out a lie she hoped would help.

His eyebrows rose, creasing his pale forehead. "You saw it?"

"I think so."

"Can I get a description of the other vehicle?"

Her acting skills failed her in that moment, and she couldn't hide her surprise. "What?"

"You saw someone hit him from behind?"

"Um, no. I don't think so." He cocked his head, taking another look at her, so she spoke in a torrent before he tried to pin the accident on her. "I was coming the opposite direction, probably about a hundred feet back. I saw the truck dropping into the creek, but that's it."

"And you didn't notice the other vehicle behind it?"

She carefully shook her head. "You think someone hit him?"

His face was closing down again. "Ma'am, if you'll go speak to Deputy Sullivan over there, she'll take your report."

"Thanks," she said, but she didn't look at Deputy Sullivan as she walked. She'd reached a vantage point that offered a view into the open door of the crashed truck, and she could clearly see an orange canvas bag that had tumbled to rest on a white airbag on the passenger side.

That was Daniel's bag. She was sure of it. And apparently someone had run him off the road.

For a moment the trees lengthened in her vision, stretching out and beginning to tilt into a slow spin. Elise closed her eyes and took a deep breath. Maybe this wasn't what it seemed. Maybe Daniel hadn't been targeted.

When she opened her eyes, she felt better. Not because she was calm but because her adrenaline had cleared her vision and focused her mind.

She sprinted through the last of the traffic to head back to her car. She kept her head down and tugged her knit cap lower to hide as much of her face as she could, half-convinced a car might swerve onto the shoulder at any moment and cause another "accident." She held her breath so tightly for the last dozen feet that she was left gasping next to her car by the time she reached it.

Someone had run Daniel off the road. There could be only one reason, and it didn't have anything to do with him helping his cousin out with a gig. He'd lied about the funeral. He must have. Somebody was tying up loose ends, including Daniel, and that meant this conspiracy went deep and dark. Elise couldn't trust anyone.

The moment she'd locked her car door, she reached out to touch the plastic packet of letters, shocked that she'd left them visible on the seat for anyone following her. Stupid. She had to start thinking like someone who was in serious trouble.

Still, she had a brief thought that she should drive toward Tahoe, track down the hospital, and see if Daniel was okay. If he'd gotten mixed up in this, that didn't mean he knew how bad it was, how dangerous. Maybe he was hurting for money and figured information was a fair enough trade, even if it involved old friends.

Her heart pulled her toward him, toward the spark between them and the sweet possibility of something good. Toward that happy teenage boy who'd always been kind to her and had supported Kyle through his toughest years. But the hospital wouldn't give out information, and someone else might be waiting there, checking on the job they'd just done.

She drove straight to Kyle's instead, past Daniel's place and their mom's house and all the way to the hills at the far end of the town where Kyle had bought a run-down box of a house years before. The light-blue paint had faded from the sun on one side and accumulated a haze of moss on the other, a strange gradient from north to south.

His place looked deserted, but that was a year-round issue. Tall grass in the summer, drifted leaves in the fall. It wasn't that Kyle was lazy or even that he didn't like being outdoors; he simply got too caught up in the minutiae of life and forgot about everything else. He occasionally still went camping with old friends—very occasionally—but once he was inside in front of his computer, he lived in another world.

She picked her way through a patch of dry thistles to knock at the door, keeping an eye on a wasp's nest a foot above the jamb. Neither Kyle nor the wasps emerged. She knocked harder, then rang the bell, to no avail. Though she told herself he was likely out running errands, she couldn't be sure. What if he was inside and needed help?

After cautiously approaching the garage, Elise got up on her tiptoes to look through one of the tiny windows.

"Whew," she whispered when she saw that his car was gone. Her panic faded a little, and now she felt foolish running to her big brother for protection. She needed a beer, anyway. And lunch, she promised herself. That too.

Creekside Cabins looked empty and peaceful when she arrived. No assassins that she could see, and no one waiting in a vehicle to confront her either. She wanted to rush right in and dump the letters onto the table, but she forced herself to take it slow, checking the locks on both doors to be sure they were fully engaged.

When she grabbed a beer from the fridge, she realized how parched she was, her mouth dried out from adrenaline and bad choices, and she downed half of it before she even sat down at the table.

Opening the letter first, she saw that it was from Valeria and skimmed it quickly. The entirety of the two pages focused on Valeria's new life in Los Angeles, with no gossip at all about the boys back home.

Two of the other notes were creased at sharp angles and had obviously been folded into triangles or polygons before, but one was creased into a simple folded square. She opened it to see a photocopy of a crudely drawn map.

Elise identified Cold Creek immediately, as well as another small town farther down the winding line of the highway. But the big *X* was higher on the page, and a quick study of the other squiggles of roads made clear that Deer Flats Camp was the target of this map. Her breath left her.

This was the last place Robin had been seen. That night, there'd been a huge gathering at the private campground, land that had been owned by a local family for generations. There was an ancient outhouse and a big clearing for bonfires. Huge piles of dirt had been sculpted into BMX jumps, and a stream flowed through the place, crisscrossed by ATV trails.

Elise had been to several parties there in her youth, drinking way too much so she'd stop seeing flashes of her sister through the trees. But no one had ever determined whether Robin had actually vanished from there or left to go somewhere else. Everyone knew everyone, so people came and went with various groups all night long, and lots of people brought tents or slept in their cars. Even Amber had left with another friend who offered a ride around eleven.

The map seemed like a clue, because Robin hadn't needed this map to find Deer Flats any more than Elise would have needed it. So why had she had it? It must have been meant for someone else, and maybe that someone had been Christian.

Elise set the paper carefully on the table and looked for any markings, but nothing had been written on it. There was also no indication it had been checked for fingerprints, no powdery smudges, no scraps cut out.

The old anger welled up like the yawning mouth of a monster. Her sister might have been saved if the police had taken their mother seriously. Maybe she'd only been injured when she'd been dumped. Maybe she'd held on, dying over a couple of days.

Elise finished her beer and grabbed another.

If they'd done a real investigation, there'd be evidence pointing to *someone*. There'd be something solid to hold on to, something to save her from this tarpit of fear and doubt and grief. She and Kyle were both being pulled under, and no one could reach them now.

She shoved the map aside and pulled out a note. This one was from Amber, and Elise's heart squeezed in pain at the sight of her friend's handwriting.

> *On my way to work and you're still sleeping. My new Miracle Bra just came in the mail! Did you ever get yours? So glad Dad wasn't home. He would have FREAKED if he saw mail for me from Victoria's Secret. Can you even imagine? I would NOT have been going to that party tonight. "You turn eighteen on September 2, and you're still living under my roof and my rules until then." (Can you hear him yelling in your head?) You're lucky your dad is gone. Yeah yeah, I know that's rude, but honestly they're not worth the trouble. He still thinks I have a special flower to protect. (As if.)*
>
> *Wear your pink button-down tonight, ok? I'll wear my blue one. We'll look super cute and we'll need them when the sun sets. Watch out for my bodacious tatas tho. Hope I don't upstage you. (As if, again.)*
> *Amber*

Everything had been so good and right and hopeful for Robin that summer. She'd been hurtling through space toward her life, ready to shoot the moon. Instead she'd dropped out of the sky and fallen into a cold river to be eaten by crawfish and currents.

Had she worn the pink button-down? Most of the reports had described her as wearing a denim miniskirt and a white tank top, but she could have taken off the pink shirt. It had been a warm night.

Elise stared at the wall, trying to picture that shirt, but she had no memory of it, and that blank space felt like a betrayal. Another piece of Robin she'd let go of, a tattered string trailing through the dirt.

She picked up the paper and carefully folded it along old lines, trying different patterns until she'd finally matched up the edges. Once it was no more than three inches tall, the paper made a flat little house. Or maybe it was an arrow, pointing her toward something. She laid her hand on it for a long moment before moving it aside.

The last note was bent at one edge. She smoothed it out and looked for a signature. Brittany. Frowning, she tried to remember a face, but all she could picture was red hair cut into a bob. Robin had been friends with nearly everyone in her high school. There were too many to recall.

Eeeee! Call me when you're home. Billy gave me his cell phone number, and I CALLED HIM.

Elise's heart picked up speed. A boy named Billy with enough money for a cell phone way back then? "Billy Jackson," she hissed. It had to be him.

I invited him to the party tonight and YES he's going to come! So do not go without me. I need a pep talk on the way. You know how weird and awkward I get around guys I don't know. I'm a dweeb. Maybe he'll bring his friends. I saw one of them checking you out!

Did Valeria write back to you? She's going to come see me at UCLA next month! We'll take a million rolls of pictures and send you extra prints. Love you, babe. See you tonight! I'll drop by the sub shop and talk to Amber about who's driving.

Stay cool,
Brittany

Which one of Jackson's friends had been checking out Robin? Christian or Quinn? She could feel the truth of it now. That they'd all been there. That they'd done something to her sister. Rich older guys and a throwaway local girl. Anything could have happened.

No one had taken date rape or roofies seriously back then. Predatory behavior had been part of the game, and a girl who drank too much was asking for trouble. Maybe they'd assaulted Robin and thought nothing of it until something had gone wrong. Maybe Phoenix had been involved too.

Or maybe Phoenix had witnessed something. He could have tried to extort them all those years later, three uber-rich executives with a secret that would destroy them.

Elise dropped her head to her hands, trying to think of what exactly she'd told Christian. *I had a big sister. She died when I was ten.* She squeezed her forehead, hoping to dislodge the rest of their conversation. *She vanished from a party.*

And then? He'd expressed horror, of course. Sympathetic exclamations she couldn't recall now. But he hadn't said he'd been here. Why? A missing girl must be something they'd all remember.

What had he *said?*

She squeezed until her fingers hurt, but the pain didn't help. When she finally let go, she slid her hands down to cover her eyes as she cried. The doors were locked, and the blinds closed, and there was no reason to hold back, no reason to hide her anguish behind anger or sarcasm, so she let it out. She wailed; then she screamed.

"Why?" she sobbed. Why, why, *why?*

She'd finally been healing, finally been doing the hard labor of crawling away from the wreck of her first thirty-five years. The abandonment by her father, the struggle of her single mom, then the unexplained vanishing of her only sister. All those years of fury and fear and grief and trauma. The emotional neglect. The unfulfilled needs. The fight to find a spark of happiness once a day, once a week, once a year.

Why couldn't Christian have been real and right? Why couldn't she have anything good?

Throat aching from her screams, she dropped her head to the table and sobbed, her tears and spit pooling on the wood. She'd loved him. She'd fucking loved him, and he'd been a monster.

Had he wrapped himself around her out of fascinated guilt? That was the most she could hope for. Because the truth was that he might have inserted himself into her body and her life because the idea of fucking Robin's sister had turned him on with the incandescence of a sun. He might have looked at her in bed and seen Robin all over again.

Another sob tore from her throat. She was trapped with this forever now. She couldn't ask him anything, couldn't demand an answer. He was dead, and that should have felt like vindication, but it was just another endless violation. There would never be any answers, not from Christian or Robin or Phoenix.

But Billy Jackson knew something.

Her sobbing died away. Elise gingerly raised her head and wiped her nose against her sleeve like a dazed child.

If she'd really lost everything, what the hell was she trying to protect herself from? There was no way to make this better. No way to make this any less horrifying than it was. If Savannah had been married to a monster, Elise couldn't shield her from that.

She grabbed her phone and texted Kyle. I'm sorry about last night. You're right. The whole truth needs to come out. Let me know what I can do.

CHAPTER 27

Elise was so lost in her internet research on Billy Jackson that she almost didn't hear it. Something pecked at the edge of her attention, distracting her from a short article about his charitable contributions to STEM camps for girls. Expanding STEM access was a worthy endeavor and probably not an unusual charity for a tech executive to sponsor, but the focus on teenage girls made her face twist with disgust now.

Were there other girls in his past? Other teenagers who'd never come home?

She raised her head at a small rattling sound, aware that it wasn't the first time her brain had registered it. Frowning, she held her breath and waited. When the whisper of noise repeated, she shot to her feet.

Someone was trying to open her door.

Hands raised to fight, she took one step back, then reassured herself the metallic sound had been faint. It was the door to the outside, not the one that led into her living space.

When something thumped hard against the wood, she grabbed her cell phone and edged toward the closed door to the reception area.

"Hello?" a man yelled. "Hello, are you open?"

A customer? It didn't seem likely. She'd turned off the neon vacancy sign last night.

Her brain whirred. She had, hadn't she? She could remember the intent. She even remembered standing up to go take care of it and setting her drink on the table. The memory ended there.

As quietly as she could, she tiptoed into the reception area. The front door was solid oak, and she'd closed the blinds on the adjacent window, but she could see a dance of blue light past them as someone moved. When a booming knock exploded through the small space, Elise flinched and ducked her head. The man outside muttered a curse, but she dared to creep toward the desk and the light switch next to it.

Damn it. Still switched on. She stretched her arm as far as it would reach and clicked it off. "We're closed!" she yelled. "Sorry!"

Silence. She held her breath and wondered if the man outside was doing the same, trying to plot his next sneaky move.

He finally yelled back. "I only need a room for one night!"

"Sorry! I have a family emergency!"

"Can I just come in so we can negotiate? I need a key and some towels. Nothing else. I won't bother you after that."

Elise hesitated, her instincts warring. She couldn't afford to turn away a paying customer, and she certainly couldn't afford this guy leaving a terrible review for everyone to see. Then again, she didn't want to be murdered either, and he seemed desperate to get inside.

She dared to tiptoe to the window and look out. A white man stood on the porch in the dim light of dusk, wearing jeans and a T-shirt, overweight in a way that promised lots of muscle beneath any softness. His ball cap was tugged low over his face, hiding his eyes, and wasn't that suspicious?

Elise twisted around to press her back to the door, wondering once more if she were losing her mind.

When he knocked again, the force of it shot through her spine. That settled the question. She didn't need anyone this aggressive staying at Creekside Cabins even without the current danger. This guy could fuck all the way off.

"My father's in the hospital," she yelled. "I'm shutting down for two weeks." She had no qualms about daring the universe to mess with her dad, because he deserved all the bad luck she could send his way.

"Jesus Christ," the man grumbled. "Could you at least come out and give me names of a couple of places nearby? I'm in town for a job, and I don't want to drive all over kingdom come."

She'd been right to turn him away. All he seemed to care about was getting her door open, and she imagined him pushing right through and shoving her up against the wall to find out what she knew about Billy Jackson.

"There are cabins six miles to the west, or there's Tahoe to the east. I just told you I have a family emergency. Please leave."

He started talking again, but she was already in her living space and closing the door behind her. She zipped through the kitchen into the mudroom and lifted the curtain that covered the window there. God, she hadn't even registered the sound of him pulling up, but a black Dodge Ram was parked close to her car. Maybe too close, as if he wanted to cut off a means of escape.

He'd backed in as well, which conjured up an image of him tossing her dead body into the bed of the pickup, never to be seen again. There were so many gullies and washes and canyons around here.

Too late, she saw that he'd already walked around to the lot. He glanced up when he reached his truck, and before she let the slat of the blind drop, he looked right at her.

Stifling a squeak, Elise backed away into the kitchen, but not so quickly that she didn't hear him call her a bitch.

When her phone rang, she assumed it was him calling the Creekside Cabins number, and started to silence it, but then her therapist's name flashed. Finger hovering, Elise glanced at the two beer bottles on the table, then back to the phone. She should answer, but it was getting late and she had things to do. She'd return the call another time.

"Okay," she huffed, trying to brace her nerves as she closed her phone.

She'd pack a few things and head to Kyle's if he'd have her. His spare room was currently stuffed with file boxes and weird collectibles, but

Elise wasn't above sleeping on the couch. She'd spent half her twenties on friends' couches.

She pulled a duffel bag from her closet and threw a few clothes in along with a pair of tennis shoes. She packed toiletries too, because Kyle no doubt bought the first shampoo he crossed paths with at the store along with an economy pack of the cheapest soap he could find.

Okay if I crash at your place? she texted him.

Sure, he responded immediately. But be quiet when you get here. I'm recording another interview. I'll ask if he wants to talk to you too.

I'm not up for that today. No thank you.

A few seconds later, he responded. Cool. See ya.

With another brother, she might expect a bit more protectiveness, but Kyle had his own crises to worry about. He'd put in his time raising Elise, and he seemed to think she could take care of herself now. And what was Kyle going to do that she couldn't? He wasn't a Navy SEAL, and she was definitely meaner than he was.

She dropped the duffel near the door, then headed to the kitchen to slip cans of tonic and a bottle of gin into a shopping bag before staring into her empty fridge. She'd never eaten lunch. Or breakfast. No wonder she felt so strange and woozy. She'd downed four beers on an empty stomach hours earlier.

Oops.

Maybe Kyle would have the ingredients for the comfort food he'd perfected during their childhood: tuna hotdish. Noodles, butter, and cream-of-mushroom soup would definitely be comforting. Once her belly was full of pasta, she was certain she could sleep the night through, even on her brother's old couch.

Stomach growling at the thought of a hot meal, Elise grabbed the backpack she'd stuffed with her notes, computer, and purse and headed for the door.

After peeking through the window, she shut off the exterior lights and stepped out to find that night had fallen.

The dark closed around her like a fist. God, she'd never seen her place like this before, empty and dead, all the exterior lights snuffed out. Her neck prickled at the thought of Jeremy Quinn murdered by a sniper while he was alone on his own deck.

Holding as still as she could, Elise listened. She heard the whisper of water, the distant whoosh of cars passing, leaves shaking in the breeze. A mourning dove cooed from somewhere on her roof. That was it. No guns cocking or footsteps pounding.

But damn, it was spooky. Her nearest neighbor was only a quarter mile away, but the creek and the highway were moats cutting her off from others. She felt a sudden keen awareness that even the stars above her offered cold, ancient light, and the moon peeking above a far hilltop was nothing but dead rock pretending to glow.

She resided with ghosts here, lived with them every day and every night. It was the living people who floated through, the true apparitions in her life. She inhaled the crisp night air, and when she released her breath, it clouded around her like yet another spirit. Her stupid, drifting soul, never staying where it was supposed to be.

Elise walked away and left it hanging in the air behind her. She didn't need a soul. It'd be easier to go on without it.

Screw these assholes. She'd fight until the bitter end.

CHAPTER 28

At the end of her driveway, Elise squinted toward a square of reflective light up the road. When her eyes adjusted, she could make out the shape of a dark-colored vehicle about eighty feet away.

There was no crossroad there, just a rutted path to a crooked structure that barely deserved the title of house. A thin old man owned it, though she couldn't quite name him a neighbor. She'd caught only brief glimpses of him hauling a trash can out to the shoulder every couple of weeks.

The shape looked like an SUV, but it could have been a pickup. Its lights were off, and the nose faced out so she couldn't trace the silhouette of the back half. Could it be the Dodge Ram that man was driving? Maybe.

When something swooped above the highway, Elise flinched, banging her elbow against the door. Her funny bone sang with the same strange, sharp ache that had taken over her heart. Just an owl or a bat. What the hell had she thought it was, anyway? She wasn't being chased by vampires.

Wrenching her attention from the truck, she pulled out and took the right turn in a squealing arc.

She alternated between watching the curves of the road and watching the rearview mirror as she sped away from her home. The truck didn't follow, or at least its lights never appeared. Was she imagining things?

To reset her nerves, she gave her head a quick, hard shake and concentrated on the drive. She'd feel better once she was with Kyle. They'd have each other's backs, and they could figure this out together.

As she drove through town, she found that every house and business had lost its familiarity somewhere on her journey from normal life to nightmare. There were two cars parked close to the road in the driveway of one home. In front of the tiny corner convenience store, several men stood smoking cigarettes and watching as she rolled past. The Alvarez auto shop was packed with cars, and any one of them could hide someone waiting behind the wheel to follow her.

The last of this gauntlet was a group of seasonal cabins at the opposite end of town from Creekside. The place was open only four months of the year and wasn't exactly her competition: ten primitive structures with a shared bathhouse. But there was a truck parked there among the locked cabins. Why? Teenagers making out? Or an assassin on the move? Moonlight reflecting off the hood marked it as a pale color, not the black Dodge.

Breathing a sigh of relief, she pulled her eyes back to the road, only to startle at the alarming glow of headlights in her rearview mirror, approaching fast. Where the hell had they come from?

She was past town now, driving alone in complete darkness. She would hit another village in a few minutes, but it was more of a wayside stop than anything, just a bridge that crossed the creek, surrounded by a few houses in the hills and a trailhead parking area.

"Shit," she muttered as the headlights drew closer. Elise turned on her brights and sped up, taking the curves too quickly. The vehicle behind her fell back.

As she bumped over the bridge, Elise reassured herself, imagining a married couple in the vehicle behind her, one of them telling the other they were driving too fast and following too close. With one last look, she continued past the houses toward Cold Creek, trying to catch a glimpse behind her in the faint glow of the bridge lighting.

Yeah, it was definitely a dark truck.

She picked up speed again, suddenly remembering that Daniel had been run off the road right on this three-mile stretch of highway. If that happened to her now, in the dark, help wouldn't be fast.

When a car honked, Elise gasped and jerked the wheel, her tires briefly skidding along the sandy shoulder, kicking up debris. The approaching vehicle flashed their brights, and Elise scrambled to turn hers off, hands shaking and heart pounding. She'd be in Cold Creek in a few minutes.

By the time she spotted the first islands of light that promised houses, her hands and shoulders sang with pain. So did her head. She was dehydrated and hungry and completely broken. She wanted to eat and drink and sleep, and maybe tomorrow she and Kyle would find a way out of this.

Cold Creek, so small and scattered during the day, enveloped her like an embrace as she finally drove into it, a galaxy of porch lights and warm windows. The car behind her drew close again, and she couldn't even summon panic about that. She was almost to her brother's house. She just had to make it through a brief stretch of darkness on his unlit road.

She was at the narrow road in no time, taking the hidden right turn as quickly as she could. The truck behind her slowed. Then it stopped. It paused right there in the main road at the turn she'd just taken, and there was no stop sign there. No reason to even slow down.

Her pulse sprang into a sprint at this confirmation that her tail hadn't been happenstance. She forced her eyes to the tunnel her headlights cut through the dark, and when she looked at her mirror again, the lights behind her had vanished. Though she wanted to feel grateful, she had to assume the driver had gone dark and could be creeping up behind her.

Stepping on the gas, she flew up the road, bushes raking her car like grasping fingers as she cut the turns too tightly. Whoever it was, they wouldn't know the route as well as she did, so she pressed her advantage and gunned the engine on the brief straightaway.

One more curve, and then she was swinging onto his driveway. Her car bounced over a slight rise, and for a moment Elise felt airborne. Then a hard jolt, a skid, and she threw the car in park. She snapped off the lights before she'd even turned the engine off, then grabbed her bags and sprinted through the weeds straight for the door. The knob turned. He'd left it open for her, thank God.

"Shit!" she wheezed as she burst through. She shut the door and pressed her back against it. After dropping her backpack and bag, she twisted her arm around to snap the lock into place.

Kyle swung around in his desk chair and put a finger to his lips, his head misshapen in the dim lighting. When she puzzled out that he was wearing bulky headphones, she pointed at the door with a violent gesture, making her eyes huge with alarm. He, in turn, pointed at one of his monitors.

Shaking, she pushed off the door and moved closer to the dining room he used as an office. The monitor showed a greenish view of his driveway and the road beyond it. She could clearly see her car, even in the dark, and nothing moved on the road. He hadn't had a night-vision camera when she'd stayed with him before, but she was thankful for it now, staring hard at the unmoving scene.

"That's exactly right," Kyle said, swinging his chair back around to face his desk. "We can't trust the authorities here. This guy could have anyone in his pocket. Certainly the local cops and the DA, but state investigators? Sure. Maybe even the authorities on a national level. Who knows? He's a billionaire."

He paused and made a sound of agreement before carrying on. "If he hired people to do this, there won't be any physical evidence that leads back to him. And I already have experience with what happens to a case when there are no leads. My sister's body still hasn't been found, and the only evidence that ever came to light was planted."

He nodded enthusiastically, clearly responding to something in his ear. Elise looked back to the security monitor. Still no vehicles but hers.

"Right! And as you can see from the picture I sent, Billy Jackson, Jeremy Quinn, Christian Valic . . . they all knew Phoenix Whit back when this happened. Feel free to share that photo on your social media. Get it out there so everyone can see the proof."

Elise winced at the idea of all of this spreading across social media, but she kept her eyes on the driveway view, her tension notching slowly down. If someone had followed her, they'd backed off.

"That isn't some kind of coincidence," Kyle continued. "Maybe Phoenix really was involved in some way or maybe he just knew she'd left with them. Maybe he even followed her. The Stratum boys could have paid him off over the years, but then decided that was no longer worth the risk, because once the company went public . . . Phoenix would have known exactly how much they were all worth. And how much they had to lose."

Elise finally gave up her vigil to move her bags and toe off her shoes.

"Yeah, man," Kyle continued. "Remember that tech executive whose throat was slit in his garage in San Francisco a few years ago? The cops tried to blame it on random street violence. Homeless people. Remember that? Turns out it was a pissed-off investor." He barked out a harsh laugh. His voice sounded stronger and deeper than she'd ever heard it. "Are we really expected to believe they would have solved that on their own if the murderer's girlfriend hadn't turned him in? They would've arrested some poor street person and pinned it on him for showing up on a Ring doorbell two blocks away. They're never looking in the right direction! Either because they're too blinded by the shine of money or because their eyes are wide open to it, right?"

Elise weaved on her feet, dizzy now from the drop in adrenaline and from her empty stomach. She moved into Kyle's peripheral vision and pointed at the kitchen. He gave her a thumbs-up, seemingly confident in whatever security he'd set up. She could only hope her tail had decided to fall back and wait, assuming she'd return to her cabin tonight.

"Not today, Satan," she muttered as she retreated to the kitchen and began opening cabinets.

His kitchen was a mess, but most of it was clutter, no moldy dishes in the sink, so she washed her hands and got out a big pot to start the noodles. She couldn't think straight anymore. She had to eat.

Once the water was heating, she mixed herself a drink and moved back to the monitor to keep watch. Kyle was still talking, but she had to swallow a groan of pleasure at the sharp bite of gin on her tongue. Her whole body relaxed for a brief, perfect moment. Then she registered what her brother was saying.

"As you know, this isn't our only familial connection to Stratum. I'll tell you more about my younger sister next week, and that part of the story is really going to blow everyone's minds."

She glared at him, but he didn't look at her. She knew she'd already given him permission, but her skin crawled as he nodded at some idea he'd just heard.

"Exactly!" he crowed. "This is the truly devastating evidence that Billy Jackson doesn't want out. It's why Christian was killed, and Quinn too. Their history, their crimes, led Christian to worm his way into my surviving sister's life. And man, she looks exactly like Robin. *Exactly* like Robin."

Elise's mouth went as dry as a desert at his words. She wanted to rush for him and pull the plug on his computer, but she couldn't be a coward anymore. She had to face this whole thing head-on. She was still a fighter. She could still survive.

"Dude, this is all insidious and disgusting," Kyle growled. "And just a quick note to Billy Jackson, because I assume he's listening: I've already sent the entire story and the evidence I've gathered to multiple sources. You can't stop this anymore, because we won't let you. Now we've got a whole audience tracking stuff down and adding to the pile of proof. And I thank them for that. I can't do this on my own. It's too deep."

When tears sprang to her eyes, she walked away. It *was* too deep. She couldn't survive this on her own either, and as uncomfortable as she was with Kyle's strategy, she needed it. If he didn't take this all public, they'd be sitting ducks.

"Yeah, thanks so much! If I'm still around next week, I'll see you then!" A few seconds later he took off the headphones and spun around. "Hey!" he called. "He really, really wants to talk to you, Sis. So think about it. You're a bigger part of this than I am."

"I'll think about it," she lied. The truth needed to be out there, but she didn't. Let them all talk about her; it didn't mean she had to offer up her softest spots as target practice.

She returned to direct his attention back to the monitor. "I think someone followed me here."

Frowning, he swiveled around. "Are you sure? I haven't seen any movement aside from you pulling in."

That harrowing drive began to feel far away as the gin did its job. She chewed her lip as she tried to replay it in her mind. "I felt sure at the time. Someone came by the cabins, pounding on the door, insisting that I open up and talk to him even when I said we were closed. When I left I saw a truck parked down the road, and there was definitely someone following way too close on the highway. They stopped when I turned onto your street."

"They stopped? All right, that's weird. I'll keep a lookout. We'll turn off the lights in a little while so no one can see a door open, and I'll walk out to the road to see if I spot anything. You okay?"

"Yeah. Thanks. Just got spooked. I'm making your old hotdish now if you're hungry."

"Starving."

"Good. Feel free to work your magic once the noodles are cooked. I feel like you have a secret ingredient."

"The secret ingredient is more butter. And extra black pepper."

She laughed, sinking into the comforting burn of alcohol glowing in her muscles. For some reason, she was overcome with an urge to hug

Kyle. To really, truly hug him, then snuggle next to him on the couch like they were kids again. They weren't a touchy-feely family, but she suddenly felt like it had been far too long.

She almost asked if he wanted to watch a movie, then realized how stupid that was. As if they could let their guards down and lose themselves in a film. She finished her drink instead. "Want one?"

"I've got beer," he responded, this time not even casting a side-eye at her cocktail. Good. Let him deal with this his way and she'd deal with it hers.

"I'll review the security feed," Kyle said. "Don't worry, it's closed circuit so no one can monitor it or mess with the files."

"Sure. Okay."

After returning to the kitchen to drop the noodles in the water, she pawed through his crowded fridge for butter before mixing herself another drink.

Her tension continued to fall, like a huge pool of murky water slowly being drained. She was here. She was safe. She'd be okay.

But then a dark thought struck her so hard she lurched. "Kyle?" she called. "Have you kept Mom up to date on all of this?"

"No. I didn't want to stress her out. I'll fill her in soon, though."

"You don't think she's in any danger?"

"I don't think so. She's barely online. She never leaves the house. I can't imagine anyone would consider her a threat."

Elise nodded, though he couldn't see her. "Still, maybe we should consider camping out at Mom's tomorrow."

"Her broadband is absolute crap."

"Well, I was more worried about her safety than your job, Kyle."

He snorted. "She's fine. Let's be honest. No one would care if something happened to me or you, but the brave mother of a murdered girl? That's gonna raise some eyebrows and only churn up more interest in this story. Especially now that I'm laying it all out there."

She turned down the burner a bit and wandered out to join him. "When you put it that way, I think I feel better about our safety too."

"You should. We're safer now than we were a week ago. When that interview airs tomorrow, we'll be safer yet. I'm not worried. But the couch is all yours. I'm glad you came to stay."

"Me too." Giving in to the warm, squishy relief inside her, Elise set down the drink and wrapped her arms around Kyle's shoulders. "Thank you, Big Brother. I'm sorry you have to take care of me again."

A flush rose up the side of his face as she pressed her cheek to his. "It's no big deal," he said.

"It was always a big deal. And I've let you do too much all these years. I'm sorry. I love you."

"Love you too," he mumbled. She decided snuggling was probably out of the question and let him go after one last hard squeeze.

Her brother wasn't a natural leader. He preferred the solitude of his work and hobbies, and he'd always been that way, reading in his room or playing video games. Still, when Robin had disappeared, he'd taken care of the family because he'd needed to. He'd stepped up. And now he was stepping up for both his sisters again. She and her quiet brother might be night and day, but those were two sides of the same coin, weren't they? They needed each other.

She was back in the kitchen and dumping the noodles into a colander when she recalled another important detail she'd shoved out of her mind. "Hey, Kyle? There was an accident earlier today. I think someone ran Daniel off the road."

"Are you serious?" That pulled him away from his desk, and he came into the kitchen, arms crossed tight. "Jesus, that's proof, isn't it? He really is involved. Is he gonna be okay?"

"I don't know, and I'm not sure how to find out. He was taken away in an ambulance, not a helicopter, so that's good. I thought about calling the hospital, but I know they won't release information. Can you, like, hack in or something?"

"I'm not a hacker, Lise. But I'll check the news."

He went silent, and she turned to find him staring at her. He looked pale with worry over Daniel. "What did you hear about the accident?" he asked.

"Not much. I came upon the scene after it happened, and the cops wouldn't tell me anything. But they did ask if I'd seen the car that hit him."

"Shit." Kyle grabbed a can opener and started on the can of soup. "I wonder if they got any information." He watched her until she shrugged. "Well, it had to be someone involved in all this, right?"

"If it was, maybe Daniel will tell the authorities about it." She thought of his sweet smile and kind eyes. She knew he wasn't a bad guy, but he'd obviously gotten mixed up in something darker than he understood. She could even imagine he thought he was helping her and Kyle in some way.

"I hope he's okay," she whispered past the thickness of her throat. "Maybe we should try to see him. He might be willing to help now. You know?"

Kyle rubbed his neck, face a pained grimace as his foot tapped the wood floor. "Maybe. Let's talk about it in the morning. There's nothing we can do now aside from checking for news. I'll finish dinner. You go relax."

He took over the cooking, and they were sitting at the table with heaping bowls of delicious mush within five minutes. Their mom had made a version of this in their earlier years, but she'd added peas and a bit of spinach for vitamins. Elise had liked Kyle's version better but still resented that he had to make it for them.

"We used to barbecue." The words sprang from her mouth before she'd even processed them.

His fork paused. "Huh?"

"When I was little, Mom used to throw parties in the yard, didn't she? She'd roll out the grill to the front walk and invite all the neighbors." Elise's heart ached, the pain so real she put a hand to her chest in alarm. "Am I imagining that?"

He glanced away, eyes distant as he nodded. "No, that's true. Memorial Day. She loved when spring finally took hold. She had tulips along the house."

"Right." Had things really been that bright and normal? She could barely remember now. "I could hear the deer outside the window at night and the tulip stems would be bare in the morning. She called it a deer buffet."

"She was a good mom," he said after a long pause, as if he'd forgotten that part of their mother too.

His use of the past tense was a vise around her heart, leaving it cramped and aching. She didn't need to defend Mom to Kyle, but the words rose up anyway. "She's doing better. She was complaining about the deer in her vegetable garden the other day. Same old grumbling."

"I'm glad she's spending time outside. Finding new things."

Elise took a bite of food and chewed slowly until she was sure she wouldn't cry. When she felt confident about her composure, she spoke again. "She finally got some kind of closure when Phoenix confessed. Maybe we'll get more answers for her, and things might . . ."

She didn't finish. Things weren't going to get back to normal. She knew that. She hadn't even wished for it after those first few years. But still. Her mom was healing.

She had another cocktail, and Kyle drank a beer, and they ate until the whole pot was empty, and that felt like healing too.

By the time Kyle turned off the interior lights and slipped out to look around, Elise could barely muster concern. She'd melted right into the couch and felt too heavy to get up and search down a pillow and blanket. She grabbed a throw pillow and curled up on her side. Her eyes closed against the dark.

"All clear," Kyle said as he shut and locked the front door behind him. "If anyone was following you, they're gone now."

"Scared of my big brother, huh?"

"Yeah, right." He switched on a light and raised his eyebrows at her position on the couch. "I'm going back to work. It's only ten."

She waved him off. "I'm exhausted. Just throw a blanket over me and wish me luck."

"Will do."

She closed her eyes again and drifted, thinking of that sci-fi movie set in a future where unwanted memories could be erased. Though it was framed as dystopian, the possibility seemed like a beautiful dream to Elise. She'd erase most of her memories if she could.

The years before Robin's disappearance had hardly been idyllic—their father had abandoned them and they'd lived on a single mother's wages—but if she could reset to that time and figure out the world from there, wouldn't she be better off? Maybe she'd have a chance to be normal, bolstered by a childhood of spring picnics and annoying older siblings.

There was no goddamn chance for normalcy now. She'd tried it and had been kicked in the gut for her stupid attempts. Now an attacker was waiting to finish the job.

Fine. If she couldn't forget everything and start from scratch, she'd have to make sure she came out on top. Destroy the monsters and win the war. Maybe she'd give that interview after all. It was time to get feral and angry again, and this time she wouldn't run away.

CHAPTER 29

Elise shoved off the rough embrace of a wool blanket and raised herself on her elbows to look around. Her eyes found nothing to focus on, dragging over woven layers of charcoal and black so lacking in definition that her brain created squiggles of light in her vision. She couldn't grab any edges, not even the shadowed corners of furniture.

Where was she? The sticky dryness of her tongue was an old memory that told stories about what might have happened, the stranger she might have gone home with. But no. It hadn't been that bad. This wasn't her old life.

Kyle's house. She was at Kyle's house, and he'd obviously turned off all the lights when he went to bed, forgetting she'd need to see to find her way to the bathroom.

Trying to orient herself, she looked toward his office area and finally saw a ray of light, the blue glow of a button on one of his monitors. The hard corner of her phone poked painfully into her hip, and she was reaching to tug it out of her jeans when something scuffed against the wall. Elise froze, fingers digging into her own stomach. For some reason, she thought of those deer outside her window when she was little, the small noises they'd make as they moved next to the house. The shush of foliage, a click of an antler. Perhaps there were deer out there.

Or perhaps something else.

Her nostrils flared as she sucked in a hard breath and held it, straining for any clue as to what that noise had been. Had something similar jarred her awake? She felt disoriented, as if she'd been snatched from a deep sleep instead of waking naturally. But she wasn't used to how this house exhaled and shifted at night.

Though her hand felt numb with cold now, she forced it lower, searching for the edge of her pocket, trying to wedge her fingers inside to get to her phone. She was too clumsy or her angle was wrong, and every fold of denim she found was a seam or belt loop. Then . . . she saw the faintest shadow shift.

All the windows were covered, but the borders offered a slight lightening of the night, and something had moved at the very corner of her vision.

She tried to tell herself it was the wind shaking a branch. Or one of those deer, maybe even a bear.

But that truck had tailed her here. They knew where she was. What if she'd only made everything easier for them by wrapping herself and Kyle up into one neat package?

An animal instinct urged her to get off her back, to be ready to run or fight. Something wasn't right. She felt watched. Hunted. So Elise eased her bare feet from under the side of the blanket and lowered them to the floor. The wood planks were ice against her toes, and her teeth began to chatter with cold or adrenaline as she twisted up to sit.

The last movement was the hardest, forcing herself to rise from the shield of the couch and expose her whole body to anyone who might be watching. But she leaned forward and pushed herself to a crouch at least, just as her fingers finally found the tight pocket of her jeans and worked their way inside.

Elise touched the unyielding surface of her phone, the glass and metal strangely warm from her flesh, and she managed to wedge her thumb beneath it and start to tug it free. The glass slipped against her sweaty fingers. She could smell the fear coming off her, feel the dampness beneath her arms, sweat pouring out despite her chill. She worked her feet along the floor until she felt open space behind her, then took a careful step toward the hallway at her back.

Once her phone was free, she hit the button and cringed frantically away from the supernova glow of the screen.

"Shit," she breathed, scrambling to slide the brightness down. The phone indicated it was 5:32 in the morning, still pitch black but not truly night.

Determined to reach Kyle's room, she slid back another step. He didn't trust the cops, but unless he had a better plan or an explanation, they'd have to call 911 if they needed help.

The wood beneath her heel squealed as she shifted her weight, but she was sure she was almost to the wall now and stretched her arm behind her to search for it. The floor popped under her foot, and the sound echoed as she winced.

But why would there be an echo inside Kyle's small house? She tipped her head, thinking. Maybe it hadn't been an echo. Maybe it had been—

Another pop sounded, but before she could even flinch, it morphed into a deafening boom. Wood splintered. A voice shouted. Elise's ears rang so hard she could barely discern any words. When she threw her hands out in front of her, her phone slipped free and flew away.

She screamed, trying to make it sound like a roar of fury instead of fear as a thousand suns beamed light into her eyes. She was utterly blind and helpless as the world crashed around her.

Words began to emerge from the cacophony, and her hands rose above her head before she even realized she'd heard *"Hands up!"*

"Kyle!" she screamed as more words began to pepper her.

"Police! Show your hands or we'll shoot! Down on the ground!"

"Kyle!"

Stunned and disoriented, she stood in a half crouch, unable to follow additional commands and unwilling to assume she should. Anyone could yell "Police!" as they stormed into a home. It'd be a damn smart way to disarm someone and take them down.

A lamp clicked on, and a world that had been only punishing beams of light suddenly opened up into a room she could see. She glimpsed five men dressed all in black with rifles aimed straight at her, and then a leather-wrapped hand grabbed her and tossed her to the floor. Her knees hit with a clunk that promised pain later, but she couldn't feel anything as her palms slapped the wood.

That wasn't enough for her captor, and he shoved her whole body into a sprawl. With her face pressed to the floor, grit abraded her cheek as one wrist was yanked behind her back and cuffed to the other. Terrified, she wanted to fight, but this must be the police, their black boots parading through her vision. There were so many of them, too many to be a fake operation.

But if the police were here, what did that even mean? That she and Kyle were safe? Hardly. Just days ago they'd accused her of murder. She thought she'd been cleared, but . . .

Oh God, they'd come to arrest her.

Past the thump of boots booming against floorboards and shaking through her head, she heard Kyle shout. The yelling of orders began again, farther from her now. Elise felt a tear trickle over the bridge of her nose and slide across her cheekbone. Other than these small details, she had no idea what she was feeling inside. She couldn't reach her own mind past the shock. But she could hear a keening in her ears and knew it was her own. That must be terror. It must be pain.

"Clear!" someone yelled. "Clear!" another repeated. And suddenly Elise was levitating, raised up by hands and set roughly on her feet. She was upright for only a moment before those same hands forced her forward and then shoved her down to the couch.

"Don't move," a man ordered, but she twisted around to look behind her. At least three of the uniformed men were packed into the hallway, and there were clearly more in Kyle's bedroom. One man had been left behind near the couch, the barrel of his rifle a dead black eye aimed at her. She stared back, as if looking toward an approaching bullet would help her avoid it.

Was it a whole fucking SWAT team? For *her*?

My God, this was all her fault. She'd led these men to her brother's home. If she hadn't come over, they would have broken into her cabin and hauled her away without involving Kyle at all. Her poor brother.

She heard him cry out. "You're twisting my arm off, man!"

Elise hiccuped on a small sob, then snapped her mouth shut when her attendant threw her a sharp look. Her mind spun, twisting faster and faster like a skater's pirouette, pulling her insides into strange shapes. What the hell was happening? Was this the end? Was her entire life over, nothing but a series of mistakes and conspiracies that would put her behind bars and keep her there?

The herd of men in the hall shifted, and Elise caught a glimpse of a familiar face in Kyle's doorway. Lieutenant Lopez met her gaze. Turning away, she squeezed her eyes tightly shut in refusal.

"You're under arrest for the murder of Christian Valic," his voice intoned. "You have the right to remain silent . . ."

CHAPTER 30

Her ears buzzed, a sound like cicadas taking over her skull. It'd been twenty-five years since the last time Elise's life had completely imploded. Perhaps it was time for a plague of locusts to descend again.

She faced the front door, her shoulders rising and spine curling to protect her softest parts as she waited for the police to surround her. Lopez droned on with Miranda rights while she braced for the violence of being yanked to her feet and dragged out the door.

Eyes closed, she heard the crowd of men moving closer, the scraping and shifting of their bodies, the shushing of uniforms against armored vests. Why the hell were they drawing this out? Her cheeks were wet with tears, her nostrils clogged with them. She couldn't do anything about it. Couldn't wipe her face or blow her nose. She was a suspect, no longer a person.

"I didn't do this," she whispered, though she knew she was supposed to say nothing, give them nothing. "I didn't kill him."

How would she find an attorney? How did this work? In the past, even her worst nights had only involved tickets or fines.

"I'm being framed!" Kyle yelled, his voice at her back.

Her eyes popped open.

"Elise, this is a setup. They've gotten to the sheriff's office!"

She twisted around as the crowd of men moved like scuffling beetles, transporting her struggling brother into the living room. Kyle wore only gym shorts and a faded-blue T-shirt stretched out at the neckline.

Bigfoot lives! it promised in Comic Sans above the face of a grinning Sasquatch.

Kyle widened his eyes at her as she gawked in dumbfounded shock. Why were they dragging her brother across the floor?

"There's a number for a lawyer on my desk, Elise!" He twisted his neck to keep her in sight as the cops forced him past the couch. "I don't trust anyone, but he's my best bet. Tell him Billy Jackson has gotten to the county. Tell him I need protection!"

"Kyle?" she asked stupidly, the cicadas swarming in her brain. Why were the cops targeting her brother?

"I got too close!" he yelled as if she'd asked the question aloud. "But they can't stop the truth. Not this time."

Elise finally found her voice. "Where are you taking him?" she cried, surging to her feet. "Why are you doing this?"

"Ma'am, get back on the couch." A hand pressed her down so hard her teeth snapped together when she landed.

"Kyle!" She was sobbing now, grieving this awful injustice and spinning with terror. "Kyle, I love you! I'm sorry!"

"Just call the attorney!" he shouted. "I love you, Sis." And then he was out the door, into the night. Headlights cut through the dark now, but Kyle had still vanished, his face hidden by the hard globes of helmets around him as if they'd already made him disappear.

"Ms. Rockwood," someone said in a voice as normal and casual as if they'd been introduced at the grocery store.

She stared through the doorway as a rectangle of the world played out in its frame. The headlights of the sheriff's trucks, the backs of the men, the pale moths fluttering and diving, some of them swooping inside to land on the living room wall. A horrible thought intruded on her mind that she would never see Kyle again. Just like she'd never seen Robin.

"Ms. Rockwood?"

When she turned her head, it moved as stiffly as a rusted automaton's, the muscles of her neck straining, creaking.

Lieutenant Lopez stood a few feet from her, his face telling a lie of open concern.

"Where are you taking him?" she demanded, her mind calling up images of a dark underground room and a solitary chair.

"He'll be booked at the sheriff's office. The same place we interviewed you last week."

"*Why?* Why are you doing this? This isn't fair!" She had no idea why she voiced the last thought. When had she last believed life was fair? At age ten? "Kyle didn't even know Christian. This is stupid."

Lopez dropped into a crouch so their faces were at the same level. He switched his concern to a slight frown of disapproval. "I need you to tell me exactly how much you know about all this, Ms. Rockwood."

"Stop calling me that as if you respect me," she snapped. "You just took my brother to jail."

"I do respect you. I respect you enough to ask if you're involved instead of assuming you are."

"Involved in what? This fucking setup?" She was angry now. She could feel that, at least, and the rage brought her body back to life, revealing the strain on her shoulders and the unyielding bite of the cuffs at the sensitive bones of her wrists. Her knees throbbed and her fisted hands cramped as pain shot through her neck.

"All right," he said, almost to himself, dropping his head for a second before he rose. She was happy to hear his knees pop and hoped they hurt as much as hers.

She thought it was time for her to be hauled away too, but Lieutenant Lopez rounded the coffee table and grabbed a dining chair that sat against the wall. He planted it across from her and took a seat as he drew a digital recorder from his pocket. Holding it up, he hit a button and put it on the coffee table.

"This conversation is being recorded. I'm here this morning with Elise Rockwood." He gave the time and date and her brother's address. She wanted to blurt out that she wouldn't speak without a lawyer, but she was desperate to find out what was going on, so she only glared.

"I assume you'd rather do this here. If not, we can take a ride and do it more formally." When she didn't respond, he continued. "We have evidence that your brother was in contact with Christian Valic in the days before his death."

"This is ridiculous," she spat. "I told you he didn't know Christian. He never even met him."

"Did you know Kyle was in contact?" he asked, ignoring what she'd just said.

"No, because he wasn't."

Lopez sighed. "Ms.—" He stopped, catching himself. "There are texts on Christian Valic's phone, and it's clear from the context that he assumed they were coming from you."

Though her stomach lurched, she raised her chin in defiance. "I don't believe anything you're saying. If there were some kind of incriminating texts from me, you'd be arresting me."

"I'm not arresting you . . . *yet*," he added, raising a finger in caution. "Because I don't think the messages came from you. It was a spoofed number that we could track back to a VoIP. That's voice over internet—"

"I know what it is."

He nodded. "The texts arranged a meeting with Christian at Midmountain Trail. We believe someone set him up. Someone who knew about your previous relationship. And that makes me wonder who all knew about your affair. It also makes me wonder if you helped with the setup."

"I didn't help anyone with anything."

"But your brother did know about your relationship with Christian Valic. Right?"

Elise rolled her eyes, attempting to hide the pain his words struck through her. Yes, Kyle had known, but how could she trust anything this man had to say? She wasn't interested in his stupid story.

A wound inside her had opened at the assertion that Christian believed she wanted to see him. Had he looked forward to the sight of her despite himself? Had he hoped for more? Yearned for old feelings? Her throat went thick and tight with grief and sick love.

But no, she couldn't think that way. Christian was a monster, and the cops were either wrong or they were lying to pull more information from her.

She cleared her throat of the awful sorrow. "Anyone who read the email he sent would have assumed we'd had an affair. Including his wife. Anyone could have texted him."

"True. Which is why we didn't jump to conclusions at the time."

"Deputy Harrison did."

"Regardless, I'd like to eliminate you from the list of suspects if you weren't involved." His expression conveyed sympathy now, and she wanted to slap the acting off his face.

"His wife probably knew about us. He was 'working' on himself. He probably told her. Maybe she set him up." All sympathy for Savannah had flown out the door with her brother as they'd dragged him to the car. She would sacrifice anyone to stop this outrage. "Savannah came to my home, you know. She wanted information, and she wasn't afraid to be alone with me. Doesn't that seem suspicious?"

"We've checked your alibi thoroughly," Lopez said, his voice a soothing promise as he ignored her attempt to spotlight Savannah Valic. "One of your neighbors has security cameras that show you were telling the truth. Your vehicle didn't leave your property. You didn't go to that trailhead."

"I was already pretty clear on that, but thanks." Still, relief flooded her, making her head feel loose on her spine.

He smiled. "I get that. And if you weren't there when he was killed, now is the time for you to tell everything you know. Things will go a lot easier for you if you cooperate, but I can't help you unless I get the truth."

This was all manipulation, an obvious attempt to get her to implicate her brother or herself. "I don't have anything to say to you. Something terrifying is going on. People have followed me, people have lied. And two men are dead. Kyle is right. This all ties back to Robin's disappearance."

"I don't disagree with you, Elise." Her heart lurched at the confirmation that she wasn't off track. Lopez steepled his fingers and leaned closer, trying to create the same intimacy he'd conveyed by using her first name. "It's just you and me here. And my gut tells me—"

Before he could finish the thought, two officers in patrol uniforms stepped through the front door. Elise snorted. *Just you and me,* as if they were friends and not adversaries. One of the men dropped a couple of creased papers on the coffee table in front of Lopez.

He sighed. "This is the search warrant. We have permission to search this entire property. If you know where Kyle keeps his guns, I'd really appreciate you helping us out."

She glared in response as another cop entered, and they began opening doors and checking behind furniture. Someone in civilian clothes came in and sat down at her brother's desk. Elise looked away from the violation and blinked back tears.

When she'd composed herself, she looked to Lopez and saw that Deputy Harrison had entered behind him. He narrowed his eyes at her and smirked. "Shaving half your head won't get rid of evidence."

She glared at him as he walked around her and headed toward Kyle's bedroom. "Asshole," she muttered before turning back to Lopez. "Am I under arrest?"

"I'm still trying to give you an opportunity to make this right," he said instead of answering.

"You can make this right by letting my brother go. You're being manipulated by an extremely powerful man. Billy Jackson had something to do with Robin's death. He killed her or one of the others did. He's the one you need to talk to."

He dropped his head and pressed his steepled fingers together until they went white. Had he actually thought she'd turn on her brother?

"If you'd just look into it," she pleaded. "They were here that summer. There are pictures. And Christian . . . I think he knew Robin. He never told me that. Why wouldn't he tell me unless he had something to hide? I didn't—" Her words cracked and let a sob free, but she drowned it out with a growl and barreled ahead.

"I didn't know about any of that until he was *dead*. Do you know what it's like to think he might have thought of Robin while . . ." She shook her head, a violent motion to stop her own brain. "No," she whispered.

Lopez watched her past his lashes. When he raised his head, his mouth was a downward curve of sadness. "Ms. Rockwood, we have video evidence of your brother driving toward the trailhead the morning of Christian Valic's disappearance. We believe he was pretending to be you to lure Christian to a private meeting place. And we believe he killed or incapacitated Mr. Valic with a blow to the head before disposing of his body in the river. The same river where your sister was left."

The idea was so ridiculous she actually cackled. "Wow. You really are setting Kyle up. I'm just . . . I'm honestly shocked." Her laughter sounded like grief. "I'd like to see this so-called video evidence."

"I can't show you that."

"Of course you can't." She felt giddy now, untethered. This couldn't be happening. "It's too late, you know. My brother has already figured most of it out. Christian wanted to talk. He wanted to come clean. And Jackson couldn't allow that."

Lopez sighed and looked around before slapping his knees and rising from the chair. "Let's go."

He made to reach for her arm, and she jerked away before using her own leverage to rock herself up to her feet.

But then she couldn't move. Her body became wholly seized by dread, an emotional possession that held her limbs in thrall.

She didn't want to go to jail. She'd shed some of her armor, dropped some of her shields, and she wanted to be rewarded for that instead of punished. She hadn't done anything wrong, and what she'd said earlier was correct; none of this was *fair*.

"It's fine," Lopez said. When she didn't move, he put a gentle hand on her upper arm. "Come on."

What could she do but follow? She couldn't fight the whole damn world. She didn't even have Kyle at her back now.

"Okay," she said, stalling, trying to think, but nothing came to her. In the end, she moved her feet and followed him to the door. She walked down the two steps, her eyes on the fleet of official vehicles, wondering which was Lopez's. But as she tried to move forward, she was jerked to a stop.

"Sorry," Lieutenant Lopez said. "You can sit here."

She blinked slowly at the dusty seat of the green plastic chair. "Huh?"

"We need to finish our search. You can wait here. I need to check your car also. It's on the property, so the search warrant covers it. Where are your keys?"

"My backpack."

He disappeared into the house, then returned to set her backpack on the step and unzip it. Feeling surprisingly impassive about the whole thing, she watched as he pawed through the different sections.

"What's this?" he asked, drawing out the packet of printouts and notes.

"Evidence against Billy Jackson."

"I'll need to keep this."

She scoffed. "Why? So you can 'lose' it? Just so you know, Kyle has already sent out copies of everything, including the photos."

He raised his eyebrows as he slipped his hand back into the bag. "Got it."

That was when Elise saw her chance. "Please," she said, all rebellion gone from her voice. "Please look at it. Really look at it."

Lopez raised his head and met her gaze.

"Please," she repeated. "I didn't believe it at first either. Promise you'll look."

Several heartbeats passed while he studied her. Finally, his chin dipped. "I promise."

Elise didn't think she trusted him, yet relief flooded her at his words. Either he was the best actor in the world, or he meant to keep that promise.

Once he'd satisfied himself by unzipping every nook, he drew out her keys and set the bag at her feet. "Be right back."

Her leg bounced as she waited; then her whole body began to tremble as the cold from the ground seeped into her feet and radiated up. The sun had only just begun to emerge, and she could see frost on the shaded weeds around her.

"Sorry," Lopez said, surprising her out of a daze. "I'll get you the blanket." He dropped the keys into the pack.

"Nothing but a paintball rifle, sir," someone said when he stepped inside Kyle's house.

"Where was it?" Lopez asked.

"Bedroom closet."

"Is there a basement? A shed?"

"Just the garage. The truck is empty, but you were right about it being . . ." The voices moved farther away, and Elise couldn't hear them over the chirping of waking birds.

She tipped her head back to stare at the leaves above her, their shapes dark against the purplish-pink light of dawn. Of course they'd found no weapons, because Kyle wasn't guilty. She wanted to laugh at their stupidity, but then she'd truly look off, guffawing to herself beneath the trees. If Lopez thought she was crazy, he wouldn't listen to the truth.

Were they arresting her? She couldn't tell. Every anxious cell in her body was scrambling to warn her she was about to be locked up and railroaded, but he hadn't put her in a car. Maybe he wanted to play good cop first, and then he'd lock her up after she spilled her secrets.

She heard his voice from inside, and then he was walking out with the blanket held high like a peace offering. "Let me get those cuffs off you first," he said, tossing the blanket over a second chair.

Though Elise wanted to ask if she was free to go, she was afraid to hear the answer. "It doesn't matter," she told him as he freed one wrist and then the other.

"What doesn't?"

She winced as she brought her arms forward, her shoulders resisting the change in position. "It doesn't matter if you have video of Kyle on the highway. That's the main road around here. He's probably on it every single day just like I am. That's not proof of anything even if you're telling the truth about it."

"There's more evidence, Elise. I can't tell you what it is, but trust me—"

"Not likely." She snatched up the blanket and wrapped it tight around her, hoping it still held some warmth from the couch. "Do you even know what Stratum does? They trade in information. They collect every moment of our lives and sell it to the highest bidder. Imagine how much digital evidence they could manipulate or plant."

He stared at her for a long time, frustration evident in the high set of his shoulders and his grim mouth. "I can't share anything more about our evidence," he eventually said, revealing nothing.

Elise finally felt confident enough to dare the question. "Am I free to go?" she asked.

"No."

Shit.

After a few moments of waiting for her to crack, he shook his head. "Your car can't leave the property until we've completed the search. I'll check on you in a minute. Think about what I said. I can help you now, Ms. Rockwood. I might not be able to help you later."

She felt thankful to be Ms. Rockwood again, despite her earlier protest. Better that he was feigning respect than pretending to be a friend. "Think about what *I* said, Lieutenant."

"I will." She was surprised when he placed her phone on her lap and walked away.

Elise snatched it up and pulled her knees to her chest to huddle beneath the wool blanket. Her feet felt numb, and she almost followed him through the door to ask if she could return to the couch, but she didn't want to even hint at weakness.

She needed to call that attorney, so she could only hope the cops hadn't confiscated the note in the search or trashed the office so badly she wouldn't find it. Her poor brother. How had she let this happen to him? How had she let any of this happen? Christian and the affair and . . .

Pressing a palm to her forehead, she tried once again to re-create the conversations they'd had about her sister. There hadn't been many. She didn't want to be defined by it the way she'd been as a kid, *Robin Rockwood's little sister* burned on her forehead like a brand.

Elise hadn't told anyone for years once she'd escaped. Some of her best friends along the way hadn't known. She'd rarely spoken her sister's name, and when people asked about family, she said she had a mother and a brother. That was it. She'd drowned Robin's memory in tequila and gin and let her float away on that river.

When the true-crime boom had started up, Elise had despised it, snidely cutting the legs out from anyone who professed an interest. "Just another way to jerk off on the bodies of dead girls," she'd snarled more than once. That had shut them up.

But she'd been different with Christian. Softer. Younger. She'd craved his touch on every part of her, body and soul. Elise pulled the blanket over her head like a cloak to weep.

I had a big sister. She died when I was ten. That part was clear. She remembered the weight of it rolling off her, the gulp of breath she snatched from the air. They'd been naked, twisted in sheets, the breeze a kiss over the twine of their limbs.

"Oh," Christian had responded on a sigh. "Jesus, Elise. I'm so sorry. That kind of trauma . . ." He'd pulled her a bit closer, arms that had been loose around her now gathering her up. She'd melted into him, relieved to have spoken her worst curse aloud.

"Her name was Robin," she'd rasped. "She was only eighteen. She vanished from a party. I never saw her again."

But after that . . . after that . . . something about the cops, something about Phoenix, something about the weeks of searching every shadow of these mountains.

In return, she remembered him asking a lot of questions about Robin. What was she like? What were her plans? Did Elise look like her?

She'd been so touched at the time that he'd wanted to know about the sister instead of the crime. But now the memory made her dig her fingertips into her arms hard enough to hurt. When the pain seemed too much, she pressed harder. He'd wanted stories about Robin because he'd wanted to remember her, not through Elise's eyes, but through his own.

If Kyle hadn't spotted the truth, she'd still believe the lie. That Christian, bold and handsome and so fucking smart, had loved Elise, a lost and angry girl of average face and body. That she'd been enough, even for a little while, to throw that man off kilter and disrupt his life. That he'd wanted and he'd *needed*, all because of her.

But that hadn't been it at all. The love had been nothing more than obsession. A craving to own an old pleasure, or maybe a need to repair something he'd broken. Whatever it was, it was sick, and it was destroying her family yet again.

She scrubbed the blanket over her face and drew in a shuddering breath as she sat straight. No more tears. No more sorrow. She didn't have time for it, because right now she had to save the brother who'd always saved her, and she might be the only person in the world who believed in him.

CHAPTER 31

The last of the sheriff's techs were still packing up when Elise pulled out her laptop and opened that cursed email from Christian to once again search for clues in his words.

After she'd first received it and read it and spilled most of her bile out in draft responses, Kyle had advised her to delete the vitriol and try again, so she had. In the end, she'd been scrupulously polite in her reply, sending a clear message.

> Happy to hear things are going so well for you! I'm good but busy. I don't think I have time to meet up, and it probably wouldn't be the best idea anyway. I'm sure you'll keep growing regardless. And hey . . . we can talk when you're dead, right?

Friendly, as if she didn't care. Distant, as if she'd moved on. It had been an unsatisfying pill to swallow, dragging the whole way down, but Christian had taken the hint. His response in return had been brief and light as a feather.

> Got it. I understand and I'm really glad you're doing well. Please reach out anytime if you change your mind and want to talk.

She'd changed her mind several times, but she'd never reached out to make contact. Still, if Lopez were to be believed, someone had. Jackson or Savannah or . . . Kyle?

No, that wasn't possible. And the so-called proof wasn't proof of anything. Kyle had been driving down the highway at a perfectly normal time of day? Hell, that was evidence of nothing, and she couldn't even trust it was real considering that asshole tech bro Jackson could have faked the video. A few keystrokes, an unprotected Wi-Fi system, and boom: digital images of Kyle whizzing by on the road at any time of day that Jackson chose.

And if they'd faked that, what would they fake about her?

Her arms peppered with goose bumps as the last officers pulled away, and no amount of rubbing made them subside. If someone had sent those texts, routing them through a VoIP, they could have left bread crumbs leading the network back to her. Something hidden and subtle that would eventually be "discovered" by investigators.

Elise could see it all play out in her head. That she'd plotted with Kyle, arranging for him to do the dirty work while she stayed at her business, posting pictures and helping guests.

But what the hell would be her motive or Kyle's? Savannah Valic was the one who would inherit a fortune; she was the one who'd been betrayed. Christian's former business partners would've benefited too, free of any possible secrets of that summer. All Elise would get was the same outcome she'd already had: separation. Why the hell would she kill Christian?

Then again . . .

Elise bolted up, her spine a steel rod of tension, mouth opening in an O of horror. Oh no. Oh no, no, no.

This was all coming together perfectly to absolve Jackson of his long-ago crimes. She could picture it, a staticky, jerky snuff film stuttering out against her lids when she closed her eyes. Christian had been here in Willow Canyon with Jeremy Quinn and Billy Jackson. They'd lived in the same cabin and gone to the same parties. They'd all seen Robin, and maybe they'd all wanted her.

After all, what had Robin been but a loud local girl heading for a small life, a speck in their eyes? She was drunk at the party, and they spiked her next drink. One of them felt bold and led her deeper into the woods, Robin weaving and stumbling, getting nervous as the darkness closed in. A skirt was shoved up, a belt unbuckled. Afterward the first guy egged on the others. Maybe she'd woken up then. Maybe she'd tried to scream.

Then what? An arm across her throat? A fall against a sharp rock? Even if only one of them had killed Robin, all of them had been there to witness, watch, cover up. All of them had looked into the blackness between the trees and seen their futures flying away. And for what? Some trashy slut who was already dead?

Nothing to be done but make it go away. Make *her* go away. Hadn't it happened a thousand times before? A million? A woman's life was nothing compared to a man's future.

But now . . . now with only one man left and the truth spitting out in bits and pieces, Kyle and Elise were the perfect fall guys. Elise's motive didn't have to be betrayal or heartache or being scorned by a married man. Her motive was the same as Kyle's: *revenge.*

Jackson could come clean now. Maybe he already had. *Christian* had killed Robin. *Christian* had disposed of her body. *Christian* had set up Phoenix. And then he'd pursued Elise, obsessed with a younger sister who looked like the girl he'd raped and murdered.

Billy Jackson could argue that Christian had finally confessed to Elise in some misguided pilgrimage toward absolution. He could even claim Christian had told him as much. Then Elise had obviously talked her brother into killing Christian and going after the others who'd never turned him in.

"Oh Jesus," she breathed, fingers pressed to her lips. How the hell would they ever get out of this? She *did* have a motive, and she could never prove she hadn't known the truth until after.

273

She'd had opportunity too. Christian had asked her to meet him in private.

And the means? She had her brother's hands and his love for his sisters. That was all the means needed to kill.

By the time this all ended, there'd be buckets of digital evidence against her. She had no doubt of that. What proof might exist that could even absolve her? She'd assumed the police might eventually listen about Robin's murder, but now that would only point back to her and Kyle.

It was the perfect setup. The perfect conspiracy. Small and logical and easily coordinated, all the witnesses implicated or eliminated.

She jumped up from the chair and raced inside to search for the attorney's number. She found it, but he didn't answer, probably because it was only seven thirty in the morning. In that line of work, emergencies were likely dealt with between the hours of nine and five. She left a message with all the information she could, hoping the man would head right to the jail and sort this bullshit out.

She hung up and ordered her brain to *think* as she paced, but the more she tried to force it, the more it conjured up a montage of decades in prison. A few years ago that might not have seemed so far-fetched. She might have slipped up and hurt someone while driving drunk, or lost her temper and kicked some raging boyfriend down the stairs. But now she was so normal, so boring, so *innocent*. Her mind spun on a slippery surface.

Giving up, she went to the fridge to grab a beer, only to find herself staring dumbly at two empty six-packs, the bottles long gone. "Damn it," she said as she searched around for the bottle of gin, but it was gone too. Maybe she'd finished it last night.

She could go to the store. It was early, but she needed it, and she didn't have anything else to do. She could call . . .

Oh Christ, she could call her mother. Because she was going to have to tell her mom about Kyle.

How the hell was she going to explain all this? It touched on every subject she never wanted to discuss with her mom. Robin. Grief. Fear. Her own terrible decisions. And the worst truth of all: that Lucinda Rockwood might lose another of her children. Maybe even both of them.

But Elise had to tell her. The only other option was to get in her car and drive far away, the way she'd done seventeen years before. Repeat another cycle of adolescence, still the same lost girl.

But she wasn't. She wasn't that angry, broken girl anymore, because she knew she wouldn't flee and abandon her mom and Kyle. This time she'd stay and fight.

"I don't want to," she whispered, clutching at a fistful of hair, twisting until it hurt. But no one ever wanted to. People fought because they had to. Her mom hadn't wanted the crippling fear brought on by losing hold of her oldest child. Her brother hadn't wanted the burden of caring for a little sister in a scary world. And Elise didn't want to face a hundred violations rolled up into one huge conspiracy that dug into her oldest wounds. But here she was.

She grabbed her backpack and headed for the door, feeling a brief certainty that there'd be someone waiting when she opened it. Lopez or Jackson or Savannah Valic.

Savannah.

Just minutes ago, Elise had thrown the woman under the bus as another suspect. And maybe she was. But if she wasn't involved in this, she could be an ally.

It was a ridiculous idea, the betrayed wife helping out the other woman. But what the hell did Elise have to lose at this point? She was utterly screwed and her entire family along with her.

She opened the door and rushed outside, pulling up her call history as she walked. She hit Savannah's name and slid into her car as the phone rang.

When the woman didn't answer, Elise felt a wave of relief that she could leave a message instead of speaking to her directly.

"Hi, this is Elise Rockwood. I'm sorry to reach out like this, and maybe I'm just being naive . . ." Laughing at her own stupidity, she shook her head. This was the longest of long shots. "Did Christian ever talk to you about a girl named Robin? Or a girl who went missing when he was here all those years ago? Because . . . God."

She pulled in a deep breath and pushed on. "Something happened, Savannah. That summer they were here. I think Jackson might have hurt a girl, and now he's trying to pin it all on Christian. Please don't—" Her voice broke, a crack like something fracturing inside her. "Please, if Christian told you anything, if Jackson was the one who did it, you have to tell the police. You have to tell the public! I didn't know about any of this until after he was dead, but you were his wife. Maybe he told you something important. Maybe . . ."

When she couldn't think of anything else to say, she sat quiet for a few moments, her brain losing traction again.

"Anyway . . . I'm sorry for calling. I'm sorry for everything. But I hope you'll reach out again."

After she hung up, she started the car and headed for the store for a drink, the hands of the clock be damned. But she wasn't even all the way down Kyle's street when her phone rang. She pretended to be brave and answered it without flinching, even knowing exactly who was calling. "Hello."

"How dare you?" Savannah snarled.

"I'm sorry," she said calmly, still hoping. Even if Savannah were willing to help, she'd have her anger, and Elise deserved to endure it. She pulled to a stop beneath a huge pine tree.

"Did you think you'd get away with this? You think I'm stupid?"

"No, it's not—"

"You deserve everything that's coming to you. You're a monster!" She was sobbing, screaming, and if Elise had been in the same room with her, she would have felt genuine fear instead of this wincing discomfort.

"You tried to take him away from me," she sobbed, "and you *failed*! So you decided to try again. To take him from me forever."

"I never—"

"His fucking life coach came to see me yesterday. His *life coach*, can you believe that? Some ultramarathoning, yoga asshole who probably only came by because he hadn't gotten payment for their last ridiculous retreat. For all I know, Christian was screwing him too."

This wasn't going as planned, but Elise swallowed her protests and let Savannah rage. Because maybe, *maybe*, she'd get it out of her system and listen to reason.

"I told him I knew about you. Oh, you all think I'm so clueless. Did you and Christian laugh about that? Stupid Savannah?"

"No. Never."

"But I can take care of myself when I need to, Elise Rockwood." The way she sneered her name sent prickles of apprehension racing over Elise's skin. She said *Rockwood* as if she knew exactly what it meant. Who Elise was. Who Robin was.

"I knew something wasn't right, so I let that loudmouth talk. And you know what he said? This asshole pretending he was here to comfort me? He said, 'Sometimes love hits us whether we want it to or not. But Christian chose you, Savannah. That was an active choice, a *hard* choice. It tore him up, but he said it was worth it. Try to remember the twenty-two good years, not the one bad year.'"

She paused, panting, and Elise's body rang like a bell had been struck. Because the words were terrible and beautiful, but Savannah's voice promised pain.

"One bad year," she snarled, her throat grinding out the words.

"It wasn't a year," Elise tried, but it had been close.

"I'm supposed to be honored that he *chose* me? His own wife? The mother of his son? The woman who helped him build everything?" Her cry spoke of something thrown across the room, and a belated crash confirmed Elise's suspicion. "You took everything from me!" she screamed.

"That's not true. If Jackson manages to—"

"I hope you and your psycho brother rot in jail. I'll do what I can to keep you there."

Savannah knew about Kyle's arrest. Fear stabbed deep and spread through Elise's gut. Had the police told her? Or had it been Jackson? "Please—"

But Savannah was gone, the phone a dead silence in Elise's ear.

Oh God. This was so bad. If Savannah hated Elise that much, would she let Jackson defile her husband's memory just to keep Kyle and her in prison? Surely not, not if she knew the truth. But if she didn't . . . ?

If she didn't know, she'd demand Elise's head on a platter. And it seemed she might very well get it.

CHAPTER 32

When she pulled into her mom's driveway, Elise was surprised to find the garage door open. She unsealed the bottle of vodka and gulped down a huge mouthful, ignoring the shame of knowing she'd chosen it because the smell of gin would be too obvious. She hadn't had the chance to brush her teeth, so really it was more like mouthwash than a cocktail. She took another sip.

Once she felt more ready, she stepped out of the car and paused to listen, wondering if she should head around to the back. When she took a step toward the front door, a movement inside her mom's ancient Camry drew her eye, and Elise nearly jumped out of her skin.

"Holy shit," she breathed, a hand to her chest to cover her galloping heart. The top of her mom's gray head was just visible past the driver's seat of her thirty-year-old car. The thing probably didn't even run anymore.

"Mom?" she called as she approached, worried she'd startle her mother's heart into the same scramble. She saw the hands strangling the steering wheel, saw her head bowed toward her chest. "It's just me, Mom."

She heard a low murmur through the glass. Her mom didn't make any more movement, so Elise reached to ease the door open. "Hey, are you okay?"

Her mother's soft sob answered that question. "I'm sorry," she managed to say, the words querulous and broken. "I'm sorry."

Elise rushed to touch her arm, her shoulder, everything inside her going rigid with alarm. "What's wrong?"

"I want to go. I want to help Kyle. I just c-can't. I can't even help my own son."

Elise squeezed her eyes shut to stop her own tears, but they leaked free anyway. Their mother already knew about his arrest. "It's okay. Kyle had me call an attorney."

"But he needs me!"

That might be true, but there was no changing twenty-five years of paralysis in one moment. "He understands why you can't come. Come on. Let's go inside. It's okay."

As heartbroken as she was for Mom and for Kyle, she felt a rush of selfish relief that she didn't have to drop the news on this woman like a bomb. Elise would still have to explain, but that was a far lighter duty.

"Did Kyle call you?" she asked, helping her mom out of the car. She seemed weak, her body taut and trembling.

"No."

Elise glanced over her shoulder. Surely the press hadn't already reported this. Perhaps a neighbor with connections to the sheriff's office?

"The police came," her mom explained as Elise opened the door into the house.

"Oh, Mom. I'm so sorry."

The house was in more disarray than usual. It had never been neat as a pin, but now the couch was pulled out from the wall and drawers were open. "They searched here too?"

"Yes. They asked and I let them. I have nothing to hide, and it's not like they could find their own butthole with both hands, anyway."

Elise smiled in relief that her mom's feistiness was returning. "When were they here?"

"They just left."

That might mean they were on their way to Elise's next, or maybe they'd gone there first. She didn't care. Like her mom, she had nothing to hide. Her biggest secret was out now. Actually, not quite. Her biggest secret had been an affair with a local married man. Now the truth was larger, a demon doubling in size. But Kyle had meant to reveal that in his next interview: Elise Rockwood had an affair with her sister's killer.

There would be no hiding that now. Christian was an accomplice at least. Let them comb through her life and see if they could find anything more damning.

Hands shaking, her mother collapsed into her recliner and wiped a hand over her glistening forehead. Elise left her there but returned quickly with a glass of water. "I'm waiting to hear back from the attorney. Hopefully he's already taking care of things on Kyle's end. I can . . ." She hesitated to say it, afraid to even voice the words. "I can check on Kyle myself later if that's allowed."

God, she truly didn't want to set foot on law enforcement territory, but she'd need guidance from Kyle at some point. Should she contact the podcaster to get the word out? Alert the press and give interviews? Or should she go into hiding?

"I'll take a sedative if you can drive me," her mother responded. "You can drop me off."

"Let's wait and see what the lawyer says. Why didn't you call me in the first place?"

She shrugged a thin shoulder. "It didn't occur to me. I don't know why."

Elise knew why. Her mom would never think to call for help because Elise had never helped her. Robin had been her joy and Kyle her rock, and now they were both gone. Even if Elise wasn't arrested, what comfort would that be? Her mother would be left with the angriest of her three kids, the one who couldn't even bring herself to be responsible for a pet, much less her family.

She didn't have time for that sorrow, but it still welled up in her. She'd been the baby of the family once, the carefree youngest who got too much attention. Perhaps having that yanked from her at age ten had twisted her into this ugly, unlovable shape.

"What did they tell you?" Elise asked quietly.

"They say your brother killed a man. Someone I've never even heard of. And they think maybe . . ." She shook her head, a tiny jerk of denial. "They're looking for a rifle."

The rifle again. But Christian wasn't shot. That meant they were definitely trying to tie him to Quinn's death as well. "Did they find anything?" she asked, feeling like a traitor for even voicing the question.

"No. Only a big carpenter hammer they took from the garage even though it was covered in cobwebs. How stupid is that?" She gulped her water before setting it aside, her body wilting into the chair. "Kyle isn't like that. He's never been violent or a bully. Even after your sister . . . He just got quieter. He took such good care of you." She began to weep. "I'm sorry, Elise."

Elise wasn't sure if she was apologizing for crying or for neglecting them during her quest to find Robin, but either way, there was nothing to forgive. Not really. Maybe that was why Elise had never been able to make peace with it. Her mother didn't need forgiveness, so what could Elise do with all her hard feelings?

"Why would your brother kill some stranger?" she wailed. "That doesn't even make any sense!"

Elise had to tell the truth now. Her mother needed to know that Kyle was innocent. "That man was . . . He was someone I dated a couple of years ago. He'd recently gotten back in touch. But the thing is . . . he was here that summer, Mom. He and his friends rented a cabin for a month that August."

"So? Phoenix killed her. He confessed."

"He did. But they knew Phoenix too. There are pictures of them together."

"I don't understand."

Her laugh sounded wild and lost in her own ears. "I don't either. But they knew Robin, went to the same parties. And this man—Christian—he never told me about that. Kyle is sure he was involved."

New tears pooled in her mom's eyes and spilled over. "And that's why Kyle killed him?"

"No! No, it's not like that. The other two friends, they were involved too. One of them might be trying to set us up. Christian wasn't even shot. He had a head injury."

Nodding, her mom pressed a hand to her lips. "I don't even think he still *has* that old rifle," she said past her fingers.

Elise froze, the Kleenex she'd grabbed crumpled in her hand. The nape of her neck prickled, hair rising like she was a mad beast pushed into a corner. "What rifle? His paintball gun?"

"No. He went deer hunting a few years in a row with Zed. You remember him? Not my favorite of your brother's friends, but I was glad he was involving Kyle and getting him out. He bought an old bolt-action rifle, but that was almost ten years ago now. If they didn't find it at his place, I imagine he sold it."

Elise's fingertips went cold; then the chill spread to swallow both her hands.

No. It meant nothing. The majority of people in this area owned a gun of some kind. And her mom was right. If it wasn't at his place or Elise's or here, then it was gone.

Maybe because he hid it, an evil voice whispered inside her.

"No," she said aloud, drawing a questioning look from her mom. She cleared her throat. "He wasn't involved. I'll find some way to prove that."

"Who was this man? Christian?"

What could she say to that now? He'd been a man Elise loved, and now he was someone she might murder herself if he appeared before her. "Christian Valic," she said softly. "One of those Silicon Valley guys with a home here. He's no one."

"I just don't understand," she whispered, hands twisting the tissues until bits began to pepper her lap.

"It's complicated." It was a pitiful attempt to halt the conversation, and it worked about as well as expected. Her mom stared at her, waiting. Elise gave in with a sigh. "Kyle believes Phoenix Whit did know about what happened to Robin. Maybe he was even there. Regardless, he thinks these men set Phoenix up to take the fall to protect themselves when their company went public. Kyle's been talking about it on a podcast—"

"The podcast!" Her mom leaned forward, the recliner rocking violently with the shift. "Someone messaged me about it on Facebook. I assumed it was just another one of those damn shows."

Elise saw an out and snatched for it. Let Kyle's voice do the hard work. "You should listen to it. It will explain everything far better than I can. Kyle is the one who did all the research. You know how he is. Do you have a pair of headphones somewhere?"

Her mom rolled her eyes at the question. "Of course. There are earbuds on my dresser."

"I'll get them." She was fleeing again, but she didn't care. She couldn't handle the burden of explaining the unexplainable while also thinking about this new revelation.

No, not a revelation. Just a fact. The gun didn't mean anything. So why did it feel like a weight had been chained to her heart, pulling it down?

She retrieved the earbuds and was met with another eye roll when she asked her mom if she knew how to find podcasts. Elise gave her the name and episode information, and her mom lit a cigarette and settled in.

Elise checked her phone as if she might have missed a phantom call. Still nothing. Her need to try the attorney again was outweighed by her fear of making a nuisance of herself and scaring him off, so she paced into the kitchen and stared out the sliding glass door.

Pierre twined himself through her legs, and she gave him a distracted scratch, trying not to imagine he could be the last cat she'd ever pet. She also tried not to imagine the exact words her mother was hearing as she started the podcast. Elise had listened several times already and didn't want to spend the next hour re-creating the entire interview.

With one glance back at her mom's still figure, cigarette smoke rising above her like mist, Elise opened the sliding door and stepped outside for some needed breaths of crisp air. Passing into the backyard was a relief. That step had been freedom when she was young, like slipping through the bars of a prison, her brother usually the one to break her free.

Kyle.

Her gaze fell on the remnants of the old shed, just a few cement blocks embedded in the ground, too heavy for kids to drag up the mountain.

"Oh." Her eyes snapped to the gap in the bushes, camouflaged by years of growth. Her feet took slow steps without her permission. Her arms pushed aside foliage that was already draining from red to brown.

The forest swallowed her, still cold and quiet at this early hour, the sunlight barely managing to slide past the tops of the trees. A woodpecker tapped on a trunk to her right. A dozen birds sang to her left. The pine scent promised calm and beauty, but she had a terrible premonition that the promise was about to be broken.

Brushing morning spiderwebs off her arms, she stepped up the trail, goose bumps rising along with her heart rate.

The fort came into view too quickly, the stained and crooked walls speaking of hundreds of years of history instead of two dozen. For a moment, her vision warped to show Kyle standing there, waving an impatient arm for her to hurry before he ducked inside. She could smell a wisp of woodsmoke, then hear the hiss of the can of mosquito repellent he kept inside the doorway because Elise suffered huge welts when she was bitten.

A foreshadow of a breeze touched her ear, treetops that were a quarter of a mile away beginning to shush and rustle. The sound moved in a wave toward her until a gust of wind finally snuck past. Branches clicked, rubbing against each other like tapping fingernails.

Elise shivered.

She didn't spot any new beer bottles in the leaf litter. Still, she approached cautiously, listening for anything out of place. No footstep broke through the other sounds of the forest, and no boogeyman peered out through the narrow opening of the door, so Elise took the last few steps and reached out to pull it open.

The flimsy wood stuck on the uneven ground, but not much. One good yank and she made a wide enough space to fit past. If she wanted to.

Did she? Aside from the thousands of creepy-crawlies that must be lurking inside—above, below, and in every possible direction—she wasn't sure she wanted to know what else was in there. But she'd come here for a reason. A terrible reason.

Elise crouched low and eased inside, wincing at every imagined brush of bristly legs against her hair. She slapped at a tickle on her neck, ordering herself to believe it was only her imagination. Keeping her body as small as possible, she shuffled in until she was in the center of the crooked shack.

It didn't smell of anything dead, at least, just dust and mildew. A quick glance around revealed no surprises. An ancient paperback in the corner, the pages grotesquely swollen and the cover bleached to a blank by water damage. Three dusty beer bottles against one wall. A stump they'd used as a stool. A skeleton of an ancient camp chair. And one small chest made out of raw wood.

She reached toward it. The chest was more of a packing crate than a piece of furniture, and it took some effort to pop off the top and ease it up to look inside. Nothing but an old pint bottle of off-brand whisky, long drained of its contents. Her teenage years had taken over anything left of her childhood here.

She'd known in the back of her mind that the chest wasn't large enough to hold a rifle, but looking inside it, she still slumped a little in relief. Sometimes old memories played tricks. What if it had been the size of a steamer trunk and she'd simply forgotten?

But Kyle hadn't hidden anything here. She'd likely been the only one to break any laws inside the fort.

When she moved to press the top back on, Elise's legs wobbled, and she grabbed at the chest to stop herself from falling into a pile of spider-infested leaves. The chest slid toward her, but she still caught enough support to stop herself from tumbling.

After rebalancing herself, she rose, hunching over and shifting her weight to turn toward the door. But the chest had pulled away from the wall, and Elise saw a flash of pale, polished wood behind it. She froze and stared hard into the shadowed space.

There were bits and pieces of timber everywhere in here, but this was smooth and glossy, not faded and splintered. She slowly crouched back down and pulled the chest farther out.

A straight line of black metal lay against the dirt.

"Oh, Kyle," she groaned, shaking her head as if she could deny the rifle that stood out against the buckled wall, set apart from its surroundings by its shine. Every other surface was dust or rust or mildew. But not this. The gun hadn't been here long. She tugged the chest all the way out, then sat on it, her legs collapsing, muscles burning, heart breaking.

It looked to be a bolt-action rifle, solid and unadorned aside from the scope mounted on top. A scope for hunting. For killing.

"No," she insisted to herself, dropping her head to the knuckles of her fisted hands. "This isn't happening. This can't be happening, Kyle."

Because this rifle in this place couldn't be part of a setup. No one else knew about their childhood fort. Not Christian, not Jackson, not . . .

Her head popped up, eyes opening wide. Daniel. Daniel would have known. She couldn't picture him here, couldn't make a memory rise, but Daniel must have come here at least once or twice, maybe much more often. Kyle took good care of his baby sister, but he hadn't included her in everything.

Elise pulled her phone from her pocket to open Facebook, but there was no signal here, tucked against this remote hill.

She lurched to her feet, shoved the chest back against the wall, and burst out of the fort to sprint toward the trail. Her feet slipped on loose pebbles as she ran around a switchback, nearly sending her face-first into a thick tree, but she managed to catch herself and stumble back onto the path.

She finally rushed through the bushes and into the backyard, but she didn't stop there. She cut straight across the yard to the side gate and pushed through to the front.

Three bars.

She searched for Daniel on Facebook and found him, but he'd only posted once in the last month. There was nothing about the accident or a hospital stay, just a picture of the kitchen of his dad's old house. *Before the reno!* Daniel had captioned it.

She spotted a local event company listed on his page and clicked it. The owner appeared to be a woman named Clara Russell. Was she really his cousin? It was possible, but that was an old question now. She hadn't posted anything about Daniel's status either.

Elise moved back to his page and saw another familiar name in his followers. His sister. Jackpot. Elise clicked over to her page.

Thank you all so much for your prayers and support of Daniel! He's doing much better and should be out of the hospital soon, maybe even tomorrow! Surgery on his leg went well, and the rehab has already started. Not sure he's appreciating that. Ouch. More soon.

The update had been posted this morning. A picture showed Daniel in a hospital bed with a black eye, giving a thumbs-up and a tired smile. Elise's heart wobbled between sympathy and fear. But he couldn't hurt her now. Not with a broken leg.

Elise circled around to the back door of the house and waved once she was inside the kitchen to get her mom's attention. "I need to go take care of a couple of things. I'll call if I hear anything from that lawyer. You call me if you hear from Kyle, okay? I'll come right back here when I'm done."

Her mom nodded in silent agreement before slipping an earbud back in, her mouth bracketed by deep lines as her gaze grew distant again.

Each step toward the door added a pound of guilt to Elise's shoulders. She hadn't bothered asking her mom if she was okay, because how could she be? Not only was Elise abandoning her during this awful moment, there was a good chance this errand would ruin everything for all of them. But she had to know, even if every possible revelation meant dropping her heart in a blender.

"I love you, Mom," she said, knowing her mother couldn't hear her. She closed the door and moved toward a truth that might kill whatever hope she had left.

CHAPTER 33

Had she driven to the hospital? Parked in the garage? Taken the elevator up? Elise remembered none of that. She'd simply opened her eyes and found herself in this hallway, shoulder pressed to the wall on the third floor of the hospital.

The air smelled like tragedy. She could taste the bleach on her tongue as she stood slack-jawed and exhausted, her adrenaline used up long before. She had nothing but anxiety and stubbornness left for this task.

Before she'd left Cold Creek, she'd zoomed in on the Facebook picture to find the logo of the hospital printed on a brochure on Daniel's bedside table. And now here she was in the orthopedic wing, frozen outside Daniel's room with only a vague memory of peeking past several doorways in her search for him.

He was alone, his sister seemingly taking a break somewhere now that he was out of danger. Elise wished she could feel that, a moment of safety, but instead she was suspended over a boiling lake, the rope fraying as she swung. There was no ignoring the problem or hoping it would go away. The rope would eventually snap whether she walked into Daniel's room or not.

Better to get it over with. She pushed off the wall and let momentum take her tired body through the doorway.

His eyes were closed, his skin paler than it should be and purpling around the edges of the bruises on his face. God, he looked young and vulnerable. Like the teenage boy she'd secretly adored so long ago. Poor Daniel. She wanted to smooth his messy hair and tell him how sorry she was for all of this.

She must have made some noise, either a shoe scuff against the floor or a mourning sigh for her lost youth, because Daniel's eyes opened to slits.

For a moment, his face softened into pleasure at the sight of her. Elise's heart twinged, wanting to soften too. But then his eyes widened and his gaze moved to the door behind her as if searching for help.

"Daniel," she said, her voice as quiet as she could make it over the noise of the building. "Are you okay?"

"Hey." The careful cheer in his tone contrasted with the tight lines around his eyes. "I'm all right."

She looked down at the cast on his leg and the metal rods coming out of it. He wasn't hooked up to any scary wires or tubes, at least, just an IV line she imagined was delivering some good painkillers. "I saw you might get out tomorrow? That's good."

"Yeah. The surgery went well. The doctor says I should fully recover. But the home renovation might have to wait a few months."

"I'm so sorry," she said. But should she be? Was he friend or foe or some mix of the two? "What happened?"

"Car accident." He looked to the doorway again, but his fear told her nothing. He damn well should be scared if he'd done the things she suspected. But if he was actually innocent and still watching the doorway so carefully, that meant . . .

"Did Kyle ever take you to our old fort?" she blurted out. "Up on the hill behind our house?"

He frowned. "Elise . . ." After a very long pause, he seemed to give up on whatever he was thinking and deigned to answer. "Yeah. Sure. I remember that place. We tried our first cigarette there."

"Have you been there recently?"

A spasm of pain crossed his face, his eyes clenching shut. He shook his head again. "No. No, I haven't. And I hope you're not inviting me, because it could be a rough hike."

She crossed her arms, hugging herself against the cool hospital air. When could he even have gone there to plant evidence? Not anytime in the last two days. It would have been before, but the podcast had only aired three days ago. Surely that interview was the catalyst for ratcheting up the conspiracy against Kyle.

Still, it was possible Daniel had gone up that very day. But why the hell would he do something so obviously dangerous and corrupt? Planting a gun on his old friend's property? That wasn't like doing a little reconnaissance for extra money.

"Daniel, I'm just so . . ." She felt her face crumple and tried to breathe past the breakdown. "I really don't know what's going on."

"Shit," he whispered. "Elise, listen. Please. I don't know what's going on either, but something is wrong with Kyle. I'm sorry to say it that way, but it's true."

"What do you mean?" She wiped her eyes. "Why do you think that?"

He cursed again, craning his neck to stare past her, though this time he looked more cautious than afraid. He lowered his voice to a rumble just above a whisper. "Did they arrest him? Is he in custody?"

"Yes," she croaked, horrified to admit it. "There was a search. They broke down the door. We were both sleeping. They let me go, but Kyle . . ."

"Jesus." When Daniel put down the call button, she realized he'd been clutching it the whole time. Her eyes filled with tears again, but she couldn't name the emotion swelling up to overtake her.

"The accident," he started before pausing to push out a loud exhale. "I didn't remember much at first, to be honest. I could recall what I'd been doing around the house but had no memory of getting into the truck. Then it was like I woke up when the sirens started and help arrived." He pointed to his face. "I've got a concussion and a broken orbital bone."

She touched her own face, wincing.

"It would've been much worse without the airbags, so I'm thankful."

"Yeah. Me too." Elise drew closer but didn't get within touching distance. She assumed he wanted to be within her reach as little as she wanted to be in his.

"But then the cops came by yesterday, asking more questions. When they asked about Kyle, I had a flash of something. And then . . . Shit, it was all there. I saw it."

She lifted her chin to encourage him to continue. "Saw what?"

"A car coming up fast behind me on the highway. I glanced into the mirror, and . . . It was him, Elise. I saw Kyle looking right at me."

Elise shook her head. "No. You can't be sure. They put that in your head when they asked about him. Cops do that kind of shit all the time. They're trying to frame him. And me too."

His face twisted with grief. "I'm afraid it's a real memory, Elise. I know I saw Kyle, because for a second I thought he was playing a joke, coming up fast so he could honk and scare the shit out of me. I was starting to laugh when he hit me."

Her body was sinking. Though her view stayed the same, she felt like a puddle on the floor. "Daniel," she said. "No."

"Jesus, he must have been going eighty. I tried to steer, but my wheels were already sliding. I had no control at all. Then I was falling."

She shook her head again. If Kyle had run Daniel off the road only because Elise had seen him at the memorial . . . then his accident hadn't been part of a conspiracy. It had just been Kyle.

And if Daniel had really shown up at the service to support his cousin Clara, then that hadn't been part of the conspiracy either.

So what was a part of the conspiracy? Christian and Jeremy Quinn had been killed and then . . .

That was it. Only her own fears spurred on by her brother.

"Oh my God," she whispered, closing her eyes as she reached out to hold the frame of the bathroom door for support. The car following her to her brother's? That had probably been the police planning for the raid in the morning. The stranger insisting on a room? Could have simply been an asshole looking for a room. And Christian's connection to Robin . . . ?

Christian had been in Willow Canyon then. He could have killed Robin. He could have watched a friend kill her or just helped hide the crime. But even if that was true . . . it might have been Kyle who'd decided to make him pay. It might have been Kyle the whole time.

"I need to go," she said. "I'm so sorry."

"Elise, wait a—"

"I'm really sorry, Daniel. I need to call someone. I need to . . ." She drifted from the room as he protested, asking her to hold on a second. But her body was floating out the door, down the hall, onto the elevator.

She wasn't sure if she'd pushed a button, but the elevator opened on the first floor, so she got off and aimed for the bright sunlight beyond the main doors. Her footsteps moved faster, faster, until she burst through the doors as if she were running toward something. Yet once she was outside, she stumbled to a halt.

What was she doing? She looked around in a daze as if she might spot a sign that read "County Jail" on the street in front of her.

Where the hell was she? Still on the California side of the lake, which meant the jail must be somewhere close by, but for a moment she couldn't think how to find it. She couldn't think of anything at all, except that she wanted to go home. Back to her cabin to crawl beneath the covers, or back to Seattle to pick up life in her old ruins, or even back to her mom's big bed that had become her own. She just wanted to be away, gone, *before*.

She took her phone out and stared at it dumbly for a long minute before she opened the map and typed in *jail*. The building popped up nearly a mile away, but she set off toward the west and hit the phone number listed.

"County jail, this is Deputy Burns. If you have an emergency, please dial 911."

"No, I need to see an inmate. Can I do that?"

"Sure. Today? Next visiting slot is at eleven thirty, but you'd need to be here in fifteen minutes to check in. After that is lunch, so your next slot is 2:00 p.m."

"Eleven thirty," she repeated, giving her brother's name. After she hung up, she plodded on, traffic roaring past her on the highway. When the sidewalk ran out two blocks later, she stayed to the shoulder, wondering why she'd left her car. She should have turned back, but the puzzle of finding her car within the dark levels of the parking garage felt unsolvable. So she just kept walking, arms loose and lips parted in shock.

She eventually spotted the line of police vehicles ahead that signaled her destination, the same sheriff's office where she'd given her interview. The county lockup lurked behind it, far enough off the road not to disturb visitors with thoughts of local crime.

Elise felt no fear for herself as she walked through the double doors into the reception area and told the man at the desk that she needed to visit an inmate. She was too afraid of something worse than being arrested now, and she barely looked at the officer as he directed her through a door that led to a wide hallway.

The rustic decoration of the front office didn't extend to these halls, which had industrial gray carpeting and cream-colored walls, and no aerial shots of the town to distract from the endless walk toward the jail entrance.

A female deputy sat behind glass and watched Elise with hard eyes when she approached. "I'm here for an eleven thirty visiting slot. I need to see Kyle Rockwood."

The woman typed blankly away for a moment, then handed Elise a clipboard with several sheets of paper and requested her license.

She was surprised to find she was wearing her backpack and had all her essentials. She recalled nothing about taking it from the car earlier and had never registered the weight against her shoulders.

Twenty minutes later, her pack stowed in a locked cubby, Elise made it through a metal detector and a pat down before being led past a visitors' room with tables and chairs. The room smelled vaguely of vomit and something acrid like roach spray. She was shown to a separate room with a plexiglass rectangle set into a wall next to a telephone receiver. Apparently Kyle was too dangerous for direct contact. Elise was shocked by the wave of shamed relief that washed over her.

She lowered herself stiffly into one of the two chairs, then picked up the phone to hold it tightly like a club. She was alone, separated from everyone else in the jail, but she still felt like wielding a weapon as she glanced at a camera. She didn't think about who she needed to defend against.

When they led Kyle in on the other side of the thick glass, he looked confused and tired, but his face lit up when he saw her. "Hey!" he said, his voice tinny as they both raised phones to their ears. "I'm surprised to see you. I thought maybe my lawyer was back. Don't worry. He's on it. I have a bail hearing scheduled for tomorrow. Did you talk to Mom yet?"

"Kyle," she said, stopping his strangely cheerful chatter. "I went to the fort."

"Oh." He watched her, waiting, eyes guileless and wide, and how the hell was that possible? "Okay."

"I went to the fort," she growled. "I was there."

"Okay," he said again, and it felt like a slap in the face. The plastic of the receiver creaked in her grip.

"That's all? Just *okay*? I saw what you . . . I'm going to have to tell them, Kyle! I have no choice, because I think maybe . . ." Maybe what? She couldn't bring herself to speak it. Even if there had been no cameras . . . she couldn't even make herself think it in complete sentences.

"Hey. Come on, Sis. You can't do that."

"Oh, I can't? I saw Daniel today too. I went to the hospital. He needed surgery on his leg. His face is broken!"

Kyle's mouth lost a little of its good cheer, but he didn't respond.

"I talked to him," Elise continued, hoping he'd interrupt her with a denial or explanation. "He said . . . My God, Kyle. How could you? *Daniel?*"

Eyes narrowing, her brother leaned forward. She waited for the denial. Waited for him to ask what the hell she was talking about. But Kyle broke her heart instead.

"He betrayed us, Elise. He was working with them. You know that. You're the one who told me."

"'Them'?" she whispered, a hollow forming where all her hope had been. "The same 'them' who shot Jeremy Quinn?"

The exhaustion leached back into his face, and he slouched deeper in the chair, the cord of his phone taut now. "Listen to me. Please, Sis. This is all real. All of it. I just have to *prove* it. You get that, right?"

She stared at him, blank and falling.

"I looked into Christian when you first told me about him, back when you broke up. But I let it go. I figured if he was leaving you alone, there was nothing to my suspicions. But when he got back in touch, something fucking gnawed at the back of my mind. The *why*. Why was he here at the same time Robin disappeared? Why did he return to our shitty little canyon when he retired? He could have lived anywhere. Hawaii. France. Hell, even Tahoe, right on the lake with all the other rich assholes. But *here*?"

"Kyle—"

"I knew you wouldn't believe me. Not even when I found evidence. I knew it was real. And it was! You've seen the pictures! Jackson with Phoenix. All of them with Robin! I wanted to tell you from the start, but you were clearly still all tied up with him in your head. You were in love with the fucking guy. I knew you wouldn't want to hear it. I *knew* it."

"That's all there is?" she asked. "That was all you had, and you decided to . . ." She waved a frantic hand.

"No, that's not what it was! Christian was ready to talk. It was time to get it off his chest. That was why he contacted you. It was time for the *truth*, Elise."

Her throat closed, the soft flesh beneath her tongue swelling, choking her until she felt like she might be sick. "You killed him," she whispered, hardly any space left in her mouth to push the words out.

Kyle blew out an exasperated noise that could have been a denial but wasn't. "He wanted to confess to you," he insisted. "It wasn't some idle apology. This was a confession he didn't want in writing; that's why he wanted to meet you. When he saw who was—" He spared a glance for the camera, and shook his head, but he chuckled a little. He actually *chuckled*. "Yeah, he knew he was caught, Lise. A cornered criminal will panic."

Two different scenes played out in her vision, subtle mirrors of each other. Christian, caught by mounting evidence, turning vicious and trying to hurt Kyle before Kyle could hurt him. The other was Christian lashing out in terror after being blindsided by a stranger claiming to know some sick secret about him. Which scene? Which truth?

"And Quinn?" she asked. "The shooting?"

Kyle glanced up, lips parting. Then he closed his mouth and shook his head, his nose wrinkling as if she were the one saying something foul.

"I don't care," she growled. "I don't care if they're listening. You owe me this. If you . . . Jesus, Kyle. You have to tell me the truth!"

"They did it, Elise. Don't you get that? They *killed* Robin. But the police would never look at them. According to them, the case was solved and closed. They certainly weren't going to reopen a closed case just to make themselves look like fools. Not without new leads."

She sucked in a shuddering breath. He was being careful with his words, but this was a confession. Kyle had killed Christian and Jeremy Quinn. Maybe he'd planned to kill Jackson too. No one was after her. Those men had been the only ones in danger the whole time.

Were they actually guilty? Did that even matter?

"And they were looking at you!" he insisted. "But then Quinn died while you were with the police—"

Elise stood, weaving a bit, the phone still a club in her fist.

Kyle's face, every expression familiar to her, twisted with fear. "Wait!" she heard his faint, broken voice leaking from the receiver. "I love you, Sis! You and Mom. You both deserve the truth!"

She dropped the phone and shook her spinning head. No, it hadn't been for her or Mom. It had been a way to patch over his own pain. To make sense of the senseless. Wasn't that exactly what she'd known at the start of this? What Kyle was reaching toward and why?

And then she'd done the same fucking thing. She'd wanted a reason for all this aching hurt. Someone to blame for her own mistakes. Kyle had pointed her right to the villain who'd broken her apart.

A bang jerked her from her daze. When she looked up Kyle slapped the glass again, hard. *"Listen,"* he was yelling. *"Listen!"*

His same old refrain, which made it so easy to read the word in the shape of his mouth. If she'd just listen better and be smarter, she'd understand that he was right. He was right and everyone else was wrong. But she *had* listened, and he'd ruined her.

"No," she said. Then "No!" again louder.

"Elise!" she heard from the phone, so she snatched it up and hit the window with it.

"No!" She punctuated each word with a blow. "No, no, no, no, no!" The force of it rang up her arm and jarred every bone in her body.

Hands grabbed her from behind and pulled. She kept a tight grip on the phone, but she was jerked away so ruthlessly that her fingers felt snapped by the violence.

Kyle was being hauled away by two armed men on the other side. "I hate you!" she screamed. "I hate you!" At the men, at her brother, at the hands holding her down. At the whole goddamn ugly world. "I hate you all!"

She twisted and screamed until everything around her disappeared and she sank into a world without any of them.

CHAPTER 34

Fourteen months later

"Do you still suspect the Stratum men of having anything to do with your sister's disappearance? Anything at all?"

Elise sat back in her chair and looked out the window of her apartment. The place was dingy and small, halfway between a studio and a one bedroom, a partial wall separating her bed from the rest of the space. But two drafty windows came together to form the corner of the room, and she could make out a sliver of the bay when the glass wasn't too grimy.

She was back where she'd started, back in a city, renting again, her life a giant question mark with dirty edges.

"Elise?"

She forced her eyes back to the woman on her computer screen who sat in front of a huge microphone. Elise had a microphone too and cushioned headphones to cut out the city noise. She shook her head.

"The police say their cabin rental ran through August 21, which means they left three days after my sister went missing. The sheriff's department didn't bother looking for Robin for several days, so in all likelihood, Christian and his friends heard nothing about a local girl who disappeared while they were there. I have no reason to believe they'd remember a random girl they met at a party if they didn't know she went missing. So while I was convinced Christian had hidden something from me, there's no evidence any of them knew anything about it."

"So why was your brother so sure?"

Elise shrugged before remembering this interview would be audio only. "I don't know. Robin's loss felt so meaningless to him. That he could lose his big sister, that we could all lose her, and never get real answers. It was a wound that never healed. It festered."

"But you do believe that Phoenix Whit did it?"

"Of course. But the *why* of it? The *how*? We'll never get that. It's morbid, I guess, but the questions are real. Was she afraid? In pain? Was she still alive when he threw her into the river? Could any of us have done anything to stop it? It's torture. What if Kyle had asked her to stay home and watch a movie? What if Mom had given her a curfew? The doubts are maddening. I mean that literally. If you follow them down, you'll free-fall."

"Do you think your brother should have pled insanity?"

Elise stilled her tapping foot. "No. Not at all. He was tormented, not insane. He knew what he was doing was wrong, which is why he hid it, even from me. But no one ever found my sister's body; she has no resting place. I think Kyle's mind couldn't rest either."

She took a deep breath and tried to slow her accelerating heart rate. She'd refused to speak a word to the press until now. But she'd recently decided to do one interview so she could answer some of these questions once and for all before fading into the ether under her new name.

Elle Johnson. She thought Elle suited her better, anyway. One syllable with no frills, nothing to shorten, nothing to draw out. A name that might even be mistaken for a random letter. And Johnson, her mother's maiden name, just common enough to hide a few sins.

"It fell on Kyle's shoulders at such a young age," she said, staring out the window again, seeing that little boy. "That he was the quote-unquote man of the house. He wanted to fix things. For Mom, for me, and mostly for Robin. But he couldn't fix what was irrevocably broken. Phoenix was already dead when we found out, and his note revealed nothing. Made no sense of *anything*. So Kyle tried to make sense of it on his own."

Priscilla Nguyen, a reporter who wrote thoughtful, in-depth investigative pieces about the root causes of violence, nodded sympathetically. "And what do you think of the rumors that Kyle is actually the one who killed Robin, and he lost his mind from guilt?"

Elise blew out a scornful sound. "Ridiculous. He was a scrawny thirteen-year-old child who was home with me and Mom the night Robin went missing. He was a good brother and a sweet boy, and he would have had a peaceful, unremarkable life if this meaningless violence hadn't been dropped on our family like a bomb. Those rumors are fucked up and cruel."

The reporter blinked and smiled. "The police have said the same, though not quite in those terms."

"They have."

Priscilla frowned down at her notes for a moment, studying them. "It's been a year since your brother's guilty plea, and more than a year since this story took on a life of its own. Your brother's conspiracy interviews have become infamous. There are two different podcasts doing whole seasons about Robin's disappearance and Kyle's crimes, and probably a hundred individual episodes on different shows, ranging from one extreme to the other. What has your life been like since then?"

"It's been rough," Elise admitted, "but to be clear, I'm not a victim of Kyle's crimes. He has real victims, real lives he ruined. I love my brother, and I don't expect the actual victims to forgive him or anything he did. But this has been another explosion in our family's life. And hey, I've been painted as a villain too, but I totally understand that. It's uncomfortable, but I've accepted it."

"You even accept the people who are absolutely sure you helped your brother kill Christian?"

Elise sighed. "Look, I've made a lot of mistakes in my life. I'm hardly an innocent bystander in this story. I hurt Savannah Valic and her family. I got sucked into Kyle's spiral. But hurting Christian? That's one mistake I didn't make. I'd made my peace with him and hadn't seen him in a very long time. I didn't want to meet him, and that was the end of it. But of course people hate me. I can't fight that. I don't even want to. Like I said, I'm not one of the victims, and I don't want to take up space that's meant for them."

"So why did you decide to do this interview? Don't get me wrong. I'm grateful. But you haven't given any comments to the press until now, not even at your brother's sentencing."

Elise took a moment to think, taking a slow sip of water before she spoke. Why now? As Priscilla had said, the story of what Kyle had done had exploded into an out-of-control frenzy, but Elise had kept her mouth shut, first out of horror, trauma, guilt. But later out of desperation.

She'd been afraid to say the wrong thing. Afraid *anything* she said would be wrong regardless of what it was. Afraid she'd only cause more pain on top of all the seething pain she'd already filled the world with.

Because it was her fault, wasn't it? If she'd never flirted with Christian, never slept with him, never loved the man . . . he'd still be alive. Jeremy Quinn would be alive too. Kyle would be free and as normal as he was ever going to be. And her mom would have her little garden and her quiet life. All that was gone now.

But she couldn't take any of it back, so here she was.

"I wanted to speak because I want to talk about violence and victims and generational pain. Not just the moment of violence, but the after. The butterfly effect. The permanence of loss. That one assault against a teenage girl, my sister, has affected a hundred lives and destroyed dozens. That's why I wanted to talk to you specifically. You're doing important work on framing victims' stories and the causes of violent crime."

"Thank you."

"At its core, my sister's murder was an act of domestic violence. Phoenix and Robin had dated, and he felt some ownership of her. He had a deeper attachment than she did, and God, he wanted to punish her for that. He needed to control her *and* his own feelings. It's a tale as old as time, right?"

"Right. As they say, in abusive relationships the most dangerous time is when you're walking away."

"Exactly. But I think there's sometimes a moment. A moment when things are starting to spiral out of control, and the perpetrator thinks he's gone too far. He thinks there's no going back, and he decides he can't leave her alive. But that's never true. It's *never true*. There is still a chance to save a life and to save a hundred lives around her."

"You think Phoenix made that calculation?"

"I do. I think he hurt Robin or scared her, and then he imagined the trouble he'd be in because she could identify him, so he murdered her instead of risking punishment. But murder is something you can't ever escape. Phoenix couldn't get away from it, even though no one knew what he'd done."

"For those who don't know," Priscilla cut in, "and I can't imagine there are many of you, the man who murdered Robin Rockwood took his own life ten years later and left a confession identifying himself as the killer."

"I just wonder if he truly understood the damage he was about to do in that moment," Elise said. "Maybe if someone hears a hundred of these stories, if people really take them in, there might be a hesitation. If only one in a thousand times . . . as I said, that's not only one life ruined. It's dozens of people who love that person and the people who love them too. Ripples upon ripples. Everyone is affected."

"Tell us about that. Your sister was only eighteen. You and your brother were ten and thirteen. You were so young."

"We were. And my sister . . . When you're eighteen, you feel so grown up, so brave and capable. But now that I'm in my late thirties . . . my God, an eighteen-year-old is still a baby. But yes, Robin was spectacular. She would have had a great life, done amazing things, but that doesn't even matter, does it? Whether she planned a big life or she wanted to live the quietest life on record, she deserved that. And my family deserved to be whole. My mom was turned inside out, my brother took on the family grief, and I became selfish and desperate. Stunted."

Stunted. The word hurt coming out, because that was exactly what she'd been. She swallowed hard, tears burning her eyes. She'd never know who she could have been before Robin's murder. But she was trying to find out now.

"Beyond us . . ." Elise stopped to clear her throat. "Beyond us, Robin's best friend never left town for college. Her other friends lived with terrible guilt. Horrible what-ifs. I mean, imagine being the friend who thinks they saw her last. The boy who didn't offer her a ride. The girl who didn't check in with her before leaving. There could be a dozen people who saw her in those last few minutes at the party, and they live with that. I've heard from them."

"That's an awful burden they don't deserve."

"Exactly. Even girls who never knew Robin lived with fear in our community for a decade after. And Phoenix ruined his own life too. He couldn't contain the horror of what he'd done. The horror was too big for that, and it grew instead of getting smaller with time. It swallowed my whole family, and then it swallowed Christian's family too. And Jeremy Quinn's. And Daniel Serrano's. One stupid, terrible act by a young man in a small town . . ."

"So you blame Phoenix Whit for the murders of Christian Valic and Jeremy Quinn?"

"No. No, Kyle has to own his crimes, and I'm glad he pled guilty instead of drawing out the pain with a trial. But I don't think anyone could dispute that he wouldn't have committed those murders if Robin were still here. My point is that this is a horror that never leaves. For some people it never even fades. And that's what I wanted to share today."

"And does your brother still believe in his conspiracy theory? That Billy Jackson or one of the other two killed your sister?"

Elise didn't look away to gather her thoughts this time. She stared directly into her laptop's camera, face earnest and calm. And she lied.

"I'm not sure. We don't speak much about it when I see him. I know he regrets what he did."

"He's given at least one interview that indicates he's still pursuing an investigation."

"I haven't heard it, but I know he's going to group therapy and working on himself. He's teaching computer science to other inmates in the prison classroom. Kyle can't ever make up for what he did, but he's trying to give something positive back now."

Elise tapped her wrist to indicate the time, and Priscilla nodded. They'd already gone past the hour, and Elise needed to get going.

"Thank you so much for being with us today, Elise Rockwood. And thank you all for listening . . ."

Once she'd wrapped up with Priscilla, she removed the headphones, closed the connection, and tried not to replay every word in her mind. She'd done the best she could, and that was all she'd say about it for a very long time. She wanted to do her small part to help people move on, but she couldn't save anyone. She couldn't even save herself. Still, she was trying.

No more screwing around with casual therapy once a month. She did the hard work for two hours a week now in addition to group meetings, and she'd given up her half-assed, white-knuckled sobriety for the real thing. These days, drinking only made her wallow in thoughts of Christian and Kyle and every other mistake she'd made. And boy, she'd finally hit rock bottom, hadn't she? The shrapnel of her crash had killed two people.

She'd reconnected with Amber for a few months, but their bond had been frayed too thin by the scandal. Elise had felt the coolness on the other side of the phone, either from Amber or from the disapproval of her husband, so she'd stopped calling, and Amber had never bothered picking up the lost thread.

But Daniel? She shook her head, the thought too tender to approach.

With a glance at the clock, she grabbed her bag and headed down to the parking garage beneath her building. The winter day was bitterly cold but bright and gorgeous. The highway to Vacaville took her along wetlands filled with white egrets and gray herons milling among every kind of duck she could imagine. She wondered if they ever flew over Kyle's prison, if he got quick glimpses of beauty from the yard. She'd have to ask.

When her thoughts veered back to the interview, Elise turned up her music and lit a cigarette to stop her mind from racing. An unhealthy vice, but she needed something. She didn't consider the cigarettes a crutch. More like a shim to help straighten her tilting framework. And hell, maybe it meant she wasn't running away from her mother anymore, though she'd drawn the line at smoking menthols.

Forty-five minutes later, she pulled into a single-level complex of garden apartments. They were nothing special, all of them painted dark brown with little decoration, but each had a nice fenced yard in back for a garden. More important, there was a shopping center around the corner with a grocery store and several take-out restaurants. It took six minutes to walk there, six minutes back. And her mom seemed willing to venture out more and more often.

Whatever she couldn't get in the shopping complex was easily deliverable right to her door.

"Ready?" Elise asked when her mom answered the knock.

"Ready as I'll ever be," she muttered, digging through her purse before triumphantly pulling out sunglasses. She smoothed down the new short bob she'd gotten after Kyle's sentencing. With the glasses on, she was barely recognizable even to Elise. "Let's go."

Staying in Cold Creek had become impossible for her mom. First the press had camped out in front of her home; then the podcasters and obsessives had arrived, knocking on her door nearly every day and roaming around in the woods behind the house. They wanted to see where Robin had been raised, where Kyle had hidden a murder weapon, where he might have killed more people or plotted more crimes. Her mother's world had spun out of control.

Between the sale of the home she'd lived in for forty years and her social security, she was doing okay in her new place. She'd even made a friend she invited over for coffee on occasion to work on jigsaw puzzles together. Her world was more open now, but she'd lost her son.

The prison was a ten-minute drive away, and Elise knew the route well enough to zone out as she drove. She picked up her mom once a week to see Kyle, though she'd get too busy for that soon. Mom had promised she'd be able to do it on her own. It would just take her a while. But she was making progress, and she'd even found a therapist who did video visits.

Better late than never. It had taken her only twenty-six years. Not that Elise had been much quicker about it.

After finding a parking space, the gauntlet to see Kyle took thirty minutes to navigate, but once they were inside, they could sit with him for an hour and even exchange hugs.

"You go ahead and sit next to him," her mom said, her eyes crinkling at the corners a bit. "I saw him three days ago."

"Mom! What?"

"I did it. I drove over by myself. I only stayed for fifteen minutes, but I did it."

"I'm so proud of you! That new therapist is kicking your ass, huh?"

"She's pushing me. But I'm ready. Kyle needs me."

"He does."

He needed Elise too, but she wasn't sure if she was doing the right thing. He asked a lot of her, and she didn't indulge him. She couldn't.

"Hey, Sis," he said when he arrived, giving her a perfunctory hug. Kyle looked heavier and paler, with new bags under his eyes. The physical isolation of prison suited him fine, but he was a little lost without internet access. "Mom." He hugged their mother a bit harder, inhaling as if he missed the scent of her. "You look good."

"So do you," their mom said with false cheer.

"Did you bring me those printouts?"

Elise shook her head. "I couldn't find anything," she said, telling the lie easily. "Except one article on a missing girl, but they wouldn't let me bring that in. Too crime adjacent, I guess."

"Hm. Maybe I can get it through discovery if they let my lawsuit go forward. They can't keep denying me access to information I have a legal right to."

She made a noncommittal sound. "I won't be out here every week after this. I start classes in three days. But you can write to me."

"Sure. Yeah." He chewed on his thumbnail for a moment, eyes distant. "I just really need that flight-tracker information."

Kyle didn't accept that Christian or Jeremy Quinn were innocent. He couldn't. Because if he accepted it, that would mean he'd murdered two men in cold blood and done the same thing to two families that Robin's death had done to theirs.

"Hey, Daniel came to see me," he said.

Elise actually jumped in surprise. "He did?"

"Yeah. Yesterday. I wrote to apologize for what I did. I didn't expect an answer, but he actually came here."

"Did he look good?" she asked, her heart lurching a little. She'd seen him once or twice before she'd sold the cabins, but not since then.

"He's good. He said he forgave me, which I didn't expect." Kyle's eyes filled with tears, but he cleared his throat and shook off his emotion before going on. "So that was good. He sold his dad's place and moved up north. Working for the forest service now."

"That's great." Elise swallowed back her own tears.

Their mom wrapped her hands around Kyle's. She didn't like to speak about his crimes, so she changed the subject and asked about the books she'd brought last time. They'd started a three-person book club to occupy Kyle's mind, but Elise hadn't read the last one. She'd been too busy with college orientation, luckily a small affair for students starting classes in the spring semester. She was the oldest one by far, but that meant she was almost invisible to the other students. Not a bad thing.

Regardless, she was finally starting college, determined to learn how to be a journalist. To hone her writing skills and learn the ins and outs of actually doing her own research. Of tracking down facts and backing them up so she'd never be fooled again.

She'd told Daniel about it in one of their late-night text exchanges. He'd reached out a few months before to ask how she and her mom were doing. Their texting felt painfully natural, and they'd been talking on the phone for a couple of months, keeping it light. No mention of Kyle or conspiracies or even the car crash. But when he'd told her he'd be near the bay area this week and suggested lunch, she'd immediately claimed to be too busy working twelve-hour shifts at her fulfillment-center job. The truth was that she'd been scared. Scared that he was good enough to give her a second chance. Scared that she might take him up on it.

She couldn't ruin another life. Better to give up a shot at happiness than make everything worse. Because if her current plans came to fruition, there would be no peace for her or anyone in her life. Still, she was so glad he'd forgiven Kyle, or at least started to. Another sign that Daniel was far too good for her.

After fifteen minutes of listening to her brother explain all the errors he'd found in their last read about lost cities, Elise twisted around and stood up. "I need to use the restroom. Mom, you stay as long as you like. I'll meet you at the car."

"Oh, stay a bit longer, sweetie," her mom said.

"I need a cigarette too. I have to admit, I've got some nerves about starting school." She smiled. "Will any of the boys want to take me to the dance?" She patted Kyle's shoulder. "I'll see you again soon, Big Brother."

She hurried out, skipping the bathroom to go straight to the locker area and retrieve her things. It was after 3:00 p.m. now. She'd been promised an email sometime late today, so maybe it had already arrived.

Once she was back in the safety of the parking lot, Elise perched on the hood of her car to soak in the bright sun, lit a cigarette, and logged in to her encrypted email account. A message waited, new and unread.

Heart beating hard, she threw a guilty look at the prison where her brother lived. She couldn't involve him in this. She couldn't involve anyone. And she imagined it would take years to make progress. She'd need the access and connections that journalistic credentials could get her. It wouldn't be easy, but this could be a start.

After bracing herself with a deep breath, Elise opened the email.

There were no words, only an image file that loaded slowly, line by line. First just a black strip. Then the point of something pale yellow. The glint and shadow of pine limbs brushing fabric.

The yellow grew slowly, eventually revealing the expanding triangle of a tent.

Elise's eyes burned, but they were dry.

She'd had another reason for doing the interview with Priscilla. She wanted the world to know that she had no lingering suspicions. That she'd turned away and was no longer looking. It was safe for everyone to let their guards down and come out, because Elise Rockwood was no danger to them, and Kyle wouldn't have access to the World Wide Web for at least twenty-five years.

Things were fine. Everything was back to normal.

But when the photo finished loading, Elise began to breathe too hard, her hands fisting.

The man seated within the right side of the tent was in a shadow, his face hard to make out. But she'd been told who it was, so she could see Phoenix Whit in the weak jaw and small nose.

The other man, sitting to the left and closer to the tent opening, looked directly at the camera with a smile, and there was no mistaking that heavy brow and the small eyes aglow from a camera flash.

His hand curved over the bare thigh of a girl. The girl wore a very short skirt and nothing else, her heavy breasts exposed, one arm resting over a face that was too deep in the tent to see. Her legs were limp and spread open. Phoenix gave a thumbs-up over her crotch.

It wasn't Robin. Her skin was too pale, her waist too thick. Elise didn't know her name. She'd written anonymously to Kyle at the prison three months before, giving a PO box but nothing else. She'd claimed to have important information and asked him to get in touch.

Kyle had written back and told her that anything sent to him in prison would be reviewed by authorities and wasn't secure, so he'd asked her to communicate with Elise instead.

Elise had exchanged a few emails with the woman, then told Kyle she was a weirdo convinced she had psychic abilities and could time travel back to save Robin.

Another lie on top of a mountain of lies. But she had to protect her brother. And she had to protect the woman too. Because she said she'd been raped by Phoenix Whit and some other man she didn't know. At the time, she thought she'd made a terrible, drunken mistake with a boy she'd gone to a party with at Moon Lake. Phoenix had told her she'd been wild. That she'd wanted two guys at once. That she'd loved it.

She'd been humiliated and ashamed, and she'd just wanted to put it behind her and head back to college for her sophomore year at UCLA. It wasn't until Kyle's crimes had hit the news that she'd realized who the other man was. Billy Jackson.

It had taken nearly a month for the woman to open up and give Elise the details. Elise had believed every word but had wondered how she could be sure it was Billy when she barely remembered the assault.

That was when she'd reluctantly mentioned a picture. Months after that poor young woman returned to UCLA, the roll of film on the disposable camera she'd taken to the mountains had finally filled up, and she'd gotten it developed. The men who'd assaulted her had left the picture as a fun little surprise. It had taken her many, many years to realize what had happened to her had been rape.

She hadn't been sure if she still had the photo. If she did, it would be in a sealed box in a storage unit from when her parents had sold their house and moved to senior living. The woman had flown back to California and promised the picture today.

Elise knew what to expect, but seeing it was another matter entirely. Sweat prickled her brow, and her skin tingled. She slipped off the hood of her car to retreat to the dim confines of the interior, the glare too much for her head.

There was no question the second man was Billy Jackson, his cheeks still plump with youth, his smile tight and cruel. And the other boy was Phoenix Whit. But who was holding the camera? Was it another local boy? Or Jeremy Quinn? Or was it Christian taking the picture?

But more important, how many other girls had Billy Jackson victimized? Over that week, over that month, over a lifetime?

It might take her years, but Elise was determined to find the truth. And to let the whole world know. She'd finally found her purpose in life, and she had her big brother to thank.

She only hoped she could live up to what he'd started.

About the Author

Victoria Helen Stone is the Amazon Charts bestselling author of *The Hook; At the Quiet Edge; The Last One Home; Problem Child; Half Past; False Step; Evelyn, After; and Jane Doe*. She is a master of dark intrigue and emotional suspense, with novels published in English, Russian, Spanish, Turkish, Hungarian, Lithuanian, German, Czech, Hebrew, Estonian, and Polish, and *Jane Doe* was optioned by Sony for television.

Victoria writes in her home office high in the Wasatch Mountains of Utah, far from her origins in the flattest plains of Minnesota, Texas, and Oklahoma. She enjoys summer trail hikes in the mountains almost as much as she enjoys staying inside by the fire during winter. Victoria is passionate about dessert, true crime, and her terror of mosquitoes, which have targeted her in a diabolical conspiracy to hunt her down no matter the season. For more information visit www.victoriahelenstone.com.